HELLO, THERE

"Want one?" he asked, holding out a muffin. Not just any muffin, either. The thing had blueberries the size of gold nuggets and it was covered in lumpy sugar crystals. She was his.

"I'm Jack," he said.

She wiped her sticky fingers on her jeans and shook. "Gillian. Pleased to meet you, and thanks." *Yum. You can climb my beanstalk anytime, Jack.*

BOOK YOUR PLACE ON OUR WEBSITE AND MAKE THE READING CONNECTION!

We've created a customized website just for our very special readers, where you can get the inside scoop on everything that's going on with Zebra, Pinnacle and Kensington books.

When you come online, you'll have the exciting opportunity to:

- View covers of upcoming books

- Read sample chapters

- Learn about our future publishing schedule (listed by publication month *and author*)

- Find out when your favorite authors will be visiting a city near you

- Search for and order backlist books from our online catalog

- Check out author bios and background information

- Send e-mail to your favorite authors

- Meet the Kensington staff online

- Join us in weekly chats with authors, readers and other guests

- Get writing guidelines

- AND MUCH MORE!

**Visit our website at
http://www.kensingtonbooks.com**

He Loves Me . . .

Lucy Ann Peters

ZEBRA BOOKS
Kensington Publishing Corp.
www.kensingtonbooks.com

ZEBRA BOOKS are published by

Kensington Publishing Corp.
850 Third Avenue
New York, NY 10022

All Kensington titles, imprints, and distributed lines are available at special quantity discounts for bulk purchases for sales
promotion, premiums, fund-raising, educational, or institu-
tional use.

Special book excerpts or customized printings can also be created to fit specific needs. For details, write or phone the office
of the Kensington Special Sales Manager: Attn. Special Sales
Department. Kensington Publishing Corp., 850 Third Avenue,
New York, NY 10022. Phone: 1-800-221-2647.

ISBN-13: 978-0-8217-8033-6
ISBN-10: 0-8217-8033-6

First Printing: July 2007
10 9 8 7 6 5 4 3 2 1

Printed in the United States of America

To Buffy

Acknowledgments

Readers Tiffany Bevan and Rosemarie Deegan offered thoughtful critique of the early drafts of this manuscript. Friends Mike Jacobson and Mark Nardone assisted with technical aspects of the story. Editor Hilary Sares supplied wisdom, humor, and encouragement. L., as always, you are the solid ground at the center of this writer's life. Traveling with you has been a blessing and a privilege.

Chapter 1

The cool shadows of early morning caressed dew-spangled fields. The leaves on the stands of birch along the banks of the Mohasset River were touched with gold.

Gillian Wilcox had little time to notice. She was wrestling with the big wheel of Jasper, her cranky lumber delivery truck. Keeping the fourteen-wheeler headed where she wanted it to go was a constant process of negotiation. Who needed the gym to stay in shape?

Ah, there it was. The turnoff that couldn't come soon enough. She braked and with aching arms wrenched the old truck off the main road that ran along the Mohasset and onto the rough dirt road leading to a building site tucked back in the woods among the trees. Doug Riley's crew was waiting there for the load of lumber strapped to Jasper's flatbed. The springs of the vehicle squeaked ominously as Gillian ground along the rutted track in low gear. Something in the front end groaned. The cab lurched.

On the seat beside her, her dog Boo thumped his tail, yowled and licked his chops nervously.

"It's just bumps in the road, you big baby," Gillian scolded.

On the far side of the cab, Orville—or maybe it was Wilbur, she could never be sure when it came to The Twins—loosed a rusty snicker. With a gnarled hand, he patted Boo on the back of his neck. "Easy, boy."

Views of the river behind them receded as they followed the

road deeper into the woods. Ahead, a modern sixteen-room house was under construction. Before long, this rutted road would be graded into a smooth driveway, tastefully illuminated by lighting hidden within the landscaping. The house itself, when finished, would appear to be an authentic 1800s mansion.

"Appear" was the operative word, thought Gillian.

The truth of the matter is that some flush yuppie would buy up the giant, generic Federal-period mock-up, keep it for two years then flip it. Sell it for half again what he paid for it.

The real estate equivalent of the cycle of life. Progress.

Maybe, according to some people in Rocky Falls. True, all the building in town was dropping some serious change in the coffers. Even into the till at the ailing Wilcox Lumber Company, Gillian had to admit. But at what cost to the town? Peacefully out of the mainstream, Rocky Falls had been minding its own business for over two hundred years. It kept its own counsel. Thought its own thoughts. Times changed, it didn't. Until lately.

As if the spirit of Rocky Falls knew it was in a fight for its life, the dirt track grabbed at the front wheels of the truck. Gillian threw her weight into the steering wheel, veering the corroded bulldog on the hood of the truck away from the trees at the side of the road.

God, her arms hurt. And her shoulders. And her back. And one knee was feeling a little weird lately. This prodigal daughter gig was hard. She'd been home now for what? Yes, two years last month. Busting her ass to bail out the vineyard. She'd left her pretty interesting job at the community planning office in Augusta to come back here, because that's what a Maine girl did when the call went out. When the velvet ties of family and loyalty beckoned you answered. Now, two years later, Rocky Falls, the town that never let go, once again had her. It was good at that, keeping things here. Bending rivers to its own ends, jailing giant boulders within its twisted roots. She was but the latest specimen in its collection.

Jasper bounced out of the cover of trees and lurched onto the building site. Gillian stuffed her musings deep.

Time to make the donuts.

Chapter 2

"Quit staring at my ass, Riley."

"I wasn't."

"Was."

"Wasn't."

Gillian sliced through the steel bands binding the load of floor joists and with a satisfying *Thwap!* one of the metal strips sprang loose and viciously thrashed the ground inches from Riley's boot toes. She straightened and vertebrae in her lower back popped. "Was."

"Was not."

She and Riley had been going at it since the sixth grade when they'd gotten into a killer argument during a snowball fight in the Rocky Falls Elementary School recess yard. He tackled her, she punched him in the ear, and then they bonded by rolling in dog shit. Making good use of brand-new hand-knitted Christmas mittens, she had grabbed a handful of half-frozen turd when she was on the bottom of the roll and scrubbed Riley's face with it when she came out on top. Her theory was he'd been trying to get her back ever since.

Orville—or maybe it was Wilbur—had scaled the high seat of the crane mounted on the truck bed just behind the cab. He flipped a toggle switch and the stabilizer feet buried themselves in the muck at the side of the truck. Then he twitched the dangling lifting forks clear of their cradle at the rear of the flatbed. *For Sale*, Gillian composed in her head. *One flatbed diesel, gently aged. Five thousand dollars or best offer, retiree included.* Finally, Wilbur hung the forks in midair and called to her.

"Hey, Gillian. Where you want me stick this here two-by stock?" Orville-or-maybe-Wilbur asked. He twitched the forks at the load on the flatbed. One outstanding possibility passed through Gillian's mind.

Riley must have read her thoughts. "Be nice," he said, grinning. "I'm a good customer."

Gillian bit back the sarcastic reply. He was right, damn him. He was in truth her *best* customer. Riley—unbelievably—was successful. Rocky Fall's largest contractor. She looked back at him and shrugged: your call.

"Up and over, then," Riley hollered, pointing to an area beyond the freshly poured concrete wall standing waist high in front of them. "Set her down on those sleepers in there."

"Thanks, Wilbur," Gillian said, waving, to reestablish chain of command. *Her* truck, *her* crane guy, after all—even if he was old enough to be her great-grandfather.

"I'm Orville," the man on the crane said. He swung the telescopic boom through its arc. Gillian watched Orville—if it really was him—slip the lifting forks neatly between the load of wall-framing lumber and the rusty truck bed.

"You are such a dork," Riley said to Gillian. His snicker was unpleasant.

"Your snicker is unpleasant," Gillian told him.

"A *wicked* dork," he said. "Wilbur's the *other* one."

Could be. The problem was that Wilbur and Orville were identical, septuagenarian twins. The only way you could tell them apart was when they were standing right next to their equally septuagenarian wives. Although that didn't necessarily cinch the ID because the wives were sisters, too. Not twins, though, thank God. Both brothers worked for her part time on a cash basis. A nice addition to Social Security for them and Gillian had the satisfaction of screwing the government in the name of helping good people.

"I knew that," Gillian said.

"Did not."

"Did."

It was amazing she and Riley could do anything together. But alas they did. Not what Riley would have liked them to be doing, though. He had been trying to get in her pants since seventh grade. The grab action during the dog shit encounter had awakened his imagination to a wider world. Basically, Gillian thought, their relationship was a replay of the age-old story: One good roll and everything goes to shit. *Hardee-har-har.*

"You take that side," Riley said to her. He pointed to the end of the stockpile that rested squarely in the middle of a lumpy, bumpy, ankle-breaking trap of dried concrete left over from the foundation pour.

"Screw you, Riley. You're the guy. You snap the foot. Take that end."

"Baby."

"You know I love it when you call me Baby." Gillian minced—as best she could in construction boots—to the good end of the load. Why did she torture Riley so? Answer: because he did it to her. And it was fun.

And safe. As houses, no pun intended. Riley was a rock, as solid and immovable as the bus-sized boulders that had stood four-square in the middle of the Mohasset River for ten thousand years. Oh, you could get to them. Approach at low water, climb up and down, all around. Do what you would to them, you never had to fear an impassioned avalanche. They owned their spot in the middle of the flow. So in a weird way she loved Riley and the stupid game they had.

"Will you hurry up?" he said, already bent over his end of the pile, his thick hands grasping the butts of two of the lengths.

Gillian took her time slipping her callused but long—and

she privately believed, rather elegant—fingers into tight-fitting leather work gloves.

"Quality work going on here," she said. "Don't rush me." The last little pinkie took the longest. She pushed in and tugged out and pushed in again, then—there! A perfect snug fit. She made eye contact with Riley. He was somewhere way back in his imagination, his jaw agape. He was good but he couldn't hide everything. *Got you, smartass.*

"Ready," she said.

Riley mumbled something Gillian thought sounded like *Me too*, but she let it pass. There were rules to the game.

They worked together in their usual efficient way, each lifting their end of each floor joist to eye level, sighting down the lengths and Riley—because he could support the heavy lumber with just one hand—marking the crown edge of the lumber with a heavy red crayon. Each joist had to be installed in the floor curved side up or the new floor would have more hills and valleys than the Rocky Falls country-side. The work was rhythmic and graceful in its own way. Two people sensing each other's intent, timing their reac-tions, coordinating their movements. If she and Riley were as good together in the romance department, she'd be Mrs. Riley with eight kids.

Shiver.

To break the monotony, she let her gaze drift around the site. Wilbur had the load of wall framing suspended just above the wooden sleepers laid out on the ground just inside the foundation wall of the rear wing. A couple of Riley's guys had assembled at the rear opening of the house, ready to begin hauling in the pile of stock once it landed. No di-rection from Riley needed. His crew knew what to do. He picked his people well and Gillian knew he was as dedicated as he could afford to be to their welfare as she was to Orville and Wilbur and the other guys that worked for her at the Wilcox mill.

That's the way it was in Rocky Falls. In all of upstate Maine, in fact. Probably the same thing in the wilds of Texas or Tennessee or anywhere else where it had always been just you, your little town, and miles of basically nothing between it and the rest of the world.

"Shit! Ouch—Will you frigging watch it?" Riley sucked on a finger. Gillian realized she'd drifted a bit *too* far off. Lost the rhythm and jammed his hand.

"Sorry. Really." She was. Stupid of her. A recent thing, the drifting. Something was niggling at her. A preoccupation. Strange, because she'd been nothing *but* focused since coming back to Rocky Falls. The whole time she'd kept her head down, played the game right. A hardworking dad injured at the mill and prodigal daughter returns to fill in, take over, do what she should have done more of when it could have *really* counted. When her mom was still alive. Guilt stabbed at her.

She peered up at the roof of the new house. A line of guys, squatting on planks, were roofing the rear slope of the main house. Hammer blows punctuated the putter and pop of an air compressor. Set against the brilliant blue of the sky, the scene had real artistic potential except for the fact that every single butt crack was revealed in its full glory.

Gillian twitched. Girlfriends ribbed her all the time: *Whoo-hoo*, bet you get some good scenery out there on those sites. *All guy, all day?* Yeah, well, there was a downside to everything. And every one of the rear ends on display needed a good pull *up*.

Except for the last one in line.

Boots, nail apron—all the leather on the job was kind of weirdly hot, Gillian had to admit—T-shirt, dark hair—nice dark hair: kind of a what? A wave?—and jeans that properly fitted an interesting rear end. What more could you ask for?

"Chr—ackers, Gillian! What the hell is wrong with you?"

Riley cursed and slid his forearm out from beneath a collection of joists that had somehow dealt themselves out across the stock pile fifty-two pickup style. Gillian realized she had no idea how that had happened.

"Riley, why don't you effing be more careful yourself, you knucklehead? It's not like we've never done this before."

"Go," he said, pointing to the lumber truck, shaking his wounded hand. "Take your little senior citizen's center on wheels and go."

"Fine. Suit yourself."

He looked steamed. And there *was* plenty of lumber back at the yard waiting to be cut. So, really, why *did* she hang around delivery sites helping Riley stack and crown his own damn lumber when she could just drop the load and hustle her and—she glanced toward the truck—One-of-the-Twins back to doing what really made the money?

Because she'd go stir-crazy sticking around the mill all day. A gal needed some sort of stimulation other than the heart-pounding walloping of the log stripper or the mesmerizing whirl of the carriage saw. Working the desk at the planning agency might not have been any great shakes career, and Augusta itself wasn't exactly a booming metropolis, but at least it had a population greater than three thousand souls and more than two places to eat lunch.

She dosed herself with one last look at well-fitted denim and sighed wistfully. One-of-the-Twins had finished the off-loading. The crane was resting back in its cradle on the bed and he was locking it down for travel. Gillian headed over.

"Snugged down good?" she asked him.

He grunted as he tugged on a rusty lever. "Been doing this for you Wilcoxes since before you was born, Missy," he said, not unkindly.

"Sorry." Then she asked him what was really on her mind. "You ever get restless around here?"

The Twin straightened, looking confused. "Where, Gilly? Around the site, here, you mean?" He looked around vaguely. "We only been comin' here for a few months."

Gillian had to laugh. "No, Orv—I mean, Wil—"

She looked at him blankly.

"That's right. Go on."

"Wilbur?"

"Yup."

"But I thought Riley said you were—"

And then she got it. The old coot.

The twinkle in his eye lit up the day. "You see, Miss Gilly, around here a body's got to come up with their own fun." He winked, slipped a ratchet handle into a winch drum and cranked thoughtfully, drawing up the slack on a canvas tie-down. Then he said, "A few more smiles like you got on your face right now'd go a long way toward livening up things around this town."

He winked the other eye, and her pent-up nudginess disappeared in a laugh. "Thanks, Wilbur."

"None needed," he said. "But I'll pass them along to my brother when I see him."

"But I thought *you* were—"

A cry echoed down from above—"Watch it! Heads up!"—followed by a scraping, sliding noise.

Gillian filled in the picture. Somebody—and probably sharp, potentially deadly some*things*—were on their way down from the roof. And not via a ladder. She shoved One-of-the-Twins unceremoniously beneath the bed of the truck and rolled herself under behind him. A shower of tools whanged off the flatbed above their heads, and the dull thump of a staging plank rattled the frame of the truck. Horror struck, Gillian waited helplessly for the soft, wet thunk of person.

Mercifully, it didn't come.

"Get him!" she heard Riley yell. "Pull that stupid bastard up *now*."

"Like I said," One-of-the-Twins said, groaning and picking bits of hay from his tongue. "You make your own fun around here."

It took Gillian several moments to free the Twin from the grip of the undercarriage. She untangled stiff limbs, asked solicitous questions and all the while prayed he'd been keeping up with his calcium requirements. Finally, he emerged, bent up like a pretzel, but unharmed. He was cackling. She wasn't. She scraped an elbow and the incident had scared the crap out of her. She flexed her arm and glanced up.

Some progress had been made on rescuing the unfortunate roofer, but it was obvious he was not taking the experience well. He had one leg hiked up and over the gutter and was clinging onto the fragile aluminum trough for dear life. Gillian empathized. Heights were not her thing either. Of course, going up a few flights on solid staging was a world apart from hanging by your fingertips above a three-story drop.

The guy on the gutter was really just a kid. Gillian could tell from his skinny frame and the way tendons stood out tautly under young skin. He was wearing the harness which Riley insisted every crewmember wear despite the constant grumbling. It would keep the boy from sliding any farther. He was in no immediate danger, but paralyzed with fear, neither could he help himself.

"Get it up there! Come on, move it!" Two guys grabbed a ladder. Riley exhorted them to get it into position but it wasn't long enough to reach the gutter line. A wide over-hang projected out between the top of it and the frightened boy. It would be a trick convincing the young man to lower himself past it and onto the first rung of the ladder.

"They need a frigging helicopter," Gillian mumbled.

"Or him," One-of-the-Twins said.

"Him" was the crackless roofer Gillian had spied earlier. Using his own harness and rope, the guy was belaying him-self down the steep slope of the roof toward the boy.

Riley blew by gesturing wildly toward the rest of his crew on the roof. "Get that frigging guy out of there. He's gonna kill—"

Without thinking, Gillian reached out and locked a re-straining hand on Riley's arm. "Riley, shut up. Your ladder's not going to do it either. Wait."

The man on belay was lowering himself even with the boy, setting one foot down into the gutter, making himself—of all things—*comfortable* on the very edge of the drop-off. The entire site had fallen completely silent. Even then, it was difficult to make out any of the words the man was saying to the frozen boy. As relaxed as the man appeared, the two cliffhangers could have been sitting in bleachers discussing the progress of a baseball game. Finally, the man gestured over his shoulder to the crew on the roof. The nonverbal message was clear: Up *slow*.

The boy's rope tensed and his other foot hooked onto the gutter.

Gillian watched, spellbound.

More rope tension, then the boy's shirt rode down as he was drawn completely onto the roof slope. Still the man talked. Quietly, almost in a whisper, it seemed to Gillian. He had not yet moved himself. More words, another gesture, the rope tugged gently and the boy rose to his knees and began to crawl up the steep pitch. Only then did the man gather himself back from the brink and turn to follow. Foot by foot, the boy gained the ridge and the safety of the planks, the man right behind. Riley's forearm felt as rigid as a length of cast iron pipe beneath Gillian's grasp.

Just before they reached the plank staging just below the chimney, the man reached out and stopped the boy in mid-crawl and said something into his ear.

"What the hell—" Riley started.

"Riley, shut up," Gillian said. The drama had to play out. Like she'd seen it before in another life, Gillian knew how it had to end.

The boy nodded and hauled himself up onto the planks, assisted by the other roofers. He sat for a moment. Then he tentatively stood up and took stock of himself and the view. Gillian knew he could see the Mohasset, the town hall steeple, the woods, probably all the way to her mill from there.

After several seconds, the boy threw both arms into the air in the classic field-goal gesture and cried, "I'm good! Oh, yeah!"

Every soul on site cheered.

Riley mumbled, "I'm *so* frigging done with apprentices."

Gillian couldn't take her eyes off the Crackless Wonder.

Chapter 3

Riley bellowed for everyone to take an early fifteen-minute break.

Good move, Gillian thought. Change the flavor.

Guys grabbed thermoses from their trucks and everyone congregated near her flatbed for lots of backslapping, ribbing of the kid and hysterical re-enactments. Not for the first time, Gillian found herself shaking her head at male rituals. She kept her eyes peeled for one particular back. She probably wouldn't recognize the front.

Just then the most beautiful man she had ever seen was looking at her from the doorway of the house. Boy.

Dark hair—yup, there was the wave—on the long side framed an exquisitely crafted face. *Hubba-hubba.*

Eyes, as piercingly blue as the flame from a gas jet, peered out above handsome cheekbones. And the lashes! Even from ten feet away, she'd swear they were the longest she'd ever seen on a member of the male species. Luxurious extravagances on an otherwise economical face.

Handsome Man waved, then hopped down onto the roughly leveled dirt and strode toward her. Women on construction sites were definitely an anomaly and she was used to being a bright flame among the moths, but this guy's radar had definitely locked onto her early. How did he even have time to pick her out of the crowd, as busy as he'd been? And who really cared? *Look* at them lashes.

"Hey," he said, hopping the wall.

"Hey, yourself," Gillian said.

Then he walked right past her. Out to the makeshift parking area, where he reached in the driver's window of a bright yellow, 1950s-era pickup that Gillian hadn't noticed before. Hard to miss, it was, with that schoolbus paint, fat tires, and a fancy scoop thing sticking up out of the hood. His hand emerged holding a thermos and a paper bag.

He came back over and settled himself on the wall near where she was standing. She was mentally patting herself on the back when she realized he'd sat so close to her because it was the only clear space on the top of the wall that didn't have a nasty looking sill bolt poking up out of it.

"Want one?" he asked, holding out a muffin. Not just any muffin, either. The thing had blueberries the size of gold nuggets and it was covered in lumpy sugar crystals. She was his.

"You got two?"

"Big appetite?"

She blushed. She did. "No, I meant one for you, too."

A little sleight of hand in the brown bag and he was holding an identical blueberry beauty. He shifted over on the sill to make some space for her and waggled the muffins.

Salivating, and wondering over exactly *what*, she squeezed herself in between The Wonder and a protruding bolt. She dug into his offering. "Mmmf." She rooted out blueberries with her tongue, even forgetting about the Lashes of the Year temporarily. When the top was but a memory and Gillian had paused, wondering how to gracefully snarffle up the paper-wrapped bottom half, her benefactor stuck out a hand.

"Jack," he said.

She wiped her sticky fingers on her jeans and shook. "Gillian. Pleased to meet you, and thanks." *Yum. You can climb my beanstalk anytime, Jack.*

"There's nothing like homemade," he said.

"*You* made them?"

If he said yes, she decided she'd have no choice but to kill him. Nobody that looked like him, saved helpless people by defying death by gravity and could cook besides, deserved to live. Unless he agreed to be her house slave for like the next fifty years.

"No," he said, and barked out a laugh as though she'd said something hysterically funny.

"You been around here long?" she asked. Pretty generic conversation starter, but she hadn't come to work that day prepared to meet such a nice pair of cheekbones.

"A while," he said, noncommittally, like people in witness protection programs on TV did.

"Uh-huh." Mysterious. A little mystery was nice.

"You staying locally?" *Do you sleep alone? Right side or the left side of the bed? Drip or perc in the morning?* So many questions, so little time.

"Out at the Inn."

Okay. Maybe the other side of the bed wasn't already *occupado*. She'd talk to Meg. Her older sister had her finger squarely on the pulse of the town. Scope out Lynette and Arthur. Get the deets on the guy sleeping under their roof. And with whom, if anyone.

"Beautiful spot, Rocky Falls," Jack said.

"Idyllic."

"Been here long?"

"Fourth generation."

"That's right. You're Charlie Wilcox's daughter."

He was a psychic, too?

"The truck?" he said, inclining his head.

She *was* a dope. The lettering on the door panel was faded but you could still read it: Wilcox Lumber and Sons, Since 1932.

"No 'daughter'?" he asked.

"Recent addition. To the business, not the family," she added.

"Ah."

"Yup."

Jack looked from the truck back to Gillian as if sizing them both up. "Progress has kind of left this place to itself, huh?"

The remark irritated her. "Some people like it that way," she snapped.

"So I've heard." He balled up the paper bag casually, but something about the new set of his shoulders told Gillian that they might not be splitting a malt down at the Riverview Restaurant lunch counter anytime soon.

"From who?"

"Around."

This was where she'd come in. He obviously held the same attitude toward Rocky Falls as a lot of the other newbies. In the face of that, an enigma, some blueberries and nice eyes could only hold you so long. A shame. She decided the muffin bum had definitely lost its initial appeal. She wrapped it in a purloined paper napkin and unobtrusively tucked it into the side pocket of her barn jacket.

"Thanks for the snack. I got to get back." She nodded toward the truck.

She saw One-of-the-Twins detach himself from a group of guys and head toward the flatbed. Riley's crew was back to doing what they did best on break, now that the hilarity had died down and the caffeine had kicked in. They were hunkered together in a circle facing each other, hands in their pockets, one kicking at the dirt and the others watching his foot do it. Gillian wondered for the millionth time what really went on in there.

"Right. See you later then, Gillian."

That depends crossed her mind, but maybe she was just cranky about being robbed of a muffin butt. And automatically suspicious of anybody new in town, hick that she was.

"Right, later," she said. What, after all, aside from the one remark that goaded her, was not to like about the new guy?

She waved at him vaguely, then turned and made her way to the truck. This Jack guy was different from your basic Rocky Falls model. *Blessedly* different. God love them for their purity of spirit and endearing naïveté, but the men in town could bore a gal into an early grave with their earnest talk of water levels on the Mohasset and the price of diesel fuel. And the subject that absolutely every New England male north of the flatlands had an opinion on: What to do with the shattered remains of the Old Man of the Mountain over in New Hampshire? They'd be kicking the dirt around over that one for generations to come.

Almost out of earshot, she turned and called back to Jack. "Hey—what do you think ought to be done about the Old Man of the Mountain, anyway?"

"Who?"

She tipped an imaginary hat. "Have a nice day." Damn. He *was* a catch.

She gave his pickup the once-over as she passed it. God, canary yellow. *Notice me*, it screamed. Big ass chrome side mirrors, shiny moon hubcaps. The windows were down. She peeked in. Pleather seats. Retrofits, but nice. A dog sitting contentedly behind the wheel. Seeing her, it licked its chops and whinnied. Because it was her dog.

"Get out, Boo." She slapped her leg. "Here."

Boo sneezed drunkenly and whined.

"*Now*, Boo."

He whinnied and flapped his long ears idiotically against his head.

Gillian strode around to her dog's side of the vehicle and stood right next to the pickup, eye to eye with him. "Get out of the car," she said, in a voice she was fairly sure would never be heard on a Puppy Chow commercial. Boo scooted sideways on the seat, turned his back to her and thumped his tail, leaving her to stare at his scrawny hindquarters. At the self-same ones she had stood behind on countless frosty winter mornings patiently waiting for it to *faire* its *toilette*. Damn dog. Brought a whole new meaning to the phrase *man's* best friend.

"Fine, then if that's the way you want it." An intelligent animal despite his stubbornness, he knew when Mommy was disappointed in him. He yowled and shuffled his feet, his toenails scratching the upholstery. That would serve the owner of the insipid vehicle.

To the knobby backbone of her traitorous dog she said, "Find your own ride home."

Chapter 4

Gillian met One-of-the-Twins at the truck. "I'll drive," she said, reaching out for the keys.

"I ain't infirm," he said, holding them back. "Just old. Settle yourself in, Miss Gillian." He opened the passenger door and kept it from smacking against her as she climbed up into the cab. Never got that kind of service from Riley.

Gillian watched The Twin hoist himself by careful stages into the driver's seat. He hit the key and the truck belched and backfired. The Twin gunned the engine then ground the gears into reverse. The roofers were scaling the scaffolding and the rest of the guys were filing back into the main house. The Twin painfully completed the three-point turn and she waved two fingers at Riley as they bounced past the house.

The Twin had just turned back onto the main road when Gillian barked, "Watch it!"

An SUV containing several children and a mom-at-the-wheel careened around a corner and headed directly for them. The Twin was forced to squeeze the truck to one side of the narrow road as the rolling metal fortress bore down on them. It barreled past, clearing them by mere inches, with nary a sideward glance from the driver.

Like we didn't even exist, thought Gillian, ruefully. "*See,* damn it? That's exactly what I'm talking about," she said, as

The Twin wrestled the truck off the soft shoulder of the road and onto firm pavement.

"You haven't said much except 'Watch it' since we left Riley's place, Miss Gilly," The Twin said, quietly.

"Yeah, well, maybe not to you," she heard herself snarl. "Sorry," she said. "I shouldn't take my bad mood out on you." Her brief conversation with the Wonder had gotten her going. The attitudes.

The Twin grunted softly.

"I guess what I mean is, these new people in town? I am so down on them. I mean, I'm not bitchy by nature, right?" She waited for an affirmative reply. She stopped herself from screaming *"Right?"* and whacking The Twin on his bony arm. He'd been through enough trauma in one day for someone forty years younger.

Finally, a polite throat clearing punctuated the silence. "Oh, no, Miss Gilly. Not you. Never in a million years."

"Smart man," Gillian said, hearing the touch of irony in his voice, yet glad he was prepared to humor her. "But seriously, for the past few years I've really resented the new people moving in. Pretty stupid, huh?"

"Maybe." He clutched and shifted gears.

"The funny thing is that it's not really all bad that they're here, you know? Lord knows we could use some new money pumped into this place. Upstate Maine ex-logging towns haven't exactly been setting the world on fire."

The Twin snorted his agreement. "Not since *my* pappy."

She went on. "And now, a whole lot of businesses have opened in the past three or four years. Town hall's getting redone, the health clinic opened downtown. Cripes, they even paved the parking lot to Crosby's Hardware. Unbelievable." She took her eyes from the road and looked over at The Twin. "You still with me here?"

"Yup."

Looking at him, Gillian felt a little guilty laying all this on him, of all people. As if, at his age, any of her angst would seem like a real problem to him. But at times The

Twins seemed like honorary grandfathers to the whole town. They had the whole history of it locked up inside their heads because they lived it. And heck, she was paying the freight on his time right then. And he was a good listener. Something she didn't have a lot of in her life at the moment. Somebody to listen to her, that is. It suddenly dawned on her The Twins and their Sisters had been listening to each other for more than half a century. For a second, she felt a twinge of envy.

She pursed her lips. "So I guess what I'm trying to figure out is: Why do I have this petty attitude? The new people are always in a hurry, but when they come in the yard on weekends to buy stock, they're pleasant enough. No crabbing about prices. And they *do* spend a lot of money. So what's my problem?"

"Look, Miss Gilly," he said, after a few minutes of silent driving alongside the sparkling river, "Rocky Falls is going to change whether you like it to or not. I know it's like your baby, and you don't want to see it grow up. But time don't stand still. Everyday it's some new thing. You just enjoy everything as it comes along and try to do your best."

"But see, that's exactly what I'm afraid of about all these new people," said Gillian, jumping on the point. "I mean that they—the new people that is—*won't* do what's best for the town. They'll just do what *they* want with it."

"I can't believe you're talking like that, Miss Gilly," he said. "*Nobody's* doing anything to this place as long as you're around. Look at all the hell you raised at them planning meetings this summer. About developing the downtown? Jumpin' Jaysus! You about blew the roof off the town hall. The Missus and I watched you three times on the cable." He laughed at the memory.

She did like to keep her hand in. Never knew when she might end up back in Augusta, fighting to save the little guys from the landgrabbing monsters. "Well, I hope you're right. But damn it, how long can we hold out with our own people selling us out? A lot of the new people in town are ready to just hand Rocky Falls over for development. All in the name of this urban renewal, planned community crap. Truthfully, they don't give a rat's ass about the quality of life around here despite all the pretty noises they've made about it. They're in it for the dough. Period."

The Twin grunted again. "You're likely right, Miss Gilly, but maybe it's a good thing. Why, we could get a Senior Citizen's Center out of it—not that that does me any good. I do all my gossiping on the job." He winked at her.

She laughed, then had a sudden thought. "Hey, speaking of gossiping, what were you all talking about back there at the site over break? Not that I want you to break any confidences or anything."

"You fixing to get me kicked out of the Guy Club, Miss Gilly?" The Twin loosed a sly, sideways grin and upshifted with a grind.

"No, no. Really. I just always wondered what went on in there. Inside those 'guy circles,' I mean," she finished awkwardly.

He chuckled at her discomfort.

"Oh, stop. Don't you pick on me too, Orville."

"Wilbur."

It was probably not very polite to say "Whatever" to a senior citizen. "Okay, Wilbur, then. I mean, there's like a ritual, right? That hands in the pocket thing, the dirt kicking? And one guy can never look directly at another guy, right?"

He braked for a turn. *Squeal.* He snapped on a directional and leaned on the wheel.

"Miss Gillian, you haven't changed a whit since you were old enough to talk. You always had a slew of funny questions. And you sure have the most peculiar way of looking at things."

Not the first man to tell her that. She figured that was the end of it. All in all, things might have worked out better for everyone if it had been. But, no.

"Okay, Miss Gilly, I figure age has some privileges."

One-of-the-Twins let the wheel spin itself straight coming out of the corner. "And being at a ripe old one, I belong to more clubs than I got time to go to. So I guess it wouldn't hurt if I got tossed out of one." He laughed again. "We were talking about the new guy. You know, that feller that saved young Jimmy, there? Damn good thing Riley makes all his guys strap in."

Riley wasn't who she wanted to talk about. "*Re*-ally . . . the new guy. Do tell."

Wilbur—if it really was him—chuckled again. He was getting his money's worth: nontaxable cash *and* free laughs. She hoped she'd have half his spunk when she was his age.

"He's some kind of big shot," he said.

The Wonder? A "big shot"? She cocked her head, puzzled. "Like how big? And in what way?" And why was he working for *Riley*, if that were true? She sat up straighter in the seat.

Her body language must have nudged The Twin into alert mode because he nervously glanced at her. "We . . . ah . . . didn't get into details, Miss Gilly."

Her ass, they didn't. "Give, Wilbur."

"Orville."

"What*ever*. Don't screw with the boss lady. Give."

"Well, he's . . . um . . . Damn, Miss Gilly, I'm afraid there ain't no good way to say this, so I'm just going to say it." He dropped the big one. "Rumor has it he's one of the ones who wants to build next to your daddy's land."

And *on* her daddy's land. Charlie had had several offers for the mill before he was hurt, all of them from some big Boston-based development company. From this Jack guy's company evidently.

To think it had all started with a muffin. Oh well, three centuries ago in Boston it had all started with a snowball and some Yo' Mama taunts to the wrong bunch of British troops.

"Turn the truck around," she said.

The Twin took his eye off the road for just a second. "Now Miss Gilly, don't you go getting all in a—"

"*Now*, Orville."

He didn't correct her. Maybe she'd actually gotten it right, but more likely, from the concerned look on his wrinkled face, he realized he'd unwittingly loosed the genie from her bottle. He sucked his teeth.

"You know, Miss Gilly, the Missus is expecting me for bridge—"

"You don't play bridge."

"I do now."

Gillian reached across the cab and tapped on the wheel. "Turn it around," she said softly.

"Yes, Ma'am." He pulled off Route 101 and into a farm stand parking lot.

Squeak. The brakes.

Groan. The steering box.

Grind. The transmission.

If old Jasper were steam powered, Gillian could have run it off what was coming out of its ears. Finally, The Twin got the old truck's nose around.

Gillian reviewed as they retraced their route. Opening move: Her dad rejects some offers to buy the mill land. Next: The Wonder comes to town. Enter the infamous muffins. The buttering up—literally—of the daughter. Charlie Wilcox's daughter, specifically. She recalled Jack's voice. She made it say *I couldn't talk any sense into the old man, so I'll just work on the daughter*.

Sell, Dad, Gillian figured she was supposed to say on cue to Charlie. *C'mon.* Retire to Florida. Screw the town. What's four generations and a whole bunch of families stacked against a huge cash windfall?

Somehow it felt like there was a missing piece in the sequence of events. No matter, she'd find it. She smiled ruefully in spite of her simmering anger. How long could any of them in town hold off wholesale change? And then the bigger question, the really prickly one: What if some of the change wasn't necessarily bad like One-of-the-Twins said? Agh. Headache. It was so much easier to just get pissed about the whole thing.

A few minutes down the road The Twin cranked on the big steering wheel again and the flatbed slopped onto the access road. Gillian suddenly knew how MacArthur must have felt returning to the Philippines.

Her boots hit the ground before the squeal of brakes died. She had to find the Muffin Man. The Muffin Man, the Muffin Man. This in sing song. Give him a piece of her mind, and quite possibly her middle finger, all for the same price.

Her anger swelled as she imagined the Infidel dressing up like a local. Clandestinely tugging on artfully aged blue jeans over a fine but undoubtedly pasty-white corporate ass. Insinuating himself into the local culture. Onto the local construction crew. *And* putting one over on poor stupid Riley who, despite the dog shit incident and the many run-ins since, she still considered a friend. Yup, poor, stupid Riley, getting hoodwinked by a slick—

Wait. She abruptly froze in mid-step, almost flipping herself over the low foundation wall.

She pictured the circle of guys at break, the scuffing toe action, the conversation. . . . *Bingo*.

The missing piece: If the crew knew or even *suspected* who The Wonder was, Riley *absolutely* knew. That meant Mr. Big Blueberries-with-Sugar-on-Top was here by invitation.

From Mr. Douglas Dickless Riley. She was officially no longer pissed. Now she was furious.

"Riley!" she bellowed at the back of the house.

Sounds of cutting and hammering stopped. The site seemed to draw in its collective breath and hold it. In the quiet, Riley sidled out to the open back wall.

Gillian eyed him. He was a big man. Intimidating to most

people. Especially to those of her somewhat slender stature. The logo *Riley Construction* was stitched on the breast pocket of his khaki work shirt. His sleeves were rolled up, displaying large wrists and muscled forearms. A shock of blond hair capped his weathered, but basically good-natured face. He slouched against a support column.

He grinned, then, the bastard, treating her to a panorama of even white teeth. "Get back to work, you guys," he said over his shoulder to no one in particular.

The job site let out its collective breath and the work noises resumed. To Gillian's tuned ear, though, the sounds seemed artificial and manufactured. She would have bet her daddy's mill that all the hidden eyes were on her and Riley, all ears straining to hear over the strike of random hammer blows.

Riley casually shouldered himself into motion and sauntered down the planks leading from the raised floor of the house down to grade. From the big-deal way he was acting, Gillian thought it safe to assume he suspected she had something on him. He'd the same look on his face in the principal's office back in eighth grade when an unidentified someone had stuffed her locker full of condoms. She hopped the poured concrete wall, carefully avoiding the bolts, and met him halfway up the ramp.

Too late, she realized that with Riley's height, her relative lack of it and the angle of the planks, she would be forced to deliver her address to his belt line and points just south. She could have sworn she heard a snicker from inside the house. MacArthur undoubtedly had at least an empty ammunition box to stand on when he made his triumphant return speech.

She fired her opening salvo. "You swine."

The stylized deer on Riley's shiny belt buckle appeared to wink at her. A trick of the slanting fall light, she hoped.

"Back so soon? Forget something?" Riley asked, way too innocently to Gillian's mind.

"Get out of my way," she said. She wanted to rip off his

face—or anatomical parts more conveniently accessible to her at the moment—but she could deal with him anytime. She was after bigger game. Muffin Man was somewhere inside. She could smell the blueberries, but Riley still blocked her path up the narrow wooden gangway.

"Move," she said. "I'll deal with *you* later."

Riley didn't budge. A muffled guffaw leaked out of the building. Then she tried, "Get the *fuck* out of my way," in a much louder voice and added a finger poke to Riley's midsection for emphasis.

He flinched and the plank trembled. Gillian felt her knees go rubbery as her legs reacted to the bounce. Riley overcompensated too, and suddenly the two of them were fighting for purchase on the same spinning log. Brawn triumphed over brain and Gillian landed on her rear end in the back-filled muck beneath the planks.

"Ow." *That hurt.* She tried to roll onto her side. Different pain, but equally less fun.

"Ow. Ow. Ow." It had been *so* much easier wrestling with Riley back in The Day.

Suddenly Riley's face was hovering above hers. There was a look of apparent concern on it. Perfect. Fighting through a fog of pain, Gillian stretched her arm out, grabbed a clod of sodden clay and with as much strength as she could muster, smacked it squarely against the side of his gleaming, golden head.

Gillian tasted grit and mud as gunk cascaded down into her face from the resulting supernova, but her sublime satisfaction at the moment of wet sloppy contact made it all worth it. She hadn't lost her touch.

"What the *fuck* did you do that for?" Riley sputtered, spitting out dirt onto the ground—thankfully—to the side of her. Unpleasant childhood memories of him hanging spitballs down over her face came back to her. She and Riley had a truly sadistic relationship, she was forced to admit.

"Because I couldn't find a fucking rock, that's why. Now get the fuck off me." And they used a lot of bad words around each other. A *fucking* lot of bad words. Still dazed, she was forced to let her head fall back. She was wickedly dizzy.

Abruptly, another face replaced Riley's against the deep blue vault of the sky. Remarkable features on this face. *Really* marvelous eyelashes. Each one was so thick and long that together they looked like an evenly planted row of birch saplings. Stupid sounding even to her, but there it was. She suddenly appreciated how wonderful it was to be consoled by someone so terrifically good looking. Who was he, again?

"I saw your fall from grace," the face quipped. "Are you okay?"

She was now. Thick dark hair curled down to just brush the collar of his shirt.

"Can you straighten your leg?" he asked, "It's at an awkward angle. You sure it's alright?"

"Jack, it's no big deal," Gillian heard Riley say. "She's a klutz. She falls on her ass all the time." She remembered how much she hated Riley. She also noticed how he didn't bark orders at Eyelashes—What had Riley called him? Jack?—to get back to work like he would have anyone else on his crew.

Eyelash Jack was different, Eyelashes was—*Whoa!* Hang on—boosting her up by grabbing her under the armpits. She shot to her feet like she was fired out of a circus cannon. Blood rushed to her head and it all came back to her.

Eyelashes was the Muffin Man, the Crackless Wonder—pity, a waste that—but he was also The Enemy. And, when by the way, had she taken up Thinking in Capital Letters?

"You bastard," she said to Riley. That was *right* where she'd left off. She was back. "You skunk."

"Gillian," Jack began. "It doesn't seem like the time or place to be—"

"And you—" she realized she couldn't really say *Shut the hell up* to him like she could to Riley, given the newness of her relationship with The Crack, so she settled for—"Pipe down till I'm ready for you."

Both men, to her surprise, went mute. She turned to The Crack. "I'm ready now."

He looked confused. "For what?"

"For you."

"To do . . . what?"

To do *what*? Deny her accusations, of course. "Protest. Deny my accusations."

"About what?"

Unbelievable. Gillian looked from The Crack to Riley then back again. The Crack. Jack. Neither name was memorable in and of itself, but paired, they had potential.

"You look innocent, but I'm certain are not," she said to Jack the Crack. To Riley she said, "You look *completely* guilty, and sure as shit you are. You and Jack—" she stopped short of adding *The Crack* lest she be labeled The Crazy One—"are in cahoots on a scheme to develop Rocky Falls."

Gillian thought she saw The Crack shoot Riley a silencing look.

Riley shuffled his feet.

"Speak up, now," she said, in her best imitation of her sister Meg's schoolmarm voice. "Which one of you two are man enough to admit it?" She deliberately looked only at The Crack to egg Riley on. She waited. The job site again gave a world-class impression of complete ignorance of the drama unfolding in its midst. The seconds ticked off. Gillian suddenly understood the expression *You could have heard a pin drop*.

Riley shuffled his feet. Gillian remained expectantly mute.

Finally he cracked. "Aw, Gillian, now don't be getting crazy about this all over again. This town is just a pinprick on the map. It could be a whole lot more and you know it."

A pinprick.

"Well, Riley," she said, taking her time, theatrically wiping mud out of her eye with a corner of her sleeve. "I don't know much about *pin*pricks, but I do know about *pricks* and for sure you are about the biggest one I ever met." She smiled sweetly at him. To The Crack she said, "You? I'm thinking your problem is all about *not* having a very big one to start with."

There were smothered guffaws from the peanut gallery. "Back to work!" Riley screamed into the house.

"Riley's right," Jack said, ignoring her jibe. "This town has been dying on the vine for a long time. But nobody around here wants to admit it."

"Dying." The word velcroed itself to a too-soft, too-sticky, too-vulnerable place at the back of her throat. She crossed her arms. Rocked on her toes. Examined the patterns in the mud at her feet. Savored the deluge she could feel building in her chest. Loving it, desperate for the sweet cleansing release it would bring.

"It's not . . . dying," she said, forcing herself to say the word. She lifted her eyes to trace the straight orderly seams of the plywood sheathing on the rough frame of the house. "And just maybe it's none of your business *how* it is because it's not yours. That ever occur to you?"

Jack started to say something, but Gillian brought her gaze back to him and slashed her hand through the air, cutting him off. The question was rhetorical. Out of the corner of her eye she saw Riley take a small step back, no doubt catching the stench of dog shit.

She began to pace, scissoring her arms in front of her, stretching the shoulder seams of her jacket, putting distance between herself and . . . That Word. The D word. *Dying*. And the guilt that it stirred.

Building, growing, swelling, bigger, bigger . . . boom. The raging current within her burst its dam and words and emotions cascaded. "Rocky Falls doesn't belong to you, Jack Whoever-You-Are. You can't just walk in here and change it any way you want to suit you. You think you're gonna rescue us just like that? Just like that kid?" She snapped her fingers, waved at the roof. "Like some white knight on a horse? Just charge in here and change the place for our own good? Hah! As if." She noticed three guys on staging planks set up around the chimney were motionless, mason trowels poised in mid-swipe, watching her. *"Get back to work!"* she screamed at them.

"Hey, watch it," Riley said. "Those are my guys."

"Shut the hell up," she said. She stalked back and forth.

"Buy up the land," she said. She turned abruptly to Jack, the pain carried on the thought making her breath hitch. "Every frigging bit of it, why don't you? Bulldoze everything. . . . All to make money for who? *You.* Tell you right now, never gonna happen."

Yet as she said the words, her blood ran cold. What if he could? What if he threw enough money around? Beneath the yesteryear charm and the warm embrace of the river and the mountains and the woods there had always been an air of quiet desperation in town and even in her own family for as long as she could remember. How far would people go to feel solid economic ground under their feet?

But the tumult within her was running loose, crashing over rocks, throwing up fountains of spray, flinging floater logs into the air like they were matchsticks. "Big deal city guy," she said to Jack. She fought to keep flecks of spit from flying out with her words. She waggled her index finger at him. "I know all about you. You're from Boston." Turner Development, she had just remembered. "Not surprising you don't give a crap about this place."

She switched back to Riley. "But you," she said. "You grew up here. Your *family* grew up here. And now you're selling them out. *Us* out. You're despicable." She poked him in the chest. He rocked back on his heels.

She turned back to Jack. His eyes welded her to the spot. *Gas jets on high . . .*

And they seemed . . . hooded. As if a second clear eyelid had slid over them, revealing him as a true predator despite his beautiful plumage. Creepy-crawly sensations danced along her nerve endings.

He took a step toward her.

She took a step backward toward Riley.

He looked like the controller at Three Mile Island must have looked moments before the gongs went off. Then, with what Gillian could only assume was an act of iron will, he reassembled his features into the guy she had known as the Muffin Man. Banal, pleasant, harmless. Someone you'd happily share a snack with. Then he smiled. A nice change.

But then he started to laugh. He laughed and laughed, the idiot, like he couldn't stop. Like there was a great big cosmic joke going on that only he understood. He practically wet himself.

Suddenly she got the punch line. It was her. *She* was the joke.

A chorus of hoots from inside the building joined in with Jack. Riley screamed again into the dimness in the building, "Dammit all, *didn't* I tell you all to get back to it?" For all the response he got, his entire crew could have already left for the day. "Well, didn't I?" he bellowed.

"Yes, Boss . . ." and "Yeah, yeah . . . Right . . ." echoed quietly back on the cool air. Hammers and air guns started up again.

Gillian hated being the butt, but was also relieved that whatever scary thing lived in the moment she and The Crack had just shared had apparently crawled back into its hole for the time being. She realized she had been holding her breath. She exhaled. Finding herself standing close to Riley, she shoved at him. "Get away from me." *Before I tell the playground monitor.*

"But you—"

"Get away."

He stepped away from her and Jack. It was that act which clearly stated to all of them that the showdown had been reduced to the Final Two. Whatever happened between the three of them from then on, Riley would be watching from the bleachers.

"You—" she targeted The Crack with her index finger— "Probably don't know any better, but you'll find out. You just wait." For her to beat the drum again like she had back at the town meetings in the spring. Live Free or Die, New Hampshire said. Don't Tread on Me . . . someplace else they learned about in grade school said. Evidently Riley had a short memory. But Rocky Falls didn't. She didn't. Her home would not be taken over.

"Get over here," she said to Riley, pointing next to her feet like she would to call Boo. No, that wasn't exactly right. She would say it in a much kinder tone to Boo. Riley came, when Boo probably would have had the sense not to. She squared-off on him, never taking her eyes from Jack, and grabbed his shirtfront in two fists. She pulled his face down close to hers. "Him, I get," she said, angling her head toward Jack. "But *you* . . ." she snarled. "There's no excuse for you."

She shook him loose and stalked off toward the truck.

"Gillian," Riley called to her retreating back. "Wait a minute . . . Gillian! You can't say that to me and just walk away!"

"Oh, really? Fucking watch me, Riley."

Maybe he did, maybe he didn't. She never looked back.

At the truck, Gillian yanked on the driver's door of the cab and it creaked open. The Twin stared down at her from the high seat.

"By God, Miss Gillian, that there was something awesome to behold," he said.

"Keys, Orville," she barked. "And move over—I'm driving."

"But Miss Gilly, you know I'm Wil—"

She raised a warning finger. He dropped the keys onto her open palm.

Chapter 5

The leaves had already started their color change. Sunlight streamed through the high treetops crowding the river, crowning the deciduous with red and orange coronas. It was chilly in the mornings now. Wreaths of morning mist obscured the water's surface, where remnants of summer-warmed water were brushed by the cool fingers of fall.

Jack snapped the tip of his fly rod and sent a tiny lure floating out over the burbling riffles of Mohasset River. He gently touched it down on the surface of a calm pool tucked into the lee of a huge granite boulder. The flamboyant fly was irresistible to the unwary, perilous to the unwise. It floated on the swirling water, waiting, calling down into the shallows. Jack stripped line and let the current do its work.

He had stumbled upon this idyllic spot serendipitously. Getting up before dawn that morning, he'd dressed in the dark, then drove slowly along the road leading out of town. After a mile or so, he'd passed a turnoff leading into the woods. Banging a U-turn, he rolled the pickup carefully along a rutted trail that disappeared into the trees. Two white-painted boulders finally halted his progress, but ahead of him sparkled the Mohasset. He'd assembled his gear and hoofed it to the river.

He needed to fish this morning before he headed off to

Riley's job. He needed to clear his head. He supposed the ritualistic actions of choreographing the movements of the rod and lure were like a mantra, his body executed the mechanical motions without conscious thought, leaving his mind free to wander. And dawn, while most of the world still slept, was the best time for him to be alone with his thoughts.

Suddenly, the fly disappeared under the surface of the pool. Jack gave the tip of his rod a quick jerk to set the hook, then stripped line. A blue-green body broke the surface eight feet downstream and shot into the air, struggling to slip the hook. The elusive form dived back under the surface, and the line made a beeline cut through the water toward the reeds.

Jack kept the rod tip high, playing the fish. As he waded closer to it, taking up line as he went, he could see it slashing back and forth among the reeds. A rainbow trout. It seemed to be shooting him desperate, sidelong glances with each pass. He drew in still more line and when he was close enough, he unclipped the net hanging from the rear of his waders and reaching forward with it, dipped its leading edge under the water. The fish, finally exhausted, floated in.

Jack straightened and clamped his rod under one arm, then reached into the net. He grasped the fish behind the gills, and untangled the trout from the twine. Its mouth was open, gasping for air. Or maybe it was trying to talk its way out of the consequences of its hasty decision to snatch the fly.

In any case, too late. Jack slid the hook carefully out of the fish's jaw. He crushed the sharp barbs flat ahead of time, to make that part of the job easier. He took a moment to admire the trout, then lowered it back into the water and waved it gently by its tail. Suddenly, the fish revived and in a burst of speed and color, shot away into the middle of the river.

Jack checked the condition of the fly. Roughed up a bit, but serviceable. He blew on the plumage to fluff it up and set himself for another cast. He flicked the rod tip and the fly floated out again on its single-minded mission. It touched down amid the deep shadows of an overhanging birch, and lazily circled in a whorl of current.

It was really all about the bait. Dangle the right thing in front of people and they can't help but snap at it. It was just a matter of finding out what they were hitting on. Then all you had to do was be patient. Wear them down. Let them fight against the line until they were too tired to resist.

The screams woke Gillian up. They were her own.

Dazed, she shoved her hand out from under the covers and slammed it down on the alarm clock. The quiet after the storm of electronic noise hurt her ears.

She sat up groggily in bed. Riley had been in the dream, and other people from town, too. Her sister Rachel, Meg and her kids, her Dad, and someone else. . . . A menacing presence lurking. Who?

"Aaagh!" she groaned. That jerk, Jack. Jack the Jerk. He was in it. God. It was bad enough she couldn't stop thinking all yesterday about her run-in with him. Now he was invading her subconscious.

She sat up in the early morning coolness of her room and stretched. She threw the covers back and tugged on sweats over her T-shirt and underwear. Rubbing her head, she headed for the kitchen and coffee. The secret to a full, productive life was to make it the night before. Then all you had to do in the morning was hit the switch to start it perking. She leaned against the chipped granite counter while the pot gurgled. She mentally organized her day.

First, finish ripping up that load of pine. She'd dropped it on the conveyor last thing before closing up the night before, but she hadn't started on it because the Jerk Named Jack had really had her stewing and she didn't trust herself to run heavy equipment when she was distracted.

Later in the morning make yet another delivery out to

Riley at the site. *Riley.* Huh. Screw him, the louse. After yesterday's Benedict Arnold routine he could sing for his stock. Let him get his lazy ass out to the yard and pick it up himself.

Thinking back to his behavior yesterday, she was again dumbstruck. He had completely betrayed her. Obviously he knew who Jack was the whole time she was making nice with him over blueberries. Riley should have given her the heads up. Sure, they'd done each other dirty in the past, but she'd always thought they had an unwritten code. Needling was part of the game, the occasional setup to embarrass the other person, completely okay. Enjoyable even. But nothing humiliating or demeaning.

Yesterday's showdown had been both.

She reached for a cup from the oak cupboard above the chipped enamel double sink. Not to mention that Riley'd sold out the town by collaborating with The Enemy. And no doubt Jack the Crack was that. A Land Shark, and not in a funny, *Saturday Night Live* way either. In a gobble-up-whatever-he-could-take way. He'd suck what he could out of Rocky Falls and head back down south a richer man, the slimy bastard. Riley might make some money in the deal, but he'd lose everything else he ever had in this town. Evidently, he was just too stupid to see it.

But Crack's absolute gall was what most stuck in her craw. He thought he knew what was best for everybody. It didn't matter what *they* thought about. The great development Nazi. She could almost feel bad for him if she didn't despise him so much. He was probably completely cut off from normal human relations by his total conviction that he was always right. And the way his face changed toward the end of their little tête-à-tête? Spooky. Completely shut down and emotionless.

Something not quite right there.

Jack reeled in line, his mind going back to the confrontation with Gillian Wilcox the day before. She was as stubborn and intractable as they came. No ring on *her* left hand, small wonder.

He'd underestimated her at first. She came across as an unsophisticated, scruffy, small town workaholic. The type that drank beer and guffawed with the locals but never slept with any of them, preferring the chase to the capture scene.

And the chase was something he understood very well. The business world was all about that. All about compromises. Whether the purpose was monetary gain or sexual satisfaction, both parties entered it with eyes wide open and in complete understanding of the terms and conditions of the agreement. Everybody was clear about their true motivations.

But in this town, no one, least of all Gillian Wilcox, seemed clear about their reasons for doing anything. Certain things were done because they'd always been done that way. Other things were never considered because they'd well . . . never been done. The whole decision-making process was illogical and maddening.

His lure drifted into the tangled roots of a birch clinging precariously to the undercut shoreline. He slowly drew the fly back, trying not to dunk it. You got better hits on a dry lure. But the current tugged stubbornly on it and despite all of his rod-tip twitches, it was sucked beneath the surface. He swore softly and reeled in.

That wasn't to say that people in town couldn't make up their minds. They could, and had earlier in the year when he had made offers through his advance people. Floated a proposal in front of the planning board. Gillian Wilcox had screwed that up. Whipped everyone into a frenzy. Pulled up some little-used state statutes on minimum lot sizes and brought his plans to a screeching halt. Turned the town, even those who saw the inevitability in his proposal and who maybe had initially *welcomed* it even, absolutely and irrevocably against him. He'd hit a complete dead end.

But then again, maybe not. Time to rethink what he knew about her, hash over the new bits of info he'd gained by talking to her directly. He finished reeling in and brought the fly up to eye level. *Still a gamer*. He snapped the rod tip forward. The lure hung for a moment on a breath of air, then settled nicely onto the surface of the river.

Okay. Now just where had he gone off track yesterday with the feisty and unexpectedly interesting Gillian Wilcox?

First move: Disarm with charm. As an opening cast, it wasn't a bad choice. Worked before. Lots of people simply couldn't resist it. His particular brand of charm, that is, he admitted unself-consciously. It was a tool. Nothing more. In her case, it *did* bring her to the surface, but when he tried to set the hook, she shied away. The instant the conversation turned personal, she'd changed the subject.

Next: attention. To her. He gave good attention. Again, it wasn't vanity that made him acknowledge the practical advantages of being a male that many women found attractive. Listening well came second nature to him. It was automatic. You didn't get ahead in business without being tuned in to client need.

He didn't get far with that either. She was a woman that kept her own counsel. She wasn't what he'd call hard on the outside, but she was flinty and durable underneath. A survivor. Gillian Wilcox didn't put much stock in what anyone thought of her good *or* bad. That was a problem.

He saw a sparkle of color in the water close in to the bank. He reeled in, then shot the lure out toward the shadowy spot. A roil of surface water told him he was in the right place.

To be honest, he'd found it unexpectedly easy to listen to Ms. Wilcox. He'd painted an image of her ahead of time as a tough old bird with callused hands and a limited vocabulary. But she turned out to be engaging, easy on the eyes, and free spirited. So much for relying on reports from his people.

She knew her business too. And her history. *And* she'd blindsided him.

Just thinking about that made his blood boil. He who had always prided himself on maintaining control in business relationships. Who had preached that loss of emotional control meant loss of favorable terms. Suckered in by an apparently naive, blue-jeaned truck driver with one-tenth his business experience.

A flash in the water under the overhanging bank. Jack reacted a split-second too late. A trout jumped and twisted in the air and threw the hook. The shining blur landed with a splash and shot back into the shadows.

"Damn!"

He couldn't remember the last time he'd been had like he was yesterday out at the site. The Wilcox woman had handled him like the last fish he'd let go, playing with him, but ultimately she was the one in control. He'd been flipped completely onto his back like a beetle. He remembered that he'd gotten angry at some point in the discussion and had laughed like a donkey to cover it up. It had been funny, this wiry, wired woman facing off two big guys in front of a whole construction site for an audience. And the way she treated that Riley. Jack actually felt bad for him at points.

But he had gotten angry. Lost his temper. She had *made* him angry. In fact, he realized, was *still* angry. He seldom missed setting a hook. He, Jack Turner, violating his own tenets by becoming emotionally involved in a deal. He'd laughed at Gillian Wilcox because he hadn't known what else to do. He'd been at a loss.

Only momentarily, but still the trend disturbed him.

The coffee pot spat and fizzled, telling Gillian it had done its thing. She filled her cup. Oh well, Jack the Crack's pathology wasn't her problem.

Her problem was keeping him and his development corporation the hell out of town.

There were some people in Rocky Falls, she knew, who wanted to go ahead with the redevelopment project. The newcomers obviously. They wanted the convenience and up-scale of a revamped downtown. But many were old timers like Pop and Beatrice Henry, who owned one of the only two eateries in town, and the Mansfields, who ran the Eagle House Inn. They didn't want to see things change, but they were directly benefiting from the recent upswing in the town's fortunes. Their thinking was that they'd like to leave their children a thriving restaurant business and a going bed and breakfast, rather than just a struggling sandwich shop and perpetually lit vacancy sign. You couldn't blame them.

Gillian opened the door to her ancient Coldspot refrigerator. It wasn't an icebox, thank goodness, but it wasn't much above one either. But, like most of the really old things in her folks' house, it still worked and she liked it.

She reached for the milk and pulled the cardboard top off the glass bottle. She sniffed at it tentatively before adding a couple of tablespoons to her coffee. A dollop of honey squeezed into her coffee from a plastic bear container topped off the java. It was a habit that grossed out a lot of people, but the sugar got her going in the morning.

She yawned and shuffled through the pantry and into the parlor. Nowadays, it would be called a living room. The natural pine floorboards of the old house were silky under her bare feet. She'd measured some of them at sixteen inches wide. They had been cut from the virgin woods standing around the house when her great-grandfather built it. Through the living room was the mudroom. Beyond that, the door to the back porch.

Gillian lifted the latch on the back door. It was hammered wrought iron, as old as the rest of the house. It couldn't be locked, not that she'd ever felt the need to do so. She pushed on the spindle work screen door, and, as usual, only the top half swung free of the jamb. Balancing her coffee, she kneed the bottom half open.

Behind the house lay the customary old New England barn. It rose two-and-a-half stories, with generous rolling doors at ground level, and a cavernous loft. Like every other structure of its kind still standing in upstate Maine, it was once used for stabling livestock and storing hay and farm equipment. Now it had a discouraged, lopsided lean to it, slowly collapsing toward its downhill side. The roofline had a pronounced swayback, a symptom of spreading walls and rotting cross ties.

Incongruously, an ornate cupola clung precariously to its sagging ridge. A throwback to days of Rocky Falls' prosperity, rows of cedar shingles in intricately cut patterns adorned its side. A bronze rooster weathervane capped the verdigris copper roof and swung arthritically in the light morning breeze.

From her vantage point on the porch rail, Gillian drank it all in with her coffee. What would it be like to go backward through time, year by year to the point where the barn and the house were filled with life and light and sound? With sturdy, simple, people going about their everyday business? Right this minute, if she were to look out on that long-vanished scene, she'd probably see a little boy in overalls—her grandfather—on his way out to feed the chickens. Her great-grandfather would be leading horses out of the barn, preparing to hitch up the lumber wagon. The layers of bird droppings and neglect would fade from the cupola, the rooster shining bright and the shingles gleaming with paint.

But there hadn't been much life in the house or on the grounds since her mom died. She had been the glue that held everyone else together. Her family never had an over-abundance of material things, but they always felt like a family. They appreciated what they had together and, except for the usual blowups with her siblings, life was good. After her mother died, Dad still had the business to keep him going. But the heart had gone out of the Wilcox clan. Gillian had had to leave. Start anew, somewhere else. Somewhere else turned out to be Augusta, in the planning office.

Her younger sister Rachel couldn't handle it anymore in town either, after their mom. Boston had been Rachel's Augusta. Smart girl, that Rachel, if she kept her hands to herself. And the Chardonnay bottle corked. Making more down south than six Rocky Falls families put together.

Then her dad got hurt, which left . . . her. She was now Wilcox Lumber. With a fingernail, Gillian flicked at a piece of paint peeling off the turned porch column next to her. It was a ritual. Every morning she sat here, she knocked off another small patch of crumbling whitewash. Like a castaway marking time.

Ugh. Grim.

What she needed was a swim. That always fixed her up. Well-worn gum boots, their leather uppers saggy and cracked, lay next to the top step. Gillian slipped her bare feet into them, swilled the rest of her coffee and headed for the river.

Jack took up the slack in the line and pulled the fly in close. The trout had gotten the best part of the lure, leaving him with little more than bare hook. He furrowed his brows and cut it from the line.

For the life of him he couldn't understand why it also bugged him that Gillian Wilcox left the site yesterday thinking he was an unfeeling son of a bitch. He wasn't. Unfeeling, that is. True, he was a bit of a bastard not coming clean with her about who he was *before* he offered up the muffins, but that was business. You don't announce your presence to the fish by splashing around in your waders. But who was she to question his motives? That pissed him off.

He unzipped his lure case and pulled out a duplicate of the decimated one. Capturing the end of the gossamer line, he was about to knot on the lure when he changed his mind. A little ways downstream he'd spotted a rock shelf that hung out over the river casting shadows across a deep pool. Just the spot for bass. He selected a different fly and attached it.

Slowly, feeling his way across the rolling gravel of the riverbed, he made his way downstream, moving closer to the pool. He snapped the rod tip and sent the new fly drifting downstream on the breeze. It landed softly on the surface of the river.

There was a lot of money to be made in Rocky Falls. Why couldn't people see that? He stood to make a bundle, but so did they. Why were they so afraid of moving ahead? They'd be better off working with him on a mutually beneficial project than wait for the eventuality of some asshole developer—one name in particular came to mind and he shuddered—dragging them kicking and screaming to somewhere they *really* didn't want to go.

Gillian Wilcox was the linchpin in the redevelopment plan. No one downtown would budge an inch until she agreed to sell her land. At least part of it. The section adjacent to the mill. She'd never let go of Wilcox Lumber proper. But once she wavered, even a little, the rest of them would tumble like dominoes.

Everyone bit on something, he came back to. He watched his lure drift on the current. It was all in the bait. He just had to find out what would work on the lithe Ms. Wilcox.

He needed to find a weakness, a vulnerability. A way in. He could start by getting to know them. Everyone in town. Find out what was really on their minds. Where the sticking points were. Gillian couldn't be around, though, when he was schmoozing. She'd snarl his cast if she knew he was working that angle. He laughed out loud at his choice of metaphor.

She had some sisters and an aunt with a shop in town, he knew. He could probably find out more about them. No doubt all kinds of useful tidbits about the Wilcox clan would surface if he just rooted around among the townsfolk long enough. He began to relax. It was great when a plan came together.

Suddenly, a bass broke the surface and launched into the air, twisting, trying to shake the hook. Jack slipped line through his fingers. The instant the fish went under he jerked the rod tip and the hook set.

The bass gave him a good fight for a while, but it eventually tired and he slipped into his net. Jack examined it. It was a beauty, close to three pounds. He looked it right in the eye, then dropped it into his creel and snapped the lid shut.

Gillian swung her arms as she walked to get her blood moving in the chilly morning air. She flipped her hair out of the collar of her sweats and pulled the drawstring of the hoodie tighter at the neck.

The dirt road to the sawmill ran alongside the house and past the barn, and Gillian took it at a good clip, knowing its ruts and washouts by heart. Just outside the front gate, on either side of the road, stood pile upon pile of rough-cut lumber neatly stacked and air drying. The familiar scent of pine resin rose up to greet her, and with so many board feet of cut lumber in such close proximity, the odor was intense. Pungent and sweet and bitter all at the same time.

She passed the last pile and entered the yard proper. A swell of pride always rose in her chest at her first sight each morning of the red sign over the front gate with its black and gold-shadowed letters proclaiming "Wilcox Lumber Company." Maybe it wasn't much, but it was all theirs. Her and her family's.

She slipped the elastic cord with the front gate key on it from her wrist and unlocked the brass padlock. She kicked the single-bar gate back against its stop, where it clicked in with a clang. The locked gate was supposed to prevent someone from—like anyone around actually would—backing a truck into the yard and making a wholesale lumber snatch. Most people found it easier to just slip under the fence and help themselves to the bits and pieces they ran short of on a Sunday. They'd leave a note under the office door telling what they took then come around later in the week with the cash. Nobody who'd grown up in town would ever stiff anyone else from town. One more reason to keep things in Rocky Falls just the way they were.

She skirted around the front office, went past the saw shed and headed for the gap between the mulch pile and the rough logs waiting to be hauled to the conveyor. A short path between them led down to her swimming spot on the Mohasset. She'd been jumping into the river there since it was pronounced clean by the federal government. Her family thought she was crazy because she would jump into water of any temperature at any time of the year. She wasn't a mid-winter, ice-breaking fanatic, but she'd swim in the Mohasset starting just after the floes broke up in early April until it crusted over in mid-October. For her, hopping in the river was a renewal, a spiritual cleansing.

Everybody in town knew she swam here, but at this hour of the morning she'd have complete privacy. She always swam naked, too. Although she was never particularly bashful about the stray woods walker getting an unexpected eyeful, when she was younger her dad used to have paranoid delusions that every guy in town lined up in the bushes to watch the event.

In fact, she did catch Riley spying on her one day when they were in tenth grade. She ran out of the water after him, wielding a nail-studded board broken off a convenient pallet. He'd almost gotten away when he stumbled and fell. She'd caught up with him and made solid, two-handed contact on his rear end with the business end of the board.

Riley actually limped back the next day to apologize. He promised never to do it again. In fact, she'd never seen him or any other guy from town spying on her since. Riley must have put the word out to stay away. He could really be okay in some ways, more the pity. Of course, after yesterday, he was a full-fledged schmuck again.

Gillian waded through the scruffy bushes lining the river's edge and clambered up onto a huge flat rock that projected out over the flowing water. There was a deep, foamy pool below it, perfect for jumping into. The brush on shore behind her screened any view of the mill, and the rushing of the water in the pool shut out the noise from it, even when the saw shed was in full operation.

So the sense of aloneness was complete. *Like being the only person alive.* She stripped off her clothes.

She paused, nude, on the high point of the rock, arching her back with her arms behind her. Fingers woven, stretching on tip toes, working out the kinks of sleep. Then, hands pressed together over her head, she dived in.

Movement on a ledge downstream caught Jack's eye. He stared, trying to penetrate the mist rising from the water, straining to decipher the shape he'd briefly glimpsed there. So surprised was he at what he finally saw, his first thought was that the sleek body suspended in mid-air belonged to a seal.

Not in fresh water, Jack. Then: *Dear God, a child. Fallen in.*

He was already in motion to attempt a rescue when realization dawned on just what, or rather *whom*, he'd seen.

It was Gillian Wilcox. She'd taken a flying leap—or dive, rather—into the cold Mohasset River not fifty yards downstream from him.

Went right off the ledge, she did. Naked as a jaybird. He'd only been in the stream twenty minutes or so, and was already chilled to the bone. And he was wearing insulated waders.

The woman was an absolute Amazon.

Gillian surfaced, spouting water like a mermaid. She dunked her head face first, then snapped it backward, smoothing her hair tight to her skull. She drifted on her back for a few moments, letting the whorls of current nudge her around the foaming pool.

He was no Peeping Tom, but he should at least stick around to see if she ever came back up. Yes, he wanted a neat way out of the bind about her refusing to sell the family land, but death at an early age wasn't exactly what he'd had in mind.

Easing himself closer to the shore to shield himself from her view by the shoulder of the ledge, he waited.

One thousand, two thousand, three thousand . . .

One minute.

A few bated breaths later and it felt more like two.

Concern suddenly overrode personal animosity and a marked unwillingness to invade the woman's privacy. He reeled in furiously, and clutching his rod in one hand and back of his waders with the other, he charged the ledge.

Numbness crept into her limbs. Gillian kicked for shore. She levered herself up onto a low shelf of rock around the far corner of the outcropping and pulled herself backward, out of the cool breeze. The morning sun was almost clear of the treetops now, and she could feel the first warm rays tentatively caress her body. Sheltered in this pocket of rock, her legs came back to life. She braced her arms behind her, and let her head hang back dreamily, soaking up the warmth.

Jack was twenty feet from the outcropping when he threw his rod and net in the general direction of the shoreline. Splashing through the last few feet of shallows he started to scale the rocky sides.

Goosebumps were rising on Gillian's body, and she finally started to shiver. Time to get back to reality. *Just one more minute . . .*

She dreamed on.

Encased in the clumsy wader boots, Jack's feet slid every which way on the smooth rock face. He sweated and struggled for purchase. The seconds were ticking off in his head. How many minutes could the human brain go without oxygen?

He finally gained the top of the ledge and pulled himself over it on his stomach. Right at the point where he'd last seen the Wilcox woman. He peered down. The surface of the foaming pool was unbroken by a floating body. Did she get swept up in an undercurrent? Was she trapped under the surface like one of those nutballs who went over Niagara Falls in barrels? He took a deep breath and jumped.

A wall of cold river water buried Gillian, bringing her to full consciousness like a slap in the face. Her first thought was that part of the granite of the ledge above her had given way, and crashed into the pool, narrowly missing her. She scanned the surface of the pool. What looked like pieces of a blown-up sporting goods store were floating on the surface, spinning lazily in the current.

Why, there was a lure case, just like the kind her dad had. And one of those baskets fishermen put their catch in. Empty. And a green flop hat with a fishing ID pinned to it.

She pushed her dripping hair back from her face and reached out to snag the hat. A hand broke the surface of the pool and grabbed her wrist. She screamed.

It was trying to pull her in . . .

No, no, that was too crazy. Someone had fallen into the pool and was drowning. She sat down on her backside and grasped the wrist with both of her hands. Using her legs for leverage, she pulled with all her strength.

Moments later, a second hand grabbed her just above the first. The skin on her wrists felt like it was being shredded, but whatever, or whoever, it was started to rise. A dark head broke the surface. Then the eyes opened, and two blue flames leapt out at her.

"Jumping Mother of . . . !" she gave a huge tug, almost detaching her arm at the elbow and up came Jack the Crack, waders and all.

"You got a knife?" she screamed at him.

"If you think I'm gonna give it to *you*, you're crazy!" he sputtered.

"You dumb bastard, it's to cut the straps. On your waders!" She nodded at them viciously. "They're pulling you under!"

One hand let go of hers. It reemerged grasping a sheath knife. She grabbed for it and slashed the straps. The scream he let out when she went near his neck with the blade was priceless.

With a sucking sound the waders slid free, and Jack kicked them off. With the two of them pulling, they managed to get his upper body onto the rock shelf. He stayed there, half-in and half-out of the water, too out of gas to go any farther.

Gillian finally let go of him. Then let go a laugh. It grew to a howl and wouldn't stop coming. She fell on her back and rolled, crying, hugging her sides, tears on her face mixing with river water.

"I've got three words for you," said Jack, his face still pressed flat to the rock, too beat to move.

"Wh—wh—what?" gasped Gillian. She couldn't catch her breath for the hysteria.

"You're buck naked . . ." he croaked.

It was her turn to scream.

Chapter 6

Gillian desperately scanned the rock shelf for her clothes, then remembered she'd left them up above her, on the projecting ledge.

Shit! She rolled to her feet, and dashed for the strewn boulders that led upward like giant steps.

Her huffing breaths and the slap of wet feet on smooth rock told Jack that she was wasting no time making her escape.

Now there's a show too good to miss. He summoned his strength and lifted his cheek from the granite. One eye was swelling shut and blood was dripping into the other one, but neither thing prevented him from enjoying the view. The perfect, always-in-control Ms. Wilcox was picking her soggy, naked way up toward the top of the rock by jumping from one gigantic stepping stone to the next. She was erratically waving her arms to keep her balance, cursing when she landed hard on a bare foot, and wiping off dripping strands of hair out of her face.

Altogether, she looked a mess. To his surprise, however, a stirring in the lower part of his body told him that despite his immediate pain and complete prostration, the rear view of sleek buttocks and long legs flexing was not lost on him.

The stirring turned to a throbbing in spite of the frigid

water. It was amazing really that he could get hard under the circumstances, what with being half-dead and all. Even more incredible was the fact that the cranky Ms. Wilcox, whose unexpectedly pleasing physical assets were just disappearing over the crest of the rock, was the catalyst.

This renewed interest in life gave him the impetus to heave himself all the way out of the water. He flopped on his back, sucking air like a beached whale, noticing the sky was bluer than he'd ever seen it before. Yes, it *was* good to be alive.

The picture of Gillian's backside once again flashed through his mind like a subliminal advertisement, and he groaned. He was now fully erect, and threatening to burst the zipper of his trousers. He felt as hard as the stone beneath him.

Carefully, he rolled onto his side. Just in time, too, because at that moment Gillian's head poked out over the edge of the rock ledge above. From his angle, she looked upside down. He felt a wave of nausea sweep over him and he shut his eyes. Gingerly, he sat up and turned himself around so he could look straight up at her. He really didn't feel well.

At least she seemed to have her clothes on. With luck his body's rabid interest in her would diminish, and he could salvage some of his dignity. The hope was short lived.

"Hey, Jack," she said, looking down at him with a grin on her face. "You pitchin' a tent down there or are you just happy to see me?"

Okay. He was going to die right there. Not from wounds incurred in the name of chivalry, or whatever stupid emotion prompted him to jump in after the witch on the rock above, but of sheer embarrassment. He tried to save himself.

"You know it's a proven fact that in life-threatening situations, males often . . ." He stopped.

"Often what?" she asked innocently, rubbing her wet hair with a T-shirt.

There *was* no graceful way out of it.

Gillian let him swing in the breeze from the noose he'd put around his own neck, then offered up her opinion. "You look like hell, Jack."

"And feeling like it, too," he croaked, suddenly aware he was lightheaded. But she must have thought he'd live through it, because she started to tear into him.

"But what *are* you anyway?" she started in. "Some kind of pervert? Hanging around here spying on me. God, it's getting so I can't do *anything* without you invading my space." Her physical space. She'd never admit to dreaming about him, but she would make him pay in spades. For the dream and catching her in her birthday suit, true. But mostly for yesterday out at Riley's construction site.

Hunched down there on the shelf, though, he looked awfully green around the gills. And he was weaving like a top running down. Truthfully, she *was* getting a little nervous about his condition. Sure, it was funny for a minute there, seeing the high and mighty Mr. Jack Turner soaked to the bone and miserable, with a hard-on the size of a small pine tree tenting out the front of his pants.

From ogling her, the pervert. A tiny flutter danced around in her chest. Confused, she shooed it away.

But now the guy just didn't look good. Blood was dripping down his face, one eye was almost shut and he was pale as death. Damn! Of all the pools in the world, why'd he have to fall into hers?

"I'm coming down there," she said.

He was still sitting upright when she got there, but he looked even worse close up.

She knelt down next to him and put her face inches from his. "If you're gonna pass out, tell me so I can catch you. Okay?" she said, clearly and slowly, like she was addressing someone mentally incompetent, which, for all she knew, he could be at that moment. The last thing she needed was for him to tip over and split his head open on her property. He'd sue and end up with her land.

"Uh huh," he said, in a voice just above a whisper.

Through hazy veils, Jack couldn't believe he had actually noticed that Gillian Wilcox's eyes were green. They were glittering in the bright morning light.

Avoiding the blood on his face, Gillian cupped his chin and looked directly into his eyes. "You getting me here, Jack?"

The gas jets were definitely on simmer. But both pupils were the same size, thank goodness. The head cut looked superficial, and the eye would be all right in a few days. No limbs broken either or he wouldn't be sitting so still. But his skin felt ice cold and his lips were turning blue. He'd live, she decided, but he needed to get warm fast.

"Look," she said. "We got to get you out of here. You won't die, but we've got to get you warmed up. Where's your vehicle?" She scanned the opposite bank of the river. That stupid toy truck he drove should stand out like a sore thumb. . . . Yep, there it was.

Locating it in the woods was extremely easy not only because it was an obnoxious rescue-vehicle yellow but because a dog barked at her from the cab. Her dog. The one she'd let out to pee not half an hour ago.

Boo had straggled in late yesterday afternoon after no doubt having to walk home from Riley's site. Evidently the lesson she had intended to teach him hadn't taken. Wait. Had Jack Turner given Boo a ride home? God, did he know where she lived? Well, duh, next to the mill. He knew all about the land around Rocky Falls. Who owned it, who lived on it, how much they owed on it. She shivered. Whatever. The cold was making her wacky.

Jack was looking around, too, as if getting his bearings. "I parked near two big boulders," he said. "Somewhere over . . . Across the river. Look, see?" He pointed.

"Uh huh." No shit. What was she, blind? She measured the distance to his pickup with her eyes. Factored in currents, river depth. Came to the strikingly obvious conclusion that no way even with her helping were they getting Mr. Jack Turner back across the river to his vehicle. Not that he was in any shape to drive. There also was no guarantee that he still had the car keys on him after his death-defying leap. And she wasn't about to frisk him and risk a chance encounter with that lodgepole pine thing prowling around in his pants.

As if reading her mind and trying to prove her wrong, Jack stood. "Look, I'm all right. Just got the wind knocked out of me, is all. I can take care of myself—" He wobbled and she grabbed him, throwing his arm over her shoulder and cinching her arm around his waist to steady him.

"Whoa, big fella. You're not busting your ass on *my* land."

Crap. The only sane option was to drag him back to her house. Again: *Of all the pools in all the world . . .*

Not her first choice. Or second. Or even her third. But under the circumstances, the only sensible one. She'd give him some dry clothes, something warm to drink and send him packing. In and out. Practically a drive-by.

"C'mon, we're outta here," she grunted, steering him in the direction of the rock stairs.

"OK," she said, on flat land at last. "We're getting there." She had to hurry Jack along now. The stairs had taken a lot out of him. Hauling his sorry ass all the way up here had about done her in, too.

"Watch your feet around these bushes . . ." She could feel the cold in the fabric of his soaked sleeve as it pressed against her cheek. The day was getting warmer as the morning went on, but away from the shelter of the rocks, the wind was sucking the heat from his body.

They negotiated the short footpath that led back to the mill. When they crossed into the yard, Gillian could see some color had come back into Jack's face and his eyes didn't look so fuzzy. But he was shivering to beat the band

and bleeding steadily from the cut on his head. She could hear his quick intakes of breath between clenched teeth.

At the moment he wasn't exactly the godlike effigy he'd appeared to be when he was hanging off the roof edge. From the mess his blood was making all over her sweatshirt sleeve, he was definitely human. But in his defense, he'd had a busy morning so far, what with spying on her and almost killing himself. . . .

Slowly she relinquished her death grip on his waist. If he took a header now, at least he'd land on a mat of pine chips, not solid granite. By the time they reached the tall piles of air-drying lumber, he was really coming around.

"Where *are* we going?" he asked her, suddenly aware of his surroundings.

"My place," Gillian replied curtly.

"But we've only known each other, what? Two days?" he said, pretending shock. The theatrical effect was somewhat reduced by the chattering of his teeth.

"I think I liked you better when you were semiconscious," she said. "Your conversation was so much more entertaining."

He tried to think of a comeback, but he was frozen to the core and his tank was on empty.

They staggered along the rutted road, every washout seeming an impassable barrier, but they took each one in turn and gradually she felt the rigid arm around her neck loosen. They approached her back porch.

With one foot on the bottom stair, Gillian felt obliged to justify her reasons to Jack for bringing him home. "Let's be clear about what's happening here—Jack." She had almost said "Crack." "I don't want you in my house any more than you probably want to be here. But I had no choice, see? It was either come here or leave you to sleep with the fish. Why?" She paused for dramatic emphasis. "Because, *first* you fell into cold water and almost drowned. You deserved it, of course, because of your nasty little habit of spying on people, but that's for another time."

He started to protest, but decided to conserve his strength for the task ahead: climbing the two steps ahead of him.

"*Second*," she ticked off the point on her fingers like a lecturing professor, "you were in a semi-coherent state, your head was bleeding, and you looked kind of out of it. You needed to warm up quickly."

He couldn't agree with her more. He was hanging onto the newel of the porch railing for dear life. His knees were even knocking together. "Could we just . . ." he began, indicating the back door with the tilt of his head.

But she was on a roll. "*Third*, I figured what with all the other crap that you lost on your little trip off the ledge, your car keys might be at the bottom of the Mohasset. Sorry we had to leave all your expensive fishing toys back there in the drink, by the way, but I figured saving you was the priority. Where was I?"

Jack's eyelids felt like they had lead weights attached. He had to sit down or fall down sometime in the next five seconds. *Shit*, he'd lost the nice bass, too, he remembered.

"Ah, yes," Gillian continued. "Your keys. You couldn't even tell me what your name was for a while there, let alone where they were. I was *not* about to do a full body frisk for them. Know what I mean?" She bounced an eyebrow suggestively.

God, the woman could twist the knife, Jack thought.

"So *this*—" she gestured to the back door with an open hand, sarcastically welcoming him like visiting royalty, "—such as it is, was the only viable option. The bathroom is on the second floor. Go clean up. I'll scrounge together some dry clothes for you."

She seemed done. It was now or never, Jack knew. God, he didn't want to be here, but he was shivering like an old sick dog and his face was covered in blood. He could feel it tightening on his skin as it dried.

He let go of his old friend, the newel post, and lifted a shaking leg. Brought the other one up next to it. One more to go. *Clunk, clunk.* There. He was on the porch. He shuffled across the decking and leaned against the wall of the house, while she opened the screen door. It stuck when she tugged on it, and the top half almost whapped him in the face. His good eye saw it coming and he reflexively ducked out of the way.

"It jams," she said.

"Thanks for the warning," he croaked.

She flipped her head around—sprinkling him with river water like he wasn't wet enough already—and disappeared into the bowels of the house. Her voice drifted back to him. "I'll bring you up some coffee. Or would you rather have tea? Oh—never mind." He heard things scraping on shelves. "It's coffee or nothing."

He followed the sound of her voice through what he supposed could be called a mudroom because it certainly was full of that, then across the living room—tremendously wide pine floorboards, the working part of his mind registered—and into the kitchen. Cupboard doors hung open like the Huns had dropped by unexpectedly. Gillian was working at the counter and her back was to him.

"Stairs are straight ahead," she said, without turning around. Her body language was not lost on him. It was as if she thought that if she didn't look at him, she didn't have to acknowledge the fact that she had let him into her house. Feeling like a leper, Jack pressed on to the stairs and looked up.

There were your average number of steps—say *fifty million.* He began climbing. At the summit of the mountain, directly across the hall, was the bathroom. He stumbled in and shut the door behind him.

Down in the kitchen, Gillian contemplated the empty metal tea container. Why did she feel like a domestic failure? A *Good Housekeeping* "Don't" with a patch across her eyes to protect her privacy. She couldn't imagine Jack the

Crack giving a rat's ass about what hot drink she offered him. He looked like a walking popsicle, and would no doubt slurp down whatever she handed him. But it was about choice. You know. Being able to offer someone who comes into your home a choice.

She whacked both clenched fists against the sides of her head. What the hell was wrong with her? Did *she* get hit on the head and not remember? *Never* in her life did she *ever* have a thought like the one she just had. Never.

She'd warm up the morning dregs of coffee and he could lump it. She grabbed the percolator, poured the remains into a saucepan, and lit the burner.

Jack stripped off his soaked clothes and reached for a towel. His fingers were bloody and he stopped himself short of touching it. Ah, a dilemma. Pulling his clothes off had smeared blood from his head over his arms and torso. He looked like an ax murder gone bad. A fresh red drip rolled down the side of his face and fell from his chin, exploding in a tiny red bomb that burst on the cracked and faded linoleum.

It was either run to the nearest car wash or jump in the tub and shower off. Like he really wanted to be making himself this much at home in—of all people's houses—Gillian Wilcox's.

From bad to worse to just plain stupid.

He sighed, and stepped into the tub, leaving a bloody footprint behind on the linoleum. He cranked both faucets on full blast. The supply pipes running exposed along the outside of the wall banged and groaned. He backed off the valves and the water hammer stopped. He groped for the curtain. There was no curtain. How did you keep the water from going everywhere when you took a—

Ah. There was no shower. How quaint.

When the hot water finally kicked in, he plugged the

drain with the rubber stopper that hung from a chain. He let the water cascade over his wrists, warming his blood. The beginnings of heat coursed up his arms and into his fingertips, chasing away the chill of the Mohasset.

Gillian gently stirred the contents of the saucepan, not wanting the coffee to scald. She was starting to get cold herself. She had toweled off with her T-shirt down at the river, before stuffing it and her underpants into the pockets of her sweats, but her whole left side was wet where she'd been pressed up against Jack on the way back. Thinking about how closely she'd been pressed up against him suddenly made referring to him as The Crack seem a little unsavory. But he certainly wasn't The Wonder anymore. The Muffin Man had always seemed a little contrived. There had to be Something Else.

The coffee bubbled. She shut down the burner and added milk to the pan. She had no idea how he liked his coffee, so she hoped for the best and made it a little lighter than she liked it herself. She cast a glance at the plastic honey bear, but rooted around instead for her sugar bowl. One crusty tablespoon, two, then a third for good measure. It would help jump-start his metabolism. Maybe sweeten his disposition, too. Above all, get him on his way quicker.

The sooner the better.

The water in the tub was about a foot deep now, and Jack's triceps bulged as he tried to slowly ease himself lower into the steaming water, but he was flat done in and landed a little harder than he wanted. Water sloshed up the sides of the tub, over the rim and onto the floor. He was creating a federal disaster area, but *God,* the heat felt good. *Aaah . . .*

Steam enveloped him and he let himself slide to the very bottom of the deep tub. Hot water rose over his stomach, floated the hair on his chest, filled the hollows of his collar-bones. *Nirvana*.

He scooped a handful of water onto his face. It dripped pink into the clean water. Blood from the gash on his head had crusted onto his face and neck. *Soap*. He searched the floor around the tub with one hand. No dice. A hanger on the sink rim? Nope. His hand bumped a wicker basket and he hauled it up. He rummaged and found an assortment of shampoos and conditioners, a fancy pink razor, and a shower cap.

A shower cap? Somehow he couldn't imagine the sleek Ms. Wilcox, of early-morning-dive fame, wearing it. And why was it there if there was no shower? Ah, there probably was one but the contraption had broken. He had a vague picture of a curtain rail hanging from the ceiling. He looked up. Yep, there were the holes in the plaster ceiling where it had once been attached. This place really needed upgrading.

A lone bottle of bubble bath hid out at the bottom of the basket. Well, *necessity was a mother.* . . . He squirted some under the last of the hot water rushing out of the spigot. He shut off the taps. The lower half of his body had disappeared under a small mountain of bubbles. He exhaled a long breath. Not where he ever thought he'd be at seven-fifteen on a Wednesday morning.

Back in Boston, he'd be just pulling into the underground parking garage about now. George, the attendant, would wave at him five mornings a week. The weekend attendants never waved, the tiny TV in the booth tuned to a game show or the soaps, volume cranked.

Park the pickup in the spot stenciled PRES MOULT DEV. Beep the door locks. Elevator doors slide open, press "Express Penthouse." Thirty-six seconds later, the car slows, doors glide open. Jennifer at the reception desk, elegant, composed. Smile at her.

Good Morning, Mr. Turner.

Good Morning, Jennifer. How are the kids today?

Fine, thanks, Mr. Turner. Your agenda for today is on your desk. I'll be in with coffee in a minute. . . .

Twelve plush carpeted steps past the reception area, stop at the potted palm. Push on the oak paneled double door bearing the brass plate "J. H. Turner, President." On his desk, his PC already up and running. Across the monitor screen, a speckled trout unceasingly springs from the depths of a software-generated brook, twists gaudily in the air, and dives below the toolbar. Drop the briefcase on the desk. Slip the coat off, cross the office, and hang it on the brass stand. Scan the Boston skyline, curse the Big Dig mess, settle into the deep leather chair. The phone buzzes. Hit "SPEAKER."

"Mr. Turner," Jennifer's disembodied voice erupts from the speaker phone, "Mr. Blah Blah from Joe Blows Ironworks. Shall I put him through?"

And so the beat went on in a very full, very busy, very . . . *un*satisfying life.

He hated to admit that. But that was after all what brought him there. No, not to Gillian Wilcox's bathtub. To Rocky Falls.

He took a moment to appreciate the absurdity of his situation. Here he was, sitting up to his nipples in water in the bathtub of a woman whose property, tub and all, he was trying to usurp. He needed her land. It was right that he get it. *This* time, the land grab—and he was too much of a realist to call it anything else—was a good thing. Not like the last time. He'd bring progress to this one-horse place. Why this town—he glanced again at the exposed plumbing and the holes in the ceiling—needed him.

And he needed it. Something else he hated to admit. This Rocky Falls deal would be good for him, too. A chance to revitalize a place, not make a cookie cutter shit hole out of it like—

Stop. Water under the bridge. And speaking of water, he had to get himself the hell out of this warm, curiously seductive claw foot. With furious fingers he scrubbed at the blood caking him, realizing that even with starting his own company he'd been unable to completely purge the sting of the past. He dunked his head and winced, as much from the ache of recollection as from cut skin. His hand came away a shiny red when he touched the gash in his head. Still bleeding. *In more ways than one.*

He applied pressure to the cut with the flat of his hand and stood up, checking his balance prior to hiking one leg over the high rim of the tub. A knock at the door sent him diving for cover beneath the bubbles.

"It's me. I've got hot coffee."

Damn. Trapped like a rat.

"I'm opening the door a crack to hand it in," Gillian said.

"Uh—sure—" He did a quick check of the bubble coverage. "Okay." His voice sounded unnaturally high pitched to him.

The door creaked open six inches and a disembodied hand, clutching a steaming mug, poked into the bathroom. He reached out for the cup but quickly realized his trusty right arm, well, had suddenly come up short. Literally. He shifted his position in the tub. So did the bubbles.

"Well?" Gillian said, her voice muffled by the door but laced with irritation. "You gonna take it or what?"

Exactly: *Or what?* "I can't, well . . . reach it," he said.

"Why not, for God's sake? You're not on the john, are you?"

"No!" he said indignantly. "I'm in the—ah, the tub."

"What?"

"The tub. I'm in the tub. I looked like a traffic accident and there was blood everywhere and I didn't see any other way to get it off without making a mess of the place."

Gillian peeked through the crack in the door. The top half of The Man in Her Bath looked to have spontaneously generated from a mountain of bubbles.

Now this was rich. Too good to pass up. She stifled a giggle. "I'm coming in." She followed the coffee mug

through the door. He was, in fact, in the tub. Up to his floating chest hair. Nice shoulders. Dark hair just brushed them.
Unh-uh.

She needed a minute, she realized. To get her bearings. It
had been a long time since . . . never mind. She surveyed the
bathroom like it had been remodeled since the last time
she'd seen it, finally settling her gaze on the mountain of
bubbles. "Well, well. I see you've made yourself right at
home." She smirked. "Oh, but I *am* disappointed that I
won't be privy to the same caliber show you so obviously
enjoyed." She handed over the mug.

"Really funny," he said.

For once he was caught short of snappy comebacks, she
realized, although who could blame the guy? He was completely at her mercy. Or lack of it. That simple fact made her
positively gleeful. She suddenly felt better and more focused than she had for days. Orville or Wilbur or Whatever
Twin He Was had it right: You made your own fun.

Jack sipped the coffee experimentally. "Good. Thanks."
He blew across the top of it.

"No problem." She reached back to the hall table for her
own coffee, then closed the bathroom door. Wouldn't want
Little Jackie to get a chill. *Little Jackie*. Hah. Wouldn't it be
funny if she was right yesterday and he really *was* little?
That would explain a lot. She checked out Bubble Mountain. It appeared to be slowly collapsing from within. Maybe
she'd have her answer soon.

"Look," he said, "you've been really nice to go to all this
trouble, but I really am okay and I've really got to be going."

Uncanny. It was like he could see her dirty gears spinning
in her head and they made him nervous. Interesting. She
closed the lid of the toilet, sat down, and made a big show
of making herself comfortable.

Jack said, "I don't think this is a very good idea."

She crossed her legs, and propped her chin comfortably
on one fist. "What, you mean the bubble bath?" This she

said in her best Are-you-an-idiot voice. She arched an eye-brow for emphasis.

"Oh, about that—I couldn't find any soap around." He laughed nervously. "I guess I dumped in too much of that . . . stuff, whatever you call it."

"*Tender Moments*?"

"Yeah. That."

Gillian sipped her own coffee to disguise the grin that threatened to split her face in two, the grin Riley called her "shit-eating" one. She sized up the bubbles again.

Under her scrutiny Jack adjusted some.

She assessed the Man in Her Bath. His face didn't look like a failed assassination attempt anymore, which was good. He'd washed most of the crusty gunk off. But, *tsk, tsk,* the cut on his head was still oozing blood into the tangle of dark hair. She watched the gash leak out another drop of blood. Not good. She scooted forward on the seat and brought her nose inches from his scalp. She pursed her lips.

"Much as I wouldn't want you to think I was concerned," she said, "but your head is still bleeding. You probably should get stitches downtown." She moved a heavy lock of damp hair aside. Jack sucked in breath but didn't flinch. "Although, *I* might be able to patch it up." She frowned, considering him. "What's your pain tolerance?"

Another priceless look crossed his face. "You're actually enjoying this, aren't you?" he said. "Don't you have any-thing better to do than torture me? Like going to work?"

She sat back and recrossed her legs. She made an event out of picking a stray fuzz ball from the material of her sweatpants. Then she lied a little. "Nope. I got all morning."

There *was* that Riley delivery, but screw him. The logs piled up on the conveyor? They weren't going anywhere. One-of-the-Twins would open the yard for her when she didn't show up. Her bases were covered.

"Ah, I think I'll just have the doc downtown check me out," Jack said. "If you'll just step outside while I . . ." He made a show of preparing to rise from the tub, but she forced herself not to move a muscle.

"On second thought," he said sinking back down casually, as if he had only been shifting to a more comfortable position, "maybe it *would* be quicker if you . . . did something."

He *was* jumpy, Gillian thought. Ants in the pants. The plot thickened. "Sure." She scrounged in the wicker basket he'd left on the floor next to the tub.

Jack saw a flash of pink go by his ear. "Ah, what are you doing?" he asked, making a conscious effort to keep his voice steady.

"Shaving your head."

"No, really. What are you doing?"

"Like I said: shaving your head." Then she laughed. "Don't worry, Sampson, it's just a teeny bit of hair. I've got to clear a spot around the cut so I can seal it up with some butterfly closures."

She scrunched forward again on the toilet seat and pulled up the sleeves of her sweatshirt. She braced one forearm on his shoulder and steadied his head with the other. "Tip your head forward," she said. Gently, she brushed hair back and away from the wound.

She whistled softly. *Now there's a nasty cut.* Drag the blade across that and she'd be scraping Bubble Boy off the ceiling.

"What? What do you see?" Jack asked.

"Well, there's this . . . hole in your head."

"Yes. Yes. What else?"

"Well, I can see all the way inside."

"Oh, God, no. A skull fracture maybe?" Jack said, rising panic in his voice.

"I'm not sure. But I can tell you one thing, if you think you can handle it."

"Please, yes. Tell me the worst."

"Well," she shifted her hold on his head, "I'm looking right inside, now and—" She stopped.

"Tell me, damn it, *what do you see?*"

"Nothing."

"What do you mean, 'nothing'?"

"It's completely . . . hollow inside," she said, in a voice filled with awe.

There was silence for a moment.

"You know what your problem is?" Jack said. "You've been hanging around Riley too long. You actually think that kind of humor is funny."

Gillian was pleasantly surprised at his naïveté. She couldn't believe he fell for her stupid joke. He seemed like such a worldly big deal out at the site yesterday. "Hey, if you can't be cruel, you can't be funny," she said. "Now hold still."

Carefully she began sawing at the base of the hair around the gash with the razor, as close to the wound as she dared. It was tedious work, trying to trim a clear spot around the dent without giving the guy a tonsure in the process. Baby fine hair, but lots of it. Darker when wet. Natural curl.

Lovely feel to it—when you ignored who it belonged to.

The faucet dripped. Steam rose from the bath. Gillian trimmed. She held her breath in concentration.

Getting there.

Bubbles snapped and popped. Pressed closely against Jack, warm water from his head and body soaked through her sweats. Familiar scents—hers—on his skin, rose to her nostrils. Everyday smells, now strangely exotic, their intensity magnified by their closeness.

Almost done.

She relaxed for a moment to stop her eyes from twitching, but with a mind of their own, they strayed to Jack's closed ones. The left was swollen and ringed in purple. But close up, on the good eye, the lashes were resting in a dark, even row. The bottom ones curled down elegantly to brush the ridge of his cheekbone. Silently, Gillian released a cupful of air through her mouth, then slowly inhaled through her nose.

She paused, stock still, her eyes shut, and savored the heated fragrance of her bubble bath rising from him. . . .

"Is that it?" Jack asked. "Are you done?"

His voice jerked her back to reality. "Um—Yup. Just a minute . . ."

She finished the job and blew out a long breath. "OK, that's it. Just the butterflies now."

She stood on suddenly shaky legs and made her way to the medicine cabinet. Closures, closures . . . She scrounged through the shelves blankly. *What was she looking for, again?* Oh, yes, there they were. And some sponges and ointment.

She took up her spot on the seat again. "Forward," she said, pushing down on the crown of Jack's head. As gently as she could, she blotted the gash, squirted an inch of anti-septic cream across it, squeezed the edges closed and applied the strips. She could feel the tension in his body, but he didn't squirm.

"All better," she said, looking into his eyes. "You're fixed." On impulse, she patted his cheek. Jack carefully captured her hand against his face and said, "Thanks."

Condensation dripped down the open pipes on the wall, rivulets raced each other to the floor. The spigot noisily released a pent-up water plug with a gurgle and a splash.

A fine mist had settled on Gillian's skin from the humid air. Steam sent damp tendrils of her auburn hair curling around her ears. A delicate leaf earring nestled in the dimple of an earlobe. Beneath the water, Jack felt himself inconveniently rise to the occasion.

Gillian broke the moment. "Hey, if you lose any more bubbles, there, partner, you'll be scaring the women folk." She nodded toward the tub water.

Jack looked down. *Shit.*

An isolated peak of foam barely covered his own personal . . . peak.

"Ah, I really think it's time for you to be going, there, pal," he said nervously.

"Sure. Anything you say, *Buddy*." She winked and slugged him jokingly on the arm with her fist. She gathered up her coffee cup and made to go. At the door, she paused. "There is just one more thing though . . ."

"Yes? And make it *quick*," he said. The pointy crests were rounding into piedmont.

"I guess I was wrong, yesterday. You know, what I said about your . . . you know."

They both contemplated the tub water. She snickered.

The red absolutely *shot* to his face. She blew a clump of soapsuds off her index finger and pulled the door closed.

Jack, a too-small towel wrapped around his waist, stood in the bathroom waiting for the tub to slowly drain. From somewhere across the hall came the sounds of drawers and closets being vigorously opened and closed. The door opened suddenly.

"Hey—hold on a minute!" he cried.

The door closed again, but not before a soft bundle came sailing through it to land with a soft plop on the damp floor.

Clothes. The woman was a full-service organization. He shook the bundle apart. A flannel shirt and jeans. No socks, that was OK. No underwear. *Really* okay. The thought of wearing some other guy's drawers creeped him out. And speaking of other guys. . . . He held the clothes up to him. The right length for him, but a lot wider. Must be her dad's. Unless she dated a chubby guy. She didn't seem the type, though. To date, that is.

He suddenly recalled long legs nimbly picking their way up the rocks. Trim butt flexing. Jack carefully zipped the pants.

* *

In her bedroom, still grinning—Jack had been filling out
the front of that little towel for sure, the oversexed bastard—
Gillian pulled off her damp things, rubbed herself briskly
with a thick terry towel and pulled on underwear and a worn
flannel work shirt. But enough foolishness, she chastised.
She had work to do. Couldn't fool around here all day,
having what?

Fun? Good Lord. With Jack Turner? Puh-leez. What was
wrong with her? There were donuts to make. Get moving,
girl.

Should have left him to drown. Called the paramedics
from the saw shed. But no. She had to save his sorry ass.
Now she was off schedule for the day. She slid on jeans and
laced her work boots with trembling fingers. Plus, she was
freezing since leaving the warmth of the bathroom. Not to
mention that it would have been nice to rinse the Mohasset
out of her hair—*along with that jerk in the bathroom*—but
the problem was . . . that jerk was still in the bathroom. The
least he could do was hand out the hairdryer.

She crossed the hall and banged on the door to the bath.
"Hey."

No response. She put her ear close to the door. Of course.
Silly her. How could he hear her over the whine of the
hairdryer? Her hairdryer.

She hip-checked the door open. The door knob must have
caught Jack somewhere unpleasant because he cursed and
dropped the hairdryer. There was a sudden pop and a brief
flash of light and the lights went out.

She squeezed her way into the bath. Jack was sitting on
the edge of the tub looking dazed and there was a black
smear on one hand. "It smells like hell in here," she said. It
did, too.

The hairdryer was belly up in the half-filled sink.

"You could have killed me."

"Yeah, yeah, that would be like twice in one day, huh?"

"What the *hell*, Gillian? No GFI circuit in here?"

"No. Just be careful of that socket. It'll shock you. Everyone knows that."

"Too damn bad if you're not 'everybody,' huh?"

"What are you, a baby?" Really, this guy was a hazard. She had to get him off her property. Her homeowner's policy had had enough of a road test for one day. "Hey, can you wrap up your beauty regimen and get out of here because I got to get to work?"

"Thought you had all day."

"Yeah, well, Wilbur called." He hadn't.

"You sure?"

"You don't believe me?"

"No, I mean are you sure it wasn't Orville?"

"How could you tell?" This they said simultaneously. Then they both laughed. A rusty, out-of-tune duet, but still.

"Jinx ya," Gillian said, surprised.

Jack chuckled, a warm sound. He was still the enemy, but she had to admit she welcomed the temporary respite from them tearing out each others' throats. She cast a last longing look into the sink at what used to be one of her favorite small appliances and turned to leave.

Jack put a hand on her forearm and said, "Wait. There's something I've got to say to you before you go."

Gillian kept her back to him. Oh, boy, here it comes. Ruin the moment, why didn't he, with yet more Jackshit about remaking Rocky Falls in his image.

"You should know that I wasn't spying on you this morning," he said. "I was just there fishing, minding my own business, when I saw you dive in. I ran up to the rock and didn't see you in the pool. I thought you were—stuck underwater, maybe, so I jumped in to try to . . . save you."

Okay, not what she expected. She turned around and looked up into his face. Mulled over what he said for perhaps three seconds. Then found she couldn't contain the guffaws if she had wanted to. Great belly laughs folded her down onto the lid of the toilet. It was fast becoming her spot. Really, the guy was so transparent. "*You* jumped in to save *me?*" she repeated. "Yeah, right."

He was still looking intently at her.

She scrubbed her eyes with her fists and reached for a tissue to blow her nose. *Nah*. Bullshitting. That's what he was doing. It was what he did for a living. It was a reflex action for him, like breathing.

Hah! He jumped in to save her? No fucking way. She giggled some more for good measure.

He jumped in to save me. . . . What a—she struggled to put it into words—pain in the ass this guy was. First he pisses her off by thinking he knows what's best for everybody. Then he adds to it by assuming she couldn't take care of herself.

Then . . . *he jumped in to save me.*

It sounded even weirder the third time. Then she realized. Good God, he was *serious*. A hole in the earth opened and threatened to swallow her. Her chest constricted and she couldn't draw breath. She stood up, groping behind her for the door jamb. Terror overwhelmed her. Took half a step into the hall. Space. She needed space. The bathroom had shrunk to the size of a phone booth.

"Oh, well," she gasped, a palm to her chest. Could you suddenly develop asthma right out of the blue? "It's a good thing I *wasn't* drowning. We'd both be dead right now, huh?" Sarcasm she hadn't consciously intended dripped from every word.

To her surprise, Jack didn't bite back like Riley would have. Instead, a slow smile crept across his face. "You know what your problem is, *Ms*. Wilcox?"

"Why do I think you're going to tell me?" Good air in, bad air out.

"You're too afraid to trust people. It scares the hell out of you that someone might actually care about you enough to want to help you."

Hah. As if. Missed by a mile. Yet why did she feel like the anaconda around her rib cage had just laid on another coil?

Distance. She theatrically spread the fingers of the hand still pressed to her chest, arched the wrist and said, "Oh, and who would that someone be, Mr. Turner? *You*? You who wants to buy this place right out from underneath me and build what? A bunch of crappy, cookie-cutter condos?" She batted her eyelashes, what few she had.

He still didn't react. Riley would have been throwing things by then.

Give her anything but a blank stare. Suddenly, *she* became angry. Absolutely ripshit. Zero to sixty in one heartbeat. Her rage jerry-built a bridge across the chasm that had yawned before her. She stepped boldly back into the bathroom and propped her booted foot on the rim of the tub, brushing his blackened hand.

"What gives you the right to decide things for people you don't even know?" she said. "Where do you get the audacity to think you always know what's best? God! What is *wrong* with you?"

That got a reaction. "This is not about me making decisions for people," he snapped, sliding his hand away from her foot. "It's about allowing people in town the opportunity to make their *own* decisions. Free from influence. *Your* influence."

"So now you're saying that my opinion doesn't count. That I should just roll over and sell my family's land. Land that they've worked for generations. While I'm at it, why don't I just use my so-called 'influence' to convince people to sell off the downtown. Then you could put up a fucking shopping mall. Wouldn't *that* be great?"

She made a moue, slathered it in sarcasm, and pretended to think to herself. "Hmm, would there be any money in it for me, Jack? Do you think I could get, oh, I don't know . . . a kickback?" She put a naive, excited expression on her face and flapped her hands. "Gee, that wouldn't be too bad, would it? Screwing my family and friends for a bit of quick cash. People do it all the time in your world, don't they?"

"Look around, Gillian," Jack said, his eyes sweeping the bathroom, but clearly indicating all of Rocky Falls. "This place as it is now isn't everybody's idea of paradise, you know. What about Lynette and Arthur down at the Eagle House Inn? They'd love to do a little more business so they could spend a few months a year someplace warm. But oh, no. You want to put the potholes back in the streets to keep out law-abiding people with lives and families, let alone the tourist element. Did you ever stop to ask two old people who'd like a slice of the sun in the middle of the winter what they thought of bringing some new money into town?"

Quite a nice speech. Not completely unlike how she had been thinking earlier. But fuck him, she wasn't about to concede anything. She switched tracks. "Well, aren't we the man about town, now. Arthur and Lynette, is it? Getting cozy with the locals, Jack? Did they know who you were or did you just put on a disguise and sneak up on them like you did with me? Are they muffin lovers, too?"

"Don't try and derail the discussion," Jack said. "Did you ever stop to consider that the whole reason you don't want Rocky Falls to change is because *you're* terrified of trying anything new? You've let your fear of letting go polarize an entire community. Nobody can do anything different because change scares the shit out of you. That's it, isn't it? What the hell is keeping you stuck in neutral? And you say *I've* got control issues."

Jack listened to himself and realized he was ripping mad. Once again, out of control. Once again, over his head. Emotionally involved in a business discussion. Bad news. But he couldn't seem to hold it together around Gillian Wilcox. *God*, the woman got under his skin.

Why couldn't he seem to get his feet under him, no pun intended, when she was around? When he was with her it was like falling down a rabbit hole into a world where nothing worked as it should. People jumped naked off cliffs into freezing water and made irrational decisions based on ancient history. He glanced around the decrepit bath. A magic land, this, where they happily lived in poorly wired, marginal housing.

Call his bluff, Gillian thought to herself. Turn the tables on him. Customer digs their heels in about something, agree with them completely. Suddenly they're eating out of your hand, buying up whatever you got at any price.

"Okay, Jack, if that's the way you feel, go ahead and talk to other people in town. You got shut down once already, but go ahead and try it again. You'll see what people say. You think you got all the answers? Go ahead, check it out. Move in with one of our nice hick families, kind of like a cultural exchange program. Take notes on their fricking plumbing."

Jack grinned. Too late, she realized her mistake. She'd had him cornered in the tub there for a while, literally and figuratively. But he'd found wiggle room somehow, and now she had issued him an engraved invitation to do exactly what he had wanted to in the first place.

"You know," he said slowly, making himself comfortable on the rolled rim of the tub. "I think that's just what I'll do. I appreciate your offer. I'll settle into Rocky Falls for a spell. Yep, I can run the company from here. Yes, indeed." He rested his crossed feet on the edge of the john and drawled, "That sounds mighty nice. Give me time to get to know folks around here. Take me a survey, nice and slow like. Get into their heads and see what they're really thinking. Great idea. Thanks, *Gillian*."

Prick. She slammed the door behind her.

Jack tried to make the collar on the worn work shirt lie flat. It wouldn't. Like everything in the Wonderful World of Wilcox, it did exactly as it pleased. Don't like my style? Wear something else. Don't like my town? Leave.

Just like the queen of the forest herself.

Huh, Forest Queen. That was a good one. It fit. Remote,

self-sufficient. Starkly . . . beautiful, some might say. Nice
legs. Rounded little calves nicely bunched. . . . *Whoa.* Keep
it on the rails. You did *not* want to be stretching out the front
of some other guy's pants.

He wondered if he'd damaged his chances for winning the
war with his stupid survey idea. He said it just to piss her off
because it seemed like they were getting somewhere for a
while, what with calling each other "buddy" and "friend."
She'd fixed his head and got him coffee, blah, blah, blah.
But then something unaccountable happened in the middle
of the whole bonding thing. Time had frozen for a moment,
they were caught in the eye of a hurricane. They'd been left
staring at each other like they were seeing each other for the
first time. Weird. Strange. Unsettling. Not part of the plan.

She would come around and see things his way eventually. Rocky Falls had to change. He looked around the bath
again. You couldn't live in a stage set from the *Grapes of
Wrath* forever. It was just her pride propping her up, making
her reject him and his ideas. All she needed was a graceful
way out of the awkward position she'd put herself into and
she'd back down.

Maybe he'd present her with just that chance before he
left the Forest Queen's citadel for good.

Downstairs, Gillian viciously brushed her hair into a
ponytail using the hall mirror, and snapped a scrunchy
around it. A baseball hat pulled down to just above her
straight brows hid the evidence of a bad hair day. She
brushed her teeth in the kitchen sink, grabbed a suspect-
looking bagel from the bread drawer and headed out back to
the saw shed.

Chapter 7

The sun was well clear of the trees by the time she emerged from her house for the second time that day, and despite her simmering rage, her heart took a little leap at the beauty of the morning. She swung her arms as she crunched down the gravel road leading to the mill, and munched contentedly on her bagel. Rocky Falls was the most beautiful place on earth, and she would never let somebody like Jack Turner mess with it. The fucking weasel.

At least poor Riley could never be a weasel. He lacked the basic guile to gravitate that far up the evolutionary ladder. Even on her worst day, she was always two steps ahead of him. She knew his next idea before he'd even thought it up.

But with Jack Turner, she was always on shifting sands. Around him, she was her own worst enemy, constantly shooting herself in the foot, unable to hold the upper hand for more than a round. Take the way he was now planning to practically retire here. She'd forced him into a corner from which the easiest way out involved screwing her. Speaking of which, that was something else that would never happen either, despite his obvious interest in the idea. God, the man could not keep it down. He probably thought he was being clever rearranging the bubbles in the tub after she'd taped his head, but the towel thing later on said he really didn't get out much. Or in much. She sniggered, feeling better.

She slipped her key into the front lock of the Wilcox Lumber office. The bell inside jangled and threatened to slip its mooring as she heaved her weight against the sticking door. Like her dad always said, Carpenters' doors *never* worked right.

She tossed her keys on the worn pine counter, fired up the PC, and threw open the curtains. She'd taken some crap about those curtains, but she liked the ducks on them and they cheered up the place. They also screened the inside of the office from view at night. She wasn't big on security as a rule, but "out of sight, out of mind" was good policy. Not that there was much valuable in here besides the computer. The hard drive clicked and rattled like a demented gerbil. Finally the screensaver kicked in. A family of ducks swam endlessly in circles in the foreground, while a fly fisherman made casts behind them.

I've got to get rid of that guy, she thought, not sure if she'd meant the software generated one or the one schlepping around her house right that minute wearing her dad's old clothes. If only *that* fisherman could be nixed by hitting a few buttons. It wasn't fair. Just by pushing a few of *her* buttons he turned her into a raving lunatic.

She eyed the monitor critically. Hell, yes. At lunch break, the fisherman was toast. She'd miss the ducks, though.

She pulled on canvas coveralls, grabbed work gloves from behind the counter and headed for the saw shed. It was a long building, with rough pine walls and huge, dusty, single-paned windows. The original cedar shingle roof had been patched numerous times. The paint had long ago blistered from the corrugated steel side walls, leaving scabs of rusting metal showing through countless layers of flaking, bilious green paint.

Gillian rolled back the large wooden doors at one end of the shed, then walked the length of it, past the gleaming saw blade and the mechanical carriage that fed it. Beyond the operator's booth, she pushed open the doors on the opposite end. Light streamed into the building, illuminating dust clouds kicked up in her wake. She was the first one here, but no problem. The Twins and Skip knew where the place was.

She walked outside again and around the side of the shed to another pair of doors behind which a carriage conveyor ferried full-size log lengths to the stripper. She shoved aside the final set of doors and followed a narrow aisle that ran alongside the debarking equipment. Beyond that sat a second conveyor that carried the pale, stripped-down logs to the saw carriage for cutting. All in all, to the uninitiated, this section of the cutting operation looked like something out of a B-grade horror film even when the stripper wasn't running. Look out when it was churning full tilt.

Gillian contemplated the load sitting on the feeder belt. If she hadn't had the blowout with Riley yesterday, she'd leave the milling work for later in the day and get his delivery out to the McMansion house first thing, but all bets were off now what with him being such a dick. So what if he was her biggest account? She could afford to let him stew a few days. Besides, if Jack was planning on skulking around Rocky Falls for the next indefinite whenever, she'd hide out here as much as she could. That way he couldn't accuse her of "unduly influencing people against him." Some of the biggest words he knew, probably. God, she could hear him now. Plus, by sticking around the mill she could avoid being dragged into another pointless argument.

But the thought of him in her house when she wasn't there definitely made her uneasy. Not that she thought he'd swipe anything because there wasn't anything around worth stealing. Besides, he could probably top her entire net worth with the money he had in his pocket. Still, it was nice knowing her mother's silverware was safely stashed at Meg's house in town.

It was him being around her stuff that bothered her. Him

seeing how she lived. Absorbing intimate little details of her life, like what brand of shampoo she used or what color her shaving razor was. Knowing him he'd find a way to use all that innocent crap against her.

But alas, the donuts. She didn't have time to supervise Jack Turner. She opened the door to the saw booth, hopped into the operator's chair and shut the soundproof door. She fired up the computer and watched the overhead closed-circuit monitor screen flicker, then hold steady. On its screen was a lengthwise view of the saw carriage and the laser beam that showed the cutting path of the saw blade.

Customers were surprised that Wilcox Lumber, ostensibly still doing it the old-fashioned way, used laser beams and TV loops to mill their lumber. But the hoof price for the timber wasn't cheap, and every scrap of board foot had to be extracted from each log if the yard was going to turn a profit. Even the by-products of the cutting operation were sold. Bark for mulch. Wood chips went to paper plants.

She had just fed power to the four-foot saw blade and set it to spinning hypnotically, when a now-familiar set of shoulders was backlit against the open double doors at the end of the shed. Cripes. The Man in Her Bath had become The Man in Her Shed.

It was one thing to invade her bathroom. The place most women—not her, but most women—probably thought of as their personal sanctuary. But now he'd crossed a line in the sand—er, sawdust. This was different, his coming down here. This was one of the few places on earth, except maybe high up on some really stable staging, where she felt at peace. Most people were so scared shitless of the saw that they never dared come into the shed.

But evidently not Jack Turner. He was probably too brain dead to realize the dangers of the place.

Shit. He'd seen her. He was coming toward the booth. She considered ignoring him and letting the machine sounds drown him out, but distractions plus heavy-duty machin-

ery equaled permanent life changes. Witness dad. She killed
the power to the saw. An "Idle" message filled the computer
screen. *Hopefully not for long*. She cracked opened the door
to the booth and yelled over the din of the blade winding
down. "What the hell do you want now?"

"I found my car keys. I'm headed back to the pool to pick
up the stuff I lost, then I'm off."

"I'll alert the media." Good. He'd go now. He'd said his
piece. Her finger was poised above the switch on the con-
sole labeled "Resume." But no, he kept on coming toward
the tiny operator's booth.

"Look," he said, "Can't we bury the hatchet if I'm going
to be in town for a while?"

Sure, right between your shoulder blades.

"We don't have to like each other, but can't we at least be
civil?" Jack said. Evidently expecting a reply, he stood his
arms open.

Probably too chicken to come any closer until the blade
stopped spinning, Gillian thought.

The blade finally did, twirling out its last slow revolution
and coming to a stop. Jack made his way carefully toward
her. She was cornered in the tiny booth. Not that she'd let
him know she felt that way. On the other hand, she would
not get sucked into another stupid confrontation. She slid
from the operator's seat, out the door and along the outside
wall of the booth, and moved farther into the bowels of the
shed.

She was pretending to make adjustments to the surface
planer when Jack arrived. He stopped across the aisle from
her and leaned against the edge of a workbench and crossed
his arms. He looked like he was trying to impersonate the
Mr. Clean guy on the commercials, she thought, but she
couldn't help but notice how the pose *did* make his biceps
look good. Not as big as Riley's, but still worth a second
look.

But that was not the point. The point was that she was still angry at him. Now also mad that he was here. Mad that he was seemingly every-fricking-where. Could she even remember what Rocky Falls—and her life, for that matter—was like two days before? Before Mr. Jack Turner had insinuated himself into every little part of it? Damn the man's persistence.

She spun angrily toward him, unsure of what she wanted or what she was going to do next. She impulsively grabbed a small pump can of oil from a shelf behind Jack's head. He flinched as her arm flashed past his face but stood his ground. He probably still had the heebie-jeebies from the razor.

She stalked back to the planer, hunched over it, and began to furiously twirl an adjustment wheel, squirting oil around it, unmindful of the stray drops splashing onto her coveralls. She realized she probably looked like an upcountry version of the Phantom of the Opera, hunched over his piano, playing a mad rhapsody, but she needed something to keep her hands busy. A tiny, distant part of her smiled at the ridiculousness of the situation. But her face didn't have to.

"Look," she said, furiously twiddling the endless array of knobs festooning the planer and pretending she was adjusting the barrel of a huge cannon pointing right at Jack, "I've said all I have to say to you. What other people want doesn't matter a whit to you. Just so you get what *you* want. I know that now. End of discussion. Go take your damn survey." She squatted, spun another wheel farther down on the machine and blasted away with the oil. It gushed onto the thigh of her coveralls.

Jack could see the tension etched along the line of her jaw, her eyes narrowed by an emotion much stronger than the act of concentration. She didn't need to be thinking *that* hard about whatever thing she was idiotically pretending to do to that planer. Tendrils of spun gold escaped from under the edges of her cap, and the small leaf earrings, incongruent with her ragged outfit, winked in the rays of sunlight fighting their way through the dusty windows. Jack suddenly felt steam against his skin, and smelled, of all things, bubble bath.

"You know, I—" he started.

"Go away."

"No," he said. "Not without resolving this."

"There is no 'resolving this.' Don't you get that?" She peered up at him.

"There might be if you could just listen for a minute."

Pretending to would cost her nothing. Eventually he'd run out of gas and just leave.

He took her silence as permission to continue. "It could all work out for the good of everyone with the right redevelopment plan," he said.

"Hello," she said. "Do you mind: context?"

"You don't need context. It's all around us. In the air between us." He checked his hands. He'd been about to wave them in the air, a gesture that would get him laughed out of a boardroom but fast.

Even though she'd heard it from him before, even though she knew "the good of everyone" was a mainstay in his argument to develop, it always seemed to take her aback. "But you're an outsider," she said, genuinely amazed at his presumptiveness. "You have no idea how Rocky Falls works, what it's really like. How dare you assume to understand. This town's been through a lot of hard times brought upon it by people who thought they knew what was best. You know nothing about all that. The last thing we need around here is some new scheme to 'help out.'"

"Just listen to your choice of words," he said. "The very fact you use the word 'scheme' to describe a redevelopment plan says *volumes* about your prejudices about it." He realized he was heating up again.

"I'm *not* prejudiced!" she retorted. "Prejudice implies a judgment in the absence of prior experience. Believe me, this town has had plenty of experience with so-called 'improvement' plans."

Gillian noticed the muscles in the side of his jaw were beginning to work overtime. Good. "First, there was the Great Fire of 1903. A complete disaster courtesy of the logging companies. Left the logging slash laying around and lightning set half the town on fire. Only by the grace of God does Rocky Falls still exist. Then the all-knowing U.S. government got involved here in the forties. It took until the seventies to clean the place up after—" her voice hitched—"Ah . . . Never mind."

She turned and went back to her random acts of oiling.

All over again, this shit coming up. She'd grown up with it, taken it in with her mother's milk, gotten sick over it, let it break her heart. Finally ran from it. It and other things. She pushed aside thoughts of her mother. Then, when you think you've finally got your issues buried deep, the grave nicely smoothed over to where no one would ever suspect there was anything buried under there and maybe you could at last draw a semi-deep breath, move on, and think about what you were going to do with the rest of your life— Bam!—a mysterious stranger rides into town and starts rummaging around in your junk drawer. She finished her thoughts out loud, "Digging up old crap, messing up people's lives, their—" Again with the hitch—"Futures. Over my dead body."

"What do you mean?" Jack asked, puzzled, curious in spite of his anger.

"Nothing. Forget it. There's no going back."

To Jack, she sounded . . . what? Sad. Really sad. The fight had left her. An image from earlier that morning of the exhausted trout floating helplessly into his net came to mind. Surprisingly, he found the picture distasteful when applied to the normally fiery Ms. Wilcox.

"It might be better if you talked about it with . . . someone," he said.

She laughed bitterly. "Oh, really?" Yet why did that sound so good? "To who? *You*?"

She laughed again, this time throwing her head back, looking to the rafters of the shed as if for inspiration. Then she stuck a thumb in an armpit and threw her chest out and aped him. "'Yup, talk to me, Mr. Jack Turner, everybody's good buddy.' Too funny, Jack really. Talk to you. *You* who doesn't give two *shits* about any negative impact on the land or the community."

"'Negative impact.' Oh, please." He looked away briefly, then back at Gillian. "Is *no* impact better than a so-called 'negative' one?"

She went back to tinkering with the machine. He went back to his argument.

"I do appreciate your position, Gillian."

She hooted.

"Really, I do. It is not my intention to offer less than fair market value for anyone's land."

She noticed he avoided saying "your land."

"I've the acreage around here carefully appraised, I know what it's worth. This is not about stealing people's property."

"Oh, really."

"Yes, really. If my plan goes through," he said, "people in Rocky Falls would have real homes to live in. Houses with modern plumbing, for God's sake and fully grounded electrical service. Or they could use the cash from land sales to move somewhere else. Or even buy up more land that will, I guarantee, become *the* place to live in upstate Maine in five years. After we renovate the downtown and develop the riverfront area, people will flock here. You all could get off the treadmill of just working to make it through to next week."

His best argument, he thought. And it was all true. He'd bet his reputation on it. In fact, he thought, here he was doing just that. "Gillian," he concluded, "you can't make eggnog without breaking eggs."

She felt like an iron bar had replaced her backbone. Her lips seemed too rigid to make sounds. She croaked out, "Yes, you have to break the eggs. But you *don't* have to leave the shells lying on the kitchen floor."

Didn't he get it, the fool? It wasn't happening. She set down the oil can, afraid of what she might do with it.

"Jack Turner, I'm officially warning you. I've listened patiently to proposals made in your name. I've sat through your advance people's slick-as-shit arguments last spring. I've saved your sorry ass from drowning, *and* patched the dent in your thick skull *and* made you freaking coffee. But—you arrogant, entitled bastard—you are now crossing the line."

Suddenly, his own temper got the better of him. His shell of reason and cool logic evaporated. He felt his blood pressure sky rocket and the veins in his neck begin to throb. Apparently he was incapable of disengaging from this demented, diminutive Cinderella standing four-square in front of him. It was her total lack of regard for anything that he was offering her, and the community she was so obsessively protective of, that spurred him on. She just couldn't see that his plans would help her town and what she thought of as "her people."

He should leave right now. Clearly, he had lost control. That equaled Game, Set, Match to your opponent. He should cut his losses. Live to cast another day.

Instead he said, "You can't tell me that you're setting the world on fire here, Gillian." He indicated her mill yard with a sweep of his hand. "And your neighbors do what—farm a few acres, press a bit of cider, work the ski hills in the winter? Big whoop-de-fucking-doo. Oh, yeah, and don't forget: They landscape the resorts in the summer. Just pray that you can cobble together enough money to pay the real estate taxes at the end of the quarter, huh?"

"Fuck you," she said.

"Oh, no. Fuck *you*," he said.

She viciously slammed a belt tensioning lever. Her hand,

slick with oil, slid from it and collided with the side of the machine. The skin of two knuckles shredded. She watched bright red spots blossom on the back of her hand.

"*Damn* it!"

"Hey, let me see . . ." Jack said.

A searing white heat wiped out all her reason. "You wanna see? See this, you—"

She snatched up the oilcan, drew her arm back, and fired it at him, but it slipped from her hand as she released it and burst open against the edge of the workbench. Jack was showered in machine oil.

He grabbed for her then, had his hands around her, wrapping her up in a bear hug. "Where do you get off unloading like that on people," he yelled at her, shaking with fury, blinking and shouldering oil out of his eyes with his sleeve. "Don't you know I could press charges against you for that?"

"And you think I couldn't get *you* for trespassing?" she countered, trying to squirm free.

"There's only one problem with that, lady," he smirked. "You *invited* me onto your property."

"Oh yeah? I've told you to leave several times." She flailed, but long, strong fingers tightened on her upper arms like pipe clamps.

"I will when I'm through saying my piece," Jack said. "I look on this gentle restraint as self-defense. If I thought for a minute you wouldn't try to blindside me, I'd let you go." He gave her the benefit of the doubt, though, and loosened his grip.

"You know, Jack," she said quietly, "there just aren't any guarantees in this life, are there? People just do the damnedest things." So saying, she twisted free of his grip and aimed a roundhouse slap at his face.

He deflected her swing and ducked under her arm, coming up behind her to grab her around the waist. She bucked her head backward trying to connect with his chin, but he anticipated it. He pressed her against the workbench thinking only to contain her until she calmed down, but she hung herself from him and planted both feet against the edge of the bench and shoved off.

Jack lost his balance and they both careened backward.

He landed on the sawdust-covered floor with her on top of him, thrashing and snarling like a bobcat. Rolling over, he pinned her beneath him with the weight of his body. She tore at his clothes, struggling for a purchase to lever herself free.

The fight started to go out of her when she realized that try as she might, there was no budging Jack. He had her. The more she twisted, the more sawdust went in her mouth and up her nose. She stopped, her chest heaving mightily, and took stock. Surprisingly, she wasn't in any discomfort. He was taking his weight on his elbows and knees, but she was completely winded and getting claustrophobic. This part she remembered from wrestling with Riley in grammar school. Way back then she'd discovered that while might sometimes did make right, she'd never be able to take him in a fair fight.

"Okay—" she grunted, "I give. Really." She felt Jack shift some of his weight off her, enough that she could at least roll over to look up at him. He still kept a light hold on her wrists, though, not that she could blame him after her whirling dervish act.

He was breathing heavy too, she realized.

"Great spot for wrestling," he said. "We should try it in a room full of broken glass next time."

He was such a smart ass. She focused her eyes on his face. *Those lashes again . . .*

"You're a mess, I hope you know," he said, breathing down onto her. Her baseball cap was long gone in the scuffle. He gently plucked a wood shaving from her tousled hair. He let go of one of her wrists. Mesmerized, Gillian didn't move a muscle.

Chapter 8

One mile outside of Rocky Falls, Rachel Wilcox downshifted her red BMW, left the relatively smooth asphalt of
Route 101 behind her and bounced onto the dirt road leading
to the Wilcox homestead. It was known to her, Gillian, and
Meg as the Wilcox Box. Dad hated that name. Dust whorls
followed the slow progress of her low-slung convertible as
she cautiously navigated through the ruts and washouts.

Two hundred yards in, she made an abrupt turn into the
gravel driveway of The Box. She coasted to a stop next to
Gillian's beat-up Toyota pickup and killed the engine of the
BMW. The dust cloud that pursued her tracked past the driveway and followed the bumpy road that led down to the mill
yard. It finally lost the scent and settled back to earth.

Home sweet home. She should have remembered not to
wear black, never mind wool. She kneed open the car door.
She turned in the seat, placed both feet gingerly onto the
rough crushed gravel of the drive, and stood. She pinned the
loose, brass-buttoned front of her black blazer to her narrow
middle with a slim wrist and carefully leaned over the dusty
side panel of the BMW to rummage behind the front seat.
She extracted a purse and a small overnight bag.

Out of habit she checked to see if her cell phone was on.
Not that the securities company—correction, ex-company—

would be calling her any time soon. Her final check was coming by mail. No sense of humor, those people.

She keyed open the trunk and contemplated a wheeled suitcase. What good the wheels were on the rough gravel of the drive she surely didn't know. Her ankle twisted as she misplaced a narrow foot. God, it was like being on a construction sight. Forget it. She slammed the trunk lid shut. She leaned over the wheel and beeped the horn, then pushed the car door closed with the tips of two fingers.

She picked her way carefully across the drive to the front porch. The elaborately turned posts and the spindle work were even more dilapidated than she remembered. Underneath each of the railings, a line of flaked white paint lay like remnants of the last snow. The place was an embarrassment. How could Gillian have let it get so bad?

The decking was springy beneath her feet, too. Something under there needed help fast. She cupped her hand above her eyes and peered through the screen door.

Jack was so close to Gillian that he noticed the fine strands of her hair were shot through with red highlights. Totally natural, he'd bet. Explained her temper. He really looked at her eyes. *Golden flecks in emerald settings . . .*

He hovered above her, his face inches from hers, and waited for her to retreat. From him? Into herself? Somewhere. But instead, time froze, and the eye of the hurricane settled over them. She shut her eyes. Her head rose up and she brought her lips lightly in contact with his.

Jack, amazed, lightly returned the kiss. He drew the ball of his thumb across her cheek. Her free arm went around his neck, her fingers brushing the hair at his collar. She smelled like fresh pine, woodsy and warm, and something else. He tried to place the familiar scent, then, *bubble bath . . .*

He let go of her other wrist and rolled over, bringing her on top of him. She didn't break the contact, and coming out on top, she leaned into the kiss. Jack felt the tension in her thighs as she straddled his legs. Heat sprang up where their bodies touched. He slowly slid his hands up the sides of her legs, and even through the rough canvas of the coveralls, he could feel her sinewy strength. Unconsciously, he made his touch soothing rather than arousing, but Gillian responded with a passionate attack on his mouth, nibbling his lower lip, running her tongue experimentally along it. She imprisoned his head between her two hands, and deepened the kiss, exploring his mouth.

Their tongues met somewhere in the middle, and they tasted each other like treats from a candy store. He slid his hands up her back, rubbing and stroking the long muscles, like a cowboy soothing a wild mustang.

"Hello!" Rachel called into the dark depths of the front hall.

The house dozed in the early morning air. "Hey, Gilly, it's me!" Too late for her sister to be sleeping. Rachel tugged open the sprung screen door.

Old house smells—plaster and tinder dry wood and some elusive scent from her childhood—greeted her. Memories rode its coattails. She'd left here in one big hurry, that was for sure. She sighed and plunked her keys on the hall table, glancing into the antique mirror hanging above it. She was momentarily stunned to see a sophisticated woman looked back at her. Blond hair, hanging loose to just below the shoulder, pearl earrings and a matching double-strand loop accented with gold beads rested against a white silk blouse, set off by a plain black wool blazer. Simple understated elegance. She had nailed it yet again. Not that anyone in Rocky Falls would appreciate that.

She slipped the overnight bag from her shoulder. Where was Gillian? Just like her to go off leaving the front door wide open. Then again, this wasn't exactly the Back Bay of

Boston. People traipsed in and out of each other's houses anytime of the day or night and nobody thought anything of it. If she flew out on a business trip and left the door of her Beacon Hill apartment open, nobody would think twice about coming in either. But four bare walls would greet her when she got back.

Maybe there were some good things about coming home.

"Gillian?" she called up the stairs. "Gillian?" The house snored on.

The floorboards of the front hall creaked as she made her way alongside the staircase toward the back of the house. She checked out the front parlor on her way past. Her mother had always kept it as a formal sitting room. It was long and narrow, front to back, with a fireplace at the far end. Some nice upholstered mahogany pieces and three-legged tables vied for space. A typical 1800s parlor. A courting room in the old days. She herself had done her share of courting—okay, maybe a *little* more than that—on the couch that was in there now. Good thing good furniture couldn't talk.

When her mother was alive, hand-knotted damask runners had graced every table, and the brass on the period kerosene lamps glowed like fire. She ran her finger over the tabletop closest to the door. Dusty. Unused.

She stepped into the kitchen at the rear of the house. More floorboards popped. It was brighter back there, with the sun flooding in through the large casement windows of the family room addition just beyond. The kitchen certainly looked lived in. Dishes were stacked in the drying rack on the drain board. A washcloth hung over the spigot drying. Balled up dish towel on the counter. The gross honey bear thing Gillian always used, with the sugar bowl sitting next to it.

Hmmm . . .

Two empty coffee cups in the sink. How interesting.

Definitely the Gillian equivalent of empty champagne bottles on the floor and a bra hanging off the lampshade.

Big sister with a love interest? A good thing, probably. The furniture wasn't the only thing gathering dust around here according to Meg's e-mails.

Suddenly Rachel realized she couldn't wait to find Gillian. The mill, she thought.

Jack felt himself harden. He squirmed beneath Gillian as the pressure from the apex of her thighs rubbed against him, sending his desire spiraling higher and higher. By unspoken mutual consent, they both began working at the front zipper of her coveralls, suddenly as restricting as a straightjacket.

His hands, her hands, fumbling, bumping, worked the sleeves down and off of her arms. She slipped a hand into the front of his shirt, to feel the warm planes of his chest. He massaging her arms, sliding up to touch her face, moving down, surrounding the swell of her breasts. All the while, kissing, kissing, kissing . . .

Rachel took the family room in three long strides and flew into the mudroom. She kicked off her heels and tugged on a pair of Gillian's sneakers. Too small, but what the hey. *Any port . . .* Wood splinters stabbed into the weave of her slacks when she hip checked the sticky screen door, but that didn't seem as important to her as it might have a few minutes before. For better or worse, she was home. And hot on the trail of some *killer* gossip.

She headed off down the road leading around the rear of the house to the mill yard, swinging her arms and tipping her head back to let the sun warm her face.

Home.

Inhaling deeply, she savored everything that the word conjured up.

The quiet. It hurts your ears at first.

The stoplights. There was one, and it blinked.

The lines at the stores. There weren't any.

In fact, the clerks stopped reading *The National Enquirer* to wait on you and you alone, as if ringing up your stuff was the most important thing they had to do all day. Ah, service.

And they didn't ask the usual stupid question before they bagged up your stuff in the food store. They automatically gave you "paper" because you couldn't start a wood stove with a plastic bag. Of course, it went without saying that they didn't always have exactly what you wanted. *Bok choy*? Huh? *Radicchio?* Never heard of it. But hey, it was a swap-off.

And to top it all off, her sister had a *thang* going on. Rachel clapped her hands in delight. True, two coffee cups did not necessarily mean boot knocking, but in this case she'd be willing to bet last quarter's bonus that it did. She had a nose for these things, a second sense. She supposed it was from a lifetime of being the subject of sexual interest from almost every male she had ever met that wasn't immediate family. Or in elementary school. Or too old to care. Which was never, as far as she could tell.

Not that being born beautiful was the be all and end all. It had its downsides. The upkeep and so forth. But on the upside, it *had* helped to get her to where she was today. Or until last week, to be precise. Bunch of stuck-up board of director wives. Couldn't take a joke.

But back to Gillian. Who could He be?

She ticked off possibilities in her head.

Riley? Convenient, and there was history there, but nah. He'd been carrying a torch for Gillian since eighth grade, but no way. They were a dead issue. Poor Riley just hadn't figured it out yet.

Just for fun, she'd had a crack at him herself in high school on the infamous couch in the front parlor, but to her surprise, she didn't get anywhere. He had zero interest in her. He'd only hung around her as a way to get to Gillian. Actually, his disinterest in her came as a relief, because he turned out to be one of the few males that she could ever really talk to without their eyes glazing over and their mouths drooling. He really wasn't bad once you got to know him. And he was kind of sexy in an overpowering, misguided sort of way.

But that was just like Gillian. Take the hard way over the mountains when someone was right there offering to move them for you. Oh, well. Maybe she'd finally lucked into something this time.

She realized her feet hurt from walking on the rough road, but it was a good pain. They'd toughen up. She'd be here at least through the annual Harvest Fair, and that was three weeks away. Plenty of time to add a layer of callus to a cosmetically insignificant area.

Then, there it was: the good old Wilcox Lumber sign. God, Gillian was so proud of this messy, dusty little business. Rachel walked through the front gate.

It was dead quiet in the yard. Weird. People must have called in, or Gillian forgot to call them to come in. Who knew? Business in Rocky Falls and Boston were at different ends of the spectrum. But Gillian had to be around somewhere. Come out, come out wherever you are. *Tell ya lil' sis all about the stud muffin . . .*

The office door was wide open. Rachel peeked in. Empty, except for about a thousand ducks. Swimming on the curtains, paddling around the monitor screen. *Ech*. Her sister really did need to get out more often. She walked to the middle of the yard and listened. No saw going, obviously, but Gillian might just be setting up for the day. Ah, all the doors to the saw shed were wide open. Yep, she was probably holed up in there, her private little sanctuary. Just mosey on over and see.

The ground around the shed was littered with wood chips and sawdust, the accumulation of three generations of lumber cutting. It felt like heavily padded carpeting under her aching feet. Rachel enjoyed her walk across it, then left the morning sun behind and entered the shadowy coolness of the shed through the first open double door.

"Hel-*lo*, anybody home?"

"Gilly?" She waited for an answering "Hello!"

Nothing.

But someone, or something, was up back, Rachel thought. She could hear rustling noises. Some kind of controlled commotion was going on beyond the saw booth. An animal digging around? A skunk, perish the thought? *That* stink would never come out of wool.

Rustle, rustle . . .

A gasp and then a low moan escaped Gillian's lips as Jack slid his hands under her shirt. He traced the curve of her navel, slid up her ribcage, and cupped her breasts through the thin lace of her bra. She cried out with pleasure when he slid his thumbs beneath the constraining elastic and ran them over her nipples. The edges of the world melted into a blur of sensation as she and Jack fell into the fire.

Suddenly, a cheery voice rang out from the front end of the shed.

"Hel-*lo!*" it warbled. "Anybody home?"

They froze, open mouthed, staring at each other like the sole survivors of an airliner crash.

"Shit! It's my sister!" Gillian hissed.

Chapter 9

"Hey, Rachel, how you—ah, doing?" It was Gillian's voice, from the rear of the building. "I wasn't expecting you," she called.

To Rachel, her voice sounded strange.

"I'm just doing some maintenance on the planer," her sister said, still sounding weird. "I'm a little, ah . . . caught on it. Let me just get myself untangled—"

The commotion kicked up a notch.

"What the hell are you doing?" Gillian whispered hoarsely to Jack. She stared wide eyed at her body entwined with Jack's and the disarray of their clothes. Cripes, she was half-undressed. "You bastard," she whispered hoarsely. "Taking advantage of me by starting something like this . . ."

Then to her sister up front she called, "Just a minute, Rach! Don't come back here—you'll . . . ah, get stuff all over your clothes."

"Me starting things?" Jack hissed back. "You kissed me first, I hope you know."

"Oh, yeah, right. That's lame." *Had she?* She couldn't remember. They had fought, then *poof,* amnesia. "Get *off* me, will you?" she grunted, shoving at his chest below her. She swung her leg over Jack and rose onto her knees.

She hastily stuffed her shirt back into the front of her coveralls and zipped them up, staying low so she wouldn't be seen. "This is just great," she said, fighting to keep her voice low. Rachel couldn't keep her mouth shut about anything. And here, with Jack Turner of all people, she, Gillian Wilcox, had apparently been about to dance the horizontal cha-cha on the floor of the saw shed. What the hell was *she* doing? She couldn't remember now.

"I'll slip out the back so you won't have to explain," Jack whispered.

"No! Rachel'll see you," she hissed. "Get yourself together. We'll bluff it out. And oh—remind me *never* to speak to you again." She gave him another shove as she rose from her crouch and headed toward the front of the shed.

Finally.

Rachel watched Gillian emerge from the gloom. But she wasn't alone.

The most beautiful man Rachel had seen in a long while dogged her sister's heels. Tall, dark hair. Blue eyes that pierced from fifty-feet away. She pressed her fist to her mouth and stifled a giggle. This was too much. Her ultra-responsible older sister doing "planer maintenance" with a handsome hunk at eight-thirty in the morning. Oh, God, this was rich. Wait until she told Meg.

Rachel bit her lip as her sister approached. And the guy was dressed in what? Their *dad's* clothes? Nice shoulders on the guy, too, from what she could see outlined beneath the blocky flannel shirt.

Rachel pretended to sneeze from the dust in the air. She feigned a cough. She was dying. This was an absolute *howl*. There were *so* many advantages to coming home unannounced.

"Hey, Rachel," Gillian said, close enough now that Rachel could see she was wearing an atrociously grimy work suit. "Great to see you, but I, ah—didn't expect you. Did I miss a message on the machine or something?"

"Oh, no. My job—I mean, plans, were cancelled at the last minute, so I thought I'd pop up here and see if my older sister was *making out* okay." She watched Gillian squirm like a worm on a hook. Perfect. Turn about was fair play. Gillian always had plenty to say to her when she was feeling her oats in high school. Now—at long last—a chance to give tit for tat. No pun intended.

"'Pop up here?'" Gillian said, recovering quickly. "From Massachusetts?"

"I'm fast."

"Oh, I'm just betting . . ."

"Moving on," Rachel said, amused. It was hard to keep Gillian pinned for long. She took in the wood curls in her sister's hair. The collar of her shirt was jammed into the zipper of her coveralls. Her lips looked swollen and bruised, and her eyes were smudgy. She sure *looked* like she'd been making out okay. But she seemed to have lost the ability to speak. *Introduce us, already.* Gillian's social skills were an embarrassment.

Finally, the man cleared his throat.

"Oh," Gillian said. "This is Jack Turner. He's in town on business."

About time, Rachel thought, then: *Really.* What kind of business?

"Nice to meet you, Jack," said Rachel, looking down at his, or rather, her father's clothes. She stuck out her hand. He shook it. She let her grip linger on his fingers for a moment more than was customary. He didn't appear to enjoy the extra hang time. Good. Maybe Gillian had found one of the rare ones that didn't think with their dicks.

"Same, Ms. Wilcox," responded Jack. "Gillian has told me a lot about you."

That was a lie, Rachel knew. "Why, I find that so interesting, Jack, as my sister seems to have maintained an air of secrecy concerning you. And please call me Rachel." She smiled sweetly.

"Mr. Turner is in town to investigate some possible building sites," Gillian said.

Rachel watched her sister stare at the Jack guy like a dog with a leash in its mouth begging to be taken for a walk. He wasn't saying anything. Gillian was melting right in front of them. Too, too good.

"In fact, he's out here today on a walk-through of the mill," Gillian said, desperation in her voice. "I was just explaining the nature of our operation to him and why I would be unwilling to enter into any type of relationship with him."

Whew. Big emphasis on *any*. Rachel watched her sister shoot a dagger at Jack. Had she read the vibes wrong? Unlikely. But it was definitely a confusing situation. "I thought you said you were working on some equipment back there?" she innocently asked Gillian.

"Well, yes, I was. We were going by the planer, and I noticed it needed oiling so I . . . oiled it."

Yeah, right. Like that was the only thing that got lubricated. Then she decided she'd tortured everybody enough. "Well, you and I can visit anytime, Gilly," she said. "And I'm sure Mr. Turner has better things to do with his time than listen to us prattle on." She batted her own blue eyes at Jack. "So, I'll just leave you two alone to finish—" she paused, "your business . . ."

She swept her eyes briefly over Jack's clothes, making it very clear she knew all about the nature of that business.

"Actually, Rachel," Gillian interrupted, "Mr. Turner was just leaving. Weren't you?" she said.

More dark looks. The poor guy. *Don't scare him away, Gilly. This one's a keeper.*

"Oh—yes. Right." Jack said, "Yes, I am. I'll be in contact with you Ms. Wilcox." He nodded at Gillian.

Dead giveaway, his *not* shaking hands with her sister, Rachel thought. She had read it right.

He turned to her and nodded. "Nice meeting you, Rachel."

Rachel quickly redrafted the plans she'd put together on the drive up from Massachusetts. She couldn't stay at The Box now. Gillian needed room to operate. "I'll be staying at our sister Meg's, Jack. She's right downtown, so I'm sure I'll be seeing more of you. Perhaps you might stop by sometime and meet the rest of the family?"

He shook her offered hand.

"Oh, no, I don't think so, Rachel," Gillian said. "Mr. Turner is very busy."

"Actually, that sounds nice, Rachel," he said. "I'll look you up. Thanks."

"How nice," Rachel said.

"My pleasure," Jack said.

Gillian said nothing.

The Wilcox women watched Jack Turner walk away in floodwater pants, holding the baggy waist up with one hand and clutching a wet bundle of laundry in the other.

"Now there goes a guy with a lot of poise," Rachel said.

Chapter 10

Jack Turner disappeared into the underbrush at the rear of the yard.

"So Gilly, tell me. How are things?" Rachel asked casually.

"A bomb could go off and you wouldn't bat an eye, would you?" Gillian said.

"Yeah, well, you don't get anywhere in computer consulting if you panic every time the system goes down."

"And has the system . . . gone down?" Gillian knew Rachel was as much a workaholic as she was. For her little sister to show up in Rocky Falls was unexpected enough, but in the middle of the week?

"No, but the wife of one of the board members thought I had. On her husband."

"Ah. Sending your severance here, are they?"

"Pretty much." Rachel sighed. "But enough about me, for once. You?"

"I'm fine," Gillian said.

"How's Dad, Meg and the kids?"

"Terrific." Gillian couldn't seem to tear her eyes away from the bushes into which Jack Turner had disappeared.

"I'll be staying with her and Bob, by the way," Rachel said. "Meg would love to have me there for awhile."

"Are you out of your mind? No, she wouldn't." Their older

sister had a work-at-home husband, a full-time teaching job, and two young kids. Their cranky, semi-disabled father was also installed in the newly created in-law apartment Gillian had added onto Meg's house.

"Touchy, touchy. I was just trying to give you your space."

"For what?"

Rachel tipped her head toward the bushes and raised her eyebrows.

"For heaven's sake, Rachel, there's nothing going on. I appreciate the thought, but you can have your old room here."

"I wouldn't exactly call *this* . . ."—Rachel extracted a long curl of shaved pine from Gillian's tousled hair—". . . Nothing." She let it go and they both watched it flutter away.

"Cripes." Gillian viciously yanked at the scrunchie holding back her hair, then bent at the waist and furiously raked her fingers through the frizzy mess. An accumulation of saw dust and wood chips rained to the ground. She straightened, flipped the disastrous tangle backward and reinstalled the elastic.

"It's nothing and never will be," she said. "The guy's a jerk."

"And you're gonna 'Wash that man right out of your hair,' huh?"

"Shut up."

Rachel *tsk, tsk*-ed. Apropos to the situation or her hair care, Gillian couldn't tell. "I don't know, Gilly. Sorry to be blunt but attracting men never was your strong suit. Don't be so quick to throw back the shorts." She guffawed. "Get it? The shorts? His pants?" She punched her sister lightly in the arm.

Gillian looked at her like she'd never seen her before.

Rachel hung onto Gillian's shoulder and lifted up one foot. She drew an imaginary line on her leg mid-calf. "The high waters he was wearing?"

"He isn't short," Gillian said, reminded of the tub. And of what she'd briefly sized up on the floor of the saw shed.

"Aw, forget it," Rachel said. Her world was chock full at the moment with people with no sense of humor. Anyway. This Jack definitely looked to be a step in the right direction for her semi-celibate sister. The gal whom everyone had pegged as a shoo-in for late admission to the convent.

"Interesting guy you found," she said. "He's the first one in recent memory that didn't react to my patented hand action."

That got her a look.

"Not that kind. I mean the pleased-to-meet-you hand-shake thing. He didn't hang on. Not for a millisecond. It was like shaking hands with the minister. I take that as a good sign."

"How nice that I have you to vet every guy that I have absolutely no interest in seeing. Tell me, is there a charge for this service?"

Rachel said in her best hooker voice. "Honey, y'awl know me. I charge for everything."

"You really are disgusting."

"Thank you."

"And it's great to have you home." Gillian put an arm around her sister's waist.

"It's great for *everyone* that I'm home, sweetie." Rachel tossed her hair and hooked some errant blond strands behind an ear. "Say, what's this guy's name? I mean, be-sides—" she batted her eyelashes—"*Ooh, la la* Jack."

"Turner. Jack Ooh-la-la Turner."

"Ah." Now for the ten-dollar question: Was her sister *doing* this Jack guy? Nah, not yet, she'd bet, but there was definitely smoke. And a nice set of shoulders. Okay, then. How to get Gilly Girl seriously hooked up? *Hmmm*. A nice little problem. A knotty little puzzle. Just the kind she liked. Push a few buttons, set a few things in motion. Just like writing program.

"Hey, Gillian," she said, "I got a great idea. You've got a lot of work to do around here, right?"

"Yeah . . ."

She clasped her hands primly in front of her. "I could help you with it."

"Hah!" The sound was out before Gillian could bite it back. Too funny. "Ah, Rachel," she said, eyeing her sister's wool and silk. "That's nice of you, but One-of-the-Twins is coming in soon and Skip, too. I really got enough help—"

"Oh, come on, Gilly, please? It'd be fun!" Rachel hopped from foot to foot and begged in a sing-song voice. That had always worked when they were kids.

"No, I . . . don't think so, Rachel," Gillian said hesitantly. "It's really dangerous. You know what happened with Dad. You really got to watch what you're doing every minute." Good God in heaven, Rachel working at the mill. What next?

"You know what your problem is, Gillian Wilcox?" Rachel said. "You're afraid to try something different. You know, to take a chance. I've never done this kind of work before, so therefore I can't."

"Afraid to take a chance?" Gillian's temper flared. "What are you, crazy?" And who else had said that not one hour ago?

"If I was afraid to 'take a chance' as you put it, would I have come home and taken this place over from Dad in the first place?" It was an outrage, what Rachel was saying.

Then she got it. She laughed and shook her head. She'd been had—again. But point well taken. "Oh, all right, for God's sake, Rachel. You're worse than a little kid. Get changed and come back down. There are extra boots in my closet. Gloves and coveralls are under the counter in the office." She pulled on her work gloves. "But hurry up about it. The lumber's not gonna cut itself." She punched Rachel's shoulder companionably.

"Ow!" Rachel massaged her arm. Jeez, right on the bone. She caught the look of contempt on her sister's face. "Just kidding!" she said.

* * *

Gillian watched her sister walk away, still rubbing her arm. *Office wimp*. She tugged at one point of her jumpsuit collar where it felt folded under, swiped a few more errant wood shavings from the coarse fabric and went back to the operator's booth. She slipped into the seat. She glanced outside to the floor on her right. She could still see the marks in the dust on the floor from her scuffle with Jack. The creep. Going after a woman in her own saw shed.

Maybe. Truthfully, she still wasn't exactly sure *what* had happened until the sound of Rachel's voice had snapped her back to reality. She had suddenly found herself breathing heavily, half-undressed, and tangled up on the floor with Jack Turner. Some kind of fugue state going on there.

Perhaps a little review was in order. First, she tried to kill Jack Turner. Next, they were on the floor rolling around like a couple of hormonal teenagers. Then, Rachel's voice from the front of the shed brought her back to reality. Finally, she wanted to kill Jack Turner all over again.

Nothing new second time around. One thing *was* for sure, though. She was not, under *any* circumstances, speaking to that man ever again.

She flipped on the master power switch in the booth, then fired up the computer system again. She fed power to the huge saw blade, and the four-foot gleaming monster began to slowly rotate. At first, it grumbled at being disturbed from its rest, vibrating the floor of the booth as it began to spin. Then it lodged its usual litany of complaints as it warbled its way through various sound pitches on the road up operating speed. Finally it hit full RPM and contentedly settled into a steady, high-pitched hum. From her vantage point, the individual diamond-tipped teeth disappeared to meld into a blur that orbited the blade like rings around a planet. A truly awesome sight. One that never got old.

She flipped another lever, and the saw carriage slid backward, away from the blade, down the track to the head of the conveyor belt, where the logs she'd debarked yesterday were waiting for cutting. She engaged the feed lever on the conveyor, and an eighteen-foot pine rolled onto the carriage. The two-ton log dropped neatly into the center of the cradle, and Gillian engaged the drive train on the carriage.

Slowly, she inched the log up to the spinning blade, stopping just inches short of it. A ruby red beam of laser light shone down on the tree trunk. She played with a few dimensions from the cutting options displayed on the computer monitor, finally selecting the one that yielded a preselected assortment of various timber dimensions that got the most from the log.

She punched in her final answer and sat back. The saw and computer worked together from there, automatically moving the log and carriage side to side and forward and back, effortlessly slicing up the huge log like a block of cheese. The cut boards flopped loose from the main log, and fell onto a conveyor belt, which ferried them to the rear of the shed for sorting and stacking. The half-round slabs pared from the sides of the rough logs were shuttled onto separate belts leading to the chipper. They'd be chopped up into mulch and shot into waiting trailers.

Forward and back, forward and back. . . . It was hard not to become mesmerized watching the saw carriage run through its rhythmic cycle. Forward and back . . . kind of like the motions she and Jack—*Aagh!*

Rachel better get back soon. Anchor her to reality. Plus she could only dice up a few logs before the pile of accumulated boards at the end of the line would start jamming up the feed operation. Rachel could pull the cut stuff off the belts at the end of the line and stack it—usually Skip's job. With him and Joyce expecting their second, Skip's morning arrival times had been on and off lately. And where was One-of-the-Twins, if not Both-of-Them, this fine morning?

Gillian glanced down the length of the shed toward the

entrance door. No big old Caddy. No foreman's pickup. The two-year-old must be giving Skip a run for his money.

But there was Rachel. She must have sprinted to the house and back, because she had returned in record time decked out in work boots, pulling the tops of coveralls over her slim shoulders as she jogged, fluffing her hair out of the collar before zipping up the front.

Gillian had a sudden burst of affection for her. She could be a royal pain in the ass sometimes, paying more attention to other people's business than her own. But at least she was up front about it, freely admitted that other people's business was so much more interesting than her own. True, she could be a bit of a wimp at times, too. But she was a Wilcox through and through. A hustler. A survivor. She got things done. Usually not in the way you'd like, but that was beside the point.

Gillian smiled as she watched Rachel mince her way down the length of the shed, palms pressed to her ears to block out the noise of the saw. Even in drab, unisex coveralls, Rachel had style. She had that walk, a certain sway to her step, that drew men like moths to a flame. In high school, Gillian had paraded in front of the full-length mirror in her room, trying to imitate Rachel's subtle hip movements. She'd pushed her own hips forward and tried to sort of roll along, but she just ended up looking like a candidate for orthopedic surgery. Rachel did it effortlessly and unconsciously. Like yawning. You had to give her credit.

Gillian let the saw wind down to half-speed, then pushed open the door of the booth. "Hey, Rachel. You *look* the part anyway," she said, chuckling.

"Yuck, don't these things come in any other colors?" Her sister was half-serious, Gillian realized, watching Rachel rearrange the waistline of the coveralls and button back the cuffs.

"Really, huh? I know myself I just never feel ready to receive company down here when my creases aren't straight," Gillian said.

"Please remember," Rachel said, "I'm doing this to be nice, not because I have to. So you be nice."

"I am—for now. Just wait until your first screw up. You got the gloves?"

Rachel yanked them from a back pocket and held them up for inspection.

"Good. Start pulling those boards off the conveyor down there." Gillian pointed. "Skip should be along any minute. Joyce is having her second baby—you heard?—and he's late getting out of there some mornings."

"Yeah, Dad told me on the phone Joyce was close." She made to go, then abruptly turned and casually propped one foot on the first step of the saw booth. "Hey, speaking of babies and girl things, I had some ideas about getting that Jack guy all heated up about you. I was thinking—"

Gillian didn't allow her to finish.

"Damn it, Rachel! I absolutely and positively *forbid* you to so much as say his name. Cripes, suddenly everywhere I turn he's there. Even in my . . . dreams, for God's sake." She instantly regretted admitting that.

Rachel pounced on it. "Dreams? Oh, honey," she said, cocking her head and smiling slyly, "you got it *baaad*. . . . You know I read this book that said—"

Swear to God I'll strangle her. . . . "Go!" Gillian screamed, pointing to the stacking and sorting end of the shed.

"Aye, aye, ma'am." Rachel saluted. She turned to leave.

"Wait!" Gillian said. "Put these on." She tossed Rachel a set of bright yellow hearing protectors.

"Oh, cool. Tunes . . ."

"Don't be a nitwit for once in your life? Wear them when the saw's running?" Gillian took a deep calming breath. "Now really go before I have to kill you."

"Pleasure to serve, ma'am!" Rachel snapped a salute and briskly retreated.

She was up to something, Gillian thought. Rachel had always been intimidated by the mill, afraid to come down. Especially when the machinery was running. Now she was being way too sisterly and helpful. A sure sign a plot was afoot.

Gillian was about to wind up the blade again when she saw Skip's truck pull into the yard. A few seconds later he strode into the shed, waving anxiously.

"Sorry, Boss. Joyce is feeling like a house with feet lately. I've been getting Joey up and dressed and fed the last few mornings." He paced agitatedly and Gillian realized he needed to vent. "He's good for a two-year-old, but man, I'm glad I got a job to escape to. Sorry again. I'll stay late to cover the time."

"Late, and you didn't bring coffee?" Gillian said, joking to ease his anxiety. "Boy, you got a nerve. Listen, Skip, why don't you go home over lunch to check on Joyce and Joey, okay? They'd really like that I'll bet."

"Hey, thanks. Good idea." He visibly relaxed. "Okay," he said, clapping his hands, ready for business. "What's on for today?"

"Why don't you hop down the end and help my sister pull stuff off the belt," said Gillian.

"Your sister? What, the principal kick Meg out of class?" He peered down the length of the shed. "*Rachel?*" He chuckled. "Well, I'll be damned. I saw the Beamer up the house." He shook his head in amazement. "But what's she doing here?"

"Damned if I know. But she's up to something, Skip. Keep an eye on her for me, would you?"

"You got it."

Time was a-wasting. Gillian spun the blade up to maximum RPMs for the third time that morning. All the stop-and-go nonsense was making her edgy. Distractions and high-speed, people-eating blades didn't mix well. She fed logs down the conveyor and into the carriage with practiced ease, while

Rachel and Skip pulled the boards off the far end of the line. They stacked and sorted the lumber into piles by length and width, and Gillian kept the hungry saw fed.

Occasionally, she glanced over at Rachel, but her sister seemed to be holding her own. The three of them worked for a productive hour and a half, until Gillian ran out of stripped logs. She shut down the booth and climbed out.

"Break!" she hollered. Neither Skip nor Rachel responded. They continued stacking the overflow, engrossed in the work and in their conversation. The funny part was that they were still yelling to be heard over the noise of the saw. With headphones on, neither had yet realized it had stopped. Besides, Rachel always had the ability to create an impenetrable bubble around herself and any male in the immediate vicinity. Nothing else existed outside it.

Gillian stretched and grabbed a bottle of water from the fridge in the office and headed back out into sunshine for a quick break. She had just made herself comfortable on a plastic milk crate when a monstrous white Dodge Ram ten-cylinder pickup bounced into the yard and pulled up short beside too-old Jasper.

He better not dent the flatbed with his door when he got out.

Riley. She watched the dust cloud he'd created settle back down onto the gravel parking area.

Well, she had to face him sooner or later. By now he'd probably figured out that she wasn't going to deliver his stuff to him. He could have sent one of his guys over to get it, but that wasn't his style. He'd never pass up an opportunity to cross paths with her. Anybody with an ounce of self-preservation would have stayed away from her for a while after the frosting she doled out yesterday. Let her cool off. But not Riley. He always led with his head and had the scars to prove it. Then again: no brain, no pain.

He levered open the door of the truck and ambled over to her. Why did he walk like that, anyway? Like John Wayne, for Crissakes. All that was missing was the gun belt and the *"Howdy, partner."*

"Howdy, Gillian," he said.

He was so annoyingly predictable.

"Uh—howdy yourself." She choked back a laugh that threatened to bubble up through her simmering anger. She pretended to study the tree line in the distance.

"My pine ready?"

"Yup."

"No deliveries today?"

"Nope."

"I'm under a lot of pressure to finish that job, you know?"

Translation: You crazy woman, why the hell did you make me drive all the way out here when you got all the time in the world to deliver it yourself?

"Well, it's ready."

"Around back?"

"Yup."

Riley waited for her to get up. She didn't.

"Well, I suppose I could get it myself."

What he really meant: You crazy woman, I hope you know I'm doing you a favor here.

"See ya," Gillian said.

Chapter 11

Riley headed back to his truck.

What was *her* problem, anyway? After the way Gillian treated him yesterday she should be glad he was still willing to do business with her.

He heard voices coming from the rear of the shed. Skip's and somebody's he didn't recognize. A kid, sounded like. But weren't they all back in school now? Skip and whoever it was were yelling at each other. Not mad, though. Talking yelling. Weird.

Riley glanced back at Gillian. She hadn't moved a muscle.

The whole world was screwy this morning.

His skull started to ache. He was in way over his head again. It always felt like that when he was involved with the Wilcoxes, especially Gillian. Like he'd come in too late in the movie to catch up. None of the jokes made sense. And they all got bitchy at him when he asked questions. He wasn't some little kid you could just shove around.

When he hopped into his truck, he sneaked another peek at Gillian. She was still soaking up the sun, her head back against the wall of the shed, her eyes shut. She didn't even seem to know he'd walked away.

God, she still looked good. The ache of wanting her

slammed him again. She wasn't what you'd call beautiful or anything. Yeah, she had a nice face and good hair. An okay body, but nothing to write home about. But he couldn't let go of her. Or her laugh. What a stupid thing to fall for, when you thought about it. But when she cracked up, it was like the whole world was laughing. Just to make her do it he was always acting stupid. Then she'd flash that grin and her eyes'd light up and he'd fall for her all over again.

He was such an idiot.

Come to think of it, he'd been trying to get her attention just about any way he could since about seventh grade. So that made it like, what, twenty-something years? It started with teasing her, pulling her hair, stuff like that. Then wrestling. He'd piss her off with some stupid dig and she'd go after him, trying to land a punch or trip him. She'd always end up on the bottom, though, but she'd still fight like crazy, pissed, her eyes all lit up just like when she laughed, and he was a goner all over again.

Damn. She gave off energy like a little portable generator. Fire her up and everything around her—including him—got all charged up. Why couldn't she understand that he just wanted to make things easier for her? There was no reason she had to take on the world all by herself. They'd be a great team. He'd help her run the mill, it would merge with his construction business, they'd sew up major building contracts for three counties around. Cash in on this thing with Jack Turner.

So why was she always pushing him away?

He was a pretty good catch. He had a good business, more work than he could do really, since the new people started coming into town. Women went for him, too. Not that he'd do any more of that once Gillian said *Yes* to him. Heck, he'd probably gone out with more than half the women in Rocky Falls at one time or another, including almost getting it on once with her sister Rachel back in high school.

Now there was a looker. But it'd been too creepy to think about doing it with Gillian's sister. Especially right there in the front parlor. Pretty damn exciting all right, but not like it would have been with Gillian.

He hit the ignition and the big diesel roared to life. He dropped the pickup into reverse and backed out of his spot. Gravel crunched under his tires as he spun the wheel under the palm of his hand. He took a last look out the window toward where Gillian had been sitting.

She was gone. He slowly drove around the back of the shed.

There she was again.

How'd she get around so fast?

No, wait a minute, it wasn't her. Same coveralls, but a head taller woman, hair as shiny and bright as the ear protectors she was wearing. She was stacking lumber with Skip Donaldson, touching each board like it was going to bite her.

Rachel? He didn't even know she was in town. She must have come back for the Harvest Fair. And what the hell was she doing down at the saw shed? The place had always scared the shit out of her.

He braked next to the new piles of fresh-cut board. "Hey, Skip, how's it going?"

The foreman saw Riley out of the corner of his eye, and slipped off the ear protectors. "Hey, Riley. What's happening?"

"That Rachel?" Riley asked unnecessarily, nodding at her.

"Yeah. She's helping out today."

"I'll be damned." Riley snorted. "Kind of in her own world, isn't she?"

Both men stared at her as she nudged one of the piles straight with her backside, prattling on all the while.

"So I said to her," Rachel was yelling, "what have you got to lose? The guy is really cute and he's obviously hot to trot for you." She paused and looked around for Skip. "Hey, where'd you—"

Then she noticed the two men looking at her. She was used to that, but what was strange was that no sound was coming out of their mouths even though she could see Skip's lips moving. Oh, God. Had she gone deaf just like Gillian warned? Panicked, she reached her hands up to her ears, and her fingertips ran into the headphones.

Cripes, what a ditz. She pulled off the tightly fitting cups, careful to avoid mussing her hair.

"Hey, Riley," she yelled. She sauntered over and did the squeeze thing. "Long time no see, how are you?"

She realized she was yelling. He was wincing. She dropped the volume. "Oh, sorry!" she said. Her hands were damp from the inside of the gloves, but even so, she felt the tiniest of charges jump the air gap when she finally let go. Whoa, that was more like it. Thought she'd lost the knack there with Jack.

Riley was momentarily dumbstruck. *Rachel?* Yes, it was her. But why did he feel like he was meeting her for the first time? He looked at her intently. Yep, still Gillian's younger sister. Brassy, bright hair. Thin, but not too thin, with a nice set of bones. Tall, but not too tall, rounded out in all the places that counted. He could tell that even in the jumpsuit.

But something had changed. She looked . . . he struggled for the right word. Grown up? No, that sounded stupid. *Classy.* That was it. She looked really classy. "I've been, ah . . . terrific. Just terrific," he said. Great—now he was tripping over his tongue. "You?"

"Oh, I'm fine, Riley. Really fine."

Oh, I'll just bet you are. An old memory jumped to mind: The sofa in the Wilcoxes' front parlor. It had been scratchy. Did she remember? He sure did. One of the only times his own personal piece of Rocky Falls granite had refused to rise to the occasion. Rachel had been a real piece—hell, she still was—but it'd been Gillian—damn her—that he'd really wanted to roughen his backside with.

"You going to be in town for a while?" he asked.

"Oh, yes, for—a while." A really long while if the wives of the board of directors didn't rediscover their *joie de vivre* PDQ.

"Great. We—ah, should get together some time. You know, talk about old times."

"That'd be great, Riley. Really great. Hey, you remember that time—"

Skip cleared his throat noisily. "Riley," he said, "I'll start sliding this stuff up on your truck racks. Rachel, nice seeing you again after all this time."

"You, too, Skip," she replied, her eyes locked on Riley's.

On the other side of the yard, Gillian had roused herself from her funk and was coaxing the colicky log loader to life. Black smoke belched out the rusty exhaust stack when she hit the starter on the machine. The diesel engine gasped once and died. Sliding the choke button all the way in, she floored the gas pedal and hit the starter again. The motor coughed and shuddered, but held the idle when she let up on the pedal. Babying it into first gear, she rolled it over to the log piles stacked at the border between her yard and the surrounding woods.

Instead of the usual bucket, the loader had special arms, like the pincers of a beetle, which could snatch up and carry a two-ton log as if it were a broomstick. A perpendicular attack on the pile of stacked logs worked best. Gillian cracked open the hydraulic pincers and dropped the bottom forks to where they barely skimmed the ground. Then she charged the stacked logs like an enraged warthog, ramming the lowered forks into the outermost logs and forcing them into the open jaws.

She fed pressure to the hydraulics and the jaws squeezed

shut, clutching two logs. The tricky part was backing the loader off the pile. Stacks had a nasty tendency to avalanche when logs from the bottom were yanked away.

Her dad had crushed his leg in a rollover with the loader doing just what she was doing now. He'd backed away from the pile and turned too quickly, and the stack cascaded down and tipped the loader over with him still in it. He claimed he'd lost hydraulics at the wrong time, but everyone including him had chalked it up to statistics: After working a dangerous job his entire life, Charlie Wilcox's number had simply come up. Enter the prodigal daughter, Gillian.

Once she was certain the pile wasn't going to join her in the cab she dropped the transmission into reverse and hit the gas. The tires spun briefly in the mud, but the loader finally fought its way backward and the load in the forks disengaged cleanly from the main pile of logs. Gillian let out a breath. She dropped the transmission into reverse, executed a jerky three-point turn and bounced the load across the yard to the debarking conveyor. She slowly inched the forks closer to the feed belts then opened the pincers. Taps on the hydraulics let the logs neatly slide onto the conveyor. She made two more trips, filling the conveyor belt, then shut down the loader. With a final burp of black smoke, it died.

She hopped down from the tractor seat, squeezed along a narrow aisle, and climbed into the control booth of the debarker. This booth was much like the saw booth, minus the fancy electronics. A more primitive piece of equipment than the saw, the debarker, nicknamed The Whomper by Gillian when she first started working at the mill with her father in high school, was designed for one brutal task: stripping logs down to bare wood.

The saw was controlled power and you had to be careful with it, for sure. But it was predictable and dependable. As long as you didn't hit any nails, it did what it was supposed to do without a lot of fuss. She respected it, but she wasn't afraid of it.

On the other hand, The Whomper was positively medieval. As many times as she'd used it, it still scared the hell out of her. A nasty, carbide-toothed wheel scraped down the length of each log, chewing off bark like a ravenous giant chomping on an ear of corn. The noise was ungodly as the rotating teeth on the cutter head chopped and hopped their way along the log, sending bark chunks to ricochet off the Plexiglas of the control booth like shrapnel.

She gave the logs on the conveyor a quick visual inspection from inside the booth, then she was ready. Before powering up The Whomper though, she glanced around the shed to make sure no one was in range. Through the rear doors of the shed, she could see Rachel, Skip, and Riley out back loading Riley's truck. At least *Skip* was.

Rachel and Riley were deep in conversation.

Phwap! Rachel had snapped her magic bubble over a new victim. Better she was yapping with Riley than Skip. Riley wasn't on the clock and Skip had enough on his mind right now without Rachel's shenanigans. That was mean. Rachel was harmless, really. Relentless as a heat-seeking missile when it came to casting spells on men, yes. But she didn't have a malicious bone in her body.

I got them all, Gillian thought, because their older sister Meg wouldn't hurt a fly, either. Don't cross her in a classroom, though. She was hell on wheels.

It was funny how the three Wilcox sisters had turned out so differently given their common gene pool. They were all self-sufficient and capable and didn't tolerate fools gladly. But somehow Meg and Rachel turned out less crusty than she did, Gillian thought. Rachel pulled men to her magnetically. They had no choice. Meg drew people in with her warmth and concern. Again, no choice. *But I attract men in by pissing them off,* Gillian thought. Before trying to kill them with slippery projectiles.

Hey, different people, different styles.

Suddenly, the sight of Skip loading Riley's truck for him

struck Gillian as tantamount to giving aid and comfort to the enemy. She kicked open the door of the booth and bellowed across the shed. "Skip! Hey, Skip!"

Skip stopped what he was doing and put a cupped hand to his ear.

"Let Riley load his own damn truck. Fire up the saw, will you?"

He waved. She settled herself in the booth and powered up The Whomper. It spat. It chopped. It threw junk at the booth, making her flinch. For thirty heart-stopping minutes she ran it. Then she was out of logs. She let out her breath and shut down the beast.

Yes, it *still* scared the crap out of her.

Skip was running the saw, feeding the logs she'd stripped onto his saw carriage and slicing them up. Down at the far end of the saw line, Rachel was still hanging in there, pulling cut stuff off the belts and dragging them onto piles, but the stacks were becoming increasingly ragged as the morning wore on. Gillian put on headphones and went to help her. They stacked together for a while, floating away on the whine and scream of the saw. Conversation was extraneous, and soon they were both panting to keep up with the flow of cut lumber. Skip was quicker on the saw than she was, Gillian realized.

She glanced toward Rachel to see how she was holding up. Her sister looked sore as hell, but she was smiling. Like she had a secret. This was bad.

"Rachel?" No response. The saw was loud, but not *that* loud.

"Rachel!"

"What?" Her sister looked up, dreamy eyed.

"What the hell's going on?"

"A date."

"What? What date?"

"A date, Gillian. I've got a date. With Riley."

Heaven save them.

Chapter 12

"Now don't that beat all," said Art Mansfield, peering out the front parlor window of the Eagle House Inn that he and Lynette, his wife of fifty-three years, had been running since the late 1940s.

"That Turner fellah?" he said, "that left before first light with his fishing pole? Well, he's back again. Taking what looks like a bundle of wet rags out of that fancy yeller pickup of his." Arthur hooted. "And get this, Lynnie. He's wearing some other feller's clothes!"

"Oh, let *me* see Arthur," said Lynette, squeezing her silver-blue head next to her husband's in the window and surreptitiously drawing aside the lace curtain. "Yes, indeed. There he is, all right. And a-yep, he's wearing some other fellow's clothes." She cackled and drew the curtain back farther.

"Quick, Lynnie, let go of them drapes before he sees us!" Spying was one thing, but getting caught at it was another. How could he and Lynnie help it though, when the show these newcomers put on was so much better than the pap that they had on TV?

But none of the other guests could hold a candle to this one here. Drove up a few weeks ago in a showy old pickup. Paid cash for everything. Seven days, right up front, no fooling around. Cash since then, too. Week at a time. The money was a shot in the arm for the register. Especially during the off-season. Nice fellow, too. Real polite. Not one of these demanding types wanting extra towels at all hours or complaining about the free breakfast.

But this fellow was sharp as a tack underneath it all. You could tell. During check-in, this Jack Turner had *really* chatted him up about the town. Trying to be casual he was, like he was just trying to make conversation, but Arthur Mansfield was nobody's fool either. This city guy was after something out here. Dimes to donuts he was tied up with them gussied-up know-nothings that roomed here back in the spring. Their money was as green as anyone else's— he wasn't complaining—but they'd caused a hellacious commotion down at the town hall trying to get some kind of development built out near the river. On some of that Wilcox land.

But this one, yep, a real polite fellow. But be that or no, old Arthur didn't give out free information to people he didn't know from John the Baptist. But Lynnie was right. The fellow *was* walking kind of funny out there. Weaving like. Kind of early in the day to tie one on, but you never knew with these young people.

"Lynnie, please honey. He's coming up the walk. Get out of the window," he said.

Lynette made a *tsk* sound and pressed her nose to the glass. "Oh, Arthur, " she said, "You've lost all sense of adventure. I'm just curious, is all."

Arthur came up behind her to peer out over her shoulder. "Geepers, Lynnie! He's on the veranda. Look like you're busy!" he hissed.

Lynette grabbed a feather duster and traipsed around, putting on a show, pretending to dust this and that. "La, ti, da . . ." she chirped.

Arthur panicked. "Crimony, Lynnie! Quit fooling around, will you?" he pleaded. "He's opening the—Oh, hello, Mr. Turner!"

* * *

Jack shouldered the front door shut behind him and stood there unsteadily in the foyer, facing his temporary landlords and trying not to drip on their rug.

"Back so soon, Mr. Turner?" Arthur, the owner of the Eagle Inn asked. He appeared to be deliberately trying to keep his eyes on Jack's face rather than on his wardrobe. "Fish not biting today?"

"You wouldn't believe me if I told you what just happened to me," Jack replied.

"I'm sure that's so, Mr. Turner," Arthur replied, his face the picture of noncommitment.

"Would you like me to take those for you, Mr. Turner?" asked Lynette, coming from the front parlor with a feather duster tucked under one arm. She reached for the bundle of wet clothes. "You know, dry them out for you?"

"You are a love, Mrs. Mansfield," Jack said, handing over the bundle. "Are you sure you don't mind?" Fortunately he'd already trashed the shirt he'd been wearing. It had looked like evidence in a murder investigation. His hosts might have thought him an ax murderer.

"Oh, no, not at all, dear," Lynette answered. There was an awkward pause. The Mansfields continued to look at him expectantly, as if waiting for the next act to begin. He wished he knew some card tricks. He motioned to the stairs. "I think I'll just . . ."

"Oh, of course, dear, you must be tired after all that outdoor activity," Lynette said. She touched Jack's arm, her hand as frail and bony as a sparrow's foot. She and Arthur stood aside to let him pass.

Lynette didn't know the half of it, Jack thought. Halfway up the stairs, Jack heard her whisper to her husband. "Ah, if I were forty years younger, Arthur."

"Yep, Lynnie, we'd be fighting over you, all right," her husband agreed.

Jack realized Arthur and Lynette, both sporting a considerable amount of electronics in their ears, thought they were having a private conversation.

They spoke again. "He's a polite one, our Mr. Turner, isn't he Arthur?" Lynette asked.

Jack sneaked a backward glance at the couple. Lynette was looking him over like he were a mannequin in the haberdasher's window.

"Aye, that's so, Lynnie," replied Arthur, likewise assessing.

It was downright unnerving, being discussed like a storefront display. Jack rounded the turn at the top of the semicircular stairs. They didn't make staircases like this one anymore, he noted, his hand on the top newel post. Three generous balusters on each stair tread and the frame—he smacked the flat of his hand against the side of the newel—still solid as a rock.

Made for the centuries. Just like the aged couple downstairs. Jack smiled and shook his head. Would he ever be that old? Or a bigger question: Would he ever find anyone crazy enough to want to share her old age with him?

Turn left at the landing, second door on the right. His room. Slip the key in the lock. No need to lock it behind him. Toss the keys on the bed. They disappear into layers of down comforter with nary a jingle. A big old-fashioned bed dominated the cozy space. Bold, striped wallpaper printed borders below the crown molding and above the chair rail. Immaculate trim painted high-gloss white. The scent of fresh linen pervaded the room. Simple, New England country charm.

A perfect style for the condominium development, in fact. Blend the new right into the old. Slick. He just had to get around Gillian Wilcox somehow. Get to the rest of the family without Gillian around. Nice of her sister Rachel to give him a ready-made excuse down at the yard to open relations. All he had to do was "drop in" on Rachel at the third sister Meg's place.

But he couldn't do that right now. Meg taught school, Gillian had said, so she wouldn't be around until later in the day. The weekend might be better still and anyway, Rachel was his ticket through the front door, and who knew what she was up to. From the look of surprise on Gillian's face when she'd heard her sister's voice coming at them down the saw shed, Rachel's visit obviously wasn't planned and he had the feeling that neither was her next move from moment to moment. Although, like her sister, she was no dummy. There was that calculated hand thing she did. She was used to traveling in some high-powered circles.

There was an aunt, too, he knew from reports his advance team had turned in last spring. The woman had a business somewhere in town. Her name again? Beatrice? Betty? Yes. Aunt Betty. A pottery place. Shouldn't be too hard to find. He could get an inside angle on what business people were thinking about the downtown renovation from her, while he ostensibly looked for that "special something."

He ran a hot shower and whistled while he pulled off Charlie Wilcox's old clothes. No clawfoot tub, just a fiberglass stall so clean you could eat off the floor of it. For the second time in the still-young day, steam rose around him. As he lathered, he deeply inhaled the last, lingering remnants of Gillian's bubble bath. He held his head under the stinging shower spray.

The feel of her lips on his was still with him: delightful, delicious, and completely unexpected. Their bodies had fit together smoothly, shifting with the familiarity of long-time lovers, yet filled with the sharp pang of first-time desire. She was maddening. Full of fire and light—dangerous. A threat to his cultivated calm and—he hated to admit this— his need for order and predictability.

Hunger for her swept through him again. He'd felt so completely alive when he had pressed his lips to hers. He'd suddenly felt like he had been drowning for all of his life and clutching onto her could keep him afloat. Save him. Touching her made him feel at once disconnected and then in the next instant, completely whole. With Gillian Wilcox in the frame, a lot of other pieces seemed to fall into place. Or not matter as much.

Craziness.

Not what he wanted or needed right now because Rocky Falls was The Place. Frank Lloyd Wright had his places. This was Jack's Place. His chance to Get Things Right. He didn't need the complications.

Jack's Place. He laughed, rinsing. Sounded like a good place to eat. He'd known Gillian Wilcox for what, two days? Argued with her for most of that time—and now he was becoming as nuts as she was. Gillian Wilcox wasn't from his world. He was ocean, Boston, big business, getting ahead, progress. She was river and woods, Rocky Falls, country life, history, and tradition that defied change of any kind.

Opposites attract? Maybe, but it felt deeper than that. Whatever it was, *it* was running *him*—not a feeling he liked. But then again, the challenge she represented was something he'd been waiting for a long time. His life had become a familiar roller coaster. Thrilling in spots, but completely predictable. He always knew where the ride would end, no matter how wild the trip. Gillian Wilcox built her roller coaster as she went, impulsively, slamming the next section of track into place breathless seconds before the screeching, screaming car hurtled past.

Her abandon was—unfortunately—a siren call to him. A summons he apparently couldn't ignore. Take that wild ride with her. Strap in, crank to the top of the highest hill and plunge, secure in the knowledge that the universe would somehow provide. Unbelievable, him doing that, but definitely a good time. Yet he hadn't invested hundreds of thousands of dollars on research on Rocky Falls as a potential planned community site just to blow it all on an amusing ride. No matter how much fun the trip looked to be.

He rinsed shampoo out of his eyes. The town was beginning to get to him, too. After he'd gotten over the initial shock of Gillian Wilcox's upcountry world, Rocky Falls started to intrigue him as much as the Forest Queen did.

There was good fishing here, a slow pace, time to talk. And great scenery. He stiffened at the recollection of Gillian poised naked like a water sprite on the top of the rock ledge in the early morning mist.

Yet how could anyone spend their whole life trying to hold back change like she did? This town was preserved in amber like a prehistoric bug—pretty to look at but immune from any infusion of new life. Make no mistake about it though, outsiders were chiseling away at the crystal prison. According to his scouting reports, people from as far away as Canada wanted in on places like Rocky Falls, seeking a piece of a pie that had all but disappeared from much of the Northeast.

Maybe there was a way to hit a happy medium with the plan for the town. Rethink the extent of the development. He could start on some half-assed renderings tonight. Maybe downsizing a bit would lighten up the xenophobia. Doubtful though, with Gillian Wilcox squarely in the middle of the frame, wanting it all her way. Which was in essence, no way. She'd turned out to be as hard as the Rocky Falls granite.

Her family probably felt differently about things, though. Her aunt with the pottery shop was probably making out like a bandit the last few years. Yes, that was definitely the way in, through the businesses.

He gingerly explored the lump on his head. Sensations remembered from the morning came back to him. Gillian Wilcox's touch. His head held in the small, hard vise of her forearm and biceps. The texture of her shirt against his bare skin, the soft swell of her breast pressed against his chest. She was strong from lumping all that lumber around, but she was exquisitely delicate when she worked to butterfly the gash. How could such opposite traits exist side-by-side in one person? How did you go from angel of mercy one minute to homicidal maniac the next?

Jack shut off the water. He whistled as he toweled off himself. A rare thing for him, whistling. Usually reserved for those moments when a plan came together. And his definitely hadn't yet. But for some unknown reason he'd been doing a good bit of it the last few days and had shit-all idea why.

He carefully combed his hair, pulling it this way and that to conceal the butterfly closures. It would be a bad thing to look like Frankenstein when he was trying to insinuate himself into the good graces of the community. Denim shirt, jeans, work boots with some hard miles on them. A little scruffy looking. Gave the impression of someone hardworking. Which he was. But look too well-off and people got suspicious wondering who you'd screwed over to get there. Yes, humble played best. It said you made your way in the world through honest work, and that maybe your feet hurt at the end of a day the same as everyone else's. It all came down to perceptions.

Finally—ready to face the world. Fish the keys out of the comforter and tuck the still damp wallet in the back pocket. Yank the door shut and take the stairs at a brisk pace. Think about sliding the banister, but decide against it. The Mansfields didn't need any more grist for the rumor mill.

His feet sounded on the first-floor landing.

"Oh, Mr. Turner," called Lynette from out back, "I've just run your things through the washer. I'll be putting them on the line out back to dry now. Wouldn't want to chance shrinking anything, you know."

"Uh, that's great Mrs. Mansfield. I really appreciate it." People in this town really did have the gift of time. And shrinkage was always an issue.

"Except for your unmentionables, of course, dear," she said, poking her head out of the kitchen at the rear of the inn. "I'll put them through the dryer. We don't want to be embarrassed in front of the whole neighborhood, do we?"

"Lynnie, for God's sake," came Arthur's bellow from the depths of the house. Not knowing quite what to say, Jack made a beeline for the front door. He couldn't bear to be privy to another "private" conversation between the Mansfields, this time regarding the disposition of his underwear.

Chapter 13

The bright sun was blinding as he stepped off the front porch and onto the inn's walkway. It was neatly trimmed with pansies, and he paused for a moment, squinting in the brilliant fall light and getting his bearings. He hadn't paid much attention to the details of the town itself since his arrival—after all, he'd been more interested in what it could *become* than what it was at the moment.

The sidewalk itself was edged with granite curbs inset with iron rings, reminders of the horse-drawn wagons of yesteryear that once had lined the fringes of the main thoroughfare. Yet the whole avenue, as far as his line of sight allowed, would have been a side street of minor consequence were it transported to Boston. To the people of Rocky Falls, though, this was the pulse point of their world. It was where everyone came to see and be seen, to mingle, and to the extent that you could, shop. The selection of goods was limited, though, and anyone with something particular in mind would have to make the trip to Bangor to find it.

Its small size withstanding, Main Street quietly thrummed with life on this golden morning. Red and yellow brick fronts, still damp from a light rain around midnight, softly shimmered, and a light breeze flirted with the corners of buntings and banners announcing the upcoming Harvest

Fair. Distracted young mothers shooed their toddlers from store to store, while a rubber-tired, six-seater wagon, filled to overflowing with squirming, seat-belted preschoolers and pulled by two laughing young women in matching T-shirts, glided along the sidewalk toward a small fenced green. Norman Rockwell, eat your heart out.

Jack started strolling toward the river. Diagonally across the street from the Eagle House Inn stood the Majestic Theatre. One movie was advertised on the marquee, and a sandwich board out front advertised the two-dollar Saturday matinee. It was an imposing building, given the small scale of the surrounding one- and two-story awning storefronts, and a bronze plaque inset into its stucco front declared its birth date: 1895.

Just ahead, on Jack's side of the street, the ladder truck was getting a bath at the fire station. A burly, middle-aged fireman was lovingly tracing the metal curves of a cherry red fender with a soapy sponge, while a younger man neatly coiled hoses. Runoff water trickled down the sloping concrete apron in front of the station and ran beneath a sandwich board reminding the public that this year's festivities marked the 150th anniversary of the event. "Come one, come all. Games, craft booths, raffles, contests of strength and skill. Dance to follow Saturday supper," the sign read.

On the other side of the board, a cut-out of Smokey the Bear, shovel in hand, reminded passers-by that the fire index was "HIGH," and that only they could prevent forest fires.

That fair must be what Rachel said she'd come home for. Was the scene with Gillian at the mill really just a few hours ago? He was falling under the spell of this town; time was starting to lose its meaning for him. If he didn't watch it, his radio would be tuned to the same station as the Mansfields' pretty soon.

He ambled casually past the firemen at work on the ladder truck, slowing just enough to catch the eye of one of them.

"Mornin,'" he said to the rugged-looking one who was reaching down into a bucket to wring out his sponge. Layers of muscle rippled in his forearms as he squeezed. Up close, he was built like an NFL lineman: an almost nonexistent neck topped a chest thick as a barrel. Tufts of jet black hair jutted out of the unbuttoned collar of a red Union suit.

"Morning, yourself," said the fireman, straightening and waiting expectantly for Jack to pick up the conversation.

"Say, is that a hand-pump engine I see up back there?" Jack asked, thinking quickly and pointing into the depths of the station garage.

"Yes, sir, it is," replied the fireman, "We pull her out once a year and haul her across into New Hampshire for the competitions. You know, we try to shoot water the farthest?"

Jack in fact really didn't know, but an opener was an opener. "Yeah? You guys hold any records?"

"We came in first in Topsham in '92, I'm proud to say. Shot two hundred and eighty-seven feet." He rested the damp sponge on the rim of the bucket, straightened stiffly with a hand to his lower back, and took the measure of Jack. "Say, I don't believe I know you. You new in town? Just visiting?"

"Both," said Jack, sticking out a hand. "I'm Jack."

"Peter Dunn. Pleased to meet you." Dunn's hand felt like a wet bear paw when Jack shook it.

"It must be tough maintaining the hand pumper and the two new rigs in such a small town, huh?"

"Well, now, the two trucks here aren't actually new. People see a lot of shiny chrome and think a unit's new, but we keep up with them is all," Dunn said, running a hand proprietarily along a huge side mirror. "This old gal here should be on a replacement schedule, but like you say, it's tough with a small budget. Luke and me," he nodded toward the other fireman rolling hoses, "we keep the place up between us."

"Must be tough with just the two of you. Any volunteers?"

"Oh, sure. Half the guys in town are wearing beepers. In a small town, everyone's gotta chip in."

Jack peered into the gloom of the cavernous station. "That hand tub must be the dickens to maintain, huh?"

"Well, yeah, it is. We mostly take care of it with donations, winnings from competitions, stuff like that." He turned to gaze lovingly at it. "It's really just a hobby for us at the station, and an expensive one at that. But we're carrying on a tradition with it. Once you let 'em go, that's the end. Hey," he said, turning back to Jack, "it sounds like you know a thing or two about running a station."

It was amazing how people invariably credited him with understanding quite a bit about a subject when they'd just finished telling him everything he ever knew about it.

"Well, no, I really don't," Jack replied. "But money is money the world around and there never seems to be enough."

"If that ain't the truth," said Dunn, guffawing. "Well, if you'd like to see me and the boys in action with the hand tub, come to the fair. It's worth a look, our Harvest Fair. Benefits good causes. There'll be lots of extra goings on this year cause of the anniversary. Worth sticking around for."

Ask and you shall receive. "I might just do that," Jack said. "Hey, I'll let you get back to work. Oh, one thing. I'd like to pick up some pottery for a friend. She collects handmade stuff. Anywhere around here I could get something like that?"

"You've come to the right place for that," Dunn said. "Betty's shop. Called 'Riverworks.' She does all her own pots and whatnot. First left past the theatre there," he said, extending an arm that three children could have swung from.

"Thanks. Good luck at the fair if I don't see you there," Jack said.

"'Morning to you," Dunn said, renewing his attack on a mud-splattered fender.

Jack crossed the street. Two drivers, one in each lane, slowed and waved for him to cross. He almost walked right into the first car, so surprised was he by the courtesy of the drivers. He passed the theatre, presently having its sidewalk rinsed and brushed to within an inch of its life by a deter-mined-looking young man with a hose and bristle broom. He stopped spraying long enough for Jack to get by, then resumed his work like the devil was after him.

Cripes, the whole town had a cleaning fetish. Lot of civic pride. A nice change after the grime of the big city. Next left after, Dunn had said. Jack rounded the corner, and ten paces in front of him a hand-carved sign hung from chains above the sidewalk.

Riverworks Designs.

Jack cupped his hands around his eyes and peered in the front window. An array of hand-thrown pottery plates, cups, and candlesticks was tastefully displayed. Lit from above by halogen lamps, some pieces on pedestals, all were unmis-takably the product of the same sure hand. A folded placard in a corner of the display informed him the artist was one "Elizabeth Lavelle."

Aunt Betty. Bingo. *Pleased to meet you Ms. Lavelle . . .*

The soft tang scent of incense greeted Jack as he entered the shop. Wind chimes tinkled softly when the door closed behind him. Sounds of trickling water disorientated him for a second, until he spied a rough hewn but artfully arranged stack of granite rocks in a corner. Water was cascading down the various levels of the free-form sculpture and drip-ping into a pool at its base. For Jack, it captured perfectly the rippling tranquility of the early morning Mohasset. New Age music floated in and around the showroom, contribut-ing to the atmosphere of calm.

Suddenly, the peace was shattered.

"Come back here, you little rascal!" came a woman's deep voice from the back room. A toddler, toy fire truck clutched in one chubby hand, ran pell-mell into Jack's shins, rebounded, and hit the floor landing on nothing but diaper. He looked up, surprised, smiled a broad toothless grin at Jack, then burst into tears. Howls filled the small shop.

A heavyset woman with hair just finishing the change to completely gray and dressed in a long, brightly colored

Lucy Ann Peters

billowing skirt came tearing around the corner after the little tyke.

"Come over here, you," she said to the little boy, who was now gasping for breath between sobs. "You can't get away from me that easily, young man!"

She bent down and scooped the child up like he weighed no more than a loaf of bread and cradled him to her ample bosom. The hands that held the young man were as strong and sinewy as the roots of an oak tree.

"Sorry about that," the woman said, addressing Jack. "I'm watching Matthew for my niece, Meg. He's a handful sometimes. Hah! What am I saying? All the time." She chuckled and bounced the boy in her arms, finally settling him on her hip.

The handful stopped crying and gummed the front fender of his truck, eyeing Jack suspiciously.

"He looks like he's calming down now," Jack said.

"Just wait five minutes until he gets used to you," the woman said, panting a bit from her mad dash after the child, "then it's back to business as usual." The woman abruptly switched tracks. "Help you with anything?"

"I'm just looking, thanks. But I'll let you know when I find something."

"Fine, take your time," said the woman. "I'll be in the back room with this little monster if you need me. Just holler." She nuzzled the tyke affectionately. "Yes, with you my little minx, with you. . . ." The boy giggled and kicked his feet. They disappeared out back. Peace was restored.

Jack's sense of calm instantly returned. The incense, the dancing water, the music, the lighting, all worked together to create an incredibly soothing atmosphere. He wasn't an impulse buyer by nature, but he suddenly felt like he needed to purchase something—anything—just to hold onto this feeling of tranquility once he left the store.

Wait a minute, what was he saying? He was being subtly manipulated. By a marketing genius.

Not that she had to be—her pieces would easily sell them-

selves. They were really special, done in subtle natural tones
that glowed with an unearthly brilliance. Utility and function
beautifully blended in well-turned forms. The woman had a
way with clay.

Jewelry made by local artisans was also on display, along
with the ubiquitous *Sounds of Nature* CDs, the display complete with headphones for sampling passages. Among the
necklaces, pins, rings, and bracelets, Maine tourmaline figured prominently. Several pieces crafted of the rare water-
melon shade, its greens and pinks softly glowing, occupied
center stage.

Gillian's earrings were there too, the delicate gold leaves
that looked like they could blow away in the wind. An image
of her, damp tendrils of fair hair curling around the pair
she'd been wearing in the bath, came to mind. She had the
most arousing earlobes he'd ever seen. He imagined nibbling on them, drawing them in like ripe berries, caressing
the tender buds with his tongue.

He was hard again in an instant. This was getting ridiculous. It was like high school all over again. He'd have to start
wearing a jockstrap to save himself from embarrassment if
this kept up.

Betty's voice caught him by surprise. "I said, did you find
anything?"

Jack snapped out of his dream and, to hide his situation,
turned away from Betty and moved toward the window display at the front of the shop. "Um . . . that vase really caught
my eye," he said. "The one with the ducks on it." He pointed.

"Ah, one of my favorites, too," Betty replied, as if she'd had
no part in its creation. The vase was roughly finished, almost
artlessly turned, but the subtlety of the ducks scratched into
it and encircling the base at the fullest part, belied the con-
summate skill of the artist. Jack pictured it full of flowers on
Gillian's kitchen table. When he dropped his coffee cup off in
her sink that morning, he'd had a quick look around the
downstairs. The piece would fit in well. It was neither too
dainty nor too rugged. Like Gillian herself, actually.

"Gift wrap?" Betty asked.

Jack knew he had a blank look on his face.

"Is it for someone? Can I wrap it up for you?" she said slowly, as if he were hard of hearing.

A gift? The question had caught him by surprise. Yes, he supposed it was. Or could be. If Gillian didn't chuck it back at him. "Yes, please, wrap it," he said.

Betty plucked the vase out of the storefront window, and did a quick rearrangement of other pieces to cover the gap in the display. She brought it behind the counter near the register, wrapped it in tissue paper, sized a box, and gently set the vase inside. She handed Jack a flip book of sample paper. "What would you like it done up in?"

There were about eight choices, but to Jack there seemed to be eight thousand. He usually just asked Jennifer his secretary to send something nice along to his dates or clients. He wasn't sure which of those two categories Gillian Wilcox fit into.

"This one," he said finally, picking a design that looked hand-painted and featured, of all things, ducks.

"Another favorite," Betty said chuckling. Deftly, she stripped paper from a roll mounted in a rack and set the gift box down in the center of the extended paper.

"So, what do you think of our little town, Mr. Turner," she asked, her eyes busy with her work.

"How did you know my name?" he asked, mildly surprised his cover was blown so quickly. Him all the time thinking he was being clever.

"You're the victim of the small town grapevine at its best, I'm afraid," she said, smiling and cutting the paper with one quick pass of the scissors. "Quite a scene you had out at that big house Riley's building back there in the woods, I understand. With another of my nieces, Gillian, so the story goes."

"Well, yes," he admitted. "She and I did disagree on a few points."

She hooted politely. "I'm sorry, Mr. Turner," she said. "But the way I heard it made it sound like you two traded opening shots in World War Three." She cut her eyes up to his face, pinning him like a mounted butterfly with her gaze.

So that's where Gillian gets "the look" he realized. It traveled on the female chromosomes in this family. He wondered how many times the woman in front of him had pitched something at somebody. At least clay didn't have the penetration power of your average oilcan.

"Well, stories always get bigger in the retelling," he stalled. He wondered how long it would be before the story about the saw shed shenanigans got around.

"No offense, Mr. Turner," said Betty, "but I know Gillian like one of my own girls. I'm thinking you lost Round One of what she sees as the fight for this town." Betty neatly folded and taped the package.

"She feels very strongly about preserving Rocky Falls the way it is," Jack said. "That's apparent. The only problem is that this place is changing around her, whether she likes it or not."

"A-yep, that's true, Mr. Turner," Betty said, resting a hip against the counter and folding her arms comfortably below her bosom. "And I wouldn't say that I'm completely against that change either. I've had this location for fourteen years come November. Three years ago, I was about ready to let the lease expire. But my second husband Leo said to me, 'Betty, with all the new people coming to town, things'll pick up. You watch.' I played his hunch. Good thing, too. Well, look around," she said, the pride she felt evident in her gaze, "I've done more business in the last few years than in the first ten put together. Our bet paid off."

"That's what I was trying to explain to your niece," Jack said. "That developing the town didn't have to be a bad thing."

"I'm sure that's what you *thought* you were saying," Betty explained, "but what she heard was a different thing altogether I'll wager." She gathered up an assortment of thin ribbons in one sturdy hand, then snipped them from their rolls. She frizzed the ribbon ends and slid the whole affair into a string handled bag done up in a stenciled leaf pattern, with the raised logo "Riverworks Designs" woven through the drifting leaves.

"She marches to a different drummer, our Gillian," Betty continued. "She was born old, tied to this town in ways even I don't understand. Left after her mother—" Betty's voice hitched. She cleared her throat—"my sister, passed. Couldn't take it here. Rachel either. Both went off. But then, look at the way Gillian came back and jumped in to fill her daddy's place at the mill. No one else could have done that. Stepped into Charlie's shoes like that. My Leo's not a wood man, lord knows. Gillian outright saved the mill, saved people's jobs. You know about that?" she asked Jack.

"A bit," he replied.

"No dummies in that family. Gillian could have what Rachel, my third niece, has—excuse me—*had*. I hear she's back." Betty sighed, a combination of relief and regret.

For mere hours, Rachel was, Jack thought, yet word had already reached Betty here at her shop. Fiber optic quality, the Rocky Falls network.

"Gilly had a good job in Augusta," Betty continued. "Plenty of cash, freedom to come and go as she pleases." She tied off the handles of the bag with another ribbon collection. "Or she could've gone the other way. Like Meg. Matthew's mom. My oldest niece . . . ?"

She looked at Jack. He nodded. He had the cast down pat.

Betty smiled. "Meggie's settled in Rocky Falls with a nice family. Back to her roots after college, but she seems happy here. Teaching school gives her a lot of time with her family. Bob, her husband, has one of those offices at home and he's hooked up to the Internet thing. I don't really understand it, but it works for him." She used scissors to draw each ribbon out to its full length then let it go. Every one snapped obediently into a tight curl.

"The point is that Gillian is married to the town. Rocky Falls and the people in it are like her kids. You mess with them, you mess with her."

Jack laughed. "I think I'm finding that out the hard way," he said. A thin cry came from the back room.

"Oh, oh," Betty said, with a smile. "My little monster. I knew it was just the eye of the storm." She carefully handed the bag with the vase in it across the counter to Jack.

She punched numbers into the register. "That'll be $54.50 for the vase. Plus the governor's share. Gift wrapping's free."

Jack was picking through a monogrammed money clip full of bills as the front door burst open. Accompanied by a cacophony of wind chimes, a tall woman in a vivid blue two-piece business suit filled the doorway.

"Jumpin' Jaysus, Betty!" the woman cried. "Did you hear?" Her hair, probably once a golden blond, was now a soft silver. Stylishly cut, it fanned around her face as she whirled to close the shop door behind her.

"That guy—you know, the developer who sent all those corporate types down here in the spring?—well, you'll *never* believe this. He's here! Right now. In Rocky Falls. And *that's* not the best part . . ."

The woman's ornate earrings bounced around with a life of their own. Her revelation was punctuated by the jangling of numerous bracelets. She clapped her hands in delight and guffawed. "*Guess* who he's fooling around with?" She hugged herself in delight.

"Virginia," Betty began, a note of caution in her tone. "There's someone I'd like you to meet—"

But there was no stopping the tornado once it had touched down. "*Gillian*!" she crowed triumphantly. "Our little Gilly! Hah!" She skipped up to the counter, oblivious to Jack's presence.

Again Betty pointed him out to the silver-haired cyclone. "His name is Jack Turner—" She glanced at him for confirmation. He nodded. "Of Turner Development Corporation." In her tone was an attempt to bring as much decorum to the awkward situation as possible.

The stylish woman's jaw dropped and she froze for an instant, but she was good. She quickly recovered.

"And, of course, I'm just so *happy* for our niece—if the story's true, of course. One never knows with rumors," Virginia said. "Pleased to meet you." To Jack she extended a manicured hand tipped with deadly looking nails painted a brilliant coral. Jack shook it, setting the bracelet collection jangling. He wondered why he felt like he knew the woman. It wasn't like him to forget a face, but he couldn't quite . . .

She was dressed to the nines, and, although she was probably in her late fifties, was still vibrant and attractive. Thirty years ago she must have been a knockout. Her clothes and jewelry spoke money and brokered deals, things he was no stranger to, but he still couldn't make the connection.

"You know how gossip is, Mr. Turner," the woman said. "People just start it with no regard to the feelings of those involved." She batted her eyes innocently at him.

"Yes, I do know how rumors are, Mrs.—?" He let the question hang.

"Masterson. And it's Ms.," she said, fluttering eyelids heavy with mascara. "But my friends call me Virginia." She held onto his hand for just a second longer than necessary, and allowed her fingers to gently draw across his palm on release.

Ah, the squeeze thing. Twice in one day. This woman had to be related to Rachel. He looked at Virginia again. Yup, Rachel thirty years hence. So was Virginia yet another aunt? Good Lord, there seemed to be an endless amount of women in the Wilcox clan. "It's a pleasure to meet you, Virginia," Jack said, feeling that, given time, he might feel differently.

"The pleasure's all mine, I'm sure, Mr. Turner," she replied.

"Jack, please."

Another cry, plaintive and high-pitched, from the back room.

"Is that my little angel? My little Matty?" Virginia asked, her voice climbing two octaves. "Auntie Ginnie is coming, Sweetie-kins," she warbled, in a sing-song voice. Then, admonishing Betty, she said, "How can you leave him all alone like that in a strange place? No wonder he's crying."

"Ah, Ginnie, let me just—" Betty began, restraining

Virginia's arm. But the tornado was not to be denied. Virginia swept past Betty and into the back room.

Jack smiled vaguely at Betty. She rolled her eyes.

"I've got the little guy three hours a day, five days a week, but she knows best," Betty said.

The screams from the back room escalated.

"Oh, Sweetie-kins, no . . ." they could hear Virginia crooning. "You know how Auntie Ginnie hates to see her little Matty upset. There's a good boy, yes . . ."

The cry rose to a crescendo, culminating in a keening wail.

"Anytime now," Betty said cryptically.

"Oh, dear," came Virginia's voice, "I see the problem. Your poor little diaper is wet and oh—full. Oh, Betty!"

Betty smirked at Jack. "I'll be right back. Don't let my sister near the register."

Jack laughed.

With yards of flowing material billowing, Betty steamed off majestically.

"Whew, kids wear me out," said Virginia, emerging from the back room. She was dabbing at an unidentifiable stain on the side pocket of her blazer. "How about you, Jack. Any kids? It seems you're a man who . . . gets around."

So the saw shed story *was* out. Suddenly he wished he were somewhere else. Roofing in one-hundred-degree heat, stripping lead paint, removing asbestos. Anywhere but there, trapped by this . . . belle in a pottery shop. "I do a bit . . . here and there," he answered vaguely.

"So I understand."

Virginia scrutinized him. *Move toward the door*, he said to his feet. "Well, I really should be going . . ." Betty could watch her own cash register.

Virginia casually moved in front of him, blocking his exit. "I run my own real estate agency here in town. V. L. Hunt Realty. You passed it coming in on 101."

She extracted a card from a gold case.

"'Hunt' is my maiden name," she said, seeing the puzzled

expression on his face as he examined the card. "After my third husband, the names started to pile up. So I figured that when I started my own business I'd make a clean break of it. But I go by Masterson still because I actually *liked* the last one. *He* left *me* . . ." she finished, sounding subdued and maybe even a little sad, Jack thought.

"Lord, look at me yak," she said, with the air of one deliberately moving on. "You are just so easy to talk to, Jack. I can see why our Gillian—" She stopped in mid-sentence. "Well, anyway, that's really none of my business."

He was again surprised to see a soft side unexpectedly emerge in the Wilcox wolf pack. He found himself beginning to like this immaculately quaffed cyclone.

She took his smile as encouragement and went on.

"Anyway, I sat through every word of the discussions that went on at the town hall last spring, and I, for one, don't think a little redevelopment around here is a bad idea. Of course, I didn't exactly say that at the meetings." *You understand*, her expression said. "My niece laid the development people out in lavender, and I wasn't about to get caught in that crossfire."

He got that. The town was full of tripwires.

"But you have to understand, Jack," she went on, "Rocky Falls is a tight bunch. We don't take well to outsiders. Don't get me wrong—we're not uneducated hicks as some like to think. It's just that we bridle at being told what to do."

"So I noticed," Jack said mildly.

Virginia shot him what he was beginning to realize was the Wilcox woman look. "But we've been known to change our minds," she said. "Once we've had a chance to think things over . . ."

Jack realized she was waiting for him to pick up the conversational thread. No, he decided, let her put her cards on the table first.

"What I am suggesting, Jack, is that you are in need of an ally in this town," Virginia said, when it became obvious

Jack was holding out. "Someone who understands both the concerns of the people here and the opportunity that exists."

He waited.

She continued. "So I thought we might work together. You know, I could help you work with the town, and you'd . . . cut me in on the action."

Maybe he should stay and guard the register.

"That's an interesting, ah . . . proposition, Virginia," he said. "But wouldn't that put you in a rather difficult position with your family and friends in town?"

"P'shaw, Mr. Turner," she scoffed, waving her hand to brush away imaginary obstacles. "Leave that to me. What do you say? Are you in?" She cocked her head like a bird of prey, eyes bright and expectant.

He mentally scratched his chin. Virginia could alternately be a deal maker or his worst nightmare come true. He blew out a breath. Oh, well, what the hell. He was already up to his ass in alligators.

"I like your style, Virginia," he replied. "Damn the torpedoes, you're on."

"You won't regret it, Jack," said Virginia, pumping his hand. *Famous last words.*

"But keep it mum for now," she cautioned in a low voice, "until we work out the boilerplate."

Oh boy, he couldn't wait.

Bearing a squirming bundle, Betty cruised back in. "Here we are," she sang. "All clean and tidy."

The bundle held out the fire engine for Jack's inspection.

"You're a fine one," he said, awkwardly. What did you say to little children? He didn't give good coo.

"Dat!" the tyke offered.

"Ah, you've made a friend, Mr. Turner," Betty said, beaming.

"I have a feeling I may need all of them I can get," he replied, chuckling. He smoothed the baby's hair where it stuck up like the scruff of a chickadee's neck.

"Why, Jack," Virginia said. "The most marvelous idea has *just* occurred to me."

Betty cut her eyes to her sister.

"The Wilcox clan and folks from all over town will shortly begin working on the plans for the Harvest Fair. Why don't you join us at our planning meeting? Jump right in, get to know people, bond with the community."

Virginia shot Betty a forced smile, dripping with coercion. "Wouldn't that be just great, Betty?"

"I think that would be a very . . . interesting experience for Mr. Turner."

"I think he'd learn a lot, don't you think?"

"No doubt," Betty said, her smile enigmatic.

"Dat!" said Matthew again.

"Well, it's settled then," Virginia said. "We'll let you know the date and time."

Said the spider to the fly, thought Jack. The exchange between the sisters had held him in mute, horrified fascination.

"Well, my little Sweetie-kins," Virginia said, holding her blazer tight to her body and leaning over to tickle Matthew under his chubby chins. "Auntie Ginnie has to go back to work. She's got to go show a nice little three-bedroom colonial with attached two-car garage zoned for potential in-law apartment conversion, sweetie, yes she *does* . . ." She ended on a soprano note high-pitched enough to call dogs. Over Virginia's shoulder, Betty made cross-eyes at Jack. He stifled a snort. Matty clucked juicily.

Virginia's high heels tapped on the door. "*Ciao*, all," she said, giving a backhanded wave. "See *you* later, Mr. Turner." With a jangle of wind chimes and bracelets, she was gone.

Jack and Betty let out a collective breath. Jack suddenly understood how people in Tornado Alley must feel after a big one blew through.

"Whew!" Betty said, "I'm sorry about all that."

As if anyone could apologize for an act of God. "Family," Jack said. "Can't live with 'em . . ."

Gillian's aunt's laugh rippled like water over smooth stone, Jack thought. He turned to leave.

"Ah, Mr. Turner . . ." Betty said. "Did you want to pay with a credit card?"

The vase. He hadn't paid for it. He dug in his money clip and handed over a fifty.

Betty was still looking at him, her hand outstretched with the bill in it. "I give to charity," she said, "but not at the office. The total was $54.84. You need another four dollars and eighty-four cents."

"Oh, I'm sorry," he said, flustered. A rare thing for him. He fished in his pocket and handed over another ten.

"You seem a bit preoccupied, Mr. Turner," Betty said, her voice full of gentle humor. "Penny for your thoughts . . ." She punched in the final sale total and the money drawer chimed open. She held out his change.

Jack gathered up the bag with the vase from the counter. "I'm sure my, um . . . friend will like it," he said. "Thank you."

"I'm sure your, um, friend will, too," she said, her laughter rippling.

He had one hand on the front door pull when the cash drawer *cha-chinged* again and she called to him.

"Oh, Mr. Turner . . ."

"Yes?"

She was holding up a penny, shiny as a new moon. "For luck," she said, tossing it.

He snatched it out of the air. The door closed on the sounds of bubbling water.

Chapter 14

"I figured a woman like you wouldn't be caught dead doing windows."

"Very funny. Really. That slays me. I've never heard that one before." Gillian didn't look up.

Ugh. Jack Turner. On a weekend.

She picked away with a razor knife at the dried caulking adhering the casing of an old window to the clapboard siding of the Eagle House Inn. She had pulled all the nails and the ancient double-hung unit was loose in the wall, almost ready to pull.

"Want some help?"

"Go away. I'm on the clock."

"Working for Arthur and Lynette?"

No, the fucking Man in the Moon. "That's right."

She got hold of the end of a chunk of desiccated caulking and tugged gently on it. A two-foot strip peeled away. She dropped the mummified length onto the porch decking, barely missing Jack's feet. He was wearing shiny loafers. Without tassels, thank God.

She figured he'd get the hint. But no, he settled himself onto the porch rail, apparently planning to watch her.

"What, no cartoons on?" she asked.

"I didn't want to pay extra for cable."

"You could sell the hood ornament of that fancy little pickup of yours and pay for a month of it."

He seemed to ponder that. "But I like it." Winged Victory. It inspired him.

"It's stupid." Like your shoes, she wanted to say. But that would really start things up and Arthur and Lynette weren't paying for her to hang around and chuck darts and dried caulking at the paying guests.

She slipped a pry bar into a crack between the window casing and the siding and applied gentle pressure. With a soft squeak, the window unit slid toward her. She was disturbing its slumber, she thought. It had rested comfortably there in its rough opening since probably when? Just after the Great Fire of 1903? The blaze had come pretty close to the Eagle House that time, she knew, from photographs she'd pored over down at the library. There had been minor damage to the exterior of the building.

Jack arose from his perch on the rail and made to take hold of the frame of the window.

"I got it, I got it," she said. She wasn't about to let the whole unit crash down onto her. That would be better than a Saturday morning cartoon.

Instead of grabbing the frame, though, he rested an index finger against the edge of the window casing, marking off the thickness of it with another finger. He contemplated the measurement.

"Full one inch," he said. "Maybe a little more." He ran his fingers contemplatively along the paint-flaked molding that outlined the perimeter of the casing.

"Excuse me?"

"The thickness of that casing. A good inch, maybe more."

Gillian kept a steadying hand on the window unit, but had to ask. "Okay, you've got me. So *what*?"

"So the window probably went in just around the time of the big fire. Probably *because* of it. Been sitting there for a hundred years, minding its own business." He chuckled. "Until you came along."

Uncanny. Like he read her mind. And how did he know all that about the Great Fire? "How do you—?"

But he had already taken hold of one side of the old window and was sliding it out of the rough opening. He helped her lower the unit from the sill to the porch floor. They leaned it against the porch wall.

"I heard you mention the fire," he said. "It interested me so I spent an afternoon going through the archives down at the library." Gillian had a tarp spread out to protect the decking. Jack stomped his feet on it to knock off a dusting of paint flakes.

"Sorry about your, ah . . . shoes." Gillian cast a disparaging glance at them.

"Oh, quiet. Please don't start things up again. This is nice for a change."

Her start things? It wasn't *her* that had her hands all over *him* in the saw shed. Or was it? She was still hazy about that. But point taken. This *was* nice. Kind of like how she and Riley always worked together but with things to talk about other than football scores or the new cold-cut selections in the expanded deli section of the market.

Gillian uncrated the new double-insulated window unit and Jack helped her hoist it into the hole in the wall. Points in his favor: he didn't give her an unsolicited clinic on how to properly level and nail off new installations like someone *else* she knew. He just held on to the frame until she had a few nails in it. Like you'd do for anybody. Then he said, "I think I'll just go slip into something less comfortable," and disappeared inside the inn.

A statement brimming with possibilities. Gillian continued working in his absence, but after shimming the new window unit two times in a row in the completely *opposite* direction indicated by the two-foot level, she realized it had suddenly become a chore to do something she had routinely done dozens of times. She forced herself to pay attention to the bubbles in the level.

A few minutes later, she heard the screen door creak. Jack came around the corner. He had put on work boots.

Such a tease. She laughed out loud.

"What?"

She shook her head. "Nothing." They went on from there, replacing three more units on the porch wall. Then somehow Jack became the "cut guy," running her miter saw. She called out the lengths for the molding that outlined the perimeter of the new casing, he mitered it, and she shot it home with the nail gun. When they were done, a full two hours earlier than she had planned to finish, the new windows looked as though they had always been there.

He even helped her lump the heavy-as-hell miter saw table into the bed of the pickup. She'd had to slide it down a plank and onto the porch to get it out of the back of her truck that morning. So Jack Turner did have some skills. *For a contractor*, she said to herself. All they did was boss people around, tell them what to do. The make-work he was doing for Riley was probably just a sham. Left to his own devices she wondered how good a craftsman he really was.

"Hey, let me borrow this?" He'd pulled her battery-powered screw gun from a tool bucket.

"Sure." Yeah, whatever. "Just don't—" she bit back *screw me*. Too much working with Riley. Too much history already with Jack. "Hurt yourself," she ad libbed.

He climbed the porch steps and disappeared into the inn. No, she realized watching him out of the corner of her eye, he had stepped just inside the front door. It was original, an ornate, two-inch-thick monster with solid brass hardware. The thing had to weigh two hundred pounds off its hinges and it never really seemed to shut right. She watched Jack open and close it half a dozen times, standing inside and outside while he did this. Threw his hip into the bolt edge and tried it again. Backed out a couple of the top hinge screws with her battery screw gun and came back out to the truck.

"Hey, you got a couple—? Oh, great."

Sheetrock screws. Big three-and-a-half-inch bastards. She handed them to him. Okay, maybe she was interested in what he was doing.

He went back to the door and inserted the long screws into the empty holes in the top hinge. Torqued them home. Shut the door. Opened it. Torqued them again. Pushed the door shut with one finger.

Click. The bolt engaged.

Slick. Efficient. No wasted motion. Okay, so maybe he did have skills.

"That thing irritated the hell out of me," he said, dropping her screw gun back into the tool bucket in the back of her pickup.

The world needed fixers. People to make things right, she thought. Jack Turner was a Fixer. But his way, she reminded herself, always his way.

Chapter 15

That miter saw table, even with the legs folded up, was a boat anchor to deal with alone. Gillian figured she owed Jack a cup of coffee for his help with it. And on the windows. Okay, and the door.

"So, tell me about Rocky Falls," Jack said.

They were making polite small talk as they made their way downtown along one of the few sidewalks in town. It ran downhill toward the river. Gillian could feel the slope of the land tugging at her, forcing her to reach a little farther forward with every step, giving her gait a free and easy feel. Which nicely complemented her state of mind. The window job had gone well and unexpectedly she hadn't found Jack's company—or help—intrusive. She hated to admit it, but it was kind of fun working with him.

"It's been here a long time," she said, noncommittally. The pleasant day was too good to ruin.

Jack persisted. "Like I said, I saw photographs of—what is it called around here? The Great Fire?—down at the library, but I didn't have time to do much reading on it."

Not likely. All he seemed to have was time. She decided to throw him a bone. "A fire wiped out about fifteen square miles of forest around Rocky Falls. Some of it was virgin.

You know, never been cut down?" She thought about the wide pine floorboards in The Box.

"I'm familiar with the concept of virgin," Jack said.

He said that with a straight face. Gillian checked.

"Did they ever find out how the fire started?" he asked.

"Logging companies."

"Did what?"

Without breaking the rhythmic swing of her arms— Jack Turner quickly covered a lot of ground literally and figuratively—she turned her head to him.

"Jack, really. It's been a nice day. A far better one than I might have imagined it could be given . . ."

"'The circumstances?'"

"Exactly. Let's not wreck it, okay?"

"Okay."

They reached the bottom of the hill and took a left onto River Street. After what seemed like an eternity of silence but was probably no more than five minutes, Gillian decided she couldn't tolerate the absolute quiet.

"Okay, the logging companies," she said, the words no sooner out of her mouth than she regretted giving in. "They left huge piles of slash laying around after they'd removed the timber. Like I told you before." Just before she'd thrown an oilcan at his head. "Fall of 1903, one good lightning strike and *Poof!*" She pantomimed an explosion with her hands. "Instant conflagration. Eight local men killed trying to fight it. There's a bronze plaque with their names on the wall of the firehouse." Gillian pointed across the street to the station house.

Jack nodded. He'd seen it. "Yet the town survived."

"By the grace of God. We're tucked into an oxbow in the river. You know, an oxbow. A place where—"

"An oxbow. I get it. You're inside an elbow of the original path of the river. Basically, the Mohasset flows right around you, protecting you on three sides," Jack finished for her.

Explanation interruptus. Now who was touchy?

"The maps, remember?" he said.

Of course. He probably knew—at least on paper—the topography of the area as well as she.

"Un-huh. How could I forget. You've done your homework on the town."

This strained silence lasted until they reached the footbridge leading to an observation point anchored to the rocks midway across the Mohasset. Gillian could see half a dozen people of various ages and an assortment of children out on the bridge. On the shore end of the walkway, an elderly lady was posed in front of the iron sign that proclaimed the historical importance of the river in the early days of Maine logging, while an equally elderly gent who Gillian supposed was her husband snapped a photograph of the woman.

Gillian rested her forearms on the top bar of the wooden railing that prevented tourists from straying off the sidewalk and onto the tumble of granite boulders hulking along the edge of the river. She hiked one foot up on the bottom rail, realizing she was winded. Jack had long legs.

His coat sleeve almost touching hers on the rail, Jack said quietly, "They can't do that nowadays."

"What, take pictures?"

"No. The logging companies, I mean. There's regulations. About disposing of the slash, replanting—"

"Yeah, well, too late. By about a hundred years." Gillian squinted and watched two kids scurry along the walkway, point down at the rushing water and turn to exclaim excitedly to their parents.

"Sounds like there's more," Jack said.

How *did* you rationally and objectively relate a story taken in with mother's milk, fleshed out in childhood, and *acted out* in adulthood, Gillian thought. One that was so vividly and completely a part of your own subconscious and the collective unconsciousness of three generations of an entire town. And then tell all that to an almost-complete stranger? Someone who lacked the what?—*historical perspective*, she supposed—to appreciate the tangled mass of emotions.

But it appeared that Jack would not let her off the hook until the whole thing was out, so against her better judgment, she pressed on. "Okay, you asked for it," she said. "Don't tell me later that I didn't warn you."

She shot her hands out of her coat sleeves and adjusted her position on the rail fence. Now the kids were dropping leaves into the Mohasset on the upriver side of the foot-bridge and running to the other edge of the walkway to see them rush past in the flow. She, Meg, and Rachel used to do that very thing when they were kids.

"When electricity came in after the Great Fire, the logging companies didn't need to locate sawmills on rivers like the Mohasset," she said. "They dropped us like a hot potato. Little mill towns like Rocky Falls just fell out of the loop and went back to sleep."

"That sounds like a good thing."

"In one way, because the companies had stopped tearing down the forests. But only because there were no more trees left worth harvesting. And big sections of the woods were just wasteland from the fire. You ever seen old photos of that place in Russia where the meteor hit like a hundred years ago? Nothing but black matchsticks left? Well, it was like that."

"There weren't any photos of that down in the archives."

"Jack, come on," Gillian scoffed. "You're 'big business.' Think like they did. Would *you* want to advertise what your industry had done to an area? Wouldn't you do everything you could to squash any kind of negative publicity?"

Although they were barely touching, she could feel the sudden tension in his arm. The history of Rocky Falls was like a pernicious virus. It jumped from host to carrier, spreading ill-will and discontent. Served him right. He was the one dredging up the crap.

"I told you," she said.

"You're deliberately making this personal," he said.

"Whatever made you think it wasn't?"

He switched feet on the bottom rail, squinted, and began to watch the children intently. "Go on."

"Incredible poverty in town, after that. For like thirty or forty years. Appalachia-like stuff. Proof of *that* you can find in *any*body's family album." She thought of pictures of her own grandfather as a young boy. Skinny for his age, an up-ended log for a stool, outside a shack roofed with corrugated tin. No tar paper on the walls, but board and batten siding all the same. Wilcox Lumber sign in the background. A sad picture all around.

"Things eventually got better, though, yes?" Jack asked.

"Oh, yeah. Courtesy of Uncle Sam."

"There you go. There are safety nets."

"Hah." The kids and their parents were making their way toward shore.

"I'll bet you never knew that Maine wood products helped win World War Two, did you?" she said. She let the curve ball hang temptingly in the air.

"Really?" said Jack, not disguising his interest. "No, I didn't."

"Oh, yes, indeed. Uncle Sam decided to build PT boats out of—of all things—wood. The government sent surveyors and federal forest agents out here. They swarmed the woods and the river, and decided we were the perfect site for a plywood manufacturing plant."

"But if the forest was wiped out in what? The early 1900s, yes? How much had come back in fifty years?" Jack asked.

Gillian had to give him credit. He was a quick study. "The virgin stands were gone, but second-growth pine and fir had filled in pretty good."

"But why manufacture in Rocky Falls? Wouldn't the government just ship the lumber to one of the existing mills?"

Gillian laughed airily, deliberately keeping her tone light to hide her contempt. "For once, our biggest liability, being tied to water, turned into our biggest asset. Rocky Falls was deemed the perfect site. We had water to use in the laminating process. The falls could run hydroelectric generators. We were the perfect, self-sustaining solution."

"So this was a good thing for the town, right?" Jack asked.

"Oh, yeah. It was just great. You saw the newer businesses downtown, like Crosby's Hardware and Merril's Department Store?"

Jack nodded.

"Well, they're the result of Uncle Sam's interest in our little town," Gillian said. "And the tiny hydroelectric plant just upriver from here?" She tilted her head. Now that the trees had thinned, the building that housed the still-operating generator was just visible. "Put in on Uncle Sam's tab. We didn't pay a penny for our electricity for almost thirty years," she finished.

The ball hung tantalizingly over home plate. Jack jumped on the pitch, anticipating the big hit. "That's my point exactly," he crowed. "Progress isn't all bad. It's a trade-off where everyone gets a little and everyone gives a little."

Swing and a miss. Gillian looked at Jack and raised her eyebrows.

From the look on his face, she knew that Jack knew he'd fallen into the trap even before he heard the "thwack" of the ball in the catcher's glove.

"But, no, correct?"

"Oh, it was great for a while," Gillian said. "The plant put lots of town people to work. Local business picked up. Things were just dandy."

Wanting to end the inning sooner than later, Jack asked, "Okay, so what happened *this* time?"

"The government terminated its contract with Rocky Falls a few years after the war ended, but the plant ran for another fifteen years. Then, in the early sixties, people in town started complaining of having blurred vision, dizziness . . . stuff like that." She stopped.

"And?"

"And it turned out that the resin they were using to glue the panels together was toxic. People who had worked at the plant had six times the normal incident rate for neurological disorders. The river water was tested. They found super-high levels of toxins."

"Good Lord," Jack breathed. "I'm really sorry."

"Why are you sorry, it's not your fault. It's just progress, right? Isn't that what you guys always say?"

It was Jack's turn to jump ugly.

"Don't put me in the 'you guys' group, for one thing. For another, there's a big difference between bringing potentially dangerous industry to town and simply trying to make a reasonable buck and improve the living conditions for people here in the process. But you're too emotional to separate the issues out."

"Maybe I am," she snapped, "but I've got a real personal stake in this, *unlike* you. My grandfather was one of the people affected by the crap at the plant. He died when I was three. Meg—my oldest sister?—terminated her first pregnancy because of . . . complications with the baby. My Aunt Betty's first husband—my true uncle, although I think of Leo as being a real one now—died of some kind of rare blood disorder. One-in-a-million thing. 'Statistical abnormality' I hear the docs called it. Who knows if that wasn't somehow connected to the crap in the river? Stuff like that entitles me to get a little 'emotional' about the issue, don't you think?"

"I told you. I am really sorry to hear about the troubles the town's had. I am."

Gillian sensed him looking at her, but she couldn't meet his eyes. Moisture stung the corners of hers.

"Look," he said, "the government did own up to the problem, though, didn't they?" He held up a placating hand as she bristled. "I know, I know. Not that *that* helped the people already affected. But they did clean up the river, right?"

"You can swim in it again, obviously," Gillian said. She passed on the too easy, too obvious *You did.* She pictured Jack with all his equipment jumping into the treacherous, tumbling stretch of the Mohasset just in front of them. He'd be a goner. "The river ecology is squared away and now sport fishing is one of the big draws around here, as you know. And sure, all that's a shot in the arm to places like the Eagle House."

"And there was a big settlement to all the people who were affected, yes?"

"'Big' is a relative term. When you've got nothing it seems like a lot."

They were quiet again for a few minutes. The rush of the rapids underneath the footbridge was the only sound. The older folks had strolled off and the family had bundled themselves back in their car. Gillian heard an engine turn over.

"Rocky Falls is a beautiful spot," Jack said, finally. "But it can't hold back progress. Nothing can. Nobody can. It happens whether you want it to or not. You just have to make sure it happens in the right way."

Gillian thought his voice dropped off there at the end. Before she had a chance to wonder why, the crunch of tires on gravel drew her attention. The family's SUV pulled up to her and Jack. The tinted window on the driver's side powered down.

"Howdy," the Man-Who-Must-Be-Dad said.

"Hello, yourself," Gillian replied.

"I wonder if you could help us?"

Gillian approached the side door of the vehicle. Mom leaned across Dad. "We've heard that they're putting up new houses somewhere along the river here? A planned community?" she said. "Could you all tell us where that might be at?"

Amazing. Her worst nightmare arrived at her doorstep in the guise of a—she eyed the interior appointments of the car—*very* expensive, top-of-the-line, power-everything, SUV. With Tennessee plates.

She glanced back at Jack. He was leaning against the fence, an amused smile on his face. He lifted a hand up off the rail then let it drop: *See?*

"Ma'am, that planned community is somewhat of a bone of contention in these parts," Gillian said to the woman in the car. She fought to keep the twang out of her voice. What was it about Southern accents that were so seductive? "I wouldn't be holding my breath about them if I were you." She smiled sweetly and made herself comfortable leaning a forearm against the car.

Apparently, Dad felt his space had been invaded.

Gillian knew just how he felt.

He toggled the window up halfway, effectively shooing her off his window ledge. "Much obliged, anyway," he said. "You all have a nice day now, hear?"

Gillian watched the vehicle drive away. "Good thing he's got four-wheel drive," she said ruefully over her shoulder to Jack. "He's gonna need it in the winter around here." She pronounced the last word 'hee-ya'.

Jack said nothing.

"You paid those people, right? To show up on cue?" she said, although she knew he didn't. She sighed. "Let's keep walking."

They made their way farther along River Street, which eventually led them past her Aunt Betty's pottery shop. "My aunt's place," Gillian said, hooking a thumb at the storefront.

"We've met," Jack said.

Gillian cocked an eyebrow speculatively but said nothing. They stopped in the Riverview Restaurant for two coffees-to-go. One-of-the-Twins was halfway through a donut at the breakfast counter. "G'day, Miss Gilly." He smiled and touched the brim of his Wilcox Lumber baseball cap.

"Oh, hey . . ." Again, no idea which Twin he was.

"Wilbur," Jack, behind her, whispered.

"Wilbur," she finished.

"He's running an errand presently," the Twin said, "but I'll pass on your regards."

"Trust me," Jack whispered again.

"Two coffees, please, Pop," Gillian said to the owner of the Riverview, Pop Henry. Another piece of local culture,

Pop, his wife Beatrice, and the Riverview. How many hours had she spent here as a teenager, leaning on the cool granite counters, spinning in the high stools, slurping milkshakes, whispering to girlfriends she was too busy now to even talk to?

"When we were really little, our mom used to bring us here on Saturdays as a treat if we were good in school the whole week," she told Jack, remembering more.

Jack imagined the three Wilcox sisters as little girls. "Bet you didn't make it here much, huh?"

She laughed. "Not much. But there were a lot of other times when I was older. We had the motivation, but not always the means, if you know what I mean. See those donuts?" She pointed to a late-in-the-morning, picked-over stack of honey-dipped donuts inside a glass domed cake stand on the counter. "Best glaze in the world."

"Heart attack on a paper plate," Jack said.

"Damn straight. Why waste your time at a drive-through chain place?" One might come to town along with the redevelopment. Gillian pushed the thought away.

"Let's get two," Jack said.

"Good idea."

"Here's your coffee," Pop said. "Easy on the milk for you, teaspoon of honey. Good thing you're my favorite customer." He laughed, a sound that reached into every corner of the cozy eatery. "For your—I mean, the gentleman—I left it black. Fixin's are over there." He pointed to a side table stocked with cream, sugar, and stirrers.

"Thanks, Pop." She slipped a ten under the chrome napkin holder after he had left to wait on another customer. She caught Jack's puzzled look. "Pop won't let me pay, sometimes," she explained.

"Ah," he said. Another lesson in Small Town. They grabbed napkins from a chrome dispenser on the counter and selected their donuts.

She turned toward the door and bumped someone's elbow. "Oh excuse me—" It was One-of-the-Twins. Definitely—

she looked back to the counter—yes, definitely this was The-Other-Twin.

Jack was adding cream to his coffee. Softly he said, "Orville."

"Orville," she said.

"Oh, hey, Miss Gilly." He touched his finger to his Wilcox Lumber cap. "I'm Wilbur, but I'll—"

"Right. Be sure to pass along my regards."

"Happy to," he said. "G'day."

Jack chuckled and squeaked a plastic lid onto his coffee cup.

"Maybe if I stenciled their names onto the front of their hats . . ."

"You're mumbling," he said.

"No, then they'd just switch them around. Maybe I could make some kind of secret mark on them that only I could see?"

Jack opened the door for her. "You've got to let it go," he said, smiling. Then he said, "Good God."

"What?"

"She's a beauty . . ." He crossed the sidewalk to run his hand along a sweeping tail fin. Balanced his coffee and donut in one hand and got down on one knee to caress the ruby red, nose-cone tail lights. Angled his head to catch the luster of the black finish.

"It belongs to The Twins. It's the first—and only—new car they ever bought," Gillian said, feeling like a tour guide. "It's a Cadillac."

Jack whistled. "No shit . . ." Gillian didn't take offense. The guy had been transported to a far, far, better world. "Look at all that chrome. Holy crap." He ran his hand lovingly along the curved roof line. "Whew . . . Rocky Falls was doing pretty well there for a while."

"For a while," Gillian agreed. "C'mon. I gotta sit." She tugged on his arm, pulling him away from the gleaming car. They parked themselves in the center of the small common on a sunny bench facing the firehouse. Gillian settled herself onto the sunny seat with a weary sigh. She felt as old as Arthur and Lynette.

"Tired?"

"Exhausted," she admitted.

"Working Saturdays will catch up with you. I know."

"It's not that kind of tired. I'm emotionally exhausted." Not fun to admit, but true.

"At least you're not morally bankrupt as well."

"Jack."

"Sorry."

Ooh. Was that a connection she felt? Slow, girl. How good an idea was it to open up even a bit to Jack Turner? He'd turn her every vulnerability against her. She said so.

"Right. Like I was able to hide all mine from you in the bathtub," Jack said.

"Sweetie, there ain't much you hid from me in the bathtub." She waggled her eyebrows like Groucho Marx and tapped ash off an imaginary cigar.

He laughed, then asked a little too lightly, "Really?"

She took a sip of her coffee and smiled enigmatically. "You'll never know now, will you?"

He snickered.

She glanced at him. He appeared to be waiting for her to decide where to take the conversation next. She decided. "I really shouldn't be talking to you about how I feel about this place." She indicated the town with a sweep of her cup. "But I'm going to anyway." She readjusted her position on the bench.

"I have resisted facing things," she said. "Not proud of that. I forgot that the one thing that always works at the end of the day is the truth, no matter how much it may suck. You're forcing me to face some of that truth, for better or for worse."

"Like . . . ?"

She looked at him appraisingly. What was she doing, running at his lance, making it easy for him to skewer her right through the heart? He *never* ever appeared entirely harm-

less to her since she'd seen the blue flames in his eyes leap
out at her that first time. And he certainly didn't look entirely benign right now either. Yet for some reason she found
herself craving the joust, somehow sensing that Jack would
parry at the last moment, leaving her with only a flesh
wound.

Yeah, on her carotid artery. Maybe the fair committee
should think about adding a medieval flavor to the upcoming event. Women in tall pointy hats with flowing veils attached to the top. Chicken-eating contests. Mugs of mead.
Jack in tights. Anyway.

"I'm realizing it's not my job to keep the whole world
together," she said. "I can't control everything." It sucked
out *loud* not being Master of the Universe. "Hell, I can't
even control you."

"You gave it a good try."

Gillian laughed ruefully and looked up at the sky. She
tracked the clouds drifting past. "I don't have the energy to
run the whole world, you know. How does God do it?"

"He works Sundays."

Gillian chuckled, actually feeling the funny this time.

Jack recrossed his legs. His sleeve again rested inches
from hers on the top slat of the seat back. "You're deep
down weird," he said, not unkindly. "Right down to the
crunchy nugget center. You know that?"

Gillian tucked one leg beneath her and squinted up at
Haystack Mountain. The bare hiking trail up its wooded side
would be outlined in white maybe as early as next month.
"Gee, thanks, and yes. But don't think for a second you're
the first person to tell me that." She bent down and picked
up a long skinny twig that had fallen from one of the maples
that anchored one end of the small common. Being honest
was *sooo* much fun. She tapped the end of the stick on the
bench.

"You know what's even weirder though?" Jack said.

"Can't imagine."

"I thought I could change *you*."

"Good try. Didn't go unnoticed."

They both laughed.

Gillian bent over and scratched at the dirt beneath the bench with the business end of her stick. Dug canals while Jack watched. Joined the network into a nearby puddle. The canals filled. The puddle drained. She thought of her mother. Once alive, at home, working the Wilcox dirt, on hands and knees, swearing, cursing the weeds in the side garden as she ripped them from the beds, casting them onto a pile behind her. The Wilcox women were all pretty good swearers, except for Meg who hardly ever did. But then again her huge vocabulary could stop a runaway train. The gardens were a mess now. Gillian straightened some of the winding canals and watched the water follow her stick.

"You like gardening?" she asked Jack.

"I like looking at gardens. Neat, orderly."

"Disciplined. Tamed. Whipped into shape. Got it." Gillian slashed diagonally through her miniature irrigation system. Water ran every which way.

If only Rocky Falls were a miniature town and could be easily rearranged like the toy village her mother used to set up on the mantel at the holidays. One tiny bulb illuminated the interior of every frosted storefront, each Victorian house. Fake snow swathed the church steeple. Line the buildings up any way you want because you were the architect, the planner, the visionary.

If you looked down on Rocky Falls from the top of Haystack Mountain just to the east of town you could imagine doing that for real. Move things here, there. Because from up there you could see the whole town through a circle made from your two hands. Except she had never had the urge to move anything around, change a single thing, as she beheld the town through that intimate circle. Sure, maybe move Haystack in a little closer so you didn't have to walk so far to reach its base. You could pull in a few distant hills, tighten the curve of the oxbow for a little more protection, a closer embrace. But everything else was a wrap. Done deal. A place memories were made of. A place to make more of them.

Yes, she had left this place. Had *had* to leave this place. But now she was back. She'd be damned if the stuff she saw happen at the State Planning Office to other little Maine towns would happen here.

"What's that?" Jack asked, pointing to a twelve-foot diameter brown octagon stamped into the grass at the center of the common.

Gillian had forgotten he was there. "Gazebo. Or exgazebo, more like," she said. "It's sitting in my barn right now. Needs cosmetic surgery."

"And you're the doctor?"

"That's what committee work gets you."

"The one meeting you don't show up for and they stick it to you, eh?"

She laughed. That was exactly what happened. "The Rocky Falls Historic Preservation Society nominated me—in absentia—as the perfect person with the vehicle and skills necessary to recondition the thing. It's over a hundred years old. Victorian, gee-gaws sticking out all over it. A painter's nightmare. The poor bastard was who got elected to fix it up the last time probably hauled it out of here on a horse-drawn cart."

"On a Saturday. When the guy'd rather be sleeping late."

"Exactly."

Jack Turner knew her too well and he was fun to be with. Damn.

Across the street, Peter Dunn left the fire station office and walked across the concrete apron towards the first open bay door of the station garage. He looked across at the common, saw her and Jack, and waved. Gillian returned the greeting. To her surprise, Jack waved as well. How did he—?

"Friendly people in this town," he said. "All a guy's got to do is walk around and say Hey, and you've got everybody's life story." He blew across the top of his coffee. "This is a great place to live. Nice people. Nice community. If you can deal with the snow, it's perfect."

"So what's wrong with that?"

"The secret's out. Rocky Falls is in the crosshairs."

An icy blade drew a thin red line across her belly.

"And why not?" she said, surprised at the level of hostility in her voice. But churning lava was better than the kiss of cold steel any day. "All these upper-income people with their two-point-three purebred dogs? They're just dying to move in. Get the best of both worlds: Make a nice chunk of change in the city, then home to good ol' Rocky Falls in the evening where you shoo the cows out of your driveway with the Land Rover. I won't surrender the town inch by slow inch to people with that kind of mind-set."

Their disagreements about the future of the town were like subtitles in a foreign film, she realized. Even if the action onscreen paused for a moment, the dialogue just kept scrolling along beneath it.

"But look," Jack said. "What if somebody came in here with a plan to improve the town without "negatively impacting" it?" He turned to her on the bench and looked directly into her eyes. "Would you let them in?" he asked quietly.

"The day hell freezes over."

Jack hung his head.

Poor baby. He was frustrated. Gillian could see the healing dent in his scalp.

"Picture this, though," Jack said, rebounding. He set his coffee down on the bench and with his hands framed the row of ancient storefronts adjacent to the fire station.

The guy was absolutely bulletproof, Gillian realized. Unstoppable, incapable of being deflected. A one-man biblical flood. She sighed. You had to like his gumption, though. "Picturing."

"Okay. We—"

"Don't include me."

"Right. My company would combine those three units—"

He pointed to the florist's, an art studio, and a trinket shop that sold Maine souvenirs and postcards.

"Those are not 'units,' Jack. They are people's lives. Their fortunes. Their dreams."

"Let me finish. We shore up the internal party walls and combine those dinky little shops into one common area with courtyard entrance. Strip off those dangerous stone cornices— see where they're crumbling? Right there. At the top?— and carry the theme of the new exterior facade down through the next . . ." He counted with a fingertip. "Four. Yes. Four storefronts. I've kind of redone the original plans. Here."

He pulled a flattened crumpled piece of paper from his wallet and handed it to her. She unfolded it. It was a sketch of the row of shops directly in front of them.

Men always reached into their wallets right before they screw you, Gillian thought. Most for condoms, but not this one. He was a mind fucker. How do you put a rubber balloon around your brain? *Wham Bam . . .*

"Thank you, ma'am," she said aloud.

"Pardon?"

"Nothing." She grudgingly looked at the drawing. It was hastily rendered but with no little skill. She had fooled around with projections and plan views herself and they weren't easy. On Jack's drawing, color added in here and there emphasized the slope of new roofs, shadows highlighted the recessed entrances.

When she got beyond the art though, she wondered if she would be forced to throw up the coffee she'd drunk. Puke right onto the sidewalk like a little kid at a parade. "I see," she said. Oh *boy*, did she. "Your plans involve changing the downtown also. Not just putting in a planned community, but actually restructuring downtown Rocky Falls."

"Are you asking me or telling me?"

"Don't fool with me." She took a swig of coffee and shut her eyes, savoring the liquid heat as it warmed the frozen places in her innards.

"Okay," he said. "It started out with just the residential piece. Near yours? Out by the river?"

"Jack, no shit."

"Right. Then I thought about some projects I've seen that, well, let's just say they didn't turn out very good."

Her eyes still closed, feeling lead weights were attached to the lids, she said, "That's what happens when one person thinks they know best. They remake something according to what they want without consideration for what people who live there might want."

"I hate to split hairs about this, but no, that's not what screwed things up."

She fought to open her eyes. Squinted in the bright light. "Where is this 'project' you're referring to, by the way?"

"A long way from here."

She look directly at Jack. "It had better be."

"Good coffee," he said.

"Great, change the subject. Hope the whole thing just goes away." Gillian refolded the rendering and handed it back.

"Let's hope," he said.

Gillian shook her head. What an idiot she could be. Forgetting that one thing always led to another. "That drawing shocked me, Jack, I gotta say. I really thought you were in this just for the riverside development. You know, the residential piece? Bamboozle me out of my land and throw up some crappy cookie-cutter houses?"

Dominoes: give a little and piece by piece the whole town comes crashing down. She pictured the ending of *Planet of the Apes* with the town gazebo in place of the Statue of Liberty. Or maybe her barn could crash to the ground in slow motion like the Golden Gate Bridge always seemed to do in disaster movies. More heat than the coffee could have provided rose to her cheeks.

"The units—" He stopped, seeing the expression on Gillian's face—"I mean, the houses, would not be crappy. In fact, since spending time in Rocky Falls, I've changed my mind about the riverside development. There were too many homes planned originally. I've had the whole complex pulled back from the river to allow uninterrupted access to the shore line."

"How nice."

"*But*, the downtown has to be brought up to date. It's a package deal. It's not just me saying that, it's—" he found himself about to say "past experience" but instead he finished with "the numbers."

"And you live by the numbers."

"Don't we all?" Feeling on solid ground now, he turned on the bench to face Gillian. "It's like you with the mill. You have to figure out how you can support The Twins, and Skip and everybody else who works for you and still turn a profit? You've got taxes, right? On the house, the mill?"

"Of course."

He picked up his coffee and eyed her over the rim of the paper cup. "First and foremost? Numbers." He nodded. "All numbers."

A flood, she'd thought? Hell, no. The man was a full-fledged tsunami. From a distance he appeared to be just a harmless beautiful wave, but get out of Dodge quick if you lived near the beach.

"Jack, it's been fun," she said. She stood, using up what felt like the last of her strength. "But no more. Not today. I'm done."

She chucked the dregs of her coffee out onto the grass.

Chapter 16

The shortest possible route back to the Eagle House Inn was Elm Street to Maple then to Birch. Not a very imaginative bunch when it came to names, the town's forefathers. Gillian walked at a fast clip. Her legs protested but her mind, and maybe her heart, too, needed distance. From Jack, from so-called "progress," from every painful place in her head that being around him seemed to require her to revisit. Distance. Her legs groaned.

Beautiful old homes, most still in reasonably good repair, all relics of happier more prosperous times in Rocky Falls lined these streets closest to the center of town. A turn-of-the-century hodge-podge of Queen Anne shingle-styles and Gothics with fringed rake boards trimming steep gables. Mixed in were eighteenth-century saltboxes and stately Greek revivals. Fresh paint jobs gleamed on several homes recently purchased by people new to town, labor and materials supplied by townspeople, who then turned the money back into improving their own homes. What a tangled dilemma, this old town.

Reaching the inn, Gillian fired up her cranky pickup truck, then left it idling to warm up. She ducked into the Eagle House and set a date with Arthur and Lynette for her to return and finish up the interior trim on the windows. She pulled the truck out onto Route 101 and headed for home. In the rearview mirror, she saw Jack just coming into sight, his long strides eating up the sidewalk.

A mile out of town, the layout changed. The lots became larger, more random. Worker housing. Mill owners and supervisors built mansions close to Rocky Falls center, but these buildings on the outskirts were simple two-story frame houses. Everyday workmen's homes. Neat as a pin, some of them were, shored up by pensions and disability settlements. Mrs. Orville—or maybe it was Mrs. Wilbur—was bent over a flower bed in the front yard of one of the tidiest ones, edging spade clutched in a wrinkled hand. In silhouette, Mrs. One-of-the-Twins'-Wives was indistinguishable from the plywood cutouts of old women bent to their gardening sold by the souvenir shop downtown. Gillian waved and Mrs. One-of-the-Twins carefully but gamely returned it.

A few more cross streets and the mobile homes began. Again, a mix. Some whimsical with whirly-gigs filling front lawns, others with discouraged-looking fences outlining neglected patches of turf. The worst had no grass out front and vehicles in various stages of disrepair marooned in the drive. In this neighborhood lived the kids of the kids whose parents had briefly enjoyed the revitalization of Rocky Falls during the "plywood years." A lot of them were younger than she herself was, with larger families than they could afford, anywhere from two to four dogs and a double-mortgaged double-wide. Life on the margin.

Working the ski lifts in the winter, logging whenever they could. Scrounging wood to heat their homes in the often brutal Maine winter. Like Jack said, Gillian had to admit. Two children were scaling one of the towering piles of split cordwood standing adjacent to a particularly rundown trailer. Gillian recognized the kids from the odd visits she made to Meg's classroom each year. Meg always asked her to do a little show-and-tell on what she did down at the mill.

Some homesteads were looking up, though. New porches and decks, permanent block foundations, brand-spanking new septic vent pipe "candy canes" sticking up out of recently seeded ground. New money from new people cycling right into the pockets of those who'd lived here forever. You couldn't escape the math.

Damn Jack. Right again. Plain as the nose on your face, the improvement and hope emanating from these homes.

So maybe it was her that was off. So caught up in her own vision of how things had always been that she was unable to picture things any other way. Not seeing how bad things had become. Only when a visitor other than immediate family came into your home did you truly appreciate how filled with shit some of the corners were.

But the "plan" Jack had outlined? The "ripping off cornices" and "combining storefronts" sounded like more than just straightening up some clutter. More than just a nose job, it sounded like major reconstructive surgery. Would anyone recognize Rocky Falls once it was done? Would any townies want to live here? Wasn't the devil you knew always preferable?

As she vigorously downshifted for a stop sign, a thought struck her: Jack had been doing his Vandals and Visigoth routine for a while. He had a track record. He'd unwillingly admitted as much a few minutes ago.

Sure, back in the spring his team had flashed a few pictures of other projects by Turner Development. They seemed pretty nice. Nothing on the scale of a Rocky Falls redo, just a few storefront renovations and some cute, small cul-de-sacs. But those were the things he wanted everyone to know about. Somewhere out there were work samples he didn't want anyone to know about. Those were the ones she needed to focus on. Needed to see personally. Those were where—she made a mental apology to Boo—the dog died.

Nothing predicted future behavior like . . . blah, blah,

blah. Somewhere out there was a Rocky Falls done over Jack-style.

All she had to do was find it.

She accelerated away from the intersection and shifted through the gears. He'd be pissed when he found out she'd gone looking for it, though. But this was war. Never forget that. Besides, it was always gratifying to watch Jack lose his cool. It was therapeutic too, because it kept her from throwing things at him, a habit which could get a girl into trouble long term.

She checked the speedometer and realized she was going sixty in a forty zone. Having grown up with most of the cops in town, she was on a first-name basis with all of them and they were likewise friendly to her. Otherwise, she'd have had to install a new muffler on the Toyota months ago. But twenty miles an hour over? They weren't that friendly. She let up on the gas and slowed to a thoughtful forty-five. Rolled the side window down as far as it would go before it jammed in its track. Let the wind play with her hair.

Jack took the teasing much better than Riley ever did, which added a welcome level of challenge to the mind game. Maybe before she embarked on her final campaign to unhinge Mr. Turner by checking out his work samples, she'd soften him up for the big hit. Also eek out a little get-back for how he'd knocked the bloom off her fine mood this day.

She could what? Several ideas leaped immediately to mind. She giggled and bumped the truck up to fifty.

Chapter 17

"Jack, for Chrissakes. Make sure them clapboards line up around the corner, will you?" Riley bellowed.

Monday was not exactly his favorite day, but Jack didn't think his mood affected his job performance. He leaned out from the staging and eyed the wide corner board in front of him. Every clapboard course on either side of the corner lined perfectly with his squared-up pencil marks.

Damn that Riley. Riding him because he'd started up with Gillian. And damn the Rocky Falls grapevine for filling him in. Gillian and Riley might have had something going once, at least according to Riley's warped way of thinking, but to Jack it seemed like a pretty perverse relationship. They rolled in the mud, threw things at each other, cursed, swore. They were a walking, talking Jerry Springer episode.

He fished in the right front pocket of his nail apron for more stainless steel siding nails. Two, no three, left. He scrounged through the rest of the pockets. In the left rear, the really deep one, he found a nasty surprise. He pulled his hand out. It was covered with a clear, sticky mess. He sniffed. Silicone caulking. He cautiously investigated further. The pocket was chock full of the stuff.

He looked to his left. "Bud?"

Buddy, his working partner for the day, shook his sheepdog hair out of his eyes and snickered. "Not me." He bent over, held the blade guard back on a battery-powered trim saw and shaved a millimeter from the end of a clapboard.

Riley? *Too subtle.*

A tangled mass of curls came to mind.

Like she'd done hundreds of mornings over the last two years, Gillian tugged on the sliding door to the saw shed. The handle seemed to tear itself from her grasp. She lost her grip, flew backward, and landed in a pile of bark mulch. She looked around. Nobody had seen her.

She got to her feet, rubbing her rear end. She examined the handle. Then the door, then the frame. *A-yep.* Some smart ass had nailed the door to the frame with a couple of sixteen-penny spikes.

Riley? *Too subtle.*

Elegant eyelashes came to mind.

Jack was starving. When the hell was—

"Break!" Somebody down below yelled.

Jack tacked a nail in the newly installed fascia in front of him and hung his nail apron from it. The leather still had a chemical smell. At least one pocket was now permanently waterproof. He followed Buddy, along the staging and down the ladder.

Every morning the crew stashed their lunchboxes on a workbench in the rough shelter constructed to keep the plans table dry. Jack hooked the handle of his box on the way by. The handle seemed to tear itself out of his grasp and the change in momentum nearly flipped him onto his back. He staggered and caught himself on the edge of the plan table.

"Whatcha'all got in that thermos of yours, Jackie?" Riley asked, coming around the corner with a paper carton of coffee in his hand. "Vodka? You're losing your balance with alarmin' regularity."

The crew—because they were paid to, Jack thought— guffawed.

Jack approached his lunchbox as if it contained a bomb.

"*Boom!*" somebody behind him yelled and to his dismay, he flinched and jumped backward.

"You're an ass," he said to Buddy.

"Thank you." Buddy bowed and the crew laughed some more.

Jack moved in on the box again and the crew, hooked into the drama, leaned in. He unsnapped the latches and cautiously opened the metal lid. The box contained . . . two peanut butter and jelly sandwiches and an apple. Exactly what he'd packed that morning in his room at the Eagle House.

With a sigh of relief he resnapped the lid and hoisted the box. Again, the handle tore itself out of his grasp. The crew laughed uproariously.

Jack opened the lid again and removed the contents. He peered at the bottom of the box. "Son of a—" Then he had to laugh. "Anybody got a pry bar?"

Someone . . . had nailed him—or at least his lunchbox— but good.

Gillian grabbed hold of the cage of the front-end loader and hauled herself up into the cab, a self-satisfied smirk on her face. The grin had been plastered there for almost a day and a half. Try as she might to wipe it from her expression, it crept back in like a cat in a rainstorm. The lunchbox idea was pure genius. She'd almost wet herself when Buddy had told her Jack's reaction.

She turned the key in the ignition. The diesel engine belched a few times then caught. She waited a few minutes, then eased off the choke. The engine revs held steady. Today would be a good day.

One of the yard's portable generators had crapped out and she had to load it onto Jasper. One-of-the-Twins would drive it into town for service. She slipped the loader into first gear and it accelerated smoothly. So useful when in a cooperative mood. *Wasn't everyone*? She wondered what Jack was up to. Or more like: What onerous task did Riley have that needed doing that only Jack was qualified to do? Really, why didn't Jack just up and quit Riley? He had his own business back in Boston. He was supposedly a big deal. Witness that stupid pickup truck, as ugly as it was. Restorations and hood ornaments like that Winged Victory chick didn't come cheap.

But if Jack quit Riley, then he wouldn't have an excuse to hang around Rocky Falls anymore, twisting the arms of the locals to go along with his "vision." He'd have to torture everybody remotely from his undoubtedly big Boston office. Send a flock of suits back here like he had earlier in the year. And he wouldn't be able to play stupid practical jokes on her if he went back south. Apparently he lived for them. For her, they were just a hobby. She shifted positions on the hard seat. Her butt still hurt.

Coming up on the shed, she slowed and tweaked the forks to where they hung just above the broken generator. She hopped out of the cab and slung a length of steel chain around the forks and then slipped a hook through the lifting ring on the unit.

With an upward tap on the hydraulics, the generator swung from the forks. She carefully trundled it across the yard. When she reached Jasper, she tapped the controls again and the generator rose smoothly into position above the flatbed of the delivery truck. Suddenly, the hydraulics gave out. With a hiss and a burst of red fluid the forks fell. The generator slammed down onto the truck bed. It careened off the bed and smashed into the cage of the loader, then hit the ground with a thud.

The impact rocked the loader. White-faced, Gillian killed the ignition and shinnied out from behind the steering wheel.

The generator—gasoline gushing from it—lay on its side on the ground. The cage around the cab was crumpled in. The roof was skewed and dented.

For the life of her, she didn't get the joke.

Jack froze his hammer in mid-swing on Thursday. "What do you mean, 'About what happened at the mill?'" he asked Bud.

"Well, seems like Gillian Wilcox had some trouble with a loader."

Jack slipped his hammer handle into a loop on his apron and put his hands on his hips. "Give. Is she hurt?"

Suddenly, molding a piece of lead flashing to follow the contour of a cornice return seemed to take every bit of Buddy's concentration.

"Buddy. Is she okay?"

"Scared the shit out of her was all."

Jack let out a breath. Buddy worked the flashing to within an inch of its life. The message was clear if you spoke Rocky Falls.

"And you think *I* had something to do with that," Jack said. He felt himself heat up.

Buddy shrugged. "You and Gillian do seem to have a thing going on. You know, egging each other on?"

Of course. Buddy and most everybody else on site had grown up with Gillian. Hundreds of kickball games in gym and thousands of forbidden notes passed in history class got you a lot of loyalty. Why wouldn't they think it was him?

"What kind of problem was it, Buddy?"

Jack watched him work for a minute. The flashing fit about as well as it was ever going to. "Buddy?"

"Hydraulics let go."

Buddy peeled up a fiberglass roof shingle and slid the leading edge of the flashing beneath it.

Life on a shoestring. That's what this whole town was: one big jury-rigged catastrophe waiting to happen. Thank God Gillian wasn't hurt this time. But if it wasn't the loader next time—and there would be a next time—it might be the frigging electrical wiring in her house that got her. Or that piece of shit pickup she drove around in. He'd checked it out one day he'd seen it parked downtown. You could see the road through some holes in the floor.

Numbers. All about the numbers. Get more people here, get more money here. Fix the town up. Patch the holes in the floor. Get GFI outlets. Run decent machines. No more people hurt.

God this town needed him.

Chapter 18

It was Saturday afternoon and the carpenter in Gillian was pleased.

She slowed and turned off Route 101, bounced her pickup onto the Wilcox gravel drive. Today, the interior trim had gone back up on the inside of the new window units at the Eagle House the same way it had come off the old ones. Once Arthur hit everything with a bit of paint, you'd never know that the windows hadn't been living there in the parlor wall of Eagle House since the turn of the century.

She was good. No doubt about it, remodeling really challenged your skills. Throwing up cookie-cutter developments from plans was one thing, but remodeling really stretched you.

It was hard to believe that a week had gone by since she and Jack had worked together at the Inn. A prank-filled one always passed so quickly. And then there was the bit of excitement with the loader. She had taken a sledge and a breaker bar and straightened out the roll cage so you could at least get into the cab and had a service guy do a quick fix on the busted line. But any real work on the hydraulics would have to wait for another couple of weekend carpentry jobs.

She stretched, reaching forward to the windshield with

first one arm, then the other. One shoulder popped. It was still sore from her close encounter of the mechanical kind. Boo leaned over and licked her hand, almost as if he sensed her pain. She'd realized she'd need Rachel's help getting the miter saw table out of the bed of the truck.

She did a three-point turn in front of the house and backed the pickup up the slight incline that led up to the double doors of the old barn. She braked just before the rear tires rolled onto the springy wooden floor. Not worth taking a chance on sending the truck through it.

She kicked open her door. Boo followed her out, running for a quick pee. In a moment he was back, happily sniffing, hot on the trail of some varmint that had visited the barn overnight. Hopefully it hadn't been a skunk. She had trapped and released a mommy possum and her brood during the summer, but a skunk? Quick job with a flashlight and the .22 rifle, but dealing with the carcass would be unpleasant.

Boo ran into the barn and over to the old gazebo. Fun and games and pranks were all fine and good, but seeing the dilapidated structure brought her back to the thoughts that had been haunting her all week. Where was this town headed? If Jack had his way, how would it turn out? Everywhere she looked lately, it seemed she saw evidence for both sides of the argument.

Gillian watched Boo sniff around the pillar bases and under the disintegrated seats. Why couldn't people be more like dogs, completely happy living in the present moment? Ecstatically exploring, caught up in a potpourri of odors, not caring a whit about what might arise in the next moment, or hour or lifetime. The past? No worries, no regrets, no list of unchristened fire hydrants. For Boo, the best things in life were right under his nose right now. Humans could only hope to have it so good.

Gillian grabbed the bucket of hand tools from the back of the pickup and hauled it into the gloom of the barn. Making her way past a tangle of garden tools stacked haphazardly in a corner, she hooked her bootlace on something. She stumbled and stepped on the flat blade of a grub hoe, driving the thick wooden handle into her shin. Cursing, she lost control of the heavy bucket of tools and half fell to the floor.

She rose to one knee and hugged the injured shin to her chest. Mother of *God*. . . . She struggled to her feet and tried walking it off. *Ow, ow, ow* . . .

She peered into the corner to see what had tripped her. She found a small, tipped-over basket filled with gardening tools. A little pointed spade for . . . what? Putting in bulbs. She remembered the curve of her mother's back as she bent over that task. A little rake thing for scratching around the plants. A pair of cracked leather gardening gloves. A surge of emotion welled up, hitting Gillian square in the chest like a lightning bolt. *Oh, Ma.*

She hobbled to the workbench. Reached behind her to clench the edge of it for support. Let the tears fall straight to the ground. Some of the silver drops burst on her boot tops, creating salty crowns. Leaving town after her mother died, going to live in Augusta? An escape. It put blessed distance between her heart and the breathtaking razor cut of loss.

Because everyday life in a big city sterilized your psyche if you let it, and she had cherished the insulating numbness. Nurtured it like a child. Day after day, the reasoned lockstep of community planning disciplined her grief, gave it a buzz cut, told it to get in line and shut the hell up. *Move*, soldier. Assess grants, prioritize need, allocate funds. Save this town, let that one go. Left, right, left right, *hoo*-rah.

It wasn't so easy being a good soldier when you were back home on leave, away from the regimented discipline of the barracks. She looked up into the rafters of the old barn, then let her gaze travel through the jammed-open doors at the rear of it. Beyond were the piles of lumber stacked and drying outside the yard gate. Every damn piece of wood, every rock and every rafter, every thing as far as the eye could see, was saturated with memories. Of her childhood, of . . . her mother. Of all the people she'd grown up with who were now grown ups themselves. All of them busy now, locked into their own distracted orbits, only accidentally crossing one another's path even in a place as small as Rocky Falls. How had that happened? And if it happened all too easily in a *small* Rocky Falls, what would happen if the place got bigger and busier? She thought about the life they had all had once, her family, here together, in the Wilcox Box. She hadn't allowed herself to do that since her mother . . .

The cookouts. The annual lumber company picnic. She, Meg, Rachel at the Harvest Fair, throwing ball after ball at the dunk tank, trying to nail Riley or whoever was up on the seat. In high school, working with her dad at the mill in the summer. All the boys who had a sudden need for a particular piece of timber way up high on a rack and her too dumb to figure out why they got so quiet behind her when she climbed up to get it.

Rocky Falls was like a frigging snow globe. Everything stayed perfectly preserved inside it, every plastic flake in exactly the same place since the last time you shook it. Every saggy floorboard still sagged, every cracked clapboard was still busted, every feeling fresh—

Cripes. She folded her hands together on the top of her head and blew out a breath. Glistening tear drops shot out onto the barn floor. They landed on the sawdust and disappeared without a trace.

Contain. Cope. Keep it quiet. Soldier on. Wood to be cut, people to be paid. The beat goes on. God, she hurt. Tired, tired, tired. She patted her thigh wearily. "Boo . . ."

Her dog trotted over and licked her hand. She knelt down and pressed her forehead to his, his warm doggy smell enveloping, comforting. She scrubbed behind his ears. "Good, Boo," she crooned. His entire backside waggled. Gillian leaned into him and chuckled. The sound seemed to shake the building to its core. She swore she felt the ground beneath her feet tremble.

She tried another laugh, louder this time. It bounced

around the barn, leaked out the door, flew over the fields. She imagined it falling into the river with a joyous splash.

She yelled. Something, she didn't know what. It wasn't about the words, it was about the sound. After a moment, the echo reached her. Her heart expanded. She took a deep breath. Yelled again. Any nonsense that came to mind. Waited. And there it was again. She yelled again and again, over and over, listening after each time.

Holy shit. The snow globe was cracking.

"Good dog, Boo-boo."

She rubbed his chest. He waggled wildly. She threw an imaginary stick and he ran off after it. She laughed hysterically. Wonderful animal, God love him, but not the quickest greyhound at the track. She wiped her tears. Straightened up the chaos of tools in the dark corner. Placed her mother's gloves carefully on the shelf above the workbench. Went back out to the pickup and contemplated the immovable mass of the miter saw table.

She needed help. In more ways than one, but for now just with the miter saw. She yelled up at the side of The Box.

"Rachel!" The saw wasn't so much heavy as bulky. But moving it with a bad shoulder was daunting. Someday she'd rig up something permanent to help with it. Thank goodness for old Arthur, pitching in to help off-load the beast out at the inn today. She yelled again. "Rachel!"

All the windows on the first floor of The Box were open. A little cool for that, but okay. Her sister should be able to hear her.

Gillian grabbed the nail gun compressor from the tailgate of her pickup and lugged it off to the barn where she heaved it up and onto the workbench. Off the floor in case of rain. For good measure she threw a scrap of tarp over it and the bucket of tools. The roof of the barn needed looking at. Again, someday. It all came down to time. Then, uncomfortable with lying to herself, she admitted that the real issue was money. She didn't have it. And if she did, the first item she'd spend it on wouldn't be this old barn. Jack and his damn numbers.

They'd always been her dad's enemy, too, not that any of his kids had ever felt the lack of anything that really mattered. Gillian gave the saw table a half-hearted tug. It didn't budge. The thing was a frigging glacial erratic. She went to find her sister.

Stomping her feet on the back porch, Gillian noticed a spring in the deck boards under her feet. Was the whole place suddenly falling down around her ears or had that slowly been happening for a while? She kicked at the decking again in another spot. *Hah.* Solid as a rock. The old girl still had fight left in her.

"Rachel!"

Gillian hung her barn coat on a nail in the mudroom and moved on into the living room. Dumbstruck, she stopped in the middle of it. Magazines were piled neatly in the magazine rack. The slip covers on the baggy armchairs and the saggy Lazyboy were straight and wrinkle-free, the throw pillows were neatly arranged. But wait, there was more.

Fireplace ash and cold cinders had been swept up. Gillian had forgotten about the beautiful tile work set into the hearth. As a little girl she had been fascinated by the intricate pattern. Down on her hands and knees she would trace the designs with her fingertips and wonder about all the people through all the years who had sat in front of that fire on cold winter nights.

The afghan her mother made when Gillian was in grade school was perfectly draped along the back of the couch and some picture books of Maine Gillian had forgotten the family owned were arranged on the scarred coffee table. And there were flowers. Gillian touched them tentatively— fresh flowers—in the vase that for the two years Gillian had been home had held a decrepit bunch of artificial holiday greens. Hey, they were in season at least once a year.

And the place smelled good. Not that it had stunk before, but now it smelled . . . *fresh.* No wonder, with every freak-

ing window in the joint wide open. Gillian carefully removed the stick that propped the nearest sash up and eased
down the window. It froze in its track. She jiggled it and it
crashed down like a guillotine. She counted her fingers.

She glanced into the front parlor. More sparkle. More
shine. The matte finish appeared to have been removed from
everything. A drone from upstairs told her why Rachel had
not heard her named called. The vacuum. Bless Rachel, she
must have bought new bags for the little monster.

At the upstairs landing, Gillian took a left, following the
sucking sound. Then, *Thar she blew*: Rachel.

Her sister had her back to Gillian and she was leading the
aged Electrolux through an involved dance step. The musical accompaniment was supplied by a digital recorder no
bigger than a pack of gum hanging from the waist band of
an expensive looking, velour pair of sweatpants.

Why anyone would waste that kind of money on sweats
was beyond her, was Gillian's first thought. Then, what *was*
that thing playing the music? She'd seen them advertised but
the details escaped her. But the capper was the lacy, racy bra
Rachel was wearing. Gillian had a bad angle on the thing
but it seemed to have more internal supports than your average gambrel roof. You had to laugh.

Blond hair bouncing in a ponytail. The harem pants. Bare
midriff and dance antics. Barbara Eden, hang onto your fez.

Gillian tapped her sister on the shoulder. Rachel screamed,
dropped the vacuum and spun around.

"Jeesum Crow—Gillian?" She shook herself like a wet
dog. "What the hell is *wrong* with you? You scared the shit
out of me."

"Oops."

Rachel shut the vacuum off and wiped a strand of hair out
of her face with the back of a hand. "*Oops?* That's it? No
'Sorry'?"

"Sorry. But why? What do you care what the house looks
like anyway? You're not staying here."

"*Au contraire*, I am. You were right about Meggie's place.

Not going to work long term. With Dad and the kids? No way."

"Really . . ." Gillian wasn't quite sure how she felt about the idea of her sister living here with her even though she had championed the idea in the first place. And what was this "long term" all about?

"Well, that's great," Gillian said, finally. They'd make it work.

"Too long a pause there," Rachel noted.

Caught. "No really, it's fine. It'll be good. We can catch up." Gillian stuffed her hands in her front pockets. "Oh, and thanks, Rach. The place looks great. It hasn't looked this good since Ma—"

"Stop." Rachel held up a restraining hand and reached down for the vacuum. She ratcheted the handle to the vertical position. Gillian spotted the wet shine in her sister's eyes.

Gillian felt her own throat threaten to clog. She cleared it. "Right. Another day."

Rachel bit her lip and coiled the power cord onto the back of the machine. "Right."

"Anyway," Gillian said, "I've got me a plan."

"Plans? I like plans. Do tell." Rachel sounded perkier. She parked the vacuum in a corner of the hall.

Gillian told. "Jack Turner."

"Yes . . ." Rachel drew the word out as she slid the tie on her ponytail from her hair.

"I'm going to check him out."

"Thought you already did *that* in the saw shed." Rachel flashed a smart ass smile as she edged past Gillian in the narrow hall and went into the bathroom. Gillian followed her.

"I gotta jump in the shower," Rachel said, shutting the door on her sister. Then, from behind the closed door, Rachel said, "Gilly, honey, run around and close all the windows for Mommy, won't you? We don't want her to catch a chill."

Gillian knew when she was being ditched. "Right before her big date, huh?" she said to a panel on the door.

"How did you know?"

"The housecleaning? The thought being you and Riley might end up back here afterward? What's the plan? Hang something on the doorknob as a signal to me not to come barging in?"

"Ha ha."

Gillian heard the taps of the tub squeak. Pipes rapped. Water gushed. She used the time to run around and shut all the windows. Grab a snack. Sit for a moment in the living room, munching and taking in the new and improved Wilcox Box. With all Rachel's work, it had become a pleasant house to spend time in. She even shut her eyes for a quick cat nap. Eventually, she heard the drain upstairs gurgle and a hairdryer start up.

She went back upstairs and knocked on the bathroom door.

"Entrez."

Rachel was wrapped in a huge, white, fluffy bath towel and she was rummaging through the medicine cabinet. Gillian was amazed at the sheer amount of beauty products Rachel had managed to cram into the tiny space.

"Looks like you've moved in the important pieces already, huh?" Gillian said.

"Shut it." Rachel spritzed something from a spray bottle onto her hair and Gillian watched her work it in. Then the brush work started. Gillian found herself mesmerized by the process. It was amazing to watch a whole human face being built from the neck up.

After fifty brush strokes—Gillian had been counting—Rachel said, "It's funny you said 'check out Jack Turner' because I was thinking about him in the tub."

"Do I want to know in what way?"

"I'm trying to help, here, so don't be a jerk. I was also thinking about Dad. You know, his so-called accident?"

"So-called?"

"Yeah. Don't you think it's funny that he was hurt right after he turned down the offers that we now know were from Jack?"

Hmm. Funny would not be the word. Gillian had never thought about it in that way before. With a timeline attached. She had been so busy getting her feet under her when she first arrived back in Rocky Falls. What with getting the mill back up and running and filling the built-up back orders for the customers who had been good enough to wait on their stock until the situation with her dad got straightened out. On and on and on. She'd been working like a chicken with its head cut off. Leaving precious little time for reflection, let alone some days making it to the bathroom.

"Dad's accident was just a coincidence, Rachel."

"What makes you so sure?"

Another fifty brush strokes. Gillian watched, counted, and mulled.

"This conversation is making me incredibly uncomfortable," she said finally. The thought of someone deliberately trying to hurt her dad made her crazy.

"Creepy, huh? But take it to the next level and see where that gets you."

Face cream in a fancy tube came next. Gillian watched her sister rub it in using ritualistic circular motions. Forty swirls on each cheek. Fascinating. Then, delicate horizontal swipes under each eye. There were twelve of those.

With a sickening wrench in her stomach, Gillian realized she might have shared—no, *bought*—coffee for the man who could have been responsible for—

"Shit!" She slammed the meaty part of her fist into the bathroom door. The sweats Rachel had hung on the hooks on the back of the door fell and pooled on the floor. The mirror attached to the back side of the door rattled in its frame and threatened to shatter.

Rachel jumped.

"Shit, *nothing*, Gillian. Don't fucking do that, okay? I could have lost an eye." Her sister stepped back from the mirror and blinked frenetically, mouth open, mascara brush forgotten in her hand. "Shit. Right *in* my eye. I *hate* it when that shit gets in your eye."

"I wouldn't know." Which was almost true. Gillian could count on one hand the number of times she'd bothered to wear makeup. She paced the tiny bathroom, feeling like a caged, helpless animal. If Jack was somehow tied into what happened to her dad . . . "Arrgh!" And for what happened to her in the damn loader not two days ago. Going after the heir apparent, was he? But no, that was absurd. Jack responsible for all that? Gillian thought about him on the roof with the kid who almost bought it out at Riley's McMansion job. Thought about Jack and her almost . . .

Besides, why play stupid pranks like nailing doors shut then suddenly escalate to full-blown sabotage? It didn't make sense. Still . . .

"Calm down, Sweetie," Rachel said. She leaned forward into the mirror on a damage-control mission. "We don't know anything about anybody yet. All we got is speculation. Don't get your panties all in a—" she abruptly turned to face Gillian, a hand to her heart.

"Yes?"

"I just had a horrible thought."

Gillian tensed, ready for action. *Tell me.* She was ready. Ready to tear Jack Turner apart with her bare hands. *Just tell me who it was.* Snap his neck, throw him into the chipper, no one the wiser. She was a pit bull and he was—

"You do . . . wear panties, don't you?" her sister asked.

Gillian stared at her.

"I mean, Sweetie, some women prefer the comfort of commando," Rachel said. "But with all the sweating and groaning you do down at the mill—" she snickered. "I mean, in your *job* there—I'd think you'd want something absorbent under all that—What? Why are you staring at me?"

"Sometimes I am amazed that you and I share a common gene pool. And yes. I wear underwear."

Most days. Like it made a difference. With the exception

of that really weird thing with Jack Turner in the saw shed, she wasn't about to get lucky in Rocky Falls anytime soon. Nobody in town cared how she looked, least of all she. Lumping lumber all day made a mess out of your hair and your skin. Your hands turned into little crocodile feet. She itched a dry spot on the back of one.

Working in a city, in an office was different. In Augusta, when she'd slaved away at the state planning office, there were people around. There were in Rocky Falls too, of course, but in an office you had to smell at least as good as the people around you. On a construction site surrounded by dozens of guys it was a good thing *not* to smell too good or you'd never get any piece. *Peace*, she meant.

Stupid. What did it matter. Underwear. Her dad had maybe been set up and they were talking about underwear. It was a ploy on her sister's part, Gillian knew, to distract her. To derail her notoriously overactive imagination. Otherwise, Rachel knew she'd crank out one horrible scenario after another, each starring her dad, a once hale and hearty guy who now seemed all too vulnerable. Gillian found herself admitting she would have killed to protect him if she'd had the opportunity. She wondered if she could do it retroactively if there *had* in fact been foul play and she discovered the culprit. She paced some more while Rachel finished her eyes.

Rachel exhaled and clicked the mascara brush back into its tube. "How you doing?"

"Oh, you know, fighting to maintain control. The usual."

"No shit, huh? You take up all the available air when you're pissed." Rachel blotted her lashes with a tissue. "Don't go there, now, Gillian," she said. "You'll just tear yourself up for nothing. Chances are Dad's accident was just that. An accident."

Gillian stopped herself from mentioning the loader issue she had had. No sense worrying Rachel. Instead, she'd do the angry act for both of them. "I can't be as frigging calm as you when it's Dad we're talking about here. When some fucking worm might have . . ." It really was unspeakable.

Rachel put a restraining hand on her sister's arm and pinned Gillian with her eyes. "I am not calm about this, Gilly, believe me. If anybody did anything to Dad, I'll cut their heart out with a plastic knife."

Despite her heated anger, a shiver went through Gillian. Her baby sister was applying makeup with surgical precision while simultaneously mulling over the methods she would use to disembowel the opposition. Rachel would be a terrific albeit unexpected ally.

Gillian found great relief in that. Not to be alone with this . . . *situation* she'd inherited. The mill, her dad's fragile state, the people depending on her for their livelihood. Sometimes it all got to be too much.

"Are you crying?" Rachel asked her.

"No." Gillian wiped half-formed tears out of her eyes and sniffled.

"It's not just you," Rachel said, draping her free arm around Gillian's shoulders and letting it rest there for a moment.

"'Not just me,' what?"

Rachel made her voice deep. "Standing four-square in the breech, defending the fort against all comers, Yadda, yadda. You know, all that crap we learned in history class." She went back to work on her lashes. "Nobody treads on me either, baby."

"I think that's New Hampshire's motto."

"Whatever."

"I guess it's guilt, you know?" Gillian said. "For cutting out on Dad after Mom died? For not being here when Ma was sick. Leaving Dad in the lurch with it all."

Rachel snorted. "How were *you* gonna help *him*, huh? Tell me that. The original old man of the mountains, he is. But yeah, I know how you feel." Rachel batted her freshly minted eyes. "But you and Dad are two of a kind. Neither one of you is about to ask anyone for help."

"True."

"And Ma and Dad—and don't forget Meg, too—didn't have to keep Ma's being sick such a big secret," Rachel said. "Sure, Meggie took the brunt of everything being back here, but don't tell me a little part of her doesn't get off on being nailed up on that cross."

"She is a teacher, after all."

They both laughed at that.

"So see?" Rachel said, rummaging through the medicine cabinet. "Ah. There's the little bugger." She twisted the shiny lipstick tube and considered the color. "We got a plan. We find out who is *really* the dirty bird in all this shit going on then we kick some serious ass." Rachel hung a fist in the air, knuckles out. Gillian rapped it with hers.

"Some Jackass, maybe," Gillian said.

"Back at ya, Sista." Rachel leaned into the mirror and traced her lips with color. Finished, she kissed herself in the glass, smacking them loudly. "Gorgeous. But there's one thing I still don't get though," she said.

"Which is?"

Rachel held the lipstick tube erect in front of her and cranked the color stick in and out suggestively. "Why they make these things to look like little—" she leaned in and whispered into Gillian's ear.

Gillian laughed. "You are *so* strange. Do you know that?"

"Yep." Rachel laughed.

"Okay, better now," Gillian said, because she really was. Two sisters together in the alley, back to back, switch blades flashing at a common threat. It felt good. "You really have learned a thing or two since you left here," she said to Rachel.

"I know. Shame *you* haven't huh?"

"Screw you."

"Jealous?"

Gillian yanked down her sister's towel and ran.

Chapter 19

    Gillian woke up to the television blaring. Just the way it had been before she fell asleep. She clicked the volume down a few notches. Was the mill making her as deaf as her dad?

    She shook her head groggily. Another long couple of days at the yard. Made lots and lots of donuts. Overtired equals weird dreams. Before she'd drifted off, she'd been mulling over the Jack-as-saboteur angle and it just didn't feel right. Maybe somebody out there was fucking around with things, but it wasn't him. He was direct. Bore you to death, wear you down, argue incessantly. All right to your face, unfortunately. What you saw was what you got.

    It had been a warm summer day in her strange dream and she was downtown, riding in a parade, perched up high on a flower-covered float. People were cheering as she was borne majestically past them. She was wearing a medieval dress with one of those pointy-cone, flowing veil things on her head. Riley was jumping up and down at the curb, waving to get her attention. *As usual.* Pre-Rachel, anyway. She and Riley hadn't had a good go round for days. Part of her missed him, she hated to admit.

    Suddenly, the sun clouded over in the dream and the heavens opened up. People held parade programs over their heads, grabbed their kids by the hand, and ran for cover. The float stopped moving and she was alone in the street. A man with dark hair was walking slowly toward her. He was wearing a bright yellow cape and some kind of helmet with a silver-winged creature atop it. In spite of the rain soaking everything around her and running down her face in rivulets, he was completely dry.

When he got close to the front of the float, he reached his hand up to her, beckoning her to come to him. She shook her head and drew back. He let his hand drop.

Still looking at her, he reached down and picked up the front of the float in one hand. He started walking slowly backward, dragging the float with him. He was headed down Main Street toward the Mohasset. They got close enough for her to see the cold wind whipping up whitecaps on the river. He was going to pull her in . . .

She had woken up in a sweat, she realized, flapping her arms. Great. Awake at . . . she squinted across the living room at the Mickey Mouse clock on the kitchen wall—two thirty-six A.M. Tomorrow was Wednesday, for some reason often the busiest day of the week at the yard. She needed to settle down and get some shuteye but fast. She re-arranged herself on the couch, too lazy to move upstairs to her own bed.

Her sore shoulder still bugged her. She turned onto her other side. Shut her eyes. Wished she could place a personal call to Lindsay Wagner to come and adjust the Sleep Number of the bumpy couch.

The minutes ticked by. She was still hot and sweaty. She rolled off the couch and raised the slatted blinds in the window. Half moon up there. Got back onto the couch and sat hugging her knees, staring at the reflective black square of the darkness outside. Counted sheep. They all had dark, curly wool. Enough.

Get up, girl, there's no going back. To sleep, anyway. She pulled on sweats, stumbled into the kitchen, lit the burner ring with a match, boiled water, made some tea. Three A.M. now, on the stove clock. The time in the twenty-four-hour cycle that scientists claim the human body was closest to death. Tomorrow around noon she'd probably be all the way there if she didn't get some rest PDQ, but she couldn't wind down. The dream had rattled her.

She carried the tea out to the back porch and contemplated the luminous crescent hanging overhead. Just enough light for a stroll. *Careful, Gilly, a woman alone at night?* she heard her mother caution. Maybe not in Augusta, Ma, but around Rocky Falls? *P'shaw.*

She headed for the river, the moonlight faintly illuminating the path. Past the piles of stock outside the gate, then duck under the single-bar gate. God Bless Rocky Falls, she thought for perhaps the millionth time in her life. It *was* a nice place, where a woman could walk around at three in the morning and not be worried about—*clink*—a noise in the night.

Gillian ducked into the shadow of the office.

Clink. There it was again. A metal on metal strike. Soft, but purposeful. Then an equally quiet curse.

Gillian crouched down and moved slowly forward using the shadows of the office as cover. When she reached the end of the building, she hunkered down on one knee and peered around the corner. She froze, listening, allowing her eyes to adjust to the dim light in the yard.

There. By the dead loader. Movement. *Clink.* And a flash of light.

She needed a better angle. She retreated and worked her way around the opposite side of the small office building. On the way, her foot connected with a short length of reinforcing bar rusting away in the weeds along the building. She soundlessly fished it out and hefted it experimentally. Nice swing. Rust and a textured surface made for a good grip. But it would kill someone. Whoever was presently screwing with the loader, to be specific.

She set the bar down and moved on. Another flash of light, then another curse and the light flickered out. She bolted across an exposed section of yard and into the finish

pine shed. Rummaged in silence through a collection of
precut moldings. Selected a length of closet pole with the
same quiet care Babe Ruth, down by two runs in the ninth
inning, might have chosen a Louisville Slugger.

Practice swing. Perfect. A stunner, not a killer. *Batter
up . . .*

Sneak to the head of the shed. Look out. Still there, the
bastard. All alone. Unsuspecting. Idiot. The machine was
already fucked up. Didn't he realize that? What was this guy
thinking? She stared into the blackness, willing her pupils
to open wider. Yep, a guy, from the set of his shoulders. She
clutched the length of closet pole. Feel the power. Rachel's
plastic knife be damned, older sister would take care of
her own.

Careful, Gilly.

Right, Ma, but this one's for Dad. This is probably the guy
that set up Dad's accident. Mine too, maybe.

Good time to call for backup, her mother's voice said in
her head. She had been a fan of police shows. *No doubt,*
Gilly replied. Get one—or several—of the friendly men in
blue down here. Arrest the bad guy. She wouldn't have to
get involved. On the other hand, she was mightily pissed.
Which never made for the clearest thinking.

She desperately wanted one good swing, she realized.
Was that too much to ask? Stun the bastard, maybe knock
him out, maybe not. If yes, *then* call the cops. If no, run like
hell. The bastard would be groggy, in no shape to give
chase. She thought of her dad and his cane. Her blood
boiled. Serve the fucker out there right.

Let's do this, Ma. Geronimo!

A dozen quick steps to the loader. The guy was completely oblivious to her approach. The engine covers on both
sides of the loader were raised and the bastard was crouched
over one of the front forks.

An awkward angle. Tough to get a good swing in with the
cab right there. Easy to fix. Set her feet, right toe pointed

at first base, bat back and off her shoulder, eye on the skull, just like Charlie had coached her in high school softball.

"Hey, you!" she yelled. The skull turned. She swung. The skull jerked back and disappeared beneath the fork. Her Rocky Falls slugger connected with the solid steel fork and shattered into bark mulch.

Okay, maybe now she had a problem. She turned to run. Just like in a horror movie—just like in her dream, in fact—a hand reached out and grabbed her ankle. She stumbled to her knees, face planted. The hand was dragging her backward. She kicked, screamed, clawed at the earth, to no avail. The hand was dragging her under the machine.

"What is fucking wrong with you?" a voice asked.

A somewhat familiar voice, she had to admit. Nice to know that the person who was about to kill you was at least a passing acquaintance.

"Let me go, you fucker!" That was her.

"Not until you calm down." That was him. Yes, definitely a him. A her maybe she could have overpowered.

Boo howled somewhere in the distance.

"Good boy! Over here!" she yelled.

An answering bark. In seconds Gillian heard the jingle of dog tags. Saved. Her sweet Boo, thank God, come to rescue her. "Boo! Boo! Here!"

In the dim moonlight, Boo shot toward her. Shinnied under the loader on his belly. "Boo! Sic 'em!" Gillian cried. Shinnied right past her. She ended up saying it to his spastically waggling doggy behind. What the—? Her hand connected with a cool metal tube. Flashlight. She aimed and clicked it on.

Boo was licking Jack's face.

"Bad dog, Boo," Gillian scolded.

Boo paused in his ecstatic lapping. He curled his lip.

At her. At the one who fed him, made him disgusting gravy, wrapped his heart worm pills in sliced roast beef. He rumbled a not-very-friendly sound deep in his chest.

" 'Grrrrrrr' to you too, ass," she said. She kicked free of

Jack's hold on her ankle and scrambled out from under the loader. All males were pigs. She looked around for another weapon, then paused. Jack's tools were spread around the area with surgical precision. A neatly laid out row of box wrenches. A cluster of deep sockets and a couple of big ratchet handles. The boy must eat his carrots to be doing close work by moonlight. Confused, now. Stop. Think. What work? What the hell was he up to?

She swatted open handed at a dark head emerging from the gloom beneath the loader. It was Jack's head, not the other dirty dog's.

"Ow," he said.

"Shut up," she said.

Boo, unseen, still crouched beneath the loader, growled again. "You too, you traitor." He whinnied. *Baby*.

Neatly laid out tools. "What in the name of God are you up to, Jack? Screwing with the machine? Messing it up again so this time I get it for good? Charlie down, me down, the mill goes under?" She danced around in a little circle like the guys she'd seen on Fight TV. They were always good for a quick little fantasy, stripped down in the ring, before the punching and the blood started. Could she really have hit Jack with the closet pole? Yes.

She barked, "Then, when the last Wilcox is belly up, Jack Turner swoops in and scoops up all the chips on the table, right? A swoop and scoop, right? That's what you had planned?" Swoop and scoop. She watched too many cop shows. "Come on. Give." She realized she was bouncing on her toes. Fight or flight.

"Look, I—" Jack reached for her.

"Don't touch me," she said to him, taking a step back. She stopped at scrunching up her fists. That would look incredibly stupid. But that was how she felt inside. Ah, to be one of those Fight guys. A lot of life's problems just disappeared when you owned a good roundhouse kick. "Just—" *Argh*, the frustration of it all. She looked at the tools again— "Explain."

"This loader is a piece of shit. Do you know that?"

"I just had it fully serviced."

"Bullshit."

Jack turned his head toward the loader but kept one eye on her, Gillian noticed. *Coward.*

"Let's try this again, shall we?" he said. "I'm betting you just told the guy to get it running again, right?"

"Well . . . yes. That's all I—" She was about to say *could afford*, but then amended it to "Needed." Her tenuous financial situation was none of his business.

"The thing's a death trap, Gillian. Look." He pulled a long slim length of something from the seat. "See that?" She shone the flashlight where he was pointing. In the light she noticed the gash in his head was looking much better. Almost totally healed over. The dark hair was fast resodding the area she'd shaved.

"Corrosion," he said. He reached down for a screwdriver and with a grunt, pushed the flat blade right through the metal conduit. "Most of the line are like this."

Wow. That she didn't realize. "But the paint on them still looks okay."

"Doesn't matter. They're disintegrating from the inside out. You'd never know just by looking at them." He pointed. "I swapped most of those out. They were the worst of the bunch."

She ran the flashlight beam over the forks. A few of the new hydraulic lines were a slightly different color than the rest. Not enough of a difference to notice if you weren't looking for it.

"You . . . swapped them out?"

"Yes. Removed them? Replaced them?" He spoke slowly and gestured exaggeratedly with his hands.

Like she was an idiot. Which evidently she was.

"Why . . . ?" was the best she could do.

"Buddy told me the whole story about you almost buying it in this thing the other day."

Buddy. Right. "So you thought . . . ?" She realized she had stopped breathing.

"And I was . . . concerned."

And you jumped in to save me . . .

He was speaking to her, she realized. "What?"

"I said 'And I knew you wouldn't do anything about it.'"

"But I did."

"Temporarily. Until the next time this thing decided to try and kill somebody."

She narrowed her eyes. "How do you know so much about hydraulics?"

"I just do. Now, here's an idea: How about I come back in the daylight to finish this and you don't try to kill me?"

She laughed, embarrassed finally. Boo shinnied out from under the loader and came and sat on his haunches next to her, she feeling his warmth, but he looking off into the dark woods as if he could have sat anywhere really, but her legs were the closest available thing to lean against. She scratched between his ears. He tentatively lapped her fingers.

"Okay," she said. "You fix, but I pay. Cash. Not what I'd pay the service guy, but then again you're not deductible." They agreed on a figure.

Because, really, how long could you keep fighting, swimming upstream in the Mohasset? The river wins. Eventually and all the time. It was exhausting, the fighting. She'd let herself drift for a while, let the current take her, gather her strength. She held the flashlight to make it easier for Jack to assemble his tools and repack them in his tool box. He kept a weather eye on her the whole time.

That told her that the river hadn't completely won this evening. She'd cast at least a little doubt over the raging waters. *In not all seasons are you invincible,* she said to him in the depths of her mind. Head waters dry up, a tumble turns to a trickle. In the heat of summer people wade to islands which in spring time were your impenetrable fortresses. People picnicked on your territory, cavorting on your granite formations, celebrating your vulnerability. She watched

Jack casually heft his heavy tool caddy. But the smart ones never entirely forgot your power.

She laughed to herself. Must be the moon bringing out her Muse. In its silver light, they walked back to The Box together. Boo ran back and forth between them and the black woods, sniffing, tracking, delighted to be out and about at this unusual hour. The glow of the moon cast deep shadows across the dips and washouts on the rutted gravel road, making them appear to be black and bottomless. Gillian and Jack carefully skirted the dark pools, keeping to the lit edges of the track.

Jack had stashed his pickup off to the side of Route 101 on a slight downward incline a short distance from the Wilcox driveway. He slid his tool box into the bed of the truck and strapped it in tight to the rear wall of the cab. Gillian handed him the flashlight. He grasped the other end of it and they stood still there for a moment like two relay racers handing off the baton.

"Well, I gotta go," she said at last.

"Right. Riley'll be riding my ass in like—" he checked his watch— "Two hours? Holy shit, I'll never get up."

"I'll give you a wake up call at the inn."

Jack's face lit up. "Really?"

No wonder him and Boo got along so well. "No," she said.

"Good night, then."

"You too," she said. "Boo, heel." She snapped her fingers. Boo whined, but came to her and sat at her feet.

Jack climbed into the pickup, let it roll forward for a dozen feet, then popped the clutch. With a lurch and a bang the engine caught. "Starter," he yelled. He waved once and drove off toward town.

She watched the pickup grow smaller and smaller in the distance. It was somehow nice to know that not everything in old Jack's tidy little world was entirely squared away.

Chapter 20

Friday night, Gillian was minding her own business and watching *CSI* reruns when the phone rang. It was Jack. Her heart did a little somersault without even stopping to ask her permission. "Who is this?" she asked.

"Guess."

"Oh, hey, Riley. How are ya, Sweetie? You callin' for that good time I been promising you?"

"Ha, ha. Come get your dog."

Boo? No, he was right—She sleepily patted the couch beside her.

Okay, so he *hadn't* come back from his 9 o'clock whiz. She keyed the remote to get the time. 10:38 P.M. And she hadn't the foggiest idea where her child was. Reason Number 27 the State of Maine would undoubtedly take her future offspring away from her. She had really conked out. Again. Working too hard. Playing too little.

"Set the place on fire, Riley, I tell you. M-m-*mmm*," her mouth said to Jack, needing fun.

"He misses you."

"Who? Riley?" Startled, she sat up, completely awake now.

"No, you idiot, your dog. Say hello to Mommy." Woofs and flaps and sneezes fell out of the receiver.

"What the hell is he doing over there?"

"I don't know. Maybe he drove himself over. He's your dog. You're supposed to be watching him."

The little bugger must have hoofed it into town to visit with the new love of his life. "Better use a wet nap on that phone," she said.

"He's not staying over. Come and get him. He smells."

"Now?" She brushed the hair back from her face and sniffed herself. She didn't, fortunately. "It's late." She breathed into her hand. *Much.*

"And I'm up watching an educational channel with your stupid dog. Arthur and Lynette have hit the sack. I'll leave the front door open."

"And the light on."

"What?"

"Motel Six?"

"Come soon," he said, and hung up.

Educational channel, her ass. He probably had the porn network on and a stack of quarters next to the vibrating bed. Arthur and Lynette did in fact have one room that featured a vibrating bed. Lynette claimed she used it occasionally for her arthritis if the room wasn't rented out. Gillian hadn't wanted to know the details.

She brushed her teeth on the off chance it was *the* room.

She locked the front door of the Eagle Inn after her. She was halfway up the stairs when one of the treads let out a horrendous creak. A door opened. Light from within the room shone on the wall of the second floor hall. Gillian cringed. Running into Lynette or worse, Arthur in—good-*gawd*, his drawers—no, wait. It wasn't Arthur up there at the head of the stairs. It was Jack. He was wearing shorts and a T-shirt, not underwear. Maybe a good thing, maybe not.

"*Sssh!*" he said. From behind him Gillian heard a familiar snort. A dark shape brushed Jack's leg. Her traitorous dog defending his erstwhile master. "Look, it's Mommy," Jack said.

Boo took the steps to Gillian in two quick bounds and threw his front paws up on her shoulder. He licked her face like he hadn't seen her for years. As if it were covered in that disgusting, just-add-water "gravy" that he'd kill to get just one more slurp of. Tail thumping the wall, toenails fighting for a hold on the thin stair runner, dog woofies flying everywhere. The royal treatment.

Gillian sighed with relief. He still loved her. She scratched him behind the ears and made shushing noises.

Jack waved her up. "Come on up. But be quiet."

"Wasn't me that let the dog out," she muttered. She followed Boo up the stairs. *Just for a minute.*

Jack pushed wide the door to his room. Although the space was dark, illuminated solely by the light from the TV, Gillian realized it was *the* room. There was the coin box mounted on the wall right next to the bed. Boo followed her inside and hopped up on the couch. He circled twice, then settled himself with a satisfied grunt into a Boo-sized depression in the cushions.

"He seems right at home," Gillian said. Would that she were so lucky. She couldn't decide what to do with her hands. She tried crossing them in front of her, but that made her feel like an FBI guy guarding the president's suite. She crossed them behind her back. No good. She felt ten years old. She finally parked herself next to Boo on the couch and patted him distractedly. She looked up to find Jack looking at her like he was surprised to discover her in his room. If he really was, that would make two of them.

"We were watching sci-fi," he said, gesturing at the muted television. "Boo seems to like it."

"Unh huh, sci-fi. Very educational."

"It is if you have the right perspective. Popcorn?" He held out the dregs of a microwaved bag. Gillian peered suspiciously inside and shook her head. On the television screen people in cheesy space suits milled around an unconvincing rendition of a caterpillar-treaded planet crawler. It was either heavily battle damaged or the people were crappy drivers.

"Take this scene, for instance," Jack said. He squeezed himself onto the couch on the other side of Boo. "Move, you," he said. Boo whimpered and gave up maybe half an inch of cushion. On television, one of the space suits gestured officiously at the beat-up vehicle and two other planeteers gathered around to inspect what looked to be a blast hole in its side.

Jack made a scratchy noise in his throat and said in an artificially deep voice, "You there, check out the hole in that painted plywood, over." *Scratch*.

One of the suits bent down for a closer look. "Looks serious, sir," Jack said, in a lighter tone. *Scratch*. "But we could fix it with orientated strand board if this planet had a Home Depot."

Gillian snickered. Pretty funny, actually.

And he wasn't done. "Send out a search party right away." *Scratch*. "Aye, aye, sir." One of the suits on screen saluted. "And sailor, pick up some sheetrock screws and some spray paint while you're at it." *Scratch*.

Boo howled. Gillian grabbed him around the muzzle. "Shut up, you idiot! You wanna get us kicked out?" She shook his head gently to emphasize each word. When she let go, his head was still shaking.

Jack laughed. He patted Boo. "Be down tomorrow for the rest of the fix on the loader," he said.

They had already discussed this two nights ago in the yard. By moonlight. "Good," Gillian said.

"Right," Jack said. "Tomorrow, Saturday."

"Right," Gillian said. 'Tomorrow' was Saturday in her world as well.

"Buddy?" Jack said, after a moment.

"Yes?" So they were back to "buddy" now, were they? She felt foolish suddenly. Now he would be asking her to leave.

Hit the road. *Lots of work in the morning, beauty sleep,* blah, blah, blah. Politely, but still, go.

"Would he be a 'kickball' buddy?"

"What?"

"I mean, an old friend?"

"Buddy!" She got it now. "Yeah, he and me go way back, yeah." Gillian brushed Boo's shaggy eyebrows flat. He gurgled contentedly deep in his throat.

"Not like you and me, huh?" Jack said.

"Not like."

They silently watched the silent action on-screen. Gillian watched a pulse point in her wrist flutter as she stroked Boo. A large, hairy creature lumbered slowly from behind some giant Styrofoam boulders with several of his . . . hands, Gillian supposed you could call them, raised. *I come in peace,* she'd bet he said on screen. His ass was toast, she predicted. One of the silver suits blasted him with a cheesy-looking ray gun. The creature charged the wounded ship. Idiot monster. No one ever believed that old line.

"I went a little nuts when I heard about your loader . . . incident," Jack said, the random flashes of light from the television illuminating his face.

"So I heard."

"From?"

"Buddy," she said.

"Ah. Back to him."

"So it seems."

Jack smiled. "I don't want to talk about Buddy anymore."

"And I don't want to be one," Gillian heard her traitorous mouth say.

Just like that they met across Boo's shaggy back and snaked their arms around each other. Gillian found her hand behind Jack's head, his behind hers. Boo sneezed and discontentedly wormed his way out from between the two humans who were suddenly way too close together for his taste. He slinked into a corner and curled up with his tail across his eyes.

"He's jealous," Jack said, sucking on Gillian's lower lip.

Breathless, Gillian squeezed out, "Of who?" She tugged Jack's T-shirt up and ran her hands across his chest.

"Me." Jack slid his hands under her shirt and unsnapped her bra. "Me."

"That is so wrong."

"Yeah," Jack drawled. "How's this?" He teased her nipples. Gillian gasped.

"So right?" Jack ventured.

"Shut up. Use your mouth for something else, would you?" She stripped off her shirt and pushed his head down to her chest.

He lapped and licked and sucked Gillian until she thought she was probably about as hot as the Great Fire of 1903. He unsnapped her jeans and busied himself proving how good he could be with his hands. Tradesmen were just *the* best. It finally dawned on her that he was humming. Distractedly, off key.

"Hey, Sleepy," she said. "Or is it Dopey? Or Doc?"

He didn't answer, so absorbed in his work was he. She groaned. "You off to work in the mines or something? We don't need—" *Ssss* . . . Yikes. He'd hit the bull's-eye with his fingers—"a musical score already."

"I'm composing a symphony to the Forest Queen," he mumbled. "I'm happy."

Her jeans slid down her legs and out of the corner of her eye she caught her underwear flying through the air.

"And when I'm happy . . ." His mouth found her. The room spun.

". . . I hum, Your Majesty."

The man had a rich fantasy life, but his musical talent, as off-key as it might have been, went right to her head. Blood rushed. The room whirled around her. He was a good minstrel. She grabbed his hair and hung on. Buzzing, buzzing, buzzing, busy as a bee he was. Stung her three times. Right in a row.

Now pray God she wasn't allergic.

Chapter 21

Gillian heard the airplane before she saw it. The distant drone gradually swelled to a deafening roar. A burst of sunlight reflected off polished aluminum and then a silver underbelly filled the patch of sky framed by the towering pines which grew along the river. She waved, her excitement taking over, knowing full well the pilot of the aircraft would never be able to pick out a solitary figure waiting in the dense undergrowth along this stretch of the Mohassset.

She checked her watch. Eleven o'clock on the dot. Sarah was right on time. Definitely a sea change for her friend who had made it to *maybe* half her morning classes on time when she and Gillian had roomed together in college. Gillian supposed she too had grown up a lot since those days. Running a business, meeting payroll. By the skin of her teeth some weeks, but still, meeting it. People depended on her for their livelihood. Scary when you thought about it.

Which she didn't want to, right then, because today was about escape. Taking off—literally—from Rocky Falls. Leaving her cares behind.

Today was about exploration, too. Exploration of a whole new future. For Rocky Falls. For her. For her and Jack, maybe. Memories of their time together in his room at the Eagle House warmed her as she stripped down to her swim suit. God, there weren't enough quarters in the Philadelphia mint . . .

After that, they'd stayed up all night, watched the sun rise. Talked about Boo and building. Okay, geeky. Not very romantic. But enlightening. Jack had even taken Boo out for his first-thing-in-the-morning whiz. Then she'd whizzed Jack before heading back home. He'd come to the yard later in the day, fixed the loader. Then fixed her. Twice. Tsunamis could be good things.

Sunday—yesterday? yes, her head was still spinning—they'd gotten down to the real business. Climbed Haystack Mountain. Looked down at the sleepy town. Talked development. Sketched designs in the air and superimposed them on the sleepy town below. Aired her state planning office perspective: *Integrate and preserve.*

He laid out the business point of view: *Pump it up.* They circled each other like the beleaguered crew and the creature from the science fiction movie, but somehow managed to avoid blasting each other to smithereens. She was proud of them.

Them . . . How that little word tickled.

The float plane returned with a vengeance, lower in the sky now. An eardrum-splitting roar filled the channel of the Mohasset, its deepest at the point just in front of her. The surrounding trees and hills turned the noise back upon itself, intensifying it. It echoed down the valley.

Gillian was forced to halt her undressing, one foot in and one foot out of her hiking shorts, to cover her ears as the plane flashed past her on its landing run. The torrent of sound reached a crescendo, then abruptly died downstream. She pulled off her remaining clothes and stuffed them, her shoes, her wristwatch, and wallet into a waterproof dry sack that already contained a towel. She carefully mated the sealing edges of the bag, curled the top over the proscribed two times and used the velcro straps to cinch the whole package into a tight bundle.

Between a gap in the trees at the edge of the river, the nose of a taxiing twin-engine float plane came into view on the river. Gillian waved again, this time reasonably confident that her friend in the pilot's seat could see her. The engines briefly accelerated and a small curling wave formed under the benignly smiling, upswept bow of the plane. Sarah must have goosed the engines to keep Gertrude—that was the unlikely name of the plane—steady in the current. The Mohasset ran gently and deep at this point below the town, but she and Sarah, having laid out today's plan via cell phone earlier in the week, knew they had to coordinate their relative positions on the river to ensure that drifting swimmer and plane eventually met.

Gillian made her way to the river's edge and waved again. The window on the pilot's side of the cockpit slid open and a slim arm returned the greeting. Gillian tucked the waterproof sack under her arm and jumped off the river bank into the river. She clung to the bag for a moment waiting for the initial shock of cold water to wear off, then struck out for the middle of the river. She aimed for a spot upstream of the float plane, knowing the Mohasset, the surface of which appeared placid at this point, would nevertheless pull her inexorably downstream as she made the crossing.

Sarah goosed the engines briefly to keep the float plane in the channel of the river. Gillian pulled to within twenty-five yards of the plane and let the current do the rest. She drifted beneath the wide sheltering wing of the plane and reached for the grab handle just below the door set into the fuselage. The hatch hinged inward and a boarding ladder splashed into the water.

Gillian's friend popped her head out the open doorway. "Ah, how nice. You've got a suit on."

"Yeah, yeah. I thought about going buff, but old Gertie probably attracted a lot of attention coming in here. I didn't want to add to the show."

"Good call," Sarah said. She nodded toward the bank near where Gillian had entered the water.

Gillian, one foot on the bottom rung of the boarding ladder, turned to look. Two guys in orange accompanied by two adolescents similarly clothed and two avidly sniffing dogs were pointing excitedly at the plane.

"You would have made their day for sure," Sarah said, steadying the ladder.

"I've flashed enough ass around this river for one lifetime," Gillian reined in the floating dry bag and tossed it into the plane.

"Sounds like a story in there," Sarah said.

Gillian snickered. "Later." She climbed the ladder and hopped into the small cabin of the plane, ducking as she passed through the low doorway. "How have you been?" Gillian made to hug her friend then remembered she was soaking wet.

Sarah held her off, laughing. "I'm good. Everyone's good. The airfield's booming." She wrapped her fingers around Gillian's forearm. "And you're freezing. You brought clothes, yes?" She indicated the bag.

"Yep."

"Get dressed and come up front. I got to keep this baby in the middle of the river." Sarah squeezed herself between the two rows of seats and quickly made her way toward the front of the plane.

Although it was awkward moving around in the small cabin of the plane, Gillian managed to dry herself off and shimmy back into her clothes. Occasionally the engines would wind up in a brief burst of power, and Gillian had to brace herself against a high seat back. Minutes later, she traced Sarah's route forward into the cockpit.

"Whoa, pretty fancy," she said, her eyes taking in all the dials, switches, and levers. They were everywhere. Even on the ceiling.

"No more complicated than your average food processor," Sarah said. "Not that you'd know." She grinned, her eyes on the river. "Strap in."

Gillian boosted herself up into the vacant, high-backed chair on the right-hand side of the cockpit and after winning a wrestling match with the crisscrossing chest harness, announced she was ready for takeoff, captain. She was excited.

"Calm yourself," Sarah said, laughing. "You might be ready, but we're not. We got to get turned around and lined up. We clear of any traffic on your side?"

Gillian checked. No canoes, no kayaks, no Roman galleys. "Good here."

Sarah goosed the right-hand engine and Gertrude began to grudgingly rotate on her axis.

Exciting, exciting, exciting. Her friend had the life, traveling the country on assignments for a conservation journal. Flying herself to the gigs sometimes, fuel expenses a write-off no doubt. And she had what seemed like the world's best husband. "How's Logan?" Gillian asked.

"Grumpy. A pain in the ass. Too many hours at the field. He's got to get an operations manager to run the place day to day if he's going to keep his sanity, but of course, he's the *only* one in the world who can do it right." Sarah made a face. "But I'll keep him around. You?"

Gillian knew what her friend meant. "After two years of renewed badgering, it looks like there might be a change in the wind on the Riley front."

"Really?" Sarah briefly looked away from the river. "You and Riley?" Her eyes were sparkling.

"No. Him and someone else."

"Anyone I—"

"Yeah. Rachel."

"Really."

"Yes, really."

Sarah cut her eyes back to the river. "And you feel . . . how about this?"

"Fine. They were made for each other."

After some jockeying with the engine controls, Sarah asked, "Belts tight? The ride can get a little bumpy sometimes."

Gillian wondered if they were still talking about flying. "I'm good," she said.

"I hope so," Sarah said. "But follow the map, would you?"

She'd forgotten how bossy her friend could be. "Sarah, I can run my own life. I know where I'm going, thank you very much."

Sarah pointed to a mesh pocket on the cockpit wall near Gillian's right calf. It bulged with folded sectional maps.

"Oh."

"Just grab the first one for now. It'll get us out over Vermont."

Feeling the complete idiot, Gillian dutifully unfolded the map on her lap and smoothed it as best she could. It looked a lot like the ones she used when she hiked in the White Mountains except it was much more complicated. Lots of circles with radiating lines and degree markings overlaying the terrain features. Man-made landmarks were penciled in as well.

"When we get up to cruising altitude," Sarah said, "turn it whatever way you need to so it follows the course we're on. That way you can pick out the landmarks as we go."

"Okay. But what if the weather gets crappy and we can't see the ground."

"I filed a flight plan that included a route map for flying on instruments."

"Clever." Back in college, Sarah needed help getting to New Hampshire by car. She watched her friend jockey both throttles as the plane came out of its turn. "I never thought I'd figure that out," Sarah said. "Instruments, I mean. Logan had me under this hood—"

"Sounds kinky."

Sarah bumped both throttle levers forward simultaneously and Gertrude sprang forward. Gillian clutched a grab handle on the seat. "Okay, okay, I'm listening."

"Anyway," Sarah continued, "there I was flying around blind under this stupid hood. Can't see a freaking thing except the instruments in front of me, which is the whole point. After awhile, though, I just let go of worrying about where I thought the plane should be going. I just gave up and let the instruments tell me where to go. Everything worked out after that."

They were definitely not talking about flying anymore. "Weird, giving up control like that."

"Tell me about it." Sarah shot a quick glance Gillian's way. "But you should try it sometimes. It's very liberating."

Gillian forced her voice lower into an announcer's voice. "Yes, folks, we're back. And in this week's exciting show, Dr. Phil flies a float plane."

"Very funny." Sarah riveted her attention to the stretch of open river ahead and said, "Feet flat on the floor. Head back against the seat back." She reached over and gave an extra tug on Gillian's lap belt. "Airsickness bag's right there." She pointed to a pocket on the side of Gillian's seat.

"Hopefully I won't need that," Gillian said.

"You never know. Here we go."

Sarah fiddled with a few levers then shoved both throttles forward to the stops. At first, there was nothing but the roar. An all-consuming twin-engine cacophony of sound. The headphones Sarah had slipped on over her wet hair cut out much of the sound, but not all of it. Gillian heard her own breathing rasp in the ear cups.

Gertrude picked up speed, until the tree line on either side of the river became a blur. Moments later, all vibration ceased as she leapt into the air.

Gillian glanced down at the ground below. So far so good. No need for the barf bag. Below the plane was the footbridge where she and Jack had stopped to talk. Another family—if the one she and Jack had seen that day hadn't already taken up residence in "the best undiscovered little town in upstate Maine"—was out on the bridge. The kids were—what else?—throwing leaves into the river on one side of the walkway and running to the downstream side to see them flash past in the current.

A rumble from beneath the plane. Gillian's heart skipped a beat and Sarah calmly announced "Flaps up."

Gillian twisted in her seat. There was Wilcox Lumber, the yikes—scar—of the yard abutting the river. She had never seen it from this perspective. From the top of Haystack Mountain, yes, which gave you some idea of the layout, but never from directly above. Wilcox Lumber never had the ready cash to hire a pilot and photographer to do a fly over of their property and preserve the view in living color. Thank goodness, Gillian could now say.

It was embarrassing to see the lumber operation with all its warts revealed. Moldering piles of lumber she had never gotten to and had since become infested with bugs due to lack of regular wet-downs. She had a very green thumb apparently when it came to raising insects. Was that the loader? Of course, its yellow smear haphazardly abandoned in the last place she'd used it. A woman of her age still not straightening up her toys after playing with them. Embarrassing. The lumberyard slid from view.

A few more tweaks to buttons and levers around the cockpit and Sarah spoke. "This place we're going to see? Greensville? What's there? You were very mysterious on the phone. There's no airfield within fifty miles of the place, by the way. No bodies of water big enough to set Gertie down in either. I checked."

Good old Sarah. Took a person at their word, did all the checking and double checking, so conscientious, so . . . *different*.

"You've changed, you know," Gillian said.

"You're welcome. Think nothing of all the research I did on your behalf without even asking *why*?"

"Thank you. I appreciate it. But what I mean is, you're *organized*." Gillian watched her friend lean over to glance at a compass set into what Gillian would call a dashboard if they had been in a car. "You've got your shit together. You know where you're going, for heaven's sake."

"Jealous?"

"Don't smirk. It reminds me of Riley. And yes, I guess I am, a bit. That Logan seems to have done wonders for you." Gillian had only spoken with Sarah's new husband briefly at the wedding but knew all about him from her friend's descriptions and stories.

Sarah's laugh was a bark. "*I* did wonders for me, kid," she said. "He was just along for the ride."

"He seems like a great guy, though."

"Again: he's a royal pain in the ass. He works too much, gets crabby and takes it out on me. But yes, he is." She backed off on the throttles and Gertrude's nose leveled off.

Gillian scanned the ground below. It was amazing how much progress they were making without her having even being aware of the movement of the plane, because there, almost directly below, was Riley's construction site. A yellow grader or bulldozer or something was working on the approach road. All the staging on the roof was gone. Some kind of effort was under way on the hardscape in the middle of what Gillian could now appreciate was a circular drive just in front of the house. Please tell her they *weren't* installing a fountain.

"Why? Would that be so bad?" Sarah asked.

"First sign of senility," Gillian said, "talking out loud when your mind swears your mouth is on "mute." And yes, it would be."

"Explain." Sarah glanced over at the map again and fiddled with what looked like a radio set into the instrument panel. There were two radios, actually, Gillian realized, taking stock. Two of them, side by side. Two **of** everything, in fact. Everything was backed up. Clever. You needed back-ups in life. Plan Number One went wrong all the time.

"There's this whole . . . thing, this whole . . . development craze, I guess you'd call it, going on in Rocky Falls. All kinds of building. Everybody's caught up in it. Riley's got that McMansion going on down there and that's just the first of a string he's got planned. All kinds of new people in town. With lots of money."

"And poor Cinderella's stuck home sweeping the hearth while everyone else goes to the party."

Gillian laughed. "My sister's doing that." She explained about Rachel's housecleaning and everything else she was up to since her return to Rocky Falls. "She's only hinted at the real reason she's back, but I think she was 'encouraged' to leave the firm she was working at in Boston by the wives of the board of directors," Gillian said.

"One can only imagine the 'compromising position' she must have found herself—no, been *found* in," Sarah said primly.

Gillian guffawed. She and Sarah considered a few possibilities. The laughter that filled the cockpit was just like old times. "Am I that obvious about the Cinderella thing, though?" Gillian asked, after the snorting died down.

"Well, you have had this early Christian martyr thing going on since your mom passed away, no offense."

"None taken." Gillian thought for a moment. "Funny, though, that's what I said about Meg." Off in the distance, cumulus towers were feathering their icy tops into the jet stream. Gillian said quietly, "But I did leave her in the lurch, Sarah. My mom, I mean. My dad, too. That's not something you just walk away from."

"Says who?"

Ouch. Gillian watched Sarah thumb a button on the control wheel. She checked the compass for the millionth time. Fooled with the radio. They flew in silence for several minutes.

"Pull out the next map," Sarah said finally. "We're almost off this one."

"For sure."

"Too blunt, right? Logan says I am. Time has not dulled the edge, unfortunately."

"Hey, the truth always hurts. It's not your fault." Gillian stared out the window. She wanted to cry. Here, a couple of thousand feet in the air? She looked around for an altimeter. What difference? The point was: *here* was *away*. Completely. From what? The responsibility? Yes. And the crushing guilt. Her eyes watered.

Sarah handed over a pair of sunglasses. They were yellow with palm trees on the bows. Gillian let her eyes drip behind the mirrored lenses. She stared off into the deep blue emptiness surrounding the plane. Fat tears ran down her cheeks.

Sarah spoke, her voice trickling into Gillian's headphones. "Sometimes I'll be flying along up here, all by myself, not a care in the world and all of a sudden, for no reason at all, *I* start crying. It's that kind of place."

Gillian hiccuped. "It's beautiful. You feel like you could be anything you want when you're up here."

"You can be on the ground, too, I found out."

"Easy for you to say." Gillian wiped her eyes on her T-shirt.

"Don't use your sleeve. It's gross," Sarah said. "I've been there." She handed over a box of tissues.

Gillian laughed. "Again, prepared."

"Like I said, it's that kind of place." They flew for a while longer, then Sarah said, "So about this Turner guy. He seems to be squarely at the center of the shit storm you're going through down there."

Sarah meant "in Rocky Falls." It took Gillian a moment to make the leap. She had mentally detached from the world below. "He's right in the eye. The one relatively calm place in the whole damn system. Safe from everything. He just sits in the middle of everything and throws shit out at people around him."

Gertrude's throaty, steady drone filled the cockpit. Sarah said, "You might be surprised."

"At what?"

Her friend held up a finger while a message squawked in the headphones. To Gillian, it was unintelligible gibberish. Sarah unclipped a microphone and responded in kind. A secret language these people had. The transmission ended and Sarah signed off.

"Who is this Roger guy all you pilots are talking about, anyway?" Gillian asked.

"Very funny. Not. We were talking about you, here, I believe." Sarah replaced the mic in its holder next to the radios. "It might not be as calm as you think in that eye, is what I meant."

"Meaning?" Gillian eyed a gathering wall of clouds ahead. It seemed to be growing outward from the middle.

"I don't know. All I do is fly the damn plane."

Her friend was maddening at times. Bring her this far then drop her? "You know, Sarah, you're even more close-mouthed than you say Logan is. You two are actually the perfect couple."

"On some days. Lay out the next map, will you?" Sarah said succinctly.

Gillian laid the second map over the first and smoothed it. Sarah was irritated with her. Not that you could blame her. Dragging a person all the way out here with virtually no explanation and then expecting therapy in the bargain. "Okay," she said, "sorry. I'm being a jerk. It's just that the guy had great muffins." Gillian explained about the blueberries and the roof rescue.

"Hubba, hubba," Sarah said, her voice light again.

"I know, you'd think, right? Then I found out that he was actually the one behind all the crap that went on earlier in the year. The land buy proposals, the housing development next to the lumberyard?"

"Right, you were in a lather about that."

"Damn straight. Thought we'd put it to bed for good. But no. Jack was back. In the flesh." Gillian shared the Crack jokes.

Sarah struggled to keep the plane on course. "*You* should be the writer," she said, gasping for breath.

"I'd laugh too if it was somebody else's life."

"Sorry."

"It gets weirder. Boo seemed to think Jack was the cat's pajamas. He was always jumping into his truck, laying around on Jack's stuff, bothering him at home. We all know Boo isn't the brightest pup in the pound, but he is an excellent judge of character."

Sarah held up a hand. "I'm . . . confused. You're telling me your *dog* set you up with this guy?"

"Not exactly. I more . . . took Boo's opinion under advisement. Besides Jack is relentless when he wants something."

"And *you* is what he wants."

It was a statement, not a question, Gillian realized. She felt the shock all the way in her toes.

"My gosh."

Maybe he did.

Her?

He always said that he did, right from the start. *I jumped in to save you . . .*

Her breath caught in her chest. Had Gertrude climbed that high? Should they be on oxygen?

She asked Sarah. Her friend's voice crackled in the headphones. "Don't make me slap you."

He jumped in to save me . . .

"Gillian?"

"What?"

"You have that look."

"Because I guess he . . . does," she said.

Sunlight filigreed the edges of the cumulus towers, but the center of the massed wall was darkening ominously. Sarah must have caught her staring at it. "Nothing to worry about," she said, nodding at the angry purple of the cloud mass. "We're giving it plenty of room. Finish the story."

Gillian shifted in her seat. Wrapped her fingers around a grab handle overhead. Wiggled her toes. The physical sensations grounded her. *Breathe.*

"We have completely different ideas about the town," she said, her voice sounding to her like it was coming from a great distance away. *Maybe he really did want her.* "But we actually get along okay lately. If you discount the incessant bickering."

Sarah laughed. *A case of misery loves company,* Gillian imagined. "The problem is he can be so damn . . . attractive. And aggravating. And overbearing. And so positive he's right and knows what's best for everybody."

Sarah chuckled, the sound deep in her chest.

"Then Rachel got me thinking that maybe someone was behind the accident at the mill. The one that hurt my dad. I was ready to rip off his face." Gillian glanced at her friend. Sarah's eyes were boring holes into her.

"It hooks you, doesn't it?" Gillian said.

Sarah gave her head a little shake as if trying to clear it. "This part is just . . . eerily familiar, is all."

"Right. You and Logan." Sarah and her new husband had also had some colorful "issues" between them.

"Well, I thought about Jack and about the roof rescue," Gillian said. "About Boo and how he wanted to have Jack's babies."

Sarah hooted.

"In the end, the whole thing didn't add up to Jack having been involved. But still, it bothered me. Then, late one night . . ." She explained how she'd almost whacked Jack over the head in the lumberyard at two in the morning. "A couple nights after our rendezvous at the loader, I actually

ended up whacking him in the nicest way possible. Two—
no, three—times in a row."

"Ouch."

"It was worth it."

"Evidently."

Okay, so it had been a while since the last time. "Boo was
there, too."

"Ah, Jeez, Gillian—that part I didn't need to know."
Sarah busied herself adjusting a knob on the instrument
panel. "Your dog needs to find his own action." The engines
seemed to smooth.

"He's a good boy. The only problem left with us—me and
Jack, that is—is that he's got this plan—*scheme,* I call it—
to redo Rocky Falls in his image. Woo-*hoo* . . ." Gillian waggling all her fingers in the air.

Sarah laughed.

"What's funny here? I'm pouring my heart out."

"Nothing, nothing. I just wondered if Jack had a long-lost
brother."

"Logan."

Sarah laughed again. "No shit. Go on."

"Part of me says it's a good thing," Gillian said. "Rocky
Falls isn't exactly setting the world on fire." She thought of
the shabby trailers and the scrawny-looking kids in Meg's
classroom. "But another part of me is suspicious. I don't
want things to change. And yes, I know that my motivations
for that aren't completely healthy. I know that I feel I'd somehow be abandoning my mother—again—if I let anything
change. And I know that's a totally messed up way to feel."

She took a deep breath, then blew it out noisily. The noise
exploded in the headphones.

"Cripes! Gillian—" Sarah grimaced.

"Ow. Ow . . ." Gillian slipped a cup off her own head and
massaged her ear. She gingerly recentered the strap of the
headphones against her scalp. "Sorry. Where was I? Ah, the
town. I don't want it getting worked over like all those times

before. After all, I have to live there long after Mr. Jack Turner has made his money and screwed."

"You and the town, huh?"

"Shut up."

"Just trying to keep things light."

Sarah probably feared she would launch into another rave about Rocky Falls's history as she had done to her too many times in the past, Gillian realized ashamedly. Sarah. Another good girl in an alley fight. Gillian wondered if she had done enough to deserve her friendship.

"What makes you think he's planning to leave?" Sarah asked.

Gillian looked to the clouds again. "Well, why would he stay in Rocky Falls?" Her stomach flipped. "Oh, shit."

"Oh, yes." Sarah chuckled. " *Oo-lala*, just maybe."

Gillian blushed, dumbstruck.

Jack *staying*? In Rocky Falls? She had never once considered the possibility. Not like temporarily bunking in a crappy construction trailer while the redevelopment happened and then leaving to go back to Jack Land, wherever that was, but *staying?* In *her* town?

That he wanted her was hard enough to believe. But he did, apparently. But then to think of him living—actually *residing*—in town? With her? Brushing his teeth every morning in . . . what sink? Hers, with the green lime stains and the chipped porcelain? His . . . somewhere in town? Theirs . . . who knew where?

She flattened a palm against her chest. She was all aflutter. She had never fluttered in her life before. "That is so stupid," she said.

"Why? Guy meets girl, falls in love, lives happily ever after."

"With the Forest Queen," Gillian finished dreamily.

"You're positively humming," Sarah said after a few moments.

"Funny you should choose those words and, yes, I know. I can hardly sit still."

"No, I mean, you're really humming. Off-key. It's driving me nuts."

"Oh—sorry." Gillian laughed and splayed the fingers of each hand on the arm rests of her high-backed seat. This changed everything. Jack actually concerned about the town? Involved in not only her life, but in *its* life? Was it possible?

Yes, a voice inside her said. Because when you put the sun smack dab in the middle of the galaxy where it belonged everything else around it operated in a completely sensible way. Give Jack the benefit of legitimate motives and move him onto the chessboard. *Shazaam*, everything else worked. Maybe it was Gillian Wilcox that was whacked, trying to make all Jack Turner's behavior fit some weird and convoluted motives? Maybe he really *was* thinking of staying and really believed his plans *would* make for a better place to live. Thinking of staying . . .

Jumped in to save her . .

It followed.

Jumped right in. To save her . . .

She smelled bubble bath.

"You still with me?" Sarah asked.

"It really is different up here, isn't it?" Gillian said.

One hour and four maps later put Gertrude over the eastern edge of upstate New York. A close call with a thunder cell had been avoided. A perky tail wind had them ahead of schedule. Gillian scanned the sky ahead. She could see clear to the curving horizon.

"Look sharp, now," Sarah said. "We're getting close. I'm going to lose some altitude, get us down lower. See if you can match up some features on the map with what's under us. You can draw our course on those maps with that erasable pen there if you want."

To amuse herself, Gillian used the folded edge of a used map as a straight edge and on the current one drew a line directly through their last two landmarks. She extended the line to its natural conclusion at the edge of the coated paper.

Five minutes later Gillian found another landmark. Right where it was supposed to be. "Those three smoke stacks? At the edge of the river?" She pointed excitedly.

"Got it," Sarah said.

"To hit Greenville, we should be on a line connecting those stacks with . . ." With a fingertip Gillian followed the line she had drawn. "Ah. Got it. That line of low hills." She pointed again.

Gillian watched Sarah twitch the wheel in front of her and nudge the rudder pedals with her feet. The identical set of controls on Gillian's side of the cockpit mirrored Sarah's actions.

"I'm thinking about twenty minutes at our present heading," Gillian said.

"You make a pretty good copilot," Sarah said.

"That's me. Always a bridesmaid, never a bride."

But what if that *weren't* true this time? Gillian thought. What if, instead of a Riley relationship where both parties circled each other for more than two decades, eyes peeled, searching for the next convenient pile of excrement to throw at each other, Jack was the real deal? What if he really *was* in it for the long haul? And how stupid—how *suspicious*— of her not to even consider that as a possibility.

Somehow the last hour had changed her life. A new and improved version of Gillian Wilcox had dropped from the sky, so to speak. Gillian 2.0. She realized she was in the middle of one of those moments she'd so often heard about but had never personally experienced. One of those special moments when all the random pieces fell suddenly and completely into place. The flying, the new perspective,

Sarah's seemingly offhand remarks. All had contributed. Her friend was deeper than she had ever given her credit for, Gillian ruefully admitted.

She snuggled back into the seat cushions. She allowed herself to picture a renewed downtown Rocky Falls. A choice of several kinds of coffee wouldn't be a bad thing. Her Aunt Betty's store expanding into the vacant storefront adjacent to her. Leo would be delighted. Never a "front man," he was nevertheless as dedicated to the books of the business as she was to its art. Arthur and Lynette off to Florida every winter. A reasonable, not ugly, under-control housing development *adjacent* to the mill. Not on her land. Never. But next to it. It could work. It was their lookout for the noise, of course. She had a business to run. But it could work.

She allowed herself to picture the shabby trailers replaced with modular homes. Better dressed kids in the classrooms. Full-time work with benefits for a lot of people. She ticked off family names in her head.

She imagined her and Jack together. In the Vibrobed the other night. In the saw shed. Maybe in his pickup. That would be kind of hot in a retro sort of a way. Ah, and don't forget her tub. It was a big tub. And the sofa in the front parlor of The Box. Scratchy, but she'd always wanted to christen it. If Rachel hadn't already beaten her to it years ago.

"So how are we doing?"

Gillian had completely forgotten where she was or the job Sarah had given her to do. She looked around the cockpit at its myriad of dials, levers and gee-gaws, then down at the ground rolling by beneath them, then back to her friend in the seat beside her. "Wow," she said.

"You feeling alright?"

"Better than I have in a long, long time." Gillian sat up and checked the map and glanced at the ground again. "We follow the river below us for maybe . . . fifteen more minutes? Then we're there."

"Now will you let me in on the big secret?"

"Which is . . . ?"

"Why we're here? My journalist's nosey nose is twitching."

"Oh. To see a development. A planned community. Jack Turner was supposedly one of the key players in it."

"Supposedly? He told you about it?"

"No. I dug up the connection through a few of my friends back at the state community planning office in Augusta. Sure, he gave me a few places to check out when I finally dropped the sword long enough to hear him out. You know, projects that he'd worked on. 'Get a feel for my style,' he said. But this Greenville deal wasn't on his list. He might have thought it was too far off for me to ever get to, so it wasn't worth mentioning."

"He was wrong, huh?" Sarah said, grinning. "Tours Are Us."

Gillian laughed. "Yep." She let her head rest back against the seat. The reassuring rumble of the plane's twin engines was soothing. She hadn't realized how drained she was. But she was happy. Happier than she'd been in a long time. Maybe happier than she'd ever been. Maybe.

"I'm looking forward to seeing this place," she said sleepily.

The possibilities for her and Jack and the town loomed so large and bright. Just one last thing to do. One last check.

She was exhausted. Her eyelids drooped.

Then home free.

"Oh-oh."

Sarah's voice in the headphones. Gillian heard herself snort. She inelegantly wiped drool from a corner of her mouth. Just like her to fall asleep at the really exciting part. But, wait. *Oh-oh?* In the airplane disaster movies that was never good.

She sniffed. No smoke. She looked around the cockpit. No flames. She peered blearily out the Plexiglas windows of the cockpit and counted the wings: Good, two of them in the same place they were the last time she checked.

She scanned the ground below. They were flying over a sprawling development. A vast network of interconnected spidery streets crawled up and down gently rolling hills that must once have been open farm land. In places where the land was steeper, terraces had been cut into the sloping grades and there were more houses. Houses on top of houses on top of pools and driveways and streets. It seemed to go on forever.

"What a disaster," Gillian said, rubbing her eyes and staring, horrified but still not completely awake. "But what's the *oh-oh*?"

Sarah pointed to the topmost map on the pile on Gillian's lap.

Gillian looked down at it. She followed the bold black line she had drawn on it with dry erase pen fifteen minutes or so ago. The line cut directly through a shaded area outlined by dotted lines. The word "proposed" was written within the shaded area. For a moment she was confused, but then: "No."

"I'm afraid so," Sarah said.

It couldn't be.

With a shaking hand, Gillian turned the map over searching for a date.

Sarah answered her unasked question. "It's three years old."

Gillian flipped the map face up and compared the dotted lines and the shading to what she was seeing on the ground. Matched the blot on the coated paper to the shape of the sprawling horror below. Like identical images of a perverse Rorschach inkblot, the two shapes melded into one. Proposed had become Real.

"Oh my God," she said. "It's Turner Town." She grabbed for the air sickness bag.

Chapter 22

Gertrude gently bobbed on the deep water in the middle of the Mohasset. Gillian clung to the sides of the open fuse-lage hatch, fighting to clear the pain-wracked haze from her mind.

"Here's your swimsuit," Sarah said. Numbly Gillian accepted the bundle. Spat into the water. Scanned the river bank with unseeing eyes.

"You gonna put it on?"

"Fuck it," Gillian said. She gathered up the vomit bag. She readied herself to jump into the river.

"What, no kiss?"

Gillian hung her head, let her arms flop to her sides. Each of them weighed four thousand pounds.

"Sorry about the smell," she said. "I just . . . lost it."

"Literally. Brings me back to Sunday mornings in our dorm room," her friend said.

Gillian clenched her teeth. Her bile threatened to rise when she thought of gently rolling hills tortured and strangled by the spiraling arms of Turner Town. She eyed the barf bag. Her hopes and joys reduced to one nasty little package.

"You gonna make it?" Sarah eyed the distance to shore.

"Yeah." Gillian said. Back to the river. Thank God for the river. "What about gas money? For Gertrude?"

"Deductible expense. Logan'll love it."

Gillian smiled, despite her pain, hating to let her friend go. "I won't hug you," she said.

Sarah wrinkled her nose. "I'm flying back with all the windows open."

"Can you do that?"

Sarah laughed. "Go," she said. She'd gently shoved Gillian on the shoulder. "Call me."

Gillian tossed both bags into the water, dived toward them, reined them in before the current took them away. She treaded water, looking up at her friend framed in the hatchway.

"What are you planning to do with your precious cargo?" Sarah asked, one eyebrow raised.

"Oh, you mean my hopes and dreams?" Gillian contemplated the rapidly dampening sack full of vomit. She poked it with a finger. "Sink it with a rock when I get to shore."

"Polluter."

Gillian snickered. "With all the shit dumped in this river over the years, a little more's not going to hurt anything."

"Don't turn into a bitter old woman on me," Sarah said.

Caught in a whorl of current, Gertrude began a slow rotation. Gillian swam a few strokes away from the plane to avoid a pontoon. A dozen yards out, she turned around in the water to wave to her friend, but Sarah had already levered the hatch shut. Through the row of windows in the passenger cabin, Gillian watched her make her way forward to the cockpit. Gillian waved once anyway, wondering why. Then she struck out for shore.

She sank the barf bag under a rock at the edge of the river. Her body on autopilot, she trod the path leading back to the parking area where she'd left the pickup. Silly ditties filled her head. There wasn't room for anything else.

Out of the river and through the woods . . .

Sick in our guts we go along, go along . . .

Shivering, she rooted around in the dry bag for keys to the ignition. Hopped in the truck. Revved the engine. Ran

the heater full blast. Cried in the opaque privacy of the rapidly steaming windows. Deep, wracking sobs.

So close.

Only to get kicked in the teeth. That's what happened
when you allowed yourself for one minute—one lousy, *tiny*
minute—to imagine what another life than the one you already had could be like. She cursed and cried and cursed
some more. Spiraled down into a dark place full of self-pity
and reproach.

What an idiot. Boo's mother she was, trusting anybody
who'd rub her ears—or other body parts—like they meant
it. *Stupid, stupid, stupid.* Her life was an absurdity.

Maybe half an hour went by. Gillian couldn't tell exactly.
She raised her forehead from the steering wheel and
squinted out at the river. Sniffed hard and wiped her nose on
her damp T-shirt sleeve. Thought about Sarah's warning to
her about becoming old and bitter. She pictured herself sitting alone in a dim pool of light on a winter's night fifty
years hence, penciling in a crossword with a bony hand. You
had to laugh. Or go crazy.

She scrubbed her eyes.

Through the trees the Mohasset sparkled as only it could
on a sunny day late in autumn. This really was her favorite
time of the year. The sharply angled light seemed to slice
through to some part of her that was solid flesh in all the
other seasons. She let her head relax back into the seat. She
massaged her temples.

Dust motes floated in the still air of the cab. She reached
out and grabbed at them. When she opened her fist there
was nothing there. For a minute there up in the plane it
looked like she had had it all. Like in the movies, this great
glittering *thing* happened with her and Jack. Against all
odds somebody meets someone in a totally unexpected way

under totally unpredictable circumstances and everything magically works out.

Right. In the movies.

Rocky Falls wasn't a movie set, although on a beautiful day like today it could be. Jack Turner was anything but Richard Gere rescuing a woman from a dirty business. And turning lumber wasn't turning tricks.

But there were comparisons.

Shit. Note to self: Get *Pretty Woman* back to the rental place *today* or get yet another late charge. Why didn't she just buy the damn flick?

Comparisons, Gillian thought. There were some. She defended her work at the mill as irrationally as Julia Roberts had defended *her* trade in the movie.

Wilcox Lumber made a living, kept me independent, Gillian could hear herself saying. A good side business, her carpentry, too. Second-oldest profession, the script read. But Julia wasn't working her dirty business because one of her parents couldn't anymore. Or because she felt she owed it to a dead mother to carry on as if nothing had changed.

Gillian Wilcox had fallen off the perch, she decided. Turned weird and twisted. Like the figure that sat unmoving in the upstairs window in *The Sentinel.* Keeping watch over Rocky Falls. Always remembering *The Way We Were.*

She was pitiful. In *The Final Analysis,* she watched too much TV. She came to a decision.

It was time to pull on her tall, black hooker boots and go kick some ass.

Chapter 23

The drive home required little conscious thought. Gillian mindlessly climbed the steps of The Box, pulled off wet clothes, bathed, and was back behind the wheel of her pickup in record time. Thankful for the company of an old friend, Gillian allowed herself to be borne aloft on the arms of rage. Life began anew.

As she was about to make a left turn onto Route 101 to head north to Riley's site to confront and possibly disembowel Jack, a keening wail brought her abruptly to her senses. The town's sole police cruiser flashed past, siren screaming, closely followed by the ambulance that Rocky Falls shared with Bertram, the next town over.

Gillian cautiously joined the slower traffic traveling behind the speeding vehicles. One by one, the cars in front of her took rights or lefts, leaving open road between her pickup and the cruiser, its flashing lights still clearly visible in the distance.

Never one to inject herself into other people's misfortunes—not that she wouldn't be there with a cord of firewood or a purchased casserole after the smoke cleared—she was surprised to find herself feeling a deep sense of unease. She accelerated to keep the police car in sight. A mile outside of town, it turned left onto the drive leading to Riley's construction site. Her mind flying with possibilities, none of them pleasant, most involving death or dismemberment, Gillian nailed the accelerator.

Her pickup had clawed its way up to seventy when Gillian came upon the road leading to the construction site. She slammed on the brakes, sending the rear of the truck into a skid. She downshifted, gunned the engine and bounced the front tires onto the lane.

Asphalt had replaced rutted gravel. Unobtrusive landscaping lamps dotted beds of new plantings along one side of the drive. Despite her panic, Gillian found herself impressed. Up ahead, the cruiser, its strobes still firing and the driver's door ajar, was haphazardly parked among an assortment of Bobcats, front-end loaders, and other pieces of landscaping equipment. No fountain in the turnaround, thank God.

Gillian stashed the pickup off to the side out of the way and ran to the nearest landscaper.

"Anybody hurt?"

"Yeah. Some old guy." With a dirty hand the worker pointed toward the front door of the house.

Despite her anxiety, Gillian found herself noticing how well the half-columns on either side of the six-panel front door and the blown glass transom lights above it complemented the entryway of the house. Very authentic details. Riley was upping his game.

The good news was, apparently, the injured party wasn't Riley or one of his crew. The only "old guys" working construction in town worked for Gillian and they were safely tucked into a checkers tournament two counties over. "What happened?"

"Some mucky muck guy working for Riley beat the shit out of this old guy."

"Which one of Riley's guys? What 'old guy'?" This dude didn't exactly have a master's in Botanical Science.

"Lady, for Crissakes, I don't know. I just work here." With a snort of disgust, he hefted a flat steel shovel and went back to scraping bark mulch chips into the bucket of a front-end loader.

Hating herself for being a busy body but having to know all the same, Gillian tentatively entered the house through the impressive front entrance. Inside, things got even better. Period moldings and staircase parts. The stairway banister started with a full volute centered over a first step with a steam-curved riser. Good scale on the parts, not overdone but not dinky either. Nice. Just right.

The house demanded your attention. It didn't holler "Notice me" like a lot of the new ones, but if you appreciated architectural detail in the slightest, this place had it all and wouldn't let you forget it. She forced herself to concentrate on the sounds of commotion coming from the rear of the house.

A wall of broad shoulders clad in plaid fenced off her view into the great room at the back of the house. She tapped one of the pickets on its right shoulder and when the guy turned to see who it was, she slid into the crack that opened up on his left.

Some guy, undoubtedly the "old guy" of mention, was sitting dazedly on the floor of the great room, his back resting against a half-plastered wall. The paramedic team and all their gear prevented Gillian from getting a good look at him, although she caught a flash of coifed silver hair matted with blood.

Riley and the cop from the cruiser were on top of a man who presumably was the Mucky Muck Guy. He was lying face first on the floor, looking very, well . . . mucky. Blood was smeared around the subfloor near where he lay. The cop had one of the guy's arms twisted behind the guy's back, and Riley was lying across Mucky's legs.

"Settle down, *now!*" the cop was shouting into the prostrate man's ear.

The man thrashed his legs as if he really didn't want to hear what the cop was suggesting. "Fuck you! Get the fuck

off me! That fucking sonofabitch came after *me*!" was what
Gillian thought she heard, but only the subfloor knew for
sure. Then, with Riley apparently applying more pressure,
the struggling guy finally went limp.

Gillian heard the *Snick!* and ratchet of a set of handcuffs.

"You can let up. I got him now," the cop said to Riley.

Ron Southland was the cop, Gillian could see now. Nice
guy. Two kids. Good kisser. Not that anybody but his wife
would have cause to know that now. Gillian had dated him
once. They'd called it quits because they both agreed it was
a strange-but-not-in-a-good-way experience. Small town,
too much weird history between them. Missing scissors in
kindergarten? Tactical booger reprisals? Something like
that. Neither of them could remember the exact details.
Thank goodness for small favors, as they had been eating
dinner during *that* stroll down memory lane.

Old Ronny had definitely put on some muscle since his
dating days, Gillian could see. His biceps bulged under his
navy blue jacket as he hauled Floor Guy to his knees.

Gillian cocked her head sideways. Floor Guy actually had
a nice ass for a felon. Not that she wasn't glad that she had
a whole plaid wall at her back. Floor Guy had a *lot* of rage.
Made hers look like kid stuff. He was bloody, too. From a
cut on his jaw. Not as bloody as the Old Guy being tended
to, but enough that it took her a second to comprehend that
Floor Guy was actually . . .

"*You!*" she hissed.

"Gillian." The familiar voice sliced through her shock.
"Talk to this guy." The bastard nodded savagely at Ronny,
which was tough to do from a kneeling position. "Tell him
what I'm like."

Happy to.

"Officer, this man is bad news," Gillian said to Ron.
"Don't trust him for a second." She thought of cookie-cutter
houses set cheek to jowl on endless streets of sprawling
sameness. She squatted and pointed directly into Jack's face.

"Not for one *second,* I tell you. He'd stab you in the back as soon as he'd look at you. He's a worm, a conniver, an untrustworthy toad, a—"

"I'm getting the picture," Ron Southland said. "I think." He looked like he really didn't. "Step away, now," he said.

"Gillian, what the hell—?" Jack said.

"And he has a dirty mouth," she said, not backing up.

"What is wrong with you?" the bastard said, his eyes flashing, blue flames set to rolling boil.

"Greenville." She squatted on the floor next to Jack, the toes of her boots but inches from him.

Ron Southland put a restraining hand against her shoulder. "Back up, Gillian," he said. "Now."

"Greenville is what's wrong with me." She looked Jack dead in the eye.

"I can explain," he said.

"I doubt it," she said.

"Get moving, Gillian." Ron pushed her away none too gently. She rocked back on her heels and stood up. Ron rose from his crouch on the floor and hauled Jack to his feet. "You, too," he said. "Move. Toward the door." He kneed the back of one of Jack's legs for encouragement. Jack grimaced.

"Yeah, get moving," Gillian said. She wished it could have been her doing the kicking. Ron shot her a look on the way.

She watched the two men make their way to the front of the house, Jack struggling and protesting all the way. Mr. Turner didn't seem to appreciate the personal escort. To the closest Plaid Guy she said, "What the hell happened here?" And then, in a quieter voice, "And who the heck is that?" She nodded at the Old Guy.

"That guy's old man." Plaid hooked a thumb in the direction of Jack Turner's back. Gillian turned. Jack had disappeared.

What the—? His *father?*

Chapter 24

"Well, son, you really did it now, didn't you?"

"You're not my real father, so don't call me that. And stop with the phony Southern accent. Why do you do that, anyway?"

"Puts people at ease, boy." Dodge Holt paced the narrow corridor outside the holding cells at the Rocky Falls police station. His steps were careful, measured, his weight always over the balls of his feet.

"It's moronic," Jack said.

Jack, perched at the very edge of the jail cot, clenched the metal bar underneath his wafer-thin mattress with both hands. With his glare, he traced lines in the cracked concrete of the floor. Even the pokey in this town needed a remodeling, he thought. He looked around his cramped concrete cubicle. The dented stainless steel toilet with no seat had certainly seen better days.

He looked everywhere but at Dodge Holt. Maybe if he didn't look in his direction he could pretend that the man wasn't mocking him from a scant half-dozen feet away. Regretfully, solid steel bars separated him from his stepfather.

Dodge hadn't looked good, Jack thought, when that cop, Ron something, had ushered him into the holding area. His face had been as gray as the concrete walls of the jail and he'd shuffled his feet wearily. But when the grilled gate that separated the two holding cells of the Rocky Falls jail from the rest of the Public Works building clanked shut, Dodge Holt promptly revived and began torturing his stepson. Ten minutes later, color was back in the man's face, making the big bandage above one eye appear even whiter by contrast.

"Look, boy—" he said.

"I'm not your boy," Jack snarled. *Hold it together,* he told himself. He glanced beyond his stepfather to the surveillance camera set into a wall pocket and protected by thick Plexiglas. *If you ever want to get out of here, hold it together, Jack.*

"All I wanted to do was come up here and have a little business discussion with my stepson," Dodge said, "and he almost takes my head off. Swinging at an old man like that. Now, how nice is that? Poor old guy like me, twice your age. You ought to be ashamed."

"It's you who ought to be ashamed," Jack said through clenched teeth. Dodge had practically thrown himself onto his fist, Jack thought. Ex-boxer, old Dodge, his nickname aptly earned. The cops should have checked *him* out for a criminal history, instead of wasting their time on his stepson. Jack wondered if he was warping the frame of the bed with his death grip.

"*Forgive and forget* is my motto," Dodge said. "I was ready to overlook your . . . 'trespasses,' I guess we could call them—on my Vermont project. Sugar in the gas tanks, a few hydraulic hoses loosened, surveying stakes pulled up and moved just for fun." He contemplated the fingernails of one hand. "All that I was ready to overlook. Water under the bridge. You were pissed, so was I. Old times all over again." He waved a hand dismissively.

For no reason apparent to him, Jack suddenly thought of the Mohasset and imagined he heard rushing water. But the jail was too far from the river for that. Maybe it was just the blood rushing in his ears. He realized Dodge was still talking.

"But what I will *not* abide by, son, is you going to those damn tree huggers. They're talking about going for an injunction against my project. You were just making a point before, boy. I understand that. But now there's a real chance of me getting shut down while they do some damn wetlands survey. Supposedly I'm bothering some kind of damn swamp frog that nobody gives a shit about anyway."

Jack tried hard to hide his grim smile of satisfaction. The publicity storm he'd stirred up with a couple of Vermont-based ecology clubs had done the trick a lot better than a few hydraulic system blowouts ever could.

"And don't you be smiling like such a smart ass," Dodge said. "It's us against them and don't you forget it."

In his stepfather's lexicon, "us" was anybody who developed land and "them" was anybody who stood in the way of it. Ironically, Jack thought, he had staked out a middle ground for himself between the factions and *that* was his problem. He was a Quaker, standing between the Blue and the Gray, taking cannon fire from both sides. He would not soon forget the look of rage on Gillian's face as he was hauled away. No wonder the Native Americans always turned their prisoners over to the women of the tribe.

"You made yourself a pile of money on that New York job, Jack," Dodge said. "Enough to get you your own start, may I remind you. That and the loans your mom and I cosigned for you? You weren't exactly yelling "exploitation" when I had that banker's pen in my hand, were you, boy?"

"Yeah, well, that was early days in Greenville," Jack said. "If I'd have known what you were going to turn it into, I never would have signed on. I didn't know how far it would go."

"Well, neither did I, Jack. But if people want to just keep selling you their land—at a fair price, I remind you—" Jack winced to hear his own words from his stepfather's mouth— "then who am I to stop the building? Economy of scale, Jack. Bigger is cheaper. It don't make sense to stop once you're up and going."

Again, Jack felt the razor of his stepfather's words cut deep. Jack had lived in Greenville in the early days of the project. In the beginning, it was a low-key, upscale development on the edge of a pretty little village. Seemingly, overnight it became a many-headed hydra, reaching out in all directions to consume the original town, bury it under "necessary infrastructure" like strip malls and convenience stores, gas stations, and car dealerships. Left the place a disaster area.

"So." Dodge held his arms out expansively and feigning good cheer, "What I'm saying to you is lay off, boy. Just lay off. Very simple. Stay out of my way. Out of my hair. For good. You do your little . . . *thing*," he sketched an arc in the air, "here in this little town. But you stay the hell out of my way."

He crossed his arms, waiting.

Jack finally looked up and met his stepfather's stare. "Don't count on it, *Dad*." The last word was laced with acid.

His stepfather scratched his chin thoughtfully. He chuckled and scratched it again. "Can't say as I didn't see that coming," he said. "I as much as told your mother that's what you'd say, but she made me come all the way up here in person to try and persuade you otherwise."

Jack waited for the other shoe to drop. This couldn't be good. His mother loved Dodge, Jack knew, but she also knew the consequences of crossing him. If she had jumped in the middle to play peacemaker, the shit must be pretty close to the fan blades. Dodge could pull the loans he'd cosigned. Then everything Jack had worked for would go down the drain. No one in New England would do business with anybody blackballed by Dodge Holt. Everything would be lost. The Boston office, the secretary, the current contracts.

He just as quickly realized that he'd miss absolutely none of it. Again he heard rushing water. A deep sense of calm came over him.

But then Dodge ruined the moment, as he had so many times in the past. He turned his back to the surveillance camera and in a voice so low Jack had to move closer to hear him said, "Then I'll just have to put my own offer in on the Wilcox land."

In a millisecond Jack was on his feet. The cold steel of the cell bars bit into his cheek as he stretched his hands to their farthest extent, savagely growling, clutching at Dodge's throat. Too late, Jack realized his stepfather had anticipated the reaction. With two quick steps belying his age, he had danced backward and out of reach.

The grilled door crashed open and in an instant the cop Gillian had called Ronny and another older one had Jack's flailing arms pinned against the bars. The last thing Jack heard as he was shoved backward against the cot was the echo of his stepfather's laughter.

Chapter 25

"What the hell are you doing?"

Gillian was staring numbly at the television. "I'm thinking I need a peel."

Rachel walked around to see the screen. An infomercial. In its forty-eighth minute according to the countdown clock in the corner of the picture. Two heavily made up, wasp-waisted women were hawking pots of something.

"It's on stretch pay and there are only twelve minutes left before they're sold out," Gillian said.

"I see." Her sister had lost it. Gillian had finally gone around the bend. And not the one in the Mohasset either.

"That stuff in the jars sloughs off dead skin cells," Gillian said. "See the card that dried-up-looking woman is holding? Covered in dead skin cells. Nasty, having that stuff hanging off you."

"Too bad it didn't slough off dead brain cells, huh?"

"Leave me alone."

"Hard to do that when it's coming up on noon on a work-day, the help is calling asking *me* of all people what to do down at the mill and all I can tell them is you've got a case of the Topsy Turner whim-whams." She snapped off the television.

"Hey!"

"Get up." Rachel slapped at Gillian's knee.

Gillian pulled her legs up underneath her and crossed her arms. "No."

"Now."

"No."

"What?" Rachel took a menacing step toward her.

"You're not Ma and you can't make me—Whoa! Cut the shi—" Rachel grabbed Gillian by one ankle and hauled her off the couch onto the floor.

"Ow!"

"Ow, nothing. Get up and get to work. You've got a business to run. People depend on you."

"Like they used to depend on you until your little high jinks with the board members, Rachel?"

Rachel's eyes narrowed. "Nice. You're bitter about your life, so you take it out on me." Her eyes landed on a stack of printed e-mails that had slid to the floor along with her sister. "What are those?"

"Receipts."

"For what?"

"A drawer organizer, some bags for storing sweaters, a thing that removes grout—it has seven other attachments all included in one low price—and a four-disc set of Pilates workouts. The same ones the stars use."

Rachel snapped. "Gillian, I swear to *God* if you don't get up off your ass and get a life, I'll star *you*." She moved in and swiped open handed at Gillian's head. Gillian ducked but felt the wind. "Get on with your life, for God's sake. You used to have a pretty good one, remember? Before you let old *Jackie*—" she sang the name and with her hand mimicked a shark biting the air—"chew you up and spit you out."

Gillian wiped her cheek with the back of her hand. "*You're* spitting. Do you know that?"

Rachel felt the blood shoot to her temples. "Argh! Jumping—Is this what it's like dealing with me? If it is, I am *so* sorry. But for God's sake Gillian, you are being such an ass. And this shit you bought?" She snatched up the receipts and leafed through them. "Drawer organizers. Hah! Half the kitchen drawers in this house don't even open anymore, let alone nobody knows what used to be in them the last time they did." She threw the paper into the air, and Gillian watched it spiral down into a corner behind the end table. "Sweater storage? You don't own anything but fleece." *Fwap*.

That one settled in gently behind the magazine rack.

"The grout thingie? The only cure for the grout in this place is a fucking sledge hammer." *Flick*.

The wide mantle had a new resident.

"Nice shot," Gillian said.

Rachel ignored her. "And the Pilates?" she said. She hiked up her short top and flexed her midsection. "You ain't touching these, so don't even try."

"Whoa." Gillian reached out a tentative finger and gently poked. Impressive.

"All they do is get a girl into trouble, I can tell you. Just ask the wives of the board members."

Gillian laughed despite herself.

Rachel got a hand under one of Gillian's armpits and hoisted her to her feet. Gillian leaned on her sister for a moment. "This hurts."

"Love stinks. But not as bad as you. Whew. You need a bath." She fingered a limp strand of Gillian's hair. "And some kind of conditioner. I think your hair is having sawdust separation issues."

"Shut up. I really thought he was the one, you know?"

"Love is weird." Rachel thought of Riley. Of how he was about the last person she'd ever imagine showing up on her list.

"Tell the guys I'll be down right after lunch?"

"You bet. Shower happy."

Like there was actually one in the house. "I'll try," Gillian promised.

Chapter 26

It was hard to believe it was two weeks to the day since Turner Town. Two weeks of no Jack. Of no infomercials. She'd managed to cancel the orders on all but the grout thing and who knew? She might use it on a job someday.

She slicked her wet hair out of her face and let her head rest back against the rim of the clawfoot tub. She'd been a mess there for a while. Thank God for Rachel. Kicking her in the butt when she needed it. She was back on track now. Her life back to what she used to call normal.

The mill was running right again, too. Orville and Wilbur were contentedly messing with her mind now that she'd apparently reclaimed it. Skip was home with the new baby. He and Joyce had had a beautiful girl, Melissa. Gillian's second cousin Luke was filling in for Skip at the yard. Like Skip, Luke was an easy guy to work with.

Gillian planted her feet on either side of the dripping faucets. She groaned, letting the sound rumble, watching the tub water ripple. God she didn't want to go to Meg's house tonight to work on plans for the Harvest Festival. She was dog tired. The effort of digging something presentable to wear out of her tiny, jam-packed bedroom closet—then ironing whatever she unearthed—seemed overwhelming. It'd be nice to just hang out in this wonderful warm tub for another hour or two or four, then maybe sit out on the back porch and finish reading that romance, catch up on some laundry . . .

But she knew better. That would be the first step down the path to waking up on her seventy-fifth birthday and wondering where the hell her life had gone. She had promised to appear at Meg's and she would because it was a *really* bad idea to hang around the house every night. An open invitation to unproductive brooding. She desperately needed a distraction. Something to get Turner Town off her mind.

The memory of that mess, that debacle, that *horror* continued to cling to her like a bad smell. Row upon row, parallel streets with ninety-damn-degrees the angle of the day. Like something out of *The Matrix*. Uniformity, conformity, row upon row of identical units. How could people live like that? Especially folks who had been living in what once must have been a beautiful little country town a lot like Rocky Falls. How they must have suffered as the old place changed around them. Where did you go once your own nest was irrevocably fouled? She shuddered, almost physically ill again.

Once, when she was little and going for her Girl Scouts swim badge, she had to prove that she could stay afloat for ten minutes. She practiced in shallow spots on the Mohasset, in calm pools, psyching herself up for the moment on test day when she would jump into water that was way over her head. That moment finally came and she leaped, hopeful and confident. She sank like a stone. That feel of no bottom, of nothing under her feet, of liquid suction pulling her down, down, down to her doom, remained with her for years, until Riley one day threw her back into the same deep pool. She bobbed to the surface, terrified but delightfully and wondrously buoyant.

Right now she needed something like that amazing feeling. Something that would lead her out of the sickened haze she'd been in since the flyby. Something like . . . socialization. Crap. With real people. Make small talk, smile through the pain. *Ouch*. But, yup, that would definitely do it.

Turner Town wasn't the only tragedy, she hated to admit. For a moment there in the plane, she had allowed Jack Turner to become the real deal. An early Christmas. A Disney fireworks show. It just went to show you.

Since then, in spite of her best efforts to put him out of her mind, he had been randomly intruding into her thoughts. The saw shed episode. Like constricting steel bands, his arms had seemed at first. She'd felt straightjacketed in their grip, like all the breathable air in the shed had suddenly been sucked out. Instinctively she'd fought to escape. Then *bam*, right out of the blue, the passion. Just like in a romance novel. *Sleepless in Sawdust*. A much younger Fabio could do the cover.

She felt her face smile, remembering the early fun of dubbing Jack "The Crack." The later fun of kneading the intriguing little loaves on either side of it. She laughed bitterly.

Now she knew why she had fought against him in the beginning. Always trust your first impressions. Or at least your second. Or even your third. That was the problem, she now realized. She had had so many different impressions of Jack that it was hard to keep track of them all. He shifted in the light like the colors in Maine tourmaline. Hold it this way and you had one shade, turn it that way for another. No matter now. The bottom line was the guy was bad news.

Yet she couldn't let go of the bone, no pun intended. The second he'd released her in the saw shed, it had been *she* who had climbed all over *him*. She could admit that now. Craving the closeness, the sensation of his flesh beneath her fingers. She'd kissed *him*. Over and over once she had been free to choose it. Desperately sucking his lips, drawing in great, gasping, lungfuls of breath, of air, of *life*.

She ran her hands over her belly and on up to her neck, her throat suddenly tight from a sound trapped there, primitive and dark, a hangover from the moments she laid beneath Jack Turner, his weight pressing down onto her, shifting against her hipbones. Him rolling her on top and she straddling his lean frame. The frustration of zippers, the feel of wide, warm hands sweeping up her rib cage, surrounding her breasts.

It was pure madness, of course—devoid of reason. A dizzying rush into bright white light. It had almost been her downfall.

She shook her head to clear it. Reluctantly she shut off the trickle of warm water with the toes of one foot and stood up slowly. Her knees were rubbery and not just from the heat of the water. Lightheaded and disconnected from her surroundings, she put a steadying hand on the edge of the sink cabinet and stepped out of the tub.

The reflection staring back at her from the medicine cabinet mirror looked unfamiliar. The individual features were the same as always, but the whole was different somehow. Something had shifted inside. Her Aunt Betty would talk of auras and *chi*, no doubt.

She looked different in the mirror because she was different, she realized. Forever changed. Battle weary, recovering from defeat like Washington's army licking its wounds through a brutal winter, she was living through her own personal Valley Forge.

Right. That's what a love of history got you. One-act plays in your own bathroom. She growled in frustration and the noise echoed in the tiny space, scaring her.

Get moving, she heard Rachel's voice say. *Get out*.

Now if she could just find the damn iron.

Chapter 27

"Honey!" Meg called to her husband. "Oh, honey!"

"No answer, huh?" Gillian said. That was strange. Her brother-in-law Bob's office was just at the rear of the house. Well within bellowing distance.

"Yeah, weird," Meg said.

Gillian winced as her sister yelled for Bob again. For a small person, Meg had a voice that could travel the breadth of a noisy playground and still draw blood. Gillian supposed you needed it in the teaching biz. Working with children all day? No, thanks. But summers off? Couldn't beat that.

"Hey, Meg, what's the three biggest reasons to go into teaching?" Gillian asked, smirking.

"June, July, and August. Watch what you're doing to those carrot sticks. They're looking like they came out of the chipper."

Gillian put down her paring knife and eyed the vegetable platter she was throwing together. Meg was right about the carrots. "Throwing" was the operative word. Gillian sighed and started on some radish roses. The people on the cooking channel made them look easy to do. Maybe they really were. Maybe they'd draw attention away from the pile of orange compost.

"Now where the hell did that man get to?" Gillian heard

her sister ask of no one. Meg rinsed onion dip off her fingers and dried them hastily on a dish towel, before heading out to find her husband.

A moment later a soft laugh drifted into the kitchen. Gillian gave up on the radish she was emasculating and headed out back to investigate. Meg was posted outside Bob's office door, which was slightly ajar, and she was peering in. Gillian tiptoed up next to her. Giggling and smothered laughter emanated from the room beyond. Lots of shushing sounds from Bob. Over Meg's shoulder, Gillian peeked inside.

The back of Bob's high office chair was to the door, but Gillian could see the top of her brother-in-law's head above the back of it and two diminutive rear ends protruding beyond each arm rest on either side. One behind was innocently curved, vaguely reminiscent of the posterior of the man seated in the chair. The other, unnaturally enhanced by a diaper, looked like an overstuffed hassock.

Bob's computer screen, usually filled with columns of figures and stock quotes, was awash in a riot of color and animation. Minnie Mouse was chasing Mickey around a garishly colored amusement park. The pair jumped on and off death-defying rides, as Gillian's niece and nephew squealed in delight.

Meg seemed to have lost her irritation. Gillian grinned at the cozy domestic scene. As far as she knew, Meg had made Bob promise that the computer, when the kids were old enough to use it, would be reserved for educational purposes.

On the screen, Minnie finally cornered her sidekick in the Tunnel of Love, and the kids clapped their hands in delight. *Girl chases boy. Catch the guy and your life is complete. How educational.* Meg must be flipping out. To Gillian's surprise, her sister's shoulders shook with silent laughter. Ah, but would Bob still be dancing to the same tune when daughter Jessica hit sixteen? Gillian thought not. Charlie hadn't.

Meg shut the door quietly, stomped her feet loudly in the hall a few times, then knocked. "Bob, have you seen the kids?" she asked innocently, stepping into the room.

Gillian waited in the hall, not wanting to interrupt the family drama. There were sounds of a mad scramble, then Bob's voice. "Oh—hi, honey! Just a minute—they're in here with me. I was—er . . . showing them how Daddy uses his computer, wasn't I, kids?" More sounds of shushing.

"Yes, Daddy," Gillian heard Jessica say.

Gillian bit her lip. How much would *that* cost Bob? Jessica's complicity wouldn't come cheap. Poor Bob. He should know better than to strike a devil's bargain with females of any age.

"Dat!" Matthew was going along with whatever his dad said, Gillian surmised. Already he was turning into one of the boys. She peeked into the office. A spreadsheet innocently filled the twenty-inch monitor screen. It was hard not to crack a smile.

"Well, I'm glad to see everyone hard at work," Meg said. "But Bob, did you remember that we're having everybody over to put the finishing touches on the Harvest Fair plans tonight?"

Bob spun his chair around. "Ah . . . of course, I did, honey."

No, he didn't, Gillian thought.

"Okay, kids," he said, kissing each of them on the crown of their heads, "time to go. Daddy's got to get some supper into you."

Bob stood, his two children cradled one under each arm like footballs. He swung them this way and that and made monster noises. "Hey, Gilly," he said, noticing her standing in the doorway.

"Hi, Auntie!" Jessica cried.

"Dat!" Matthew sputtered wetly.

"Hey, Bob." Gillian tweaked the noses of her niece and nephew as they were borne past her at the open door. "Behaving yourself, you two?" she asked. The expression on her sister's expression said *Not*. The trio lumbered off toward the kitchen. There was a crash down the hall, then sudden silence. Hushed giggling, more shushing, then more monster noises, fading away down the hall.

Meg laughed and her raised eyebrows said it all: *Situation normal at the Ericsons'*. "Why is it I can control a whole room full of other people's kids but not two of my own?" she asked.

"Like Dad says: Carpenter's doors . . . ?"

"Right." She chuckled.

"You're a lucky woman, Meg Ericson," Gillian said, feeling a tender gush for her sister accompanied by . . . what? A speck of jealousy. Yikes. *Thy shall not covet thy sister's lifestyle*.

"Tell me about it," her sister said. Then, "Speaking of Dad, would you go find him?"

Gillian was about to tug open the door that connected the in-law annex she had built—with only a little bit of Riley's help—onto the rear of Meg's house, when a series of rhythmic thumps announced the immanent arrival of her father. The doorknob spun in her hand and the door swung abruptly open. It slammed into her foot. Before she even had time to snap off a curse, a voice growled from the other side of it.

"Damn sticky thing," it said. "Family's full of tradesmen and none of our damn doors ever work right!"

"Dad . . . " Gillian said in a strangled voice. She was pinned against the wall. "It's me. Dad! Jeez, Dad—stop pushing, you're crushing me like a bug." The physical therapy had done wonders for him.

"Eh? Oh, sorry, Meggie," grumbled the force behind the door. "Didn't realize . . ."

The pressure let up and Gillian slid her tender foot back out of the way. The door opened and her father's large frame filled the opening. "Oh, Gillian! Why didn't you say so? Thought it was your sister."

"And you'd rather smush her? I always knew Meg was your favorite." She rubbed her shoulder. The mill accident had slowed him down there for a while, but lately he was getting to be as stubborn and willful as ever. Marge, the therapist down at the clinic on Main Street, must give good rub. *Eek.* Gillian abruptly halted that train of thought. This was her Dad here.

She was getting used to seeing him with a cane. They were all adjusting. Change was good. The natural way of things. Someday maybe she'd succeed in convincing herself of that.

"How are you, Dad?" Gillian asked, hopping on one foot while she massaged the other.

"Something wrong?" her dad asked.

"No."

"What?" He cocked his head.

"I said 'It's fine,' Dad." Gillian gingerly put weight onto her throbbing foot. It held it. She'd survive. Just like her dad. Survivors both, just like Rachel had said.

Charlie had certainly weathered his share of storms, and stubbornness and tenacity were his living legacy to her. The same qualities that had contributed to him being too hard-headed to bother with ear protection down at the mill. Now his partial deafness was almost more limiting than the cane.

"Hey, you're just in time, Dad. I was coming to get you."

"For what?" he asked, propelling himself into the hall.

"You know, the last fair meeting. It's tonight."

"*Tonight?* Why didn't you tell me?"

She and Meg both had. Not two days ago. They had inherited their planning gene from their mother. "Oh, gee, Dad, it must have slipped my mind. Sorry. Glad you're here anyway, though. C'mon down to the kitchen. Meg needs help."

Making their father feel useful was a game Gillian and Meg were old hands at since his injury. Charlie chaffed at living in the in-law apartment grafted onto Meg's house. He hated accepting what he called "charity" from his kids. But the Wilcox Box, especially with Gillian out so much, was too difficult for him to get around in by himself. Besides, he stayed a lot more active living next door to Meg. Plus, since the arrival of his two grandchildren, he didn't have the luxury of sinking into melancholia. The little buggers kept everybody on their toes. Especially that little Matthew, Gillian thought. He was either going to grow up to *be* a good lawyer, or *need* one someday.

She stood on tiptoes and kissed her father's cheek. "We've got to get a move on, Dad. People are here in half an hour."

"People? What people?" She loudly explained while they walked to the kitchen together.

"Ugh!" Would she never get the wood dust out of her hair? Rachel thought. And her nails. They looked like she'd tried to chip through concrete. No wonder Gillian didn't seem very concerned with fashion or looking nice. You'd have to own shares in a salon to keep ahead of the daily beauty insults of that damn sawmill.

The perks were good, though. She smiled into the mirror over the double sinks in Meg's bathroom where she had been ensconced for the last half-hour and admired the way the golden rope of her hair flowed through her hairbrush as she dragged it slowly through her shiny blond cap. That Riley—*Mm, mm, mmm.* Where had he been hiding himself since high school? There was something about a man in khaki. Gillian's developer was handsome all right, but Riley was a Grade A certified hunk.

Bizarre, really, that Riley had asked her out after he'd been so hot to trot for Gillian all these years. But there you go, people change. And since that Jack Turner blew into town, the Riley and Gillian scene was as cold as yesterday's dinner.

Gillian never would have landed him anyway even if she'd wanted to. Her idea of leading a guy on meant secretly nailing down his lunchbox? What was *that* all about? Luke had said that Gillian had practically laughed herself sick over that little prank. Definitely not the way to a man's heart. Then she'd heard Jack had pulled a few fast ones on her. Strange relationship. They were obviously made for each other.

Fifteen more brushstrokes to go. Half the town, including Riley, would be showing up downstairs soon. What to do about her nails . . .

"Damn!" Meg said, when the doorbell chimed.

She hastily set the bowl of onion dip down in the middle of the vegetable platter, scattering carrot bits.

"Hey, careful," Gillian said. "I put a lot of work into those things."

Meg drilled her with one of her patented "teacher" looks that spoke silent volumes. "That has to be Virginia," she said, "arriving what she calls 'fashionably early.' It would be great, actually, if she came in ahead of time with her sleeves pushed up, ready to roll cold cuts or mix the potato salad. But *no* . . ."

With amusement Gillian watched the fuel rods in her sister's nuclear core begin to melt. The woman could control whole tribes of ten-year-old banshees with just an eyebrow, but she met her match in her family. Welcome to the club.

Their Aunt Virginia seemed to think that food materialized out of nowhere without anyone having to create it. Even Gillian knew that didn't happen. Virginia invariably showed up in the kitchens around town ten minutes before the party started. She would drop off three bottles of expensive wine, rummage through drawers, and crab that people never kept the corkscrew in the same place. She was about as useful as tits on a bull at times like this.

"Hel-*lo*!" Gillian heard Virginia trill, from the front hall.

Her father was beside her popping ice cubes out of a tray. He grimaced. "Oh, boy."

"Yeah, something like that." You had to love the woman, but she was exhausting.

"Anybody home?" Virginia called again.

"No, Virginia, Bob and I are out fucking water skiing just now. . ." Meg muttered quietly. "Cripes." She slammed the oven door shut on two trays full of miniature frozen quiches.

Charlie laughed. Gillian kicked him. Her sister hardly ever swore.

"Charlie, Meggie, Bob, kids! It's Aunt *Gin*-nie!"

"She think we're deaf?" Charlie asked.

Gillian's turn to snicker. She watched her dad wrestle the ice cubes into a small serving pail. Most of the contents of half-a-dozen trays got safely corralled, but a few soldiers jumped to the floor.

"Why don't you see if you can find the corkscrew in the drawer next to the sink, Dad?" she said. While he rummaged, Gillian grabbed the errant cubes and tossed them in the sink. She realized she missed working with her dad, although not necessarily in the kitchen. He wasn't the domestic type. Something else she'd inherited.

Summers in high school, right up through college, she'd been a yard dog for him. Starting in the office taking orders, handling the register. Then, bit by bit, learning to run the saw, the Whomper, the loader. When she was only fourteen, he'd let her drive Jasper around the confines of the yard. The son he'd never had.

"Well, here's everybody," Virginia cried, entering the kitchen. "Hi, Meggie, hi, Charlie." Virginia pecked her brother-in-law on the cheek and set a clinking bag down in the middle of the counter. She bent down and kissed the air next to Meg's cheek. Meg pressed her forearms to Virginia, not wanting to get her doughy hands near her aunt's smart wool blazer.

"Nice to see you, Ginnie," Meg said, sliding the bag of wine bottles to one side so she could continue working. "How's the real estate racket?"

"Selling like hotcakes. Oh, thanks, Charlie," she said,

accepting a corkscrew. She set herself to peeling away the seal on a bottle she slid from the bag.

Behind her, Meg announced, "Watch yourself." With a dishtowel she yanked open the oven door. She poked one of the mini-quiches with a fork. "Five more minutes should do it."

"Oh, what adorable little quiches," Ginnie said. "Did you make them yourself?"

The thought of Meg running home from a day at school, throwing down her armload of books and papers to grade, and hand-making trays of quiches with Jessica and Matthew running around loose made Gillian smile. Meg had obviously made the forty-minute run over to the Shop Rite in Bangor. If Rocky Falls went the way of Turner Town, why you could get anything you wanted without leaving town. The thought made Gillian ill.

"She's wacked, Virginia, isn't she?" Charlie said to Gillian, a little too loudly, she feared.

"Dad, ssh!" But even he got it. That said something.

"But you know," he said, "it might not be a bad thing if we had a few more places to shop around here. We wouldn't have to make the damn expedition all the way to Bangor. Getting my ass in and out of the truck isn't as easy as it used to be. I could get those cashews I like right here in town. You know the ones."

"Right, Dad. And the kids would have a movie theatre to go to. And a mall. Just drop them off on a Saturday night. Think of the little friends they could make there."

"Don't be a wise ass."

"Then don't be an idiot, Dad. I never thought I'd hear you of all people jumping on the development bandwagon."

"I'm not doing any such thing, Gillian. I was just saying—"

"Hey, do me a favor, you two, huh?" Meg said. She pulled a butter dish, pots of ketchup, mustard, and relish, a cold-cut platter, and a big bowl of salad from the fridge and set them on the counter. "How about you and Dad take this stuff out to the dining room?"

Chastised, Gillian started to fill her arms. When she could grab no more, Charlie balanced things on the top of the pile. Gillian made a quick trip into the dining room.

"So, Meggie," Virginia was saying as Gillian reentered the kitchen, returning to earth after the wine had passed her initial taste test, "Who's coming tonight, besides The Usuals?"

"Rachel, for one," replied Meg, squeezing herself past her aunt who was leaning comfortably against the counter. "She's primping."

"No, she's *n-ot!*" The sing-song cadence of Rachel's voice was syrupy sweet enough to make a yellow jacket gag.

"Rachel?" Virginia cried, her voice an echo of Rachel's. She turned with arms outstretched toward her niece standing in the doorway with her arms out.

"Aunt Ginnie?" cried Rachel.

"*Yes!*" they cried simultaneously, coming together in a hug and kissing the air around each other's faces.

Now *that* was obnoxious, thought Gillian, grabbing a ketchup bottle. The universe had a truly tweaked sense of humor. Suddenly, the kitchen felt overstuffed. Too damn many people just standing around.

"Hey, come on, you guys," she snapped. "Get this stuff into the dining room like Meg said. Let's go."

"Sure, sweetie," said her dad.

"Of course, dear," said her aunt.

"*What a crab!*" said Rachel in an aside to Virginia. Gillian handed things to the two women and shooed her dad out with them. From across the kitchen Meg mouthed a silent *Thank you.*

Gillian grinned. *You're welcome.* Her older sister put up with a lot.

The doorbell rang again.

"*Door!*" Meg shrieked. Bob came around the corner and squeezed by Gillian, a jar of baby food with a spoon in it in one hand, and the crusts of a peanut butter sandwich with a perfect set of tiny teeth marks in it in the other.

"Oh, thanks, honey, you're a love," Meg said, leaned up and delivered a noisy smack to her husband's lips. "Did Matty eat anything?" she asked, eyeing the jar.

"The cherry cobbler's history. The peas are on the floor. Most of the potatoes are in his hair. But, *oh* yeah, he ate," Bob said chuckling. He grabbed a wet towel and made to leave.

"Oh, honey, check the front door on your way by and see who's there. Try and get Rachel and Aunt Ginnie to at least greet people as they arrive."

He smirked. "I shall do my best, my lady," he said, with a mock bow. "But better men than I have found their match in those two." He swept out, brandishing an imaginary sword in front of him.

Meg laughed and said, "I thank God for giving me a husband who can—once I've ignited the fuse on the keg of dynamite under his rear end, mind you—make himself useful at times like this."

Gillian felt another tiny kick from the green-eyed monster. She thought of Jack Turner for an instant, then banished the thought by handing another tray of food to Virginia who had returned all too soon.

Meg untwisted the ties on three bags of rolls and unceremoniously dumped them into a large basket lined with a dish towel. Gillian bundled up the trash in the kitchen can and slid in a fresh plastic bag. From the sounds out front, folks were arriving in force. *Hello's*, and *How are you?'s* abounded. There was a *Hello, Mr. Holt.*

"Mr. Holt?" Gillian asked.

"Some guy Bob met down at town hall. In the tax collector's office. He's just visiting Rocky Falls, but he seemed really interested in maybe moving here and he wanted to get a glimpse into 'the small town life' Bob said he called it. So Bob invited him to the fair meeting tonight."

Gillian's stomach tensed. "What was Bob doing down at the tax collector's office? You're making the mortgage, right?"

Meg waved a spatula airily. "Heck, yeah. The town

subbed out some of their financials to Bob to try and cut out a half-time position down there."

"Bastards. They don't want to pay benefits on the job is what it is," Gillian said.

"I hear you," Meg said, "but it's the same old, same old. Struggling all around to keep the services going in this town. They're talking about cutting a kindergarten teacher next year."

"No shit?"

"No money."

"How about you? You're safe, right?" Gillian couldn't employ another sister at the mill. One was enough. Besides, there wasn't enough margin to cover another salary. Rachel's long-overdue work on the company books had made that abundantly clear. But what would Meg and Bob do if Meg lost her job?

"I'm okay for next year," Meg said, "but who knows after that? Look at those towns petitioning to disband as a town. They become unincorporated. Collectively bid for services along with other towns caught in the same circumstances."

Gillian's stomach lurched again. It was getting an unexpected workout.

"Sure, they get snow plowing and trash pickup done on the cheap," Meg said, "but then the State of Maine can tell them what to do in their own town. No more town meetings, kiss self-government as we know it goodbye." Gillian was all too familiar with the disbanding movement from her work at the state planning office in Augusta. The trend scared the crap out of her.

"Let's change the subject," Meg said, concern creasing her forehead. "I've got enough on my mind right now."

"Ditto."

A *"Pleased to meet you"* drifted to the kitchen. Followed by a *"Same"* from her brother-in-law. Odd. Who had come that Bob didn't know? She and Meg exchanged looks.

Meg shrugged. "Set out some silverware!" she called into the dining room. She yanked open the oven door, removed the trays of miniature quiches and slid them onto a warmed serving plate. Cursing a hot metal tray, she dropped it into the sink, then grabbed a bunch of parsley and arranged it around the edge of the pastries. Gillian scooped up the tray and turned toward the dining room.

She ran solidly into a trim midriff whose owner said "Oof!" Startled, she looked up into the bluest eyes she'd ever seen. With lashes to beat the band.

"I can get these started around, if you'd like," Jack said.

Shit. The appetizing aroma of the mini-quiches suddenly made Gillian feel ill.

"I don't care what the fuck you do with them," was out of her mouth before her mind was even aware she'd formed the words. She shoved the plate hard against his stomach. A quiche fell to the floor and rolled under the television cabinet. Gillian realized Rachel, Charlie, Virginia, and assorted people from town were staring openmouthed at her, drinks and hors d'oeuvres frozen midway to their mouths.

"Waggles will find it," Gillian said into the hush. Howls from the Ericson family's pet mutt, banished to the backyard for the evening, could be heard plainly in the shocked silence.

Must escape. Before she filled another bag for the Mohasset. She grabbed a quiche from the tray. Bit into it, tasting nothing. "Good," she said to the crowd, raising it high in tribute. She fought the impulse to run and instead took a few steps backward, then turned and slipped out the back door with as much grace as she could muster.

The flood lights in the back yard weren't on, but the moon was just working its way above the tree line. A dinner platter, so low and huge it seemed she could reach up and touch it. If Jack Turner followed her out here, she could slip away through the woods. She whistled softly. "Waggles. Here, boy." She heard the jangle of dog tags then a deep voice.

"Evening, Miss." The voice came from the shadow of a forsythia bush. Waggles already had company. A wiry,

silver-haired man, well-preserved—mid-sixties? Gillian
guessed—was down on one knee patting the dog.

"Evening, yourself," Gillian said.

"I think I've made a friend," the man said, rising and
walking over with his hand extended.

Gillian wasn't sure if he meant the dog or her, but she
shook his hand. His fingers were strong and the skin was
rough, the grip steely. A lifetime of manual labor written
there. He had a healing scar above his eye. She bet his hair,
done up in a style reminiscent of the best televangelists,
hadn't always looked that good. Money, it said. Gotten late
in the game, though.

Waggles, smelling the quiche, jumped on Gillian, plant-
ing his paws halfway up her thigh, his nails digging into her
skin through her thin slacks.

"Sit," the man snapped.

To Gillian's amazement, Waggles did. Unable to resist his
eyes a moment longer, Gillian tossed Waggles the remains
of her mini-quiche which he inhaled. He sniffed her hands
looking for more.

"Good dog," the man said, and Waggles looked at him.
"Just needs discipline."

Unusual conversation starter, but okay, she'd bite. "Yes,
sir. Like the rest of us, I suppose." She found herself unconsciously imitating his slow drawl. Just like she had with the
people she'd scared away from the footbridge.

"You grew up here in these parts, Missy?" the man asked.
"'Cause from the sound of it, you got a little bit of Southern
belle in you." The man grinned. He had teeth like Riley's,
even and white and large, forming an enamel picket fence in
his mouth. Real? she wondered. Riley's were, but she'd bet
this guy got his from the same parts factory his hair came
from. Still, she found herself rising to his obvious attempts
to charm her.

"No, no. Just an upcountry girl through and through.
Gillian Wilcox is the name." She batted her eyes in what she

hoped was an appropriately belle-like manner. Give the guy
his props, he had to be thirty years older than her.

"Wilcox . . . Wilcox." The man stroked his chin thoughtfully, then snapped his fingers. "Wilcox Lumber, right? Just
outside of town?"

"That's it. And you are?"

"Dodge Holt."

"And what brings you to town, Mr. Holt?"

"That's a mighty nice spread there along the river, Gillian.
May I call you Gillian?"

She nodded, completely aware he had avoided her question. "Yes, it is," she replied, noncommittally. "Been in the
family for generations. My mother's side, then passed by
marriage to my dad's side."

"Ah, yes, a family merger."

"Something like that." She eyed him quizzically. "What
are you doing out here, Mr. Holt? The party's inside."

He knelt again to pat Waggles, who lay on his back and
wriggled in delight. Gillian bet the man did it so she
couldn't read his eyes. *Wait for the lie*, she told herself.

"I . . . ah, came out here for some air."

And there it was. But why? Easy math: *He was avoiding
someone inside*.

Gillian tried to remember the conversations at the front
door that she and Meg had overheard. *Mr. Holt* . . . Then a
minute or so later, *Pleased to meet you*. He was hiding out
from the pleasing someone. *Click*. From—

"Get away from her."

Jack. The tone in his voice was cut from a much bigger
chunk of chaw. The words landed with a splat onto the concrete of the patio, right between her and Dodge Holt.

"Waggles is a boy, you idiot." Gillian said.

Gillian kept her eyes on the dog. Waggles writhed in
ecstasy from the ear rubbing of the enigmatic Mr. Holt. Jack
the Crack was probably jealous that the little dog hadn't immediately jumped ship and run to him. To think that she

lacked the instincts of a dumb beagle. But then again, Boo
had been fooled too.

"Jack," Mr. Holt drawled, "we meet again."

Again? Then she got it. Holt was the "old guy" who had
been lying bleeding on the floor out at Riley's McMansion.

"Don't fuck with me, Dodge," Jack said, taking a step
closer to Holt.

No love lost here, Gillian instantly realized. She scooped
up Waggles and hugged him to her chest, casually placing
herself and twenty-two pounds of baggy beagle body between the two men.

Dodge cut his eyes to her. "Wouldn't want to intrude on
anyone else's patch," he said abruptly, all trace of the Southern gentleman gone.

Now that was nasty, the innuendo obvious and gross.

Jack must have thought so too, because one of his arms
flashed past her face. She pretended to stumble, shoving her
shoulder into his chest. His fingers closed on empty air. She
pretended to fall and he was forced to grab her with both
of his arms. Waggles woofed half-heartedly. Probably the
most excitement he'd had in a year.

"Ah, why don't we all go inside and have something to
eat?" she said, recovering her balance. She stared at Holt,
daring him to make anything out of that comment. She saw
something flash in his eyes. She braced herself for a go at him
herself.

She heard the rear door of the house open behind her.
"Mr. Holt, is it?"

Gillian had never been so happy to hear Riley's voice in
her life.

"In the flesh," Dodge said. His eyes never left her and
Jack.

"Meg's looking for you. She wants to make introductions.
Why don't—" Riley hesitated, looking right at Gillian—
"y'all come in for a spell?"

Relief rushed through her. *Thank you, thank you, thank
you*, she said in a look. The big brother she never had.

Dodge hesitated. Like he hated to let go of the moment. Like an alcoholic with an open bottle in front of him, Gillian thought. Finally, he seemed to come to a decision. He sauntered past her, touching two fingers to his forehead as he went. "Evening, ma'am." The screen door hissed shut behind him.

Gillian released Waggles and sagged onto the steps. She was a rag doll. "Not a nice man," she said.

"Who?" Jack asked.

"Both of you," she said. "But him more."

And quick for his age. No wasted motion. Two little steps and Jack was grabbing at smoke. She said as much.

"He's an ex-boxer."

"Ah. Come around to collect on some shady loans, no doubt. Funny, I always pictured shady mob guys as bigger, somehow, with blue-black stubble on their chins and bulges under their suitcoats."

He ignored the jibe. "Loans, yes. Shady? No." He joined her on the steps. "Everything was completely above board. But if you really want to know, he owns me."

"I'll bet." She slid as far to her side of the steps as the railing would allow.

"Financially, at least."

"He sounds like someone I should get to know." She thought of row upon row of cookie-cutter houses. Of the power of money.

"Suit yourself," he said, noncommittally. "I heard about your flight," he said.

"Through your network of spies?"

"Through these?" He pointed at his ears. "I was fishing the river. That is the *loudest* plane . . ."

"It's an antique."

"You could have just asked me," he said.

"Oh, really. Let's try it on for size, shall we?" She made sounds like an audiotape rewinding, then flicked an imaginary switch. In an announcer's voice she said, "Say, Jack, tell us about the complete disaster you created in upstate

New York, would you? Which part would you say was more fun, Mr. Turner? Bulldozing the farmland or laying down the miles of asphalt?" She really wasn't up for this, she realized. She was swinging blindly, not even caring if she connected. All she wanted to do was to go home and crawl into bed. Or back into the tub. She smelled bubble bath.

Which is probably how Jack got past her defenses, she realized later when she thought about the evening.

"I could never convince you with words," he said.

That should have been her cue to exit, stage left.

"So I'm going to try this." Suddenly his lips were on hers. His arms went around her. Her first thought: *Bite the bastard,* but then something zigzagged its lonely way across the No Man's Land between her heart and his. Some tentative ray of hope shone in her heart. Just across a river a future dimly glowed. One she desperately yearned for. Right there, just out of reach. She reached out, feeling the air behind Jack, feeling ridiculous. But it was there—whatever it was—just on the other side, floating above the opposite shore like the dust motes in the truck cab that painful day . . .

Details, her rational mind said. *Pin him down.* She broke the kiss. Put a restraining hand on Jack's chest. It was heaving.

"Jack, Greenville was horrible. Nothing like what I thought it would be."

"For me, too," he said, unexpectedly. His eyes were huge, the gas jets cranked full on.

"What?"

He laid out the whole story. The good intentions, the frenzied land selling, the unanticipated buy-ups. He ended with "It got out of hand. Went places we never imagined. By then, I was neck deep in it. Stuck. Dodge has always been good to my mother."

His last remark would likely seem a *non sequitur* to a lot of people, she imagined, but she understood it right away. He was talking about a sense of obligation to family. Something she never imagined they'd have in common. She felt the familiar current swirl around her, pulling at her, drawing her down, down into the vortex. . . . She'd trusted her gut—and Boo's—before and look where it had gotten her. Did she dare to again? She hesitated for one millisecond before reaching a decision. She breathed against his lips, "You have *so* much 'splaining to do, Lucy."

Her hands dived beneath his shirt, the wide warmth of him under her palms. Crazy, crazy. All new somehow, but old too. *Antique*, her mind quipped. This man was a rock, his legs sprouting from the bedrock of this town like a character from a Marvel comic book. Striding powerfully across the landscape, the Mohasset streaming around his feet, Haystack Mountain only waist high to him. He held the power to crush this place to mica dust, yet Gillian sensed him stepping carefully, treading lightly, picking his spots. As he had done with his oh-so-talented tongue. She picked back with hers.

Jack lifted her off her feet, gathered her tight to his chest in his granite limbs, her feet swinging in empty air. She threw her arms around his solid neck. Her elegant metaphors broke down when Jack attempted to nimbly hop the border of perennials at the edge of the patio. His foot slipped down into the soft bed and he stumbled forward a few steps. She braced herself for a mouthful of sod but he recovered, and with a goofy laugh that was nothing like a superhero's, made his way across the dark lawn.

"What time is it?" Gillian asked.

"Why?" he asked.

With a compressed hiss, the heads of the automatic lawn sprinklers popped above ground and fired.

"That's why," Gillian said.

"Shit." He splashed right through the Mohasset and knocked over Haystack Mountain in his rush across the slippery turf. His truck was parked at the curb just outside the spray perimeter. He set her on her feet and opened the passenger door. "Cold," she said, shivering and hugging herself. "Really, really cold."

"Get in," he said.

"Maybe it'd be better to go back to the house?"

"Like that?" He nodded at the front of her wet top.

Hot lips plus cold spray equaled extraordinary perkiness. "Right. Let's get in."

He made his way around to the driver's side and turned the ignition. The engine started right up.

"Got a new battery?" She smirked in the darkness of the cab.

"Uh-huh. With the proceeds from my second job. Shouldn't be long now," he said, flipping a selector lever on the dash.

For what? she wondered, excited, giddy, her stomach turning excited somersaults. For heat, she realized he meant. She touched the back of her hand to her forehead and found it warmer than the old truck would ever be. *Fever!*

Jack reached behind the seat back and pulled out a bag.

You'd think it was her birthday the way it was all done up with ribbons. "It's not my birthday," she said, confused. She accepted the package from him. It was heavy. Like the gears in her head. She couldn't get them to turn. He'd gotten her something. Something . . . nice. Pretty, all the ribbons. Gotten her something even before they'd made up. She had been on his mind since Greenville. *He'd jumped in to save her . . .*

"I've had it for awhile," he said. "But the time never seemed right . . . before."

Before? Then she got it. *Before Greenville.* Before she knew his dark secrets. She noticed the Riverworks logo imprinted on the side of the bag. Fortunately her Aunt Betty was probably the only person in town who could keep their mouth shut about anything.

She found she had no voice. Only one word squeaked out. "Why?"

"Just because," he said.

No one other than an immediate family member had ever given her something "just because." She struggled with the mass of ribbon until Jack slit it with a pocketknife. Gingerly opening the bag, she took out the beautifully wrapped, heavy box she found inside and held it up to her ear.

"Well, it's not ticking."

She saw an emotion flit across his face.

"I'm sorry," she said, "that was a stupid thing to say. Honestly, I'm just a little overwhelmed. I'm not used to getting gifts from—" she was about to say "handsome men," but went with "people I've just . . . I don't know. I think I'll just shut up now." Because how would she finish that? People she hardly knew yet slept with? Loved?

Moisture welled in the corners of her eyes. At that moment she wouldn't have cared if he was the ugliest man on earth, an absolute toad: he had touched her, damn it, right where she lived.

Her fingers fumbled. More quick work with the knife and the box was open.

"Oh, Jack . . . it's beautiful."

"Do you like it?" he asked. "Really?"

How much he cared if she liked it or not surprised him. And the sound of his name on her lips hit him like a powerful torrent. Yet he held himself back. *Distance*, he reminded himself. Until the day there didn't have to be any more.

"Yes, really. It's beautiful. Thank you," Gillian said.

"I'm glad. I saw it and the ducks reminded me—" he finished lamely, "of you."

She bowed her head.

"And the way you saved my sorry ass from drowning," he said, chuckling.

That made her throw her head back and laugh. To Jack's ears a delightful sound that filled the cab with life and love and sunshine.

"I don't think either of us will forget that morning," she said.

"It feels like years ago, already," he said.

"Like another lifetime."

"Like there's a time warp going on in this town," Jack said.

So he felt it too. "Right. A time warp," she said.

278 *Lucy Ann Peters*

Gillian watched Jack's long fingers flip a switch on the dash and heat blasted from beneath it. She had never seen such a doodad-free dashboard in her life. "There's only like three buttons on the whole thing," she said. This truck was its own little time warp. "Oh my Lord, Jack, is that an 8 track?"

He reached across her and thumbed opened the glove box to reveal a half-dozen clunky cartridges inside.

"Hah! What a hoot." She checked out the titles. "It's a whole Time/Life series, Jack." He looked irritated. "Sorry, sorry. I don't mean that in a bad way, it's just . . ."

Who'd have figured?

"They're also antiques," he said, a touch of pride in his voice.

"I guess. *Bread?* You've got Bread? Oh, and Cream, too. Jack—it's a complete meal in here."

He sidled over to her and nibbled her earlobe. "A yummy one."

She rummaged through the collection of cassettes, blaming her clumsiness on Jack's distracting influence, finally choosing a title and handing it to him. He pushed a few buttons. A couple on the 8 track in the dash, too, with his free hand. Ambidextrous man. A genuine multitasker. *Baby, I'm a want you . . .* crooned from hidden, kick-ass speakers.

She giggled. This was great. She leaned into him.

Abruptly he broke away and put the pickup into gear. "Jack, what the—"

He rolled the car a few dozen feet forward into the shadow of some overgrown azaleas and then put it into Neutral. And then he went into Drive. *Baby I'm a need you . . .*

The windows steamed. Gillian did too. Clothes shimmied up and shimmied down. Pure heat, dizzying. After what seemed an eternity of blowing on the kindling among other things, Gillian was desperate for the bonfire. She panted impatiently, "So, you got the thing?"

"What thing?" Jack mumbled.

His mouth was tending to a breast. *Sss!* For a guy who

sucked a little while ago, he could really, well, suck. "You know? The infamous 'foil packet'?" she said.

"No."

"No, you don't have it or no, you don't understand what I'm talking about?"

Now he was giving her other breast equal playing time. Perfectly equal, no doubt. He was *so* OCD. *Ma-an* . . . Not that she was complaining. She stroked the back of his head, the thick dark hair, and her head lolled.

"Don haf it."

"You don't have it. It. The little thingie. Which means we can't—*Argh!* I could so kill you right now." The muscles in her neck had turned to India rubber. "But I can't think."

"Then just feel," he said. His diction had improved because he was kissing her belly. Correction—her belly button—Correction: her *Oh*, goodness.

She gasped. *Oh, God.* "What kind of a man doesn't show up to these things . . . oh, Jack . . ." Her hips lifted. "Prepared?" *Ahhhh.* He licked more enthusiastically. *That* kind of a man.

"First of all," he said clearly, lifting his mouth from her.

"Hey, hey. Don't stop." She pointed downward dreamily with one hand and ran her fingers through the curls at the nape of his neck with the other.

"Right." His fingers jumped in where his tongue had left off. "First of all, I had no idea this would turn into 'one of those things.' For all I knew, you would never speak to me again."

"That's what I thought—Ugh." *Mmmm.* Oh, yeah. Right there. She told him so. The Bread guy murmured in the background. The 8 track was scratchy, kind of hard to understand the words. Normally that would drive her nuts, but—*Yees . . . right there.* She rode waves of pleasure and remembered the time she and Jack had sat in the town square and she'd thought: Most guys packed a rubber when they were planning to screw someone, but not Jack. He carried architectural renderings.

It was so what? *Romantic* that the idiot hadn't come prepared tonight. Not like he'd been in his room at the Eagle House. Big box, then. Jumbo pack. Multicolored. Completely prepared. Used up a bunch of them. *Par-tay. Fiesta.* But not tonight. That meant he really had thought he'd lost her. Which he really had for a while there, she realized. But not now. She stifled a scream, arched her back and tumbled over the edge.

The knock on the window had them sharing the same heart attack.

"What the *f*—" Jack's head flew up from between her thighs and it whacked against the steering wheel. Gillian twisted in the seat and sat up abruptly. Too late she discovered her hair had become entwined with the window crank. Chunks of it ripped out by the roots.

"*Damn* it!" She squeegeed a tiny peephole in the steamy glass with the side of her fist. "Oh, shit."

"Don't tell me."

"Oh, yes. Except this time, it's my frigging aunt."

Chapter 28

Riley mixed Dodge Holt in with the rest of the crowd inside the house. Water the man down in polite company and maybe he wouldn't start any more shit storms. Unbelievable, Jack thinking his stepfather wouldn't track him here to Rocky Falls after all the shit Jack had told him he'd done to the guy's project in Vermont. Sometimes, for a smooth operator, Jack didn't have much on the ball.

Riley went room to room searching for Rachel. He worked the crowd, easing in and out of conversations, keeping a wary eye out for Virginia. The woman made him nervous. Someone to be avoided at all costs. After a few minutes he realized neither Rachel nor her aunt were anywhere inside. Loose, together, somewhere on the property? Not good.

He gave the room a final scan. Dodge Holt was deep in conversation with Bob Ericson. He'd keep. Rachel was now the priority. He grabbed a mini-quiche and slipped out the back door.

Gillian breathed on the peephole to seal it up. The sound of expensive acrylic nails *tap, tap, tapping* on the side window and roof of the pickup was maddening. So was the giggling.

"Saw sheds, front seats, what the hell is wrong with us?" Jack panted.

"Good times," Gillian said, wrestling with her twisted pants legs. "Go away!" she bellowed at the steamed glass. "Rachel's out there, too, by the way," she said to Jack. The tempo of the tapping increased. The pickup began to rock.

"Your relatives have one twisted sense of humor," Jack said. Gillian heard his jingling belt buckle cinch home.

"And they drink like fish," she said.

More giggling from outside.

Riley tossed Waggles the mini-quiche. Good boy.

He made his way around the driveway side of the house. The automatic sprinklers had come on. He avoided the spray. The sound of raucous, high-pitched laughter drew his attention.

There was Rachel. With her aunt, unfortunately. They were having a hell of a time bumping their hips up against—he peered into the shadows—Jack Turner's yellow pickup. He heard bellowing from inside. Rachel and Virginia cackled like witches. Tanked, both of them.

"How the hell are we gonna get out of here gracefully?" Jack asked. He'd managed to get his shirt buttoned in the semidarkness. Thankfully, there were no button holes left unfilled when he was done.

"This from the man who walked off into the sunset dressed in my dad's old clothes?" Gillian turned her back to him and held out the ends of her bra. "Get me, will you?"

He kissed her between the shoulder blades and fastened her in.

"God, don't get us going again," she breathed, the familiar weak-kneed feeling sweeping her up.

Tap-tap.

"Not a chance," he said.

* * *

"Ladies," Riley said as he drew near the pickup. "Nice evening." Why did he suddenly wish he were wearing a flack jacket?

Rachel and Virginia looked at him and giggled hysterically.

"I see," he said, because he suddenly did. The two idiots had cornered Jack Turner and Gillian. Yep, there were two madly scrambling silhouettes outlined in the steamy rear window of the pickup. From how he'd seen Gillian look at Jack when she thought he wasn't looking, he hoped for Turner's sake that it *was* her in there. It'd get real ugly around here if it was someone else. Paint Rocky Falls red, Gillian would. *Welcome to Hell* sign, the whole bit, just like in one of those stupid westerns she was always watching at one o'clock in the morning.

For a second he entertained the notion of jumping in on Rachel and Virginia's action. The ultimate punk on Gillian. The dog shit-*ee* for once. Make up for a lifetime of coming in second. He sighed. No, damn it.

"Rachel, grow up," he said. "And Virginia, you should be ashamed of yourself—"

"You say *A woman your age* and I kill you," Virginia growled, pointing an imaginary gun at him. She and Rachel cackled again.

Somebody was gonna be *really* sick tomorrow. "Go," he said. "Get out of here. Get back to the house and mind the sprinklers." He shooed them like they were sheep. In their condition they practically were.

They staggered toward the house. Rachel half turned. "Don't think you can tell us whash ta do," she slurred. "We're indepindont—indupand. . . . Ah, screw it. We know whash the fock we're doing."

More hysterical laughter. The two women clung to each other for support.

"Fuckin' A . . ." Riley thought he heard from inside the pickup. He tapped on the glass. "Clear," he said.

A window rolled halfway down. "I am *so* going to beat the shit out of you, Rachel!" his oldest friend screamed in his face.

Back inside, Riley found Rachel in the kitchen rinsing dishes and attempting to put them in the dishwasher. She had cups on the bottom and silverware laying on the top rack. Even he knew that wasn't how you did it. He went to the sink and leaned over, pretending he had to rinse off his hands. There was a broken wine glass lying at the very bottom of the machine, right near the impeller.

"Hey, Riley," said Rachel. "How you doing?" She banged a dish against the side of the top rack. It took three tries for her to actually get it in the rack.

"Fine, and you, Rach?"

"Good. I'm gonna be really sick tomorrow." She grabbed the edge of the counter for support. Took a sip of coffee from a mug on the counter. Riley wasn't convinced it had started out the evening as her cup.

"Virginia?"

"Upstairs. Getting herself together for the big speech."

"Throwing up?"

"Pretty much."

Rachel looked contrite, like a little kid who knew she had gone too far. "I'm scared," she confessed.

"Don't worry, Gillian'll calm down. I can't tell you how many times she's said that to me."

"Did she ever try to make good?"

"Well, yeah. A couple. Look, let me give you a hand, here," he said. "You rinse and I'll load the machine." He surreptitiously rearranged the dishes and utensils. Fished out the glass fragments, wrapped them in a piece of newspaper and threw them into the trash.

Riley had big hands, Rachel noticed. Capable. He moved them around nicely. Economically. No wasted effort. And to think he knew his way around a dishwasher. He was obviously comfortable in the kitchen. At home on the range. She stifled an unlady-like snort. He looked at her but didn't say anything.

Sort of a surprise, really, a big, brawny guy like him. She snorted again. *Brawny.* Hah! Like the paper towel guy on TV. She was too funny. Her head spun. And she was bombed is what she was. She chugged the rest of the coffee. Riley brought her more. She helped him work through the mountain of dirty dishes and serving trays that wouldn't fit in the machine.

Neither of them said much. What was wrong with her, she wondered, to suddenly lose her gift of the gab with a guy? But was that so bad, really? Riley didn't seem to mind and this was nice, not having to keep up the chit-chat. It had been real work at times bantering with the smooth-talking three-piece suits she'd dated in Boston. From cashmere to khaki in one smooth move. Interesting. She giggled, making the room revolve. Tomorrow morning was going to suck big time.

She handed Riley the last platter to dry. Then she wrung out the wash rag and hung it over the faucet like she remembered her mother doing. There. This domestic stuff wasn't so bad once you got the hang of it. She hiccuped. The clock was definitely ticking on the old gag reflex.

Riley straightened up and Rachel heard his back crack.

"Ouch! You okay?" she asked.

"I'm fine," he said, wincing. "It's just that these damn counters are too low. They're made for midgets. I made the ones at my place three inches higher, so I'm not a cripple when I'm done fixing supper."

"You cook?" asked Rachel.

"Necessity's a mother," he said. "I don't cook, I don't eat."

"I'm impressed."

"Well, you'll just have to come by for supper one night. Hey, maybe when we go out again . . ." He hesitated. "I mean—I'm thinking there is a next time?"

"Of course." A thrill of excitement made her stomach feel better. Their first date had been . . . interesting. A little uptight, a little restrained maybe, but then again . . . interesting.

"Well, I was thinking," Riley said, "instead of us going out we could just well, stay in. I could cook for you. That is, if you're okay with that."

She batted her eyes. "That would be lovely."

Riley felt the blast all the way in his toes. Man, she was a looker, but why him? What could he possibly give her she didn't already have? He asked her out all right, but the way she'd set him up for it, he'd have to be stupid not to go for it. But she was money all over, same as Jack. They were fast trackers. Big city. He wasn't like them. Just a regular Joe with a recently successful, small-town business was what he was.

Rachel drove a BMW for chrissakes. It'd take him ten years to save up for something like that. Gillian had said Rachel got a fifty-thousand-dollar bonus last quarter. Up until a few years ago when business started to pick up, he'd have been happy to clear somewhere around that for the whole *year*.

But they ended up here tonight, doing dishes together side by side, him with a towel over his shoulder and her with an apron wrapped around her to protect an outfit that probably cost more than his truck. But it felt okay. It really did.

Suddenly inspired, he said, "Hey, why don't you come over tomorrow night? Why wait until Friday anyway?"

"Tomorrow . . ." Rachel sucked on her lower lip. "I guess I'd be free. Okay. What time?"

"I'm home at five-thirty. Come by, say, six-thirty, seven?"

"Great," her mouth said, "that'd be nice." But her brain was saying: This was *Riley*, for goodness sake.

She really, really tried to tear her eyes from the rippling muscles in his forearms as he rolled down his sleeves.

Chapter 29

Gillian and Jack ducked around the sprinklers on their way back to the house. Jack held Meg's front door open for Gillian.

"Keep your guard up," she warned.

He grinned. "Beware of the Twins?"

"Exactly. Like in *Twister*."

He chuckled. They moved into the dining room, where the initial feeding frenzy had died down. People were relaxed, talking around their last mouthfuls. They filled plates and found a quiet corner to settle into. Jack made short work of Meg's pasta, but Gillian just picked. Lack of appetite wasn't usually her problem, but her stomach felt like ball bearings were rolling around in it. She wondered where Riley was.

"You okay?"

Jack had noticed her lackluster interest in the food. "I'm fine," she said. "I just feel like we're under a microscope."

"Not to worry," Jack said. "People are probably looking at us because I'm somewhat of a bone of contention around here."

"A pretty *big* bone, I'd say," she said, assessing him over the rim of her wineglass.

He hooted.

Whatever attention she felt might have been on them shifted when her Aunt Virginia took center stage in front of the large fireplace. Amazingly, except for a slight sway, the woman seemed to have pulled herself together.

"Hello, everybody," she said to the assembled. "First, we'd like to thank you all for coming." People murmured their thanks for the dinner. Virginia accepted them as her due, Gillian noted, as if the fact that they were all standing in Meg's house and eating her cooking was just coincidental.

"Remarkable powers of recovery, your aunt," Jack said. He speared a baby dill on his plate.

"Don't talk with your mouth full."

"You didn't seem to mind a few minutes ago."

She reddened and elbowed him. It was good to have regained the crown. *The Forest Queen.* . . . It had such a nice ring to it.

Virginia said, "Now that we've all had time to socialize . . ." Did her aunt look her way on purpose? Gillian wondered. "It's time for the hard work!" The gathered laughed politely. "Now, why don't we call this meeting to order."

Rachel popped into the room, looking only half as drunk as she had sounded half an hour before. Where was Meg? Gillian wondered. Ah. In the doorway, with a kitchen towel draped over her shoulder and an exasperated expression on her face.

Virginia went on. "We'd like to start by thanking everyone who has been part of the planning of our annual gala event since last winter. All your efforts are much appreciated." She started a round of applause then killed it with a slash of her hand. "However, with the fair just a few days away, we've got some final jobs to dole out to our little army of volunteers. We thought—" Virginia said, "I mean, the *committee* thought that with the 150th anniversary and all, we needed to add a few last-minute extras this year. You know, do some sprucing up? Whip up some special touches

to set us up for another successful century and a half?"
More polite chuckles.

"Enjoying the evening?" Betty whispered.

Gillian started and sloshed some wine from her glass.
"Jeez . . ." Her aunt had come up behind them like smoke.
"Oh, hey, Betty. Hi," she said. She balanced her glass and
leaned back to kiss her aunt on the cheek. "But don't do that
to a body."

"Hi, yourself and sorry, I didn't mean to startle you." Her
chuckle was warm and deep. "Thought I'd hide out back
here with you two. Maybe my sister will overlook me."

Jack laughed. "I doubt it. Virginia never seems to miss a
trick."

"And what she misses, Rachel gets," Gillian added. The
three of them laughed as one. Gillian felt her aunt's warm
touch on her shoulder. She saw Betty's other hand come to
rest lightly on Jack's shoulder.

"You two . . . know each other?" she asked Betty.

"Oh, yes, we've met." Her aunt smiled, serene and Buddha-
like. "Heads up, you two," she said, leaning her head forward
between the two of theirs. "Rachel and Virginia have cooked
up some surprises."

Lovely. As if the ambush out at the pickup wasn't enough.

Virginia's voice boomed. "As always, Rachel and I will
handle the publicity for the fair. Ads, postings—"

"Minding other people's business . . ." Gillian muttered.

Jack almost choked on his mouthful of potato salad.

"But this year we've added a new member to our tradi-
tional twosome," Virginia said. She gestured. "You all know
Doug Riley."

There was a good-natured mock cheer from the assembled.

"Our advertising committee needs a few new last-minute
signs and sandwich boards, and a man with Doug's talent is
just the ticket for us." Rachel and Virginia grinned like a
matched pair of man-eating sharks.

Riley had come in late, and was scooping up the last of

the beans. Gillian watched his fork freeze in midair, halfway
to his mouth, the beans sliding off and dropping onto the
plate. God, poor Riley. He was screwed.

"Also, the committee thought that the making of some
new, wooden sales booths would be appropriate," Virginia
continued. "The ones we've been using are getting a bit
ratty, and we'd like to expand some of our craft display
areas."

Lynette piped up from the back of the room. "Hallelujah!
Last year we had to show the afghans the church guild made
in a shack no bigger than a three-holer." The guild ladies tit-
tered. The main body of the audience guffawed.

"And for the building committee, could we count on you—
ah, there you are, Gillian—for some lumber for the new
booths?" Virginia asked.

Gillian nodded. "Of course."

"Terrific. Now, you'll need some help with that little rush
order, so we thought that Luke could help, and Skip, too, if
Joyce will let him go long enough."

Laughter all around.

"Also—" Virginia took a deep breath, "Mr. Turner? Would
you help out building the booths?" The room went quiet. All
eyes swung to Jack.

"Told you . . ." Betty whispered in a sing-song to Jack and
Gillian.

"I . . . Uh . . ." Jack tried. Gillian could feel the stiffness
in his arm where it brushed up against hers.

"After all, there is nothing like doing common work to get
to know people, is there?" Virginia persisted. "How's that
sound, everybody?"

A round of "Here, here!" went up.

"But—" Jack said.

Gillian surreptitiously reached over and squeezed his
forearm. "We'll deal," she whispered. "Just agree."

"Okay," he said in a voice that sounded like he'd rather eat
ground glass.

"Great! That's settled then."

Peter Dunn stood at the back of the room near the buffet table, rocking on his toes, his hands comfortably stuffed into the pockets of his overalls. Her eyes found him. "Peter? You and the boys are still our musical entertainment, yes?"

He nodded. "As promised."

Virginia made a quarter turn and held out her palm in an imitation of royalty. "Lynette and the ladies of the guild? Decorations are coming along swimmingly, I imagine?"

"A-yep." Lynette and her cohorts nodded and clucked like a gaggle of matronly geese. Lots of wine being knocked back in that corner of the room, Gillian imagined.

"Well, we're all set then," Virginia concluded. She gestured toward the rear of the living room. "Let's have some coffee, shall we?"

Meg staggered in bearing a tray overloaded with cups, sugar, and cream and a bowl of fruit salad. She set it down on the dining room sideboard with a rattle, and started to slice a coffee cake.

Gillian gave Jack's arm a final squeeze. She sidled through the crowd over to her sister. "Great job tonight, Meggie," she said. She grabbed a cup and paired it up with a saucer.

Meg viciously tore the plastic wrap from a plate of brownies. One of the neat squares fell from the plate, bounced off the table and tumbled under it. "No thanks to your sister," she said. "And your aunt."

"Why is it always *my* sister and *my* aunt when they're being pains?"

Meg snorted. "You're not really going to beat her up are you?"

"Who, Rachel? You heard?" Gillian asked, amazed.

"*Ooh*, yeah." Meg laughed, her irritation dissipating. She shook her head wonderingly and affectionately rearranged a lock of Gillian's hair behind one ear as if she were a child.

Gillian had a sudden horrible thought. "Who else knows?"

"Who else doesn't?" Meg said, chuckling. "Rachel and

Virginia stumbled in the front door and practically wet themselves telling everyone about the whole thing."

Gillian felt like she had been suddenly struck by lightning.

"Don't look like that," her sister said. "It isn't worth it. You know this town. And Rachel really *was* upset underneath it all." Meg slipped a serving spoon into the fruit salad. "And not just about you threatening her. She actually felt bad that she had made things uncomfortable for you out there."

So she *hadn't* imagined all the eyes upon her when she and Jack had come back into the house tonight, Gillian thought. Then it hit her. "*Rachel* felt bad? Our baby sister, Rachel?" She shook her head in mock wonder. "I didn't think she had it in her."

Meg chuckled, an echo of their Aunt Betty in her voice. "Oh, come on," she said. "She's not all that bad." She appeared to think a minute, then added, "Usually."

Gillian laughed, then thought for a moment, getting her bearings back. "So I'm assuming it was her—or Virginia—who invited Jack to come tonight?"

"Well, actually . . ." Meg said, leaning in, a smirk lighting her face, "according to the story it sounds more like *you* did that. . ." She went back to innocently unwrapping baked goods.

Did what? It took Gillian a second to connect the dots. She felt the blush to the roots of her hair. "You are evil, do you know that? Disgusting and evil."

"Seriously, though, get a room, Gillian. Right out front?"

"It was a spur-of-the-moment thing."

"Evidently," Meg said chastely. She topped off a small pitcher with half-and-half from a carton. "By the way, what is up with you and Jack now? I mean, first the saw shed. *That* was around town within hours."

"The saw shed. Great. From Rachel, right?"

Meg raised her eyebrows. *Who else?* "Then the inn—"

"You know about *that* too?" Gillian was incredulous.

"Sweetie, love might be blind but the neighbors ain't."

Evidently neither were Arthur and Lynette Mansfield. Lynette must have emptied the Vibrobed's coin repository and thought she'd struck it big in Atlantic City.

Gillian paused, the slice of cake she was portioning out hovering in midair halfway to a paper plate Meg was holding. "Meggie—you know I don't sleep around, right?"

"I don't see how you'd have any time to because you're so, how shall I say it?, *busy* with our Mr. Turner."

"Damn that Rachel. It's like having an Eyewitness News Team in permanent residence. Cripes."

"You didn't answer my original question," Meg persisted.

"Jeepers, Meggie, I don't know. I'm embarrassed as hell to admit it, but *I* jumped *him* out there in the saw shed." Then she gave an abbreviated play-by-play of the Eagle House goings-on. Then told her sister about Turner Town. And the vase.

"Then *Poof!* this truck . . . situation tonight. Go figure."

"It sounds serious," Meg said.

"It sounds like craziness, more like. I mean, Jack and I aren't freaking teenagers anymore." Gillian could tell her sister was desperately trying to remain solemn and solicitous, but her heaving shoulders gave her away.

"Damn it, Meg . . ." Gillian said. "It's not funny. It's—"

Then she got the giggles, too. The flurry passed and she was able to go on. "I know what you mean. It's all screwed up. Laughable really. I've known this guy, what? A month? God, it seems like years. And it's not like there's clear sailing ahead of us. We've got a ton of shit between us. We gotta try to cool this until we get things straight between us."

"As if it were that easy, Gilly," Meg said. "You've got it bad. You don't control something like this. Sometimes you just meet somebody and *whammo,* you're up in flames."

"Was it like that for you and Bob?" Gillian asked, then instantly apologized. "Sorry, none of my business."

But Meg didn't seem offended, because she leaned over

and whispered into Gillian's ear. "No!" Gillian said. "In the loft? With Mom and Dad down in the yard? Yikes!"

"We were supposedly gathering up hay to stuff some Halloween dummies."

"More like having a roll in it." They cackled like old women.

"Something I can get in on?" asked a male voice.

"Um—Riley," Gillian said. "How are you doing?" Gillian sensed Meg watching her speculatively. "And no, it's definitely not something you can get in on." She and Meg had another giggling fit.

Meg recovered first. "Hey, Riley. Did you get enough food? I saw you eating late."

"Yeah, I'm all set. Thanks." He looked at Gillian, his face expressionless. "I'm taking Rachel back to your place."

Gillian fought to keep her eyebrows down.

"She can't drive, Gillian," Riley said, sounding exasperated. He knew her too well.

"You bet," she said.

"Meg, thanks again." Riley turned to go.

Gillian stopped him with a gentle hand on his arm. The novelty of her touching him in that way struck her. "Thanks again for tonight, Riley. Really. Out there and there, I mean." She pointed to the front and rear of the house.

"No sweat."

And then he was gone. Just like that. An era ended. After a lifetime of haunting her, Riley had finally let her go.

"You okay?" Meg asked.

"Yeah."

"You've still got him, you know," Meg said. "He's absolutely devoted to you."

Gillian nodded, her eyes suddenly wet, her throat tight.

Then Jack materialized at her elbow. He poured coffee. And not just one cup for himself, or two—one for him and one for her—but three. Three cups. One for himself, one for her, and one for Meg. Like he'd been doing it all his life.

Some of the breath came back into her, and she had new life in her legs.

From saw boss to Forest Queen in one magical evening. Not a bad night, all in all. She felt a thrill like champagne bubbles course right down to her toes.

Her gut *had* been right. Boo had been right. Maybe everything would be right. She didn't see how, really, but this—whatever "this" was—was so much better than grabbing at dust motes. Because incredibly, even with Jack wanting her town with everything in it that was so precious to her, she was rejuvenated by his mere presence.

What the hell had she gotten herself *back* into?

Chapter 30

The day dawned as only autumn days in Maine can: the sky as blue as Dresden china and crystal clear from horizon to horizon. Slanting shafts of light lit up the trees at the edges of the lumberyard, picking out the foremost from the reaches of dark forest beyond.

Gillian stood proprietarily on the stoop of the Wilcox Lumber office, finishing her coffee and waiting for her ad hoc booth-building crew to arrive. She and Luke had worked extra hours the last few days to get ahead of schedule so they could steal some time to work on the fair booths. They had to hustle. Saturday was coming fast.

Skip would be joining them today at the yard if all went well at home with the kids. He had already drawn up some simple plans for the booths at home and sent them in via Luke. She and Luke had stayed late last night and set stock aside for the project. With two people cutting and two people nailing today, they figured the booths would be done by mid-afternoon. Deliver them with the flatbed to the Applebee's horse farm tomorrow where the fair was always held. The 4H kids would slap a quick coat of stain on the outside of them and Lynette and the guild ladies would get the inside of them set up the way they wanted.

The weather for the rest of the week on into the fair weekend was supposed to be good, so the plan should work, but like somebody once said about New England weather: Don't like it? Just wait a day—it'll change. By that token, it would probably snow on Saturday.

That had happened before. A few years back, the fair committee had set up their infamous dunking booth early on a beautiful, balmy Saturday morning only to have flurries break out by noon. But for now, there wasn't a cloud in the sky. They'd better get some rain soon, though. The woods desperately needed a good soaking. Too, too dry a fall.

A dust cloud in the direction of the house announced the approach of vehicles. Luke's Blazer and a lower-slung vehicle crunched their way slowly down the rutted road leading from The Box. The trucks navigated their way between the piles of air-drying lumber stacked on either side of the entry gate. Gillian's heart skipped at the sight of the bright yellow pickup. To think that not too long ago she had found it an obnoxious color. It still was, she admitted, but it, like its owner, had a special place in her heart.

It'd be great to spend a fun day with Luke, just working together, not as boss and temporary employee, but as second cousins who couldn't say the last time they'd spent quality time together. Sure, she'd see him washing the trucks out front of the firehouse sometimes and she'd wave and toot the horn, but aside from the occasional chance meeting at Betty's place or the yearly family gatherings around the holidays, they didn't see much of each other. Sometimes the pace of everyday life in places as small as Rocky Falls was moving too fast. What would happen if—

She pushed the thought aside. Not today.

She smiled, remembering that she, Rachel, and Meg always forced Luke to be the daddy when he played at their house. Gillian always got stuck being one of the kids because Meg wouldn't play unless she could be the mommy. Rachel, being the youngest, was naturally relegated to the role of baby.

Pretty ironic when she thought about it. Luke had really

grown up to be a daddy. To three wonderful little girls. Stayed in Rocky Falls, married his high school sweetheart. Granted, he didn't have the opportunities to leave like the Wilcox girls had, but Gillian doubted if he would have left even if he'd been given the chance.

A small part of her envied him. His life had predictability and a direction to it. He'd grown up to be just what he pretended to be in those childhood games.

Luke rolled his pickup to a stop across the road from the office. Jack pulled in behind, his toy truck looking fragile and out of place in the rough and tumble mill, like an exotic hothouse blossom poking out from amongst thorny roses.

"Hey, boss." Luke hopped out of the driver's side and Skip came around from the other.

"Hey, Luke, Skip. How are Joyce and the kids?"

"A little kid and a baby? We're run ragged," Skip said. "One more little one and we'll have to give up playing man-to-man defense and go to zone coverage. Can't imagine."

Luke laughed the laugh of someone who'd been there and survived. "How about you?" Gillian asked him. "All set for a day swinging hammers?"

"Just point me in the right direction," he said, grinning. "We firemen are always looking to moonlight. Maybe I can pick up a new trade."

"Yeah? Pick one that doesn't have anything to do with wood," she said.

She watched Jack swing his long frame out of the pickup. He did it about as gracefully as anyone could who had that much to unfold. Quite a tall drink of water, Mr. Turner was. Amazing really how he'd managed to contort himself in the front seat the other night. Apparently he'd been highly motivated.

"Why don't you trade in that expensive tin can for a real vehicle?" she said.

"Good morning to you too," he replied. "Where's Boo?"

"Didn't come home last night. Know anything about that?"

Jack laughed. "Maybe. But I'm sure he'll be along shortly."

She had her usual morning crank on and she was crabbing reflexively at Jack, she realized, but he was taking it in stride. But that didn't excuse her uncivil behavior. Living alone did a number on your interpersonal skills.

Jack pulled a tool apron out of the bed of his truck. He turned to her. "You've got a skill saw, right?"

"Sure," she replied. "But we'll probably precut everything with the radial arm."

He nodded. "Good. We borrowed one of Riley's nail guns. A compressor, too. No sense killing ourselves hammering." Luke wheeled the air compressor. Skip followed with the gun and the air hoses slung over his shoulder.

"Right this way, gentlemen," Gillian said, heading for the saw shed.

Entering the shadows of the shed with Jack close behind her, she was acutely conscious of his presence and wondered if he had any feelings about being back in here with her. As the group threaded its way past the planer, Gillian felt a flush rise to her face, as if the cool air in the shadowy shed had suddenly risen twenty degrees. She led them to the far end of the shed, where last night she and Luke had stacked a neat pile of rough lumber just outside the double doors.

Skip and Luke set up the nail gun and the compressor, while Gillian and Jack slid lumber onto the long table of the radial arm saw.

"Here's the plan and the stock list," Gillian said, pointing to a piece of graph paper tacked to the shed wall above the saw table.

Jack glanced at it. "We should probably square up the ends of the stock first, then clamp some stops to the table so we can cut two or three boards at once and not have to measure each one."

"Okay. Let's cut the frame stuff first," Gillian said. "That way we can get Skip and Luke going with the nail gun while we chop up the rest."

"Let's do it," Jack said.

Gillian lifted each board up onto the saw table, while Jack squared up the ends. Working smoothly in tandem, they moved onto the next task, then the next. Two hours passed in a cacophony of sound, the steady whine of the saw punctuated by the staccato thwacks of the pneumatic nail gun. Everyone took a quick break at ten o'clock, and Gillian phoned in a takeout order from Riverview Restaurant. Luke went into town at noon to pick it up. Twenty minutes later he was back with their lunches and a story.

"Man, you shoulda seen Riley downtown just now," he said, barely able to contain his glee. Luke set the bags on the battered picnic table behind the office and there was a scramble as everyone grabbed for their order.

"When I was driving off after getting the lunches, I saw him—Riley, that is—out front of the Riverview," Luke said, around bites. "Up on a ladder hanging up this big banner. You know, advertising the fair?"

Gillian chewed and nodded.

"Aunt Ginnie and your sister were there," he said, raising his eyebrows at her. The way he said "your sister" left no doubt in anyone's mind as to which one he was referring. "Aunt Ginnie was yelling at Riley to lift one side of the banner higher, and Rachel was telling him to lower it. Both of them were yacking at him and neither of them was listening to the other one. It was a trip."

"I can just imagine," Gillian said. She tore open a big bag of potato chips and offered it around.

"It gets better, though," said Luke, laughing carefully so he didn't choke on his sandwich. "Riley was leaning way out to one side to try and stretch the thing tight so it wouldn't be flapping around when the *ladder* got away from him." Luke forced himself to swallow before he asphyxiated himself. "The ladder goes flying sideways. It landed against the side of that little roof over the front door. Riley was left hanging in midair on one of those ledges . . . they stick out over the second floor windows?"

"Cornices?" Jack offered.

"Yeah, that's it. Cornices. So here's Riley, fifteen feet in the air, hanging off this cornice thing. Everybody froze up for a second, like they'd been hit with some kind of stun ray. Even the people inside the restaurant stopped eating lunch to stare out the windows at him. Rachel and Ginnie screaming for help. Ah, great . . ." He chuckled delightedly. "What a scene."

Everyone forgot about their food. "So what happened?" Skip asked. "He's not still there, is he?"

"No, no. By the time I'd banged a U-turn and came back, Pop Henry had come out of the kitchen and he was boosting the ladder back up straight and Riley was getting onto it. Boy, was *he* pissed."

When the laughing died down, Luke finished the story. "You know what he said when he got back on the ladder? It was unbelievable."

"Come on, come on," Gillian said. "Give!"

"He said—" Luke couldn't get it out around the laughter. He swallowed and pounded his chest. "Riley yells out, right in front of everyone mind you, 'Not one more fucking word . . . the fucking sign is staying right the fuck where it is!'"

They howled.

"But that's still not the best part," said Luke, with tears in his eyes. "Gillian, your sister Meg was taking a field trip to the fire station today with her class, and the kids were just coming around the corner when Riley let loose. They caught the whole thing."

"Oh my gosh," Gillian said, clapping a hand to her mouth. "School Mistress Ericson? She must have been *ripped*."

"*Oh* yeah," said Luke, with a satisfied smirk on his face. "'*Mister* Riley'" he said, raising his voice an octave to imitate Meg, "'Would you *kindly* refrain from using such language on a public street. *You* should be ashamed of yourself.'"

They cried, stamped their feet, and gasped for breath. Too much, thought Gillian. Oh, to have been a fly on the wall for that one. Poor Riley, she thought for one second. But damn it all, he deserved it. It was a little bit of payback for all the humiliating scenes he'd put her through. And he better get used to things like that happening when he was around Rachel. They came with the territory.

Gillian glanced across the picnic table at Jack through tear-filled eyes. His watery outline looked relaxed, peaceful—happy. When was the last time he'd sat around a table laughing, not wanting anything from the people across it? she wondered. His obvious delight wasn't really what you'd expect from a big-city guy who probably made more in a month than anyone around the table earned in two years. Gillian considered him thoughtfully as he and the other two men wrung every last morsel of humor out of Riley's predicament.

Focusing on him so intently, she became aware that despite his outward demeanor of being the man about town, there was something about him that said he wasn't used to fitting in, or relaxing with people, or being just plain happy. Oh, he was Mr. Control himself when he was talking business or being deliberately ingratiating, but he seemed uncomfortable when the talk got loose and chummy.

He was vulnerable, too, in some ways, she realized, feeling a new kinship with him. *Fancy that*. He was really good at covering it up, but there were places in him that hurt. A warm feeling, soft and fuzzy as angora, brushed her nerve endings.

"Unbelievable, huh, Gilly?" asked Luke, still chortling over the outraged look on Meg's face.

"What? Oh—yeah. That must have been something, all right," she said, recovering.

"You okay?" he asked, noticing the faraway look on her face. The other two men stopped talking and looked at her, too.

Cripes, she'd been *way* out there. "Yeah, I'm fine. I'm just not used to relaxing in the middle of a workday, is all. It makes me sleepy and spacey."

Jack looked at her for a moment without speaking, then picked up the thread of his conversation with Skip. The group finished their lunch in casual companionship, every-one at one point or another spontaneously breaking up at their mental replay of the scene at the Riverview, enjoying a laugh at Riley's expense. But the picture of a relaxed and happy Jack Turner was the feature film in Gillian's mind.

After every last crumb in the chip bag was gone, and the oily submarine sandwich wrappers lay corkscrewed on the table, Skip ran home to check on Joyce. Luke, feeling extra-neous in the quiet that hung in the air like a mist between Jack and Gillian, mumbled something about checking out the river and ambled off.

Left to themselves, they both became uncharacteristically quiet.

From under the brim of her baseball cap, her eyes hidden and her attention seemingly devoted to tracing the deep pat-tern of grain in the weathered tabletop, Gillian studied the way the sunlight glinted off the hairs on the back of Jack's hands. The fine strands were a light reddish-brown, not at all what she would have expected given the darker hair on his head. She dared not look up to those amazing lashes, al-though she felt them calling to her.

Jack watched Gillian brush her fingers across the cracks in the wood of the tabletop separating them. When she del-icately traced the line of her lower lip with her tongue, he felt the sharp edges of rational thought blur. The scent of fresh-cut pine drying in the sun wafted to him, bringing with it the remembered feel of her thighs tight to his and the fric-tion between their bodies as they had rolled on the floor of the saw shed a scant few weeks ago. The memory bewitched him, and he felt a tightening below his belt.

Navigating the uncharted waters of their attraction was like rewiring a wet basement, he decided. The stakes were high and one false move could be your last. Patience and caution were the order of the day. He laughed within him-self. So why did they repeatedly throw both to the wind?

Gillian finally tipped her head up and forced her gaze to meet Jack's eyes. She cleared her throat. "You seem really comfortable around here. Around the yard, I mean. Working with tools, building things. I saw some of that out at the inn with the windows, but today has been fun, too." Working with Jack had all the best parts of working with Riley and more.

"Well, before I made my millions," he said, laughing deprecatingly, but Gillian wasn't so sure he was far from the truth, "I always worked construction in one way or another. For Dodge Holt in the summers during college. After I graduated, too. Did a lot of his finish work, making his new construction look old, original."

A picture clicked in. "That was your work out at Riley's site, right? The doorway, the staircase?"

He shrugged. "Yes and no. I started it, Riley liked it, I nudged Buddy in the right direction and he finished it." Then he got back on the train. "Dodge Holt taught me a lot, believe it or not. Including what *not* to do in a planned community." He glanced at Gillian, but she just nodded for him to keep going.

"I also did some life guarding."

She grinned. "I'll bet you learned a lot there, too, huh?"

"That's for sure," he said. He chuckled. Gillian Wilcox could make him laugh, and he was surprised how easily the joy came now. He hoped the cease-fire between them would hold. With every passing day it felt safer and safer to stick his head a little farther out of the foxhole. For her part, she seemed more comfortable too. He watched her, lounging across the table from him like a cat relaxing on a familiar stoop.

"What was it like, working for your stepdad?" she asked. "It was good in some ways when I worked for Charlie— sometimes I miss it—but at other times it was absolute purgatory."

Jack pursed his lips. Gillian watched his cheekbones sculpt as he considered the question. Fine cheekbones, the man had.

"It was good for a long time," he said at last. "I admired

Dodge. He was the only father I ever knew. Working for his company seemed the logical thing to do after I'd graduated."

"Greenville caused the big break between you two?"

The air between them crackled like it were saturated with electric charges. Jack shifted on the seat. "It was the straw that broke the camel's back. But there were other things. Little things. All along. Things that I forced myself to ignore out of loyalty to Dodge. And to my mother."

Gillian furrowed her brow and cocked her head. "I don't get that. In my family we go at it like cats and dogs over every little thing. God, I get sick of it sometimes, but by now it's practically a way of life. And it keeps the air clear."

"That's just the point," Jack said. "You've all got a life. Together. You fight and squabble, but at least you've got family to do it with."

"So what did you have instead?"

"Dodge and my mother."

"Not exactly a cast of characters." *Very* different from the way she had grown up. She thought of Rachel and what she was going to do to her when she finally ran her to ground.

"What about your mom? What's she like?" Gillian asked.

"My real dad's death devastated her. I wish I were older when he died. Had a chance to see the real her. But Dodge has been good to her. I can't complain about him in that respect. But Mom plays the party line. Keeps to herself. You never really know what's on her mind."

Acorns . . . Gillian thought.

"But she's feisty," Jack said, laughing at a memory. "A quality I admire." He looked up at Gillian and grinned ruefully. "Despite having Dodge between us, we're still close. We keep in touch." Jack stopped talking and studied the veins on the back of his hands.

Gillian's heartstrings twanged and jealousy swiped at her with a viridian claw. Would that it were that way with her mom.

"So what you're telling me is that it wasn't exactly the Walton family when you were growing up," Gillian said.

"That's about it, I guess. It's no big deal now, though. I mean, I don't live my life wracked up about it or anything."

Scars. He had them, too. Tender spots that still ached. He became ten times more attractive to her. She wanted to put her hand out to cover his, but she resisted. No sudden moves.

He picked at a splinter on the tabletop. "It was lonely—*I* was . . . lonely—I guess, although I didn't realize it." He shook his head and scoffed. "Why am I telling you this?" He cut his eyes to hers, and a crooked smile crossed his face. "You are luckier than you know with what you've got here in Rocky Falls."

A few days ago she would have jumped on the opportunity to turn his own words against him with *Then why are you trying to wreck it?*

But she appreciated the risk he was taking, how vulnerable he was making himself to a person who had tried to rearrange his face with an oilcan. Somebody had to lay down their Uzis when the white flags went up, and he had been the one with the guts to do it. He would get no cheap shot from her.

Besides, she could always reserve the right to kill him in the unspecified future, but for now, when she looked at him, in her mind she saw his flower vase sitting on her kitchen table. It was a simple but beautiful object that transformed her table from a place to pile the mail to a place where people might sit and linger over a meal, a conversation, a kiss . . .

She felt her body, of its own volition, lean ever so slightly across the tabletop toward him.

"Hey," he said abruptly, "let's walk off lunch. Go look at the river or something."

Gillian jumped. Snap a girl out of her reverie, why don't you?

He was on his feet before she got off a reply. "Sure . . . uh. Wait."

She swung her legs out from beneath the picnic table and

skipped a few steps to catch up to him. He seemed nervous. Pent up. So was she. Awkward. They walked past his truck. Gillian thought back to the other night in that front seat. The sights, the sounds, the—dog?

She stopped and pointed. "What is that?"

"Boo. You've been introduced before."

Her dog was sitting in the front seat of Jack's pickup, one paw resting on the steering wheel.

"I know that. What is that thing around his neck?"

"It's harmless."

"It's a bandana."

"He likes it."

"Get it off him now, please."

Boo licked his chops and whinnied. "Stay out of this," Gillian said, pointing at him. He licked her finger. She made her face and voice stern. "You know Mommy worries when you're out all night and don't call."

Boo had spent the night at the inn. He was lucky. Nobody would make a big deal out of him staying over. It wouldn't be discussed in the morning over coffee across the worn formica tabletops down at Riverview Restaurant. Please don't let her be jealous of her own dog.

She scratched Boo behind one ear. Then said, "Jack, please. Off. Take the damn bandana off."

"I think it gives him character," Jack said, reaching into the cab and rubbing Boo behind the other ear. Boo leaned into Jack's hand and looked beseechingly at Gillian. "Don't we think so, big fel-la . . ." Jack crooned. Boo's eyes glazed in pleasure.

Partly at Jack's use of the inclusive "we," Gillian imagined. "It's stupid and pretentious," she said. "He looks like an idiot."

"Hey, I sometimes wear one when it's really hot out and I'm sweating."

The visual of Jack sweating and half-naked definitely stirred things around for her, were it not for the bandana thing. Jack in a bandana. Talk about stupid. God, even if he were wearing *nothing* that would still be funny. She didn't even try to contain her amusement.

"You are just cruel sometimes, you know that?" he said.

Gillian tried to straighten up. His lower lip looked bigger than Gillian remembered it. "Does your little bandana peek out from under your hardhat like—Oh my god—" she doubled over again. Hard to get air. It was just too rich—"one of The Village People?" She strutted and mimed YMCA in the air with her arms. The Twin was so right: you had to make your own yuks. Jack was the perfect straight man.

"Okay, okay, I get your point," he said.

Petulantly, Gillian thought, he untied the bandana from around Boo's neck. Boo bobbed his head and woofed. Jack paused, the square of material limp in his hand. He thoughtfully twisted it into a tight snake, then snapped it taut between his hands. He looked at Gillian. He came around to her side of the truck.

She didn't like the look in his eyes. Scenes from *CSI* popped into her head, but no, Jack was just Jack, not some crazed nutcase with a garrote. The look in his eyes was devilish, not malicious. She wondered if given a choice she might prefer malicious. Unaccountably, her legs turned to jelly and her insides flipped. "Jack . . . down. There's a good boy," she said.

"Yes, dear . . ." He kept coming.

She circled around the rear of the pickup, but in a flash, he was up and in the bed of the truck and leaning out, in his hand a fistful of one of her sleeves. She pulled away but was stopped short by the fear of shredding her treasured John Mayer tour date T-shirt into half a wife beater.

It seemed but one second later Jack had her pinned against the side of the truck, his body tight to hers. His lips descended on her neck and the bandana—damn her smart mouth—suddenly bound her wrists together behind her back. She was— Whoa, lock up there, knees—helpless. *Mmmm.*

No choice. Best to just surrender. No oilcan handy. A

groan she barely recognized as her own filled the narrow space between her and Jack. She let herself go. Down, down, down into the vortex—then, Yes! Up, up, up! His hands, reaching to cup her bottom, buoying her up, pulling her against him.

"Jack," she muttered, lust making her lips thick, "not here . . ."

"Right."

She felt him stop and look around. Her eyes wouldn't focus. One breath later he had her in a fireman's carry. She squealed. Maybe her first time ever. He kicked the doors of the saw shed closed behind them.

Luke came around the corner twenty minutes later. "Jumpin' Jaysus, Gillian that water's freezing. I don't see how anybody can just jump in like you do—" He stopped dead in his tracks.

Window dummies.

That's what his cousin and Jack Turner looked like. Window dummies. Like in the windows of that fancy clothes store in Bangor. They were that still.

The two of them were sitting at the picnic table right where he'd left them, just staring at each other. Gilly had her head propped up on two hands, leaning a little forward with her elbows on the table, like she was watching a movie. But the only thing in front of her was Jack Turner. And he was looking back at her in the same way, like he'd been quick frozen.

Look out below.

Jack heard somebody say something about the river, but it seemed like years until he was able to turn his head and focus on the speaker. It was Luke. He turned dumbly back to Gillian. She was staring at him. He kicked her under the table.

"Oh—yeah. Right. The river," she said. "It is pretty this time of year, isn't it?" Jack could only grin, hoping what she said had passed for sensible.

The smiles didn't leave Jack and Gillian's faces for the rest of the afternoon. By five o'clock, the fair committee had its four spanking-new booths.

"They got the booths done today," Rachel said, absent-mindedly twirling linguine around her fork.

"Oh, boy," Riley said, spearing a shrimp with considerably more force than the task required.

"Still mad, huh?"

"Uh huh." He chewed vigorously, the muscles in his jaw bulging, his eyes never meeting Rachel. Let her think he was preoccupied with the mound of pasta on his plate.

She drove him completely frigging nuts, he was fast realizing. Inviting her over for dinner had seemed like a good idea a few days ago. But after today's fiasco over the banner hanging—which would take years to live down—he wasn't so sure.

He stole a glance at her under the pretense of reaching for bread. She had incredible eyes, incredible hair. In the soft twilight she glowed. Like an angel, almost.

He knew better. Her knee, pressed against his since the beginning of the meal, spoke volumes. But pissed as he was, all he could do was sit there like a lump, frozen up like an iceberg, too damn mad to take her up on what her talented little kneecap was offering. Not like him to let emotion get in the way of getting business done. He shifted in his seat.

But Christ, Rachel and her damn aunt. The tag team from hell, they were, putting him through the wringer today. Like little frigging terriers, nipping at his heels, herding him around like a sheep.

Then to have Meg Ericson ream him out for swearing in front of half the kids in town—God, he'd felt like he was back in seventh grade.

"Now young man, you stop picking on little Gillian. She's half your size!" he remembered some schoolmarm saying. He'd laid off the face scrubbing, then when the teacher had

turned away, Gillian had kicked him a good one right where it counted.

When would he ever learn? The Wilcox women were bad news. But then again, there was that knee. Shit.

"You seem kind of quiet tonight, Dougie," Rachel said. "Cat got your tongue?"

He choked down a mouthful of pasta. "Well, gees, Rachel, wouldn't you still be pissed if the situation was reversed?" His throat was tight and his voice came out squeaky. "If you'd been left hanging by your fingernails in front of half the fricking town?"

Rachel scooted closer to him and, under the table, the kneecap was on the move, sliding farther along the inside of his leg. He stifled a groan.

"Look," she said, "I'm really sorry about today. Especially after you still had me over and cooked up this wonderful meal." She speared a shrimp from his plate and delicately sucked some of the sauce off one end before drawing it slowly into her mouth through full, red lips.

A gigantic chunk calved from the ice block in his chest and landed with a splash somewhere around his belt line. His groin registered the shock wave. He seemed to lose the ability to speak.

"I'm a control freak, what can I say?" Rachel said. "And when I get together with my Aunt Ginnie, I'm twice as bad." Then she turned serious.

He didn't know she had it in her.

"I know what you're going through, Dougie. I saw how bad I can be the other night at Meg's. That thing Aunt Ginnie and I did to Gilly out at the truck when she was— ahem—'sharing a moment' with Jack Turner? My idea. I really thought she was going to punch me out over that one. Bad idea all around." She licked a drip of sauce from a long finger and worked her leg magic.

Her knee was now millimeters from the spot where her sister had landed that kick. *Shazaam* . . .

Suddenly, Riley found himself praying Rachel didn't get

312   *Lucy Ann Peters*

too worked up about her control issues. After all, they didn't seem such a big deal to *him* anymore. What a difference a knee makes. Hah, Gillian would have liked that one. Gillian who?

"Aw, Rachel. You make me crazy, you know that?" he said. "I was really pissed about today. *Really* pissed. But thinking about it now . . ."

"Yes?" Rachel moved closer to him and, under the table, her hand came to rest on his thigh.

"Well, it was kind of funny." He laughed, keeping his eyes glued to hers. As if he had a choice. She was the snake charmer. He felt his own snake strain at the basket.

"But listen—" he breathed, pointing at her nose—he was so close to her he could see golden flecks radiating from her irises and her perfume surrounded him like the morning mist on the Mohasset—"As long as it doesn't happen again."

Her pouting lips gently suctioned his fingertip.

"I'll do my best . . ." she said.

Chapter 31

The big day had finally come, the fair was here and so was he, Mr. Jack Turner of Turner Development Incorporated. Serving hot dogs to the citizenry of Rocky Falls.

"Twelve-fifty, please," he said, handing a paper box across the counter of the food booth to a heavy-set, clean-shaven man in a Polo shirt.

"Get extra napkins, honey," the man's wife said. A child with a frizzy mass of golden ringlets squirmed in her arms, while another tugged at her denim jumper.

"Oh—can we have lids and straws for those drinks?" the man asked.

"Sure." Jack snapped tops onto the cups and poked flexible straws into them. He handed them across the counter. "Quite a handful you've got there," he said.

"I'll say," said the man, pulling wads of napkins from a chrome dispenser on the counter.

"You folks lived here long?" Jack asked.

"One year next month."

"It's a great place," Jack said mildly. "But it could use a little face-lift, don't you think? Maybe a few more stores in the downtown? You know, just so you don't have to drive thirty miles to Bangor just to get a dress shirt in your size?"

"Oh, no," said the man's wife, jumping into the conversation. "We like it just the way it is. We hope it never changes. Isn't that right, honey?"

"Yes, dear," said her husband, trying to pull the older child off his wife's skirt. "We moved here because of the way it is. We've had enough of so-called modern conveniences." The woman pulled a twenty from her purse one handed and gave it to Jack.

"That's right," said the husband, scooping up child number two. "Back in Augusta we lived in a condo on the river. Nice enough place, but we never even knew the names of the people in the units on either side of us. Around here, people are a bit standoffish at first, but once they see you in the grocery store a few times, they treat you like family."

Jack made change and handed it to the husband.

"And I don't have to worry about the kids as much either," said the blond woman. "You know, who's around when they're outside playing in the yard? We wouldn't change this place for the world."

The youngest spied the drinks and began flailing to reach them.

The clock was ticking on this conversation. "How you adjusting to the change from a condo to your own house?" Jack asked. "I don't know what you folks bought into, but some of the buildings in town are absolute relics."

"Well, the place we bought does need work," admitted the blond man. "But it's got charm, you know? It's on its own piece of land and it's not a cookie-cutter copy of the house next door. We like it."

The thrashing of the youngest turned to screams and the toddler tried to scale the sides of the booth. "Well, that's our cue. The natives are restless," the woman said. "Nice talking to you."

"Enjoy your day at the fair," Jack said, waving.

He shook his head. You try to improve the place to attract new people to town when what drew them to the place was the way it already was. Go figure human nature.

With the edge of his spatula, he rolled a line of hot dogs

sizzling on the grill. Flipped a dozen hamburgers and dropped cheese on a few. It was good being a short-order cook—you didn't have to think too much.

The big dance was tonight. Forget about business for a while, Mr. Jack Turner.

Things were going along swimmingly, thought Virginia, surveying the fair from her perch in the ticket booth and checking her watch. The new booth smelled of new wood, fresh paint, and progress. She inhaled deeply.

All the hard work and browbeating of the last few days had paid off. Since early morning, a mix of old and new people had mingled in the pavilion areas between the sales tables and the games. A continuous stream of foot traffic had been in and out of Applebee's farm throughout the day. About two o'clock, the fair committee opened up the pasture across the road to accommodate all the cars.

Bad weather was always a concern, but it had cooperated beautifully today. It had even been warm enough to set up the dunking booth that Charlie had built years ago. It was always a big draw, and this year was no exception.

Doug Riley had drawn short straw for the first shift in the tank. One year he'd almost gotten pneumonia it had turned so cold. The day had started out warm and sunny, but the regional mountain weather system decided to start winter early. By three o'clock snow had swept through the fair. Of course, if Riley hadn't decided to be such a hero, he wouldn't have gotten sick. Just like at the Riverview. Hanging off the building that way, all to attract attention to himself. It was ridiculous at his age.

Virginia heard a cheer and looked over as a splash went up from the direction of the dunking booth. Her niece Gillian was pumping her fist in the air, while the small crowd gathered around her slapped her on the back. Whoever it was that was just dumped better be getting out of the tank pretty soon. Shadows were creeping in from the forest, and in another half an hour, the spotlights around the grounds would turn on. It was time to shut down the games and the sales booths and gear up for the dance.

"Aunt Ginnie!" cried Rachel, running up to the ticket booth, out of breath. "Did you see it?" she exclaimed. "Did you see Gillian dunk him?"

"What are you talking about? Him who?" asked Virginia.

"Jack Turner!" said Rachel. "His number came up and Gillian got first crack at him. Got him on the first pitch. He went down better than Riley." She flexed her arm at the shoulder. "And speak of the devil, I got Dougie myself a little while ago."

Virginia arched one eyebrow. *Dougie?*

"Well, it's nice to see that you aren't too sophisticated to enjoy yourself at the fair," she said. "But playtime's over." With a rubber band, she secured the lid of the cigar box full of admission money and hoisted up the walk-through counter. "Get back down to that booth and tell them to shut the thing down and drain it. We don't want anybody with a snoot-full out there skinny-dipping tonight. I'll check out the barn and see how Peter and Lynette are doing in there." Virginia looked at Rachel. Her niece still hadn't moved.

What had gotten into Rachel lately? Her mind was somewhere else. She and Rachel had always had . . .

She struggled for the word. *An understanding.* That was it. An understanding about how the world worked and what you had to do to get what you wanted. But this week, working with her and Riley had been pure hell. The girl had plain lost her focus.

"Rachel, did you hear me?" Virginia asked peevishly. "Go on now, we're losing the light."

"Oh—sure, Aunt Ginnie." Virginia watched her niece stroll dreamily off toward the dunking booth. Muttering to herself, she closed up the booth, hung a sign that said "Admission to Dance Free" on the front of it and struck out for the barn.

Lynette and her ladies should have everything set up by

now. Clearing out the Applebees' barn for them had been a chore, but it was well worth the effort as far as she was concerned. The 150th anniversary of the fair was a big deal after all, and they'd have it all put back together by the time the Applebees got back from their annual cross-country motor home visit to all their children and grandchildren.

The Applebees' barn had been chock full of items for the flea market they held in the field next to it every Sunday in the spring and fall. Riley had crabbed a lot about doing it, but she was glad she and Rachel had finally persuaded him to roll a couple of old two-toned Buicks out of the center of the barn and into the field, so there'd be room for dancing inside. After he'd moved some antique furniture and the flea market items into the old horse stalls under the loft overhang, there was plenty of room for a stage and a dance floor.

Virginia stepped through the open double doors of the old barn.

It was like walking into a fairyland. Lynette and the church ladies had outdone themselves. Strings of tiny white lights cascaded in dazzling curtains along the fronts of the stalls, relegating the dark cubicles to unobtrusive background. Birch tree branches were standing upright in buckets of sand, with more white lights transforming them into delicate traceries. The stage was up and Peter Dunn was setting up microphone stands. Four of them. Good sign. He'd pulled in a full band for tonight.

"Lynnie," Virginia said, catching the elderly lady's arm as she flashed past carrying rolls of crepe paper streamers. "It looks heavenly!"

A satisfied smile spread across Lynette's face. "It does, doesn't it? I think this is our best job ever." She looked up at Virginia towering above her. "And you're just the person we need. Arthur is always saying how vertically challenged I am. Come with me dear, you can help hang these streamers."

* * *

Peter Dunn sighed with relief in his impromptu hideout behind the sound mixing board as he watched Virginia being waylaid by Lynette. That was a close one—Virginia had had him dead in her sights for a minute there. He rose and greeted the rest of the band members as they stepped up onto the stage. They opened well-worn instrument cases and started to tune up.

On one side of the dance floor, Skip Donaldson finished laying a few old doors flat across sawhorses. He trimmed them with bunting to make a bar. Pop Henry wheeled in kegs of beer from the Riverview and Beatrice and Meg carted in hotplates and trays of finger foods. The lights came on around the perimeter of the barnyard as the pink-shot October sky relinquished its hold on the day.

It was almost time to dance.

"Hey, Turner," called Gillian. "You still alive in there?"

"Cold but undaunted," came Jack's cheery but chattering reply through the partially open door. Jack was in the Applebee's tack shed changing for the dance. Gillian was waiting outside impatiently. "Cripes, though," he said, "who'd a-thunk the first week in October could be so damned cold?"

"City wimp. You should be used to it after your spontaneous lifesaving plunge into the Mohasset. And besides, you ought to have enough sense not to run around in wet clothes. You should have changed before you closed up everything."

"Yeah, well, I got involved shutting down all the games and craft booths," Jack said. "I didn't want to run out on the guys."

The guys. Gillian smiled. *How cute.*

She had carefully dusted off the saddle she was leaning against before alighting on it, savoring the novel feeling of being concerned about keeping her clothes clean. She was determined to spend at least one hour in her new dress before getting something disgusting on it.

After her first pitch had sent Jack to his cold and watery demise, she'd run up to the Applebees' house to shower and get ready. Joyce had squeezed herself into the bathroom with Gillian and wouldn't let her leave until her hair and makeup were, to Joyce's practiced eye, perfect. She hadn't let Gillian look at herself until the job was finished.

"Voilà!" Joyce had cried, pulling a towel off the medicine cabinet mirror.

Gillian was floored. A ballerina, like the kind on top of a musical jewelry box, stared back at her. She turned her head this way and that, entranced by the effect. She wasn't bad looking she knew, but she never realized how she had the same high cheekbones as Rachel or how softly her dark auburn hair curled to frame her face. Any time she had ever tried for an effect, her hair had turned into a giant fuzz ball. Her wide-set green eyes were luminous from Joyce's makeup magic.

The dress itself was a wonder, too. Rachel had picked it out and brought it over to the house yesterday. A peace offering she'd said, seeming genuinely sorry about the trouble she'd caused at the fair meeting. But Gillian had been too tired from work to pay much attention to it right then.

She'd left Joyce tidying up in the bathroom and walked into the hall to spin in front of the full-length mirror, admiring herself. She would never have chosen ice blue. The dress was a shimmering, clinging jersey with a high neck and long sleeves that made it look modest until she turned around. The back was open to the waist, with a short tight skirt that shattered the demure look. She would never be able to get into her pickup in the dress without hiking the skirt up to her waist.

But her legs looked great. *She* looked great. It was worth the $75.00 she shelled out for the three-inch high-heeled sandals that Rachel insisted she buy.

Imagine me dancing . . .

For a moment, Gillian experienced a glimpse into Rachel's world, as she took in the view from the front and the back. Instead of her looking out at the world, the world suddenly seemed to be looking in at her. Heady stuff.

"Hey, hand me in my shirt will you?" Jack said. Gillian snapped out of her daydream and slid the hanger with Jack's blue button-down Oxford shirt on it through the door to the tack room.

"You really enjoyed dunking me, didn't you?" he said.

"Yup. No question," Gillian answered. It had been a ball. There was something about seeing Jack Turner drenched that tickled her pink. The man was like a cat; he hated to get wet. And yes, she did have a cruel side. But hey, if you couldn't enjoy it, what good was it? She'd gladly have stood there all afternoon pegging balls three for a buck at the dunk tank target, but she'd nailed it on the first pitch. Sufficient motivation could make up for a lack of skill any day. Seeing him hit the water a second time had been deeply satisfying.

"Come on, Jack," she said, surprised at the pouty, nagging tone in her voice. God, the dress was turning her into Rachel right before her eyes. "The band's started. I'm going to turn back into Cinderella at midnight."

"All right, all right. I'm coming," he said. She could see feet wriggling into Docksiders. He opened the door.

Before him stood a vision. Gillian twirled.

A mass of auburn hair bobbed. Long, firm legs in impossibly high-heeled sandals and a back made for touching took his breath away.

"What do you think?" the vision asked. "Pretty neat, huh?"

Jack gulped and nodded.

"Rachel picked it all out. I think it suits me." She twirled again.

Long, *long* legs.

Jack could only nod. The transformation was magical. From jump-suited saw boss to forest queen. "Wow . . ." was the best he could do. He trapped her hand carefully between two of his own and kissed her fingertips. He held her tenderly, afraid she might vanish in a wisp of smoke if he squeezed too hard. "Beautiful."

She bowed her head briefly, then blushed and smiled up at him, closing the distance between them. Gas jet blue locked with gold-flecked tourmaline.

"Like a china doll," Jack said, his voice barely above a whisper. "I'm afraid to touch you—afraid you'll break."

What she wanted right now was for him to squeeze her so hard she would break. So hard that the world would stop spinning, then kiss her like it didn't exist anymore. Gillian realized she was finding intimacy at every turn, in every mundane task she and Jack did together. She remembered the long lines of his muscles bunch and flex in his arms and shoulders when they'd worked on the fair booths in the hot sun. How desire had caught in her throat as she watched a trickle of perspiration weave its way down the side of his neck, between his pectorals and along his ridged stomach to vanish into the waist band of his pants.

The longing to trace the course of the drop of moisture with her fingertip had been almost overwhelming. Now, before her, his face inches from hers, she smelled the fresh air in his crisp shirt and soap from his hasty scrub up in the tack room.

Jack felt shimmering heat rise all around them, bring a flush to his face. He forced himself to break eye contact with her. He gently passed the ball of one thumb along the ridges of her fingernails, now gracefully rounded and varnished in clear lacquer.

"Courtesy of Joyce," Gillian said. "She's got a way with hangnails, huh?"

Always the comic, Jack thought, feeling momentarily frustrated, then he realized she was trying as hard as he not to be sucked under, right then, into the whirlpool. Wrong place, wrong time. Altogether a perfect invitation to them to be completely inappropriate in a semi-public place. Jack indulged himself in the brief luxury of kissing her fingertips again, brushing his lips to them. Gillian didn't pull away, but he did.

"My forest queen," he said in a stage voice, sweeping his arm toward the barnyard, "your pumpkin coach awaits." He held his other arm out for her to accept.

She rested her hand lightly upon it. "Quickly now, my prince," she said, caught up in the fun, "we've only until midnight."

"And then?"

"And then, I must return to plain, ordinary Gillian Wilcox at the final stroke of twelve."

God, if you only knew how much I want you, plain, ordinary Gillian Wilcox, Jack thought. *To hold you, to have you, to take you right now on the floor of this barn because tonight was truly magical.*

But the reality of tomorrow loomed just beyond it. Come the morning, how could he, like the prince in the fairy tale, ever find his way back to her with all that separated them? But unlike the prince in the fable, he knew exactly who his beloved was. What he didn't know was how to make her that forever.

A full moon was on the rise as they carefully picked their way from the tack house to the barn, gliding through liquid shadows. Gillian lurched as a high heel caught on a rough patch of ground, and Jack pulled her against his side to steady her. The soft rustle of her skirt shifting as they walked was the only sound to break the silence. One minute they were swathed in velvety black, passing the riding rings, the next, turning a corner of the old barn, blinking against the dazzling white glare spilling from its open doors. The effect was kaleidoscopic and disorientating.

The clamor of three hundred people, most of them dancing and singing along with the band, hit them like a wave. Peter Dunn was thumping out a booming beat by twanging away on a washtub bass amplified by a microphone under the tub, while Luke wailed out a lead on an electric guitar. Betty's husband Leo was fiddling like the devil himself and the sound was raucous and upbeat. The dancers, judging by the frenzied motion on the dance floor, were loving it.

"Hey, you two. What kept ya?" said Rachel, coming up to them. She was listing to one side. "Beer's cold. No cover. Ha!" Fumes from Milwaukee's finest rolled over them.

"Seems like you're having a good time, sister o' mine," said Gillian. "But what, no Riley?"

"He's going up on stage for their number. Oh—there he is!" She steadied herself by hanging onto Jack's arm. "Hi, honey!" she called. Heads turned their way. Her sister was going to have a head the size of Mount Katahdin in the morning. Rachel couldn't drink and she knew it. Funny she was so far gone, though—the dance was just starting. Something was going on.

The band wound down the Holly song and shifted into a slow blues number. Peter Dunn belted out a soulful, gravelly version of *Before You Accuse Me*. Riley stepped up to an open microphone and sawed on a harmonica.

Rachel melted into Jack, surprising him with her sudden weight shift. He compensated, but almost pulled Gillian down on top of them.

"Isn't Dougie something?" Rachel cooed. "What a hunk!" She catcalled "Woo, woo!" then put two fingers in her mouth and whistled. "God, it makes you wanna dance, don't it? Whatdya say Jack? Wanna cut a rug?" She giggled. "Or a floor, in this case?"

Jack looked down at Gillian. She rolled her eyes, at first nodding, then suddenly changed her mind. "Find someone else, Rachel," she said. "He's mine."

She strengthened her grip on Jack's arm. Tonight, Gillian Wilcox was going to do exactly what *she* wanted to do. Get everything that was coming to her. She pulled Jack away from Rachel and onto the dance floor. "Go find your own man," she called over her shoulder to her sister, surprised at how good it felt to say that.

Rachel, to Gillian's surprise, was not in the least offended and clapped her hands clumsily. "You go, Gilly girl! Atta way!"

On the dance floor, Jack found himself swaying to the music, and he was not, by nature, a swayer. Never had been. Until tonight. Until just then, in fact. He lowered his chin to rest on the warm crown of Gillian's head, pulled her close to him. Caressing her bare back. Stroked her hair with his chin, then finding the texture irresistible, lowered his lips to brush the dark strands.

She smelled delicious. Gently, he moved her head away from his chest so he could look into her eyes. All that stood between them, the development, the downtown, the whole town, ultimately, still existed. But hidden somewhere behind her gaze was a bridge, but dimly seen. A way across the gulf between them. He would find it. Tomorrow. He kissed her.

The band, the barn, and the crowd all receded to pinpoints of sensation, while the feel of her lips on his overwhelmed him. The muscles of her back were sleek and sinewy against his palm, and he let his hand slide lower to press their bodies even closer. Her slim hips lay tight to his upper thighs, and her arms tightened on his shoulders.

Gillian finally broke the contact, gasping for breath. Her eyes were smoky, the green irises dilated.

They were up to their waists now in the swirling waters, the sides of the vortex slick and slippery with nothing to cling to even if they had wanted to save themselves.

Rachel watched Jack and Gillian through slitted eyes. There was definitely Something Big happening between her cranky sister and Mr. Jack Turger. No, Turber? She burped. *Whatever.* More than just pure lust. So obvious. Drunk as she was even she could see it.

"All by yourself?" a voice behind her said, making her jump.

"Oh—Aunt Betty, hi!" Rachel said. She threw her arms around the sturdy shoulders of the shorter woman and leaned down to plant a noisy kiss on the very top of her head. "Leo's soundin' great—" she hiccuped—"tonight."

Betty laughed. "It's his big night of the year. He gets to live out all his Charlie Daniels fantasies. As if he's even *that* tall."

Rachel laughed drunkenly. "Thash a good one."

"So are you?" Betty persisted.

"Am I wha . . . ?"

"All alone tonight?"

"Well, yes and no. I came with Riley, but he's doing his *thang* . . ." Rachel unsteadily waggled her fingers in front of her mouth. "You know."

"Yes, I do. I can hear him. So what's going on with you two, anyway?"

"Betty, you keep your ear pretty—" she belched—"'Scuse me—close to the ground don't you?" She snickered and lurched. "Rachel 'n' Riley's already gettin' chewed over in the gossip mill, huh?"

"Well . . ." Then Betty shrugged and laughed. "Yes. Definitely. So what's the story, anyway?"

"What? You mean with Riley? Well it's kinda weird, you know . . . ?" Rachel glanced uncertainly at her aunt. The woman's kind bright eyes were riveted on her. "Riley was always . . . he never . . ."

"Yes?"

"I could never get him to go for me." She clutched her chest and belched again. The sound seemed to echo up from her toes. Betty winced. "God, there, I've said it. One of my only failures." She grinned sheepishly, her eyes sliding out of focus. "I always took it for granted that I could get . . . that is, I could always have . . ."

"Go on."

"You really all right with this, Aunt Betty? I mean, usually it's me and Ginnie—"

"Say no more, child. That's half the problem. Keep going, please. I don't get out much."

Rachel steamed right past the humor. "Well. I always

thought I could get whoever—I mean, you know, a man—I wanted. Like the lights. You flick the switch they come on?"

"Or 'turn on' as the case may be?"

Rachel focused blearily on her aunt. "Hey, you're pretty good at this girl talk, you know?"

Betty rolled her eyes.

Then a cloud passed over Rachel's face. "But he never went for me before, back when we were kids, Riley. All he wanted was—" she took a deep breath—"Gillian." She cut her eyes to the dance floor.

Betty followed her glance. "And now?"

Rachel burst into hysterics, doubling over and slapping her thighs. Putting her head down was a bad move. She staggered backward off balance. Betty lunged and steadied her against a wooden post.

"Budda-bing?" Betty queried.

"Budda-*boom!*" Rachel replied, tears running down her face. Was she happy, sad, just plain crazy? Maybe all of it. She tried to find Gillian and Jack in the crowd, but they'd been swallowed up. Her sister Gillian, hooked up at last, out there in the press of bodies, her hands God knew where. And she, Rachel Wilcox, bane of the frigging wives of the pencil-necked, old fart board of directors, was finally happy herself, she thought. With Gillian's cast off.

She giggled and swiped at her tears. God, what a pistol that man packed. Hallelujah to hand-me-downs. *Mmmm, mmm, mmm . . .*

"You still in there?" Betty asked, going onto tiptoes to bring her eyes to a level with her niece's.

Rachel grinned lopsidedly. "Yeah. Still here. Same address, different gal. Now I kinda realize that *I* was the one with not so many lights on."

Betty smiled and pushed Rachel's mussed hair back from her eyes. "You always were my favorite, you know?"

Rachel's eyes lit up like a two-year-old's on Christmas morning. "*Really?*" She felt her face light up. Then she realized Betty's smile had slipped into a smirk and her smile crashed. Gees. Being had by the very aunt she'd always secretly referred to as "Aunt Batty."

"You're not very nice, Auntie."

"So, now it's your old 'Aunt Batty' who's not nice, eh?"

"You knew?"

Betty grinned.

"Would you really tell me if I was your favorite?"

"No."

"Do you want to know if you're *my* favorite?"

"No."

"I love you, Auntie."

"Back at you, pumpkin. Can you stand on your own?"

"I think so—now."

"Congratulations, you're really bombed."

Rachel hiccuped and grabbed for the post. She put on her best Elvis grimace. "Thank *yew,* thank you very *much*."

Betty hovered around for a while, making small talk, waiting for Rachel's inevitable crash to the floor, but soon realized that her niece was no longer aware of anybody but Doug Riley. She hung on his every raucous note, catcalling and blowing him kisses.

Betty searched for Gillian among the dancers crowding the floor. She sighed, wishing she were taller. Ah, there, Gillian. With Jack Turner, moving to the music, as close together as two bodies could get with their clothes on. Locked in their own private world, completely wrapped up in each other. The lucky penny must have worked. If Rachel could keep *her* act together, the three Wilcox sisters might finally pull off a trifecta. Betty felt a sad but sweet smile tug at the corners of her mouth. Then, her own sister, God rest her, could be at peace. She sighed again.

"And another thing," she said to Rachel in a stern tone, as if she and her niece were actually having a rational conversation, "stop drinking. You know you can't handle it and it would be a shame if you started throwing up."

Rachel noticed her aunt as if for the first time that evening. "Oh, hi, Betty. You're here, too? Don't worry, I'm finished." She straightened experimentally and let go of the post. "At least with the booze." She giggled. "Have a great night." She waved nonchalantly and staggered off.

Betty wonderingly watched her two wayward nieces for a few moments more. Something was in the water in this town—and not like back in the fifties either. A quick chill shot through her at the memory. No, not like that. Something good.

Meg? Never any doubt there. Salt of the earth. But the other two? Jimminy. She'd been afraid Gillian would end up an old maid, married to Rocky Falls and responsibilities. And Rachel? Despite her having a successful business career Betty had always expected a call from her from Las Vegas saying she was working as a showgirl for a really nice guy named Vinnie.

Yep, for better or worse, things were afoot around Rocky Falls. Change was on the wind. Either that or she was losing the shine on her marbles. A well-groomed blond woman materialized at her elbow. She had the whitest teeth Betty had ever seen.

"This is great, huh?" the woman said moving to the beat. She was wearing blue jeans, a raw silk shirt in a vivid turquoise and a southwestern-style belt.

"Um, yes it is," Betty found herself mesmerized by the woman's dental work, watching it as the woman spoke. "I look forward to it every year."

"Oh, you must be a local, then."

"All my life. Born and raised here. Wouldn't want to live anywhere else."

A puzzled look briefly crossed the woman's face. "That's funny you say that," she began. "A few years ago, on our way to visit friends in Canada, my husband and I just happened to stay overnight in Rocky Falls. At the Eagle House Inn?"

Betty nodded.

"Well, at first we thought—" She stopped. "I mean at first impression the town seemed—"

"Like Hicksville?" finished Betty.

"No! Oh, no I don't mean that, really. It just wasn't what we were used to. We left after just that one overnight. But we kept talking about it for some reason. Like it got under our skin."

Betty smiled.

"We bought a house here about a year ago. And it just keeps getting better and better."

"I know what you mean," Betty said. "A lot of my family had chances to leave and live somewhere else, but most of them stayed. You're never ever really done with the place."

The crowd in front parted then, yielding a view of Jack and Gillian, still locked onto each other. "My niece," Betty said to the blond woman, by way of explanation.

"That good-looking guy she's with, he looks familiar. I've seen him somewhere before."

"That's the hot dog guy, honey," said a blond man, who arrived bearing two large plastic cups brimming with draft beer. His teeth ran a close second to the woman's.

"Oh, thanks, sweetie," she said.

"Can I get you something to drink?" the man asked Betty politely.

"No, thanks. Not just yet."

Introductions were made all around. "Say, don't you work at the lumberyard?" the man who had introduced himself as Harv Shackleton, asked. The blond woman gave him a withering look.

Betty laughed. "Actually, that's my niece Gillian," she said. She gestured toward the dance floor. "I own the pottery shop downtown."

"Good for you and your niece," said the woman whose name turned out to be Sue, with a meaningful glance to her husband. "Men have run all the businesses for way too long." She looked at the dance floor again. "Who's she dancing with, anyway? Oh, the hot dog guy—I remember now . . ."

"'The hot dog guy' is actually Jack Turner," said Betty. "He owns a big development company?"

"Really . . ." Harv started.

"I thought he looked familiar," Sue finished. "How come he's so friendly, if you don't mind my asking, with the locals?"

"Yeah," piped in her husband, "I wouldn't think that he'd be very welcome around here. We attended those town meetings in the spring. About the planned community development? Not pretty."

"Well," Betty said, "I don't think anyone knows what's going to happen around here, yet. Including our Mr. Turner. It's a big issue, with some good points on each side."

"No wonder he was asking me questions about how we liked it around here," Harv said. "I told him exactly what I thought, though. We moved here because of the town being the way it is. We don't want it to change into where we just came from. Isn't that right, Sue?"

The song ended on a wailing crescendo, and Peter announced the band was taking a short break. Jack and Gillian emerged from the tangle on the dance floor and moved toward Betty and the Shackletons. Gillian looked radiant, happy, relaxed. Jack's eyes never left her.

"Jack," Betty said, lightly touching his arm, "you know the Shackletons . . . ?"

Jack tore his eyes away from Gillian. He nodded distractedly. "Yes, we met over soft drinks this morning."

"We were just discussing your plans for the town, Mr. Turner," said Sue Shackleton.

Gillian widened her eyes at Jack and imperceptibly shook her head: *Don't blame me.*

"And I *won't* call you Jack if that's alright, Mr. Turner. I just want to tell you that if you turn this town into a collection of look-alike condos and fancy, upscale boutiques that don't sell a damn thing you can use let alone afford, my husband and I will be very cranky about it. Isn't that right, Harv?"

"Well—"

"Thank you, dear. Just so you understand where we're coming from, Mr. Turner. We didn't move here only to have it turn into the place we left. We'd be very upset. Remember that, Mr. Turner." She froze him with a stare. "*Very* upset. Come along, Harvey."

Harv waved vaguely. "Nice to see you again." He hurried after his wife.

Betty cocked her head, and raised her eyebrows in supplication. "I didn't start anything, Jack. I just said who you were and they were off to the races."

"Yeah, well, there seems to be a lot of that going around."

"A lot of what going around?" rumbled a deep voice behind them.

"Well, if it isn't the blues man himself," said Jack. "Mingling with us common folk are you?"

Peter Dunn laughed at him. "Where's Rachel? With all the noise she was making, I thought for sure she'd be right there when Riley got off the stage."

"She never could hold her booze. She's probably sitting on a hay bale right now waiting to get sick," Gillian said.

"Riley!" Dunn called out over heads in the crowd. "Hey, Riley! You need to look around for your lady friend. She might have passed out somewheres." No sooner had Dunn finished speaking than a gap opened in the press of bodies. And there was Rachel, sitting on a hay bale, elbows on her knees, cradling her head in her hands.

"Whoa, what happened to her?" Riley asked, coming up to the group. "She didn't look too good during that last set, but she's really out of it now, huh?"

"Comes with the territory, Riley," Gillian replied sweetly. "She's all yours now, sugar." Gillian reached for Jack's arm, waggled her fingers at him and made for the far end of the barn.

"Hey, Gillian," Riley cried. "You can't just leave her there."

Gillian half-turned, but continued walking. "You're right.

You can't." She waved again, grinning. The crowd swallowed her and Jack.

"Cripes, Pete, what's going on around here lately?" Riley said. He kicked moodily at the hay beneath his feet and then stared over at Rachel. "Everything's all screwed up. I finally decide to give Gillian the heave-ho and suddenly it's me and Rachel. And this one?" He hooked a thumb at where Rachel sat on the hay bale. "*Way* high maintenance." Then he smiled, remembering. "Hotter than a two-buck pistol, though."

"Well, I wouldn't know about that, pal," Dunn said, scratching his head uneasily. He mumbled under his breath. "Not sure I really want to, actually . . ."

"Huh?"

"Nothing. But she's your girl now, like Gillian said. You best go take care of her."

Riley hiked up his belt and sighed. "Guess you're right. There's nothing for it but to get her home. See you later."

"Good luck."

Riley waved absently and wound his way through the milling crowd toward Rachel. "My hero," she warbled, spying him. She flung her arms open wide and beamed sloppily up at him.

He glared down at her. "You're nutty as a fruitcake, you know that?"

Rachel giggled. "So are you, tiger," she crooned, dropping a hand to his thigh then dragging it provocatively across parts of his anatomy.

"Jesus, Rachel," he hissed, roughly shoving her hand away and glancing around self-consciously. "C'mon, up an' Adam."

He tugged at her arms. She tried to rise, but the connection between her legs and her brain had been dissolved in alcohol. Her head lolled loosely and she slumped off the hay bale. He had to get her home. But whose home? Not his. Not yet. Charlie. He was at Meg's house babysitting his grandkids. One more—he looked down at Rachel, unconscious and oblivious—*child*, probably wouldn't make a difference to him one way or another. He'd take Rachel to Meg's house in town.

Riley hunched down and scooped up Rachel from the straw-covered floor. He tossed her lightly into the air and settled her into the cradle of his arms, then hiked her onto his shoulder in a fireman's carry. Her long legs dangling down in front of him. One of her high heels fell off. He squatted to retrieve it.

"Pretty good carry, Riley," Peter Dunn called, as Riley passed the stage on his way toward the door. "If you ever need a job down at the fire station . . ." He smirked, mischief in his eyes.

"Yeah, yeah, very funny." Riley stuck Rachel's errant shoe in his back pocket, squared his shoulders and strode out of the barn with as much dignity as he could muster.

"Thanks for following my lead," Gillian said to Jack as they made their way across the barn through the throng of people. "Riley's a big boy. He's got to learn to pick a horse and stick with it. Rachel's his baby, now. They deserve each other." She smiled. "In fact, in a weird kind of way they do kind of fit together, don't they?"

He was staying out of this one, Jack thought. Riley and he had formed an unholy bond by becoming involved with two Wilcox sisters and Jack felt he owed the man his silence.

"What's the matter, Jack. Cat got your tongue?"

"Very funny. Where are we headed, anyway?"

"I'm dressed to kill tonight, if you hadn't noticed, and I'll be damned if I'm leaving with just one dance. I want to stake out a spot on the floor so we can be ready when the band starts up again."

"Oh." The thought of the frenzied dancing most of the crowd had been doing when they arrived put the fear of God in him. A cacophony of noise came from the stage area as the band tuned for the second set. Over Gillian's shoulder, Jack caught Peter Dunn's eye and circled a forefinger at the floor, pleading: *A slow one*. Peter smiled, nodded, and spoke to the band members. He turned back toward Jack, one giant thumb upraised.

"You know, on second thought," Jack said, "I would like to go again." He slid his arms around Gillian, ever-marveling at how well they fit together. Like a matched mortise and tenon. Behind Gillian's back, he surreptitiously waved his thanks to Peter. Peter saluted crisply.

"But can we still twirl?" Gillian asked, leaning her head back and looking up at him. "Even though it's a slow one?"

Jack's jaw dropped.

"How—?" he started.

"Jack, when are you going to realize that you are as transparent as glass to people who know you? And believe me, I know you." She stood on tiptoes and planted a gentle kiss on his lips.

He shook his head, astonished. "You know, when I first met you I felt like I'd fallen down a rabbit hole into a world where everything was topsy-turvy," he said to her. "Where everything that I thought I knew turned out to be wrong. Now I'm starting to feel . . . *comfortable* at this crazy tea party. What the hell is happening to me?"

"Jack, Jack, Jack," Gillian said, shaking her head in mock sorrow. "You're a nice guy. Face it. I have. Yeah, you've probably made a small fortune by being a bit, what's the word? *duplistic*, shall we say?"

She felt him stiffen and not in a good way. "But you know what?"

"What?" he said grumpily.

"You're okay under it all. You really are. So get used to it. And enjoy the tea."

"But why does all this," he indicated the dance around them with a sweep of his gaze, "scare the crap out of me?" And why was he admitting this?

"You've got big-time control issues, sweetie," she said,

patting his cheek. "That's all. Just relax and go with it." She squeezed his waist.

He shook his head again, like an old draft horse shaking away flies. "That's easy for you to say, you know? You've always had people behind you, around you, driving you crazy maybe, but still there for you. What I did, I did on my own."

"Jack, look. Yes, I'm lucky to have all the people around me that I have. But everybody does the best they can. Your family, they did the best they could. You've got to get off the hook. Fortunes change. Hey, you found me," she said smiling. She kissed him lightly on the lips.

"For now, yes. But cripes, Gillian, with all the shit between us? Where do we go from—"

She shushed him with fingers to his lips. "Tomorrow, Jack. Right now we've got tonight."

One piece of roller-coaster track at a time. Banged in but breathless moments before the speeding car arrived. "Maybe you're right," he said, sighing.

"Ho, ho! Get the video cameras. I want a permanent record of that."

"Shut up," he said mildly, pulling her close.

The band felt its way through a few chord progressions, then Luke settled into a slow rendition of *You Look Wonderful Tonight*.

"He's got a nice voice, doesn't he?" Gillian said, touching the side of her face to Jack's shirtfront. The heat of his chest warmed her cheek.

"How did you ever figure all this stuff out, Gillian?" he asked. "I mean, about people and the way they feel."

She laughed. "Me? With my retarded interpersonal skills?"

"I didn't say that."

She laughed again. "You'd have to get in line if you wanted to."

"So?"

She lifted her head from his shirtfront. "Jack, this is it. Last time I talk seriously to you tonight: Because I'm human." She said each word slowly. "Don't you think I've done a lot of stupid stuff in my time, too? You can be so dense sometimes, no offense."

He thought about that for a while as they swayed. "You really are pretty smart, you know?"

"Smart, huh?" She chuckled, the sound muffled by the fabric of his shirt. "If I'm so smart how come I'm dancing with a guy that wants to take my town away from me?" She said it without rancor.

"Because you see my finer qualities. Here's hoping someday I will too."

Gillian snuggled closer and murmured her agreement into the folds of his Oxford. Jack became conscious of her hot breath on his chest and suddenly found it hard to take in a deep breath. The sudden swelling in his lower body made it difficult to step in time with the music. Gillian had evidently sensed the developing situation and was making matters worse by pressing harder against him. His control was a thin thread fast unraveling.

"You better stop now, Ms. Wilcox," his last vestiges of self-discipline said.

"Oh, yeah? Or you'll what?" Gillian smirked up at him, her eyes narrowed to slits. Jack wanted her like he'd wanted no other woman in his life.

"I'll have to . . ." He thought a minute. "That's it—I'll have to pretend you lost an earring."

"What?"

"An earring." Jack let go of her and bent down, pretending to search the straw covered floor for something. He suddenly disappeared into a horse stall behind the hanging curtain of lights.

"Jack, what the—?"

A hand shot out from between the illuminated strands, grabbed her wrist and hauled her into the darkness beyond. The mustiness of old furniture assailed her, then the feel of Jack's hands on her upper arms, and his lips on hers. All else was a blur.

"Gillian," he whispered hoarsely into her mouth, "I cannot stop touching you."

"Then don't," she said.

His arms slid around her waist, pulling her close. He pressed into her through the thin material of her dress. She forced a hand between their bodies, sliding her fingers into the openings of his shirt, sampling the feel of skin against skin. His hands slid lower on her back to cup her buttocks, lifting her up and into him. She moaned, lost on a wave of heat and white light.

This time she'd ride it to the end she would, even if the road came out miles from home. But she didn't think so. This *was* home.

Jack's hands swept up her rib cage to cup her breasts. Gently kneading, his thumbs teased her nipples. In counterpoint, their tongues led and followed, tempted and tested, probed and promised. It was raw and elemental, with no end in sight save the total fusion of their bodies and souls.

Jack kissed the base of her throat, his teeth brushing her skin. He slid her dress off one shoulder and kissed his way down to the swell of her breast, all the while tasting and licking, breathing cool air across her flushed skin, raising goose bumps. Gillian ran her hands down his chest, in her mind's eye tracing the drop that had glided down his pectorals in the lumber yard. But now she followed it to its source. Pulse racing, head tipping back from the pleasure Jack was creating with his mouth, she fought to focus her attention on the bulge in the front of his trousers. With her fingertips, she lightly traced the hard outline through the material of his pants, drawing her nails across its hardness. He groaned, and drew her breast into his mouth.

"Fire!" Gillian suddenly heard through a fog of desire. Yep, plenty of it. All around her. They *had* to find better places to do this.

"Fire!"

There it was again. Somebody yelling. Good God, would

she and Jack never be left alone long enough to make love
in totally inappropriate places?

"The woods! The woods! They're on fire!"

Her heart froze.

Chapter 32

The madness, the music, the mayhem died like the last gasp of a seized engine. Dancers froze in mid-step, cups spilled on tables and beer dribbled to the floor, people, seconds before yelling to be heard above the din of sound, found themselves screaming into a sudden, deathly quiet. There was utter silence for three seconds, with only the faint wail of the klaxon at the fire station downtown echoing through the barn.

"For chrissakes, Virginia! Stop yelling 'Fire!' You'll be getting everyone in a panic," said Sam Michaels, the policeman hired to work the dance. Virginia began to bluster at him, but Betty put a restraining hand on her arm and she backed down, muttering. The crowd parted to let Michaels through to the stage.

"Peter, bad news," Michaels said, looking up at him. "The woods are on fire. Ronny Southland, down at the station, just raised me on the radio." Peter, for all his size, dropped his broomstick and leaped nimbly from the stage, pulling Luke along with him. Luke just managed to slip off the strap on his guitar and pass the instrument to Leo before his feet left the platform.

Peter landed in front of Michaels. "Where?"

"About a half mile the other side of town."

"*Which* side, Sam?" Peter asked, pinning Michaels with a look as flinty as granite. To Jack, still concealed in the stall and hastily tucking in his shirttails, it was an enigmatic question.

"The wrong one, I'm afraid," Michaels said. "Ronny figures it was lightning. Been going about forty minutes from the looks of it. Would've been reported sooner, but everybody in town older than seventeen's here right now. Downtown's all babysitters and little kids."

"What's he mean 'the wrong one'?" Jack whispered to Gillian, who was frantically pulling her dress back together.

"The wrong side of the Mohasset. Remember? I told you on our walk downtown that day that Rocky Falls survived the last fire because of the bend in the river?"

He nodded. "The oxbow."

"Exactly. Only this time fire's coming from the other direction. The river's no protection. We're a sitting duck." So was the mill and the Wilcox Box. But especially the mill. It abutted the woods. A tantalizing, high-density treat for the fiery beast in the forest.

"Shit . . ." Jack said, dawning dread etching itself into his face. Gillian made a final adjustment to the bodice of her dress. It didn't stay perfect for very long, she thought ruefully. Jack swept aside the curtain of lights and led her out by the hand in time to hear Peter Dunn call, "Leo!"

Peter talked as he walked backward toward the double barn doors. "Leo, get on the PA and tell the volunteer firemen to meet me in the parking lot. Work the mike and keep everyone else calm. Tell people to head into town to take care of whatever they have to, but tell them not to leave here until all the volunteers have cleared out. Got that?"

Leo nodded and started the announcement on the microphone. To Michaels, striding to keep up with him, Peter muttered, "Have Ron set up barricades outside of town so these people can't bring their cars in. We'll let 'em go in on

foot, though. Get what they need and get out. Last thing we
need is the downtown clogged up with vehicles."

Peter and Michaels brushed by Jack and Gillian on their
way through the crowd, and they caught most of the conversation. "Damn it!" Gillian said. "If the fire cuts across 101,
there'll be no getting out to the house and the mill from this
side of town. No way to save them. Shit! The cops'll have
the road through town blocked off anyway in the next few
minutes. Damn it!"

Gillian's face was a twisted knot of frustration. Jack
watched her rock from foot to foot, clenching her fists. "That
look's making me nervous," he said. "Don't do anything
stupid, you hear me?" He shook her arm for emphasis.

"Yeah, yeah. Look, go outside with Peter, there's probably something you can do to help in town. I've got to find
Meg, see if she needs any help at home." She brushed stray
hair back out of her face.

"Okay, but I'll meet up with you in town. I'll get to Meg's
place as soon as I can." He squeezed her arm and gave her
a quick peck on the cheek and started to walk away. Then he
turned back and stabbed his finger at her. "*Nothing stupid,*
you hear?"

"Right, nothing stupid." She waved, and clasped her
hands behind her back. "I'll see you in town in a little while.
Be careful."

Jack looked at her for a long moment, then jogged off
after Peter Dunn.

The mill, damn it, Gillian thought. She wouldn't surrender it. She couldn't. Maybe this fire tonight would turn out
to be just a flash in the pan, but it couldn't have come at a
worse time. The fire index was sky high. Thank God ground
water levels were good, though, from the wet spring and
summer. The fire guys could pull water from the Mohasset,
too, for the pumps, if it came to that.

Wait a minute, *she* could do that, too. Use river water to
fight the fire. That was it. Get on the road before the cops

barricaded Route 101. Break through the fire line somehow, get on the other side of it. Get to the mill and hook up the water cannons she should have been using all along to keep the bark on the logs moist and the bugs out. Soak the piles closest to the woods. Maybe drag them back out of the way, depending on what kind of time she had. That would set up a firebreak between the edge of the burning woods and the mill buildings. That might keep the fire from sweeping directly through the yard.

Half a mile out of town, the center of the fire, Michaels said. That meant the lightning struck right between the far edge of town and the mill. Making it through the choke point on Route 101 before the fire or the police blocked the road was going to be a close thing. She had to get going. Now.

She slipped off her high heels and dashed for the parking lot.

Jack caught up with Peter and joined a knot of men gathered around Sam Michaels's cruiser. The door was open and Michaels was on the two-way radio, relaying messages between Peter and the police station in the basement of the town hall. "Ronny, you copy? Over."

"Roger," the radio crackled.

"Ron, Peter and Luke and about twenty fire volunteers are leaving Applebee's farm right now. You meet them this side of town on 101. Let them through on foot, then set up barriers behind them. Nobody else takes cars into town. Have them leave them off the side of the road, in Virginia's realty office lot—anywhere—just so they're not blocking the way. Tell people walk to their houses and stay put until they hear from us. You got all that, over?"

The radio crackled. "Roger. You want to evacuate the downtown?"

"No on that right now, Ronny. Let's get a handle on how big this thing is first. ETA on Peter Dunn is ten minutes, what with all the jam up around here. Just keep people calm for now. I'll stay here at Applebee's and make sure everybody gets out without running each other over."

"Roger, out."

Peter started deploying forces. "Luke, grab six guys and some picks and shovels. Get the pump truck out on 101 the far side of town as far out as you can. Concentrate on keeping the road open. It's our only way through to the other side of this thing. If we can't get around it and corral it into the river, it's going to get nasty. I'm going down 101 myself right now as far as I can to figure out how big this bastard is. I'll keep you posted. Meet me out there."

Luke nodded. Peter turned to two other men in the group. "O'Donnell, Meade? Get the ladder truck out there. Same thing. Put together a crew. Chainsaws, whatever you need. Start a firebreak. Don't get trapped. We can't afford to lose any equipment and we're damn sure not going to lose any people over this. Crank the ladder way up when you get out there and see if you can get a bead on how big the bastard is and which way it's going. Radio in." The two men took off for the parking lot at a dead run.

Peter noticed Jack in the group and nodded. "Nice to see you stuck around, Mr. Turner. We need all the help we can get. I got a feeling it's going to be a long night. The rest of you: Meet at the station pronto. Luke's in charge. He'll tell you what to do. Get going."

Peter turned to Michaels. "It may be overkill, Sam, but call the Forest Service. Tell them what's going on and that we'll keep them apprised as we find out more. Tell them to get a helicopter crew together and warm up a bird. They'll be cranky about it and we may not need them, but if we can't get through to the other side of this bastard, we need eyes up above telling us which way it's going."

Michaels nodded. "I'll get some spotters with radios up on the high ground either side of 101 for now."

"Good," Dunn replied. "You called Engine Six in Bertram and let 'em know what's going on?"

"Ron Southerland did from downtown. Moment he heard. They already knew."

"Good man, that Ron. We're a hell of a lot closer to it than the Bertram unit is, but if we can't get through on 101, we'll need them on the other side."

"You gonna pull from the Mohasset and set up water cannons?"

"That we can, if the mother's burning close enough by it." Peter hitched up his trousers. "Well, I'm out of here, Sam. Mind you don't kill yourself tonight. Both of us gettin' on in years for this kind of nonsense. Keep in touch."

"I need a lift into town," Jack said to Luke.

"Jump in." Luke pointed to a dated, but immaculately maintained Ford Bronco. Jack hopped in. Luke revved the engine, hit the flashing yellow lights and pulled into the lead spot in a convoy of fifteen vehicles.

"How many vehicles you own?" Jack asked, looking around the interior of the Bronco.

"Just two. Put your seat belt on."

Jack reached for it, clicked the buckle. He was pressed back into his seat as Luke nailed the gas, hot on the trail of the 1903 blaze incarnate.

Gillian hooked a hand around a corral post to steady herself as one bare foot landed squarely on a pointy piece of crushed gravel on the last turn before the parking lot. Cursing, fashion and grace forgotten, clutching the hem of her dress high up her thighs, she limped the final thirty yards to her pickup truck.

She hopped in, scrounged under the seat for the keys and jammed them into the ignition. She gunned the engine and dropped it into first. Spitting gravel from the rear wheels, she flashed down the row of parked cars only to hit the

brakes just before she hit the pasture fence. Crap. She threw
the pickup into reverse and backed up past her original spot.
Braked again, confronted by the sheer aluminum wall of
an RV. Her escape route was cut off.

She abandoned the Toyota and frantically scanned the
aisles of cars and pickups. Her gaze fell on the Twins'
Caddy. In the front row. Backed into a space facing the road.
She limped over to it. Keys in the ignition. Perfect.

The big tires of the heavy Cadillac chirped when they
bit into the asphalt of Route 101. In a chrome rearview
mirror as big as a dinner platter, she saw men running for
their vehicles. A grim smile lifted one side of her mouth.

She'd beaten the fire guys out of the gate.

Chapter 33

"How bad is it do you think?" Jack asked Luke as they raced down 101.

"No telling. But forty minutes—an hour by the time we're on station—is a big head start in these kinds of conditions. Been bone dry too long. Crazy weather for the fall around here."

"When do you make the decision to evacuate the town?"

"That's Peter's job. Better him than me." Luke checked his rearview mirror. The last of the convoy was pulling out of Applebee's lot.

"We might just luck out, though. The heat lightning's probably what got the fire going, but with them clouds building up this afternoon we might get some rain before the night's out. Too little too late, probably, but it might take the edge off things."

"People are real jumpy around here about fire, huh?"

"Hell, yeah, after the big one in 1903 almost put paid to this place. 'Course there's not the slash piles and crap lying around now like there was then, but a big one can still do a lot of damage. It gets dicey in the middle of them things, too. The wind whips through the valley along the Mohasset, it being the low point and all. Gets shifty, too. Updrafts carry the flames to the high ground faster than people can run.

It's easy to get trapped if you don't watch it. 'Copters help, but they're not much good at spotting ground crews at night."

"The big thing's the road, right? Keeping that open?" Jack asked.

"That's exactly it." Luke downshifted. The truck took the tight turn in the road like it was on to a rail. "If we can't get through to the other side of the thing, we can't chew at the ass end of it. But Bertram—the next town over—they'll back us up. Plus Peter'll put out an 'all call' to crews in a thirty-mile radius if it gets really hairy. But yeah—the road's the thing."

Up ahead, flashing strobes marked the outskirts of the downtown. "There's Ron," Luke said, pointing with one finger lifted from the steering wheel. "He's letting us through, then putting up a roadblock to keep everyone else out. Unless they're old folks, they're walking in."

The Bronco slowed briefly as it passed Ron Southerland's post. Luke waved. The patrolman touched the brim of his cap as he spied Jack in the passenger's seat. Jack returned the salute. Southerland gestured them through the check-point, strobe flash lighting up fluorescent orange sawhorses.

"I guess it's not that far into town for people to have to go on foot," Jack said, measuring distances as they drove three blocks through eerily deserted streets.

"People around here know the drill," Luke said. "They understand it's a state of emergency right now whether anyone officially declares it that or not."

So different than in Boston, Jack thought, where every driver assumed it was their God-given right to drive around police barriers. Luke swung the Bronco into the drive of the fire station and pulled it around to the back of the building. Half the convoy followed suit and half parked at the sides of the concrete apron out front. Others bounced two wheels up and over the curb and left their vehicles parked on the sidewalk.

Luke looked over the crowd as soon as everyone was inside the station. Some men pulled on boots, coats, and oxygen bottles. Others broke shovels, extra axes, and chainsaws out of lockers. It was a hurried yet orderly scramble. Two men rolled open the station's huge front doors. Luke climbed onto the chrome running boards of the idling ladder truck.

"Hey, anybody seen Riley?" he called out.

"I heard he left the dance early to drop off Rachel Wilcox at her sister Meg's place," Jack said. The volunteer in line in front of Jack handed him a pickax. He passed it on to the next man in line.

Luke's brows knitted. "Mr. Turner, you'd be real helpful right now by taking my truck down to Meg's place and rousting Riley outta there. He probably hasn't heard what's going on yet. Tell him to trailer his bulldozer along 101 West as far as he can and hook up with Peter Dunn. He can help clear a fire break." He tossed Jack the keys to his Bronco. Jack turned to go. "Oh, and Mr. Turner?"

Jack stopped. "She's in cherry condition," Luke said. "You bring her back the same way, hear?"

Jack grinned and saluted. He trotted off toward the rear parking lot.

"All right, boys. What are we waiting for?" Luke asked. He climbed into the cab of the ladder truck and gunned the engine.

Jack pulled jerkily to a stop in front of Meg's house. He'd had a bit of trouble controlling the Bronco. It took off like a goosed jackrabbit at the slightest touch on the gas. Luke must have done some kind of work under the hood. A street legal rocket's what it was. No quaint antique here.

Lights were on in the front room and Jack could see Charlie Wilcox reading a newspaper with the TV on. Jack could hear it blaring from all the way out in the street. Riley walked by the window with a beer in his hand and sat down on the couch. He took a sip, then he must have noticed the headlights in the street in front of the house. The screen door opened as Jack was walking up the front path.

"What's up?" Riley asked warily, eyeing Luke's truck at the curb.

"They just shut down the dance. Lightning hit the woods a half-mile west on 101, between the town and Gillian's place. The woods are burning. For about fifty minutes now."

"The hell you say . . ." Riley took two steps off the front porch and sniffed. "Nothing here yet, though. Wind must be taking it the other way. Away from town, maybe, but if that's the case, toward Gillian's. Shit, I gotta get to the station."

"Wait—I just came from there. Luke says to tell you to take your bulldozer down 101 West as far as you can. Peter Dunn'll meet you out there. He wants you to start a fire break."

"Right. That makes sense. Hey, stay here with Charlie and the kids, OK? Bob's away and Rachel's dead asleep upstairs. Drunk as a skunk. She'll be no help if the shit hits the fan."

Jack nodded. "Right. Gillian'll probably come back here anyway."

"Gillian?" Riley cried. "You mean you left her running around *loose* in all of this? She's halfway to the mill by now's my bet."

"But they barricaded the town to through traffic just after we came through. There's no way she'd get through."

Riley snorted. "I figured you knew her better than that. She'll *make* a way through." He patted his pocket for keys. "Look, I gotta go. Wait here as long as you can, but if she doesn't show soon, dimes to donuts she's out at her place doing something stupid. See you later."

"Yeah . . . take care." Jack watched Riley's taillights disappear.

Shit. Blue lights. No doubt that would be Ron Southerland heading out to the edge of town to set up barricades. Gillian slammed on the brakes, skidded the Cadillac through a sharp left turn and into an alley next to the Majes-

tic Theatre, then killed the lights and ducked down below
seat level. The cruiser flashed past. Gillian gunned the
Caddy in reverse, spun the wheel toward 101 West and
pinned the accelerator.

"Now, now, everybody," Leo said to the milling, agitated
crowd in the barn. "You'll all get to leave in just a few minutes. Let's let the rest of our fire crew get out of here, then
Sam'll let us all out. There's plenty of time to get home and
check on families."

"Well, it's not the way I would have handled things," declared Virginia.

"And you would have what—sanctioned panic in the
streets?" Betty shot a frozen look at her younger sister.
"There are times, Virginia, when you would be wise to keep
it in your barracks bag. And this is one of them."

"Well, I never—" Virginia started.

Betty didn't allow her to finish. "We could only hope,
Virginia. Now, I am warning you for the last time. Do *not*
mess with me tonight. First order of business: Where's
Meg? She's got to get home to Charlie and the kids."

"Here I am, Betty." Meg emerged from the throng. "Good
God, this is nerve wracking being stuck here. I hope Charlie's making out okay. What a time for Bob to be away." She
snapped her fingers. "Cripes! Bob. I've got to call him. If
this thing makes the eleven o'clock news in Boston, he'll
flip. I wonder if they know about it in town yet?" Worry
lines lacerated her pleasant features.

"Oh, I'm sure the word's being spread as we speak," Betty
said. "Peter Dunn will evacuate if he feels it's necessary."
The fingers of one hand worried her necklace of carved an-
imals. On tiptoes, she craned her neck for a view of the
double doors leading to the parking lot. "Well, they're letting people go now, it looks like," she said to Meg. "Let's
gather up Gillian and Jack, and get out of here."

"Mr. Turner left with Luke," Virginia said. "Gillian told

him that she was going to meet up with you, Meg, and you'd go back to the house together. I wonder where she got to?"

Betty's consternation visibly deepened. "Lord knows with that girl. But let's follow this crowd out of here, maybe we'll see her on the way." The group somberly picked their way across the floor, staring in disbelief at the deserted dance floor and tables covered with forgotten raffle tickets and spilled drinks. Betty, the last person to leave, pulled the plug on the lights, plunging the barn into darkness.

Nothing beats new equipment. The diesel dump truck turned right over, then settled into a steady roar, sweet as a nut. Riley jockeyed it around in the field next to his shop, the trailer it towed with the Caterpillar bulldozer lashed onto it making the turn tighter and trickier than usual. Shit. Did he have his—? Yep, right behind the seat. The oxygen bottle, long coat, boots, helmet. All there. He crunched onto the gravel fire road leading from his place, then turned west on Route 101, toward the fire. He wound the big rig up through the gears.

"She'll be all right, don't you worry," said Charlie Wilcox to Jack, as he pretended to watch the basketball on TV. But the way he was massaging the arms of the upholstered chair spoke volumes about his concern.

"How are the kids doing?" Jack asked him.

"Eh?" Using the remote, Charlie lowered the volume on the game.

"The kids. They OK?"

"Oh, yeah. Them and Rachel. They'd all sleep through the Second Coming." Charlie chuckled. "Good kids, them," he said, his praise encompassing several generations.

Jack said, "We ought to get some of the kids' stuff together. Clothes, toys. You know, in case we've got to evacuate before the women get back."

"Yep, I suppose you're right."

Charlie heaved himself to the edge of the chair, and got his cane under his bad leg. The muscles of his right forearm bulged as he levered himself to his feet. If it was anyone else, Jack would have offered to get the things together himself. But this was Gillian Wilcox's father. Just like with the daughter, you didn't tell him what to do. Suddenly, the front door flew open and the Wilcox clan noisily flooded in.

Minus Gillian.

"Imagine him letting everyone park in my realty office lot without him so much as *asking* me," Virginia was saying.

"Ginnie, he's a police officer," Betty replied. "You know, a large man with a gun? In an undeclared state of emergency? Figure it out, for Pete's sake." Then to Jack, "Oh, hello, Mr. Turner."

Jack was on his feet in a flash. "She's not with you?" he asked, looking past them to the front walk, but gut sure of the answer before it came.

"No," Meg said quietly. The "she" was understood.

"Dammit, she told me she'd meet me here," Jack said, searching his mind and coming up with the only logical answer. "My God. She's at the mill."

"Where I'd be," Charlie said, with the selective acuity of the partially deaf. "If I could."

Betty and Meg cast dark looks at each other. Virginia shrugged and shook her head.

Jack thought out loud. "She must have blown out of Applebee's ahead of the volunteers and somehow got past Ronnie Southerland at the barricade."

"She's my daughter, Mr. Turner," Charlie said, "for better or worse. It's what I would have done."

"Jack, look," Betty said, turning and reaching out a hand, "I don't like putting you in the middle of all this. But you've got to . . ."

But she was talking to empty space. He was already gone.

". . . find her," she finished.

The screen door banged shut.

* * *

The Caddy flew past the Eagle House Inn. Hope old Arthur got the news. His place there could end up being damn close to the fire, depending on the wind. The acrid smell of smoke seeped into the interior of the car. Her heart beat faster in primitive response. Smoke clung to low spots in the road and her headlights cut swaths through it like twin bayonets. A mother deer and three foals darted out of the woods ahead of her on the left. She tapped the brakes and they charged across the road just feet from her bumper. Their white tails flashed briefly in the headlights before they disappeared into the woods on the north side of the road.

The smoke thickened farther along, lowering visibility on the road to less than a hundred yards. And then—there it was. A wall of flame in the woods. She braked to a standstill.

Gaudy tongues of flame greedily licked their way up fifty-foot pines on the river side of the road in front of her. Not satisfied with feasting on the south side of 101, the beast cast exploratory tendrils of flame across the thirty feet of asphalt to the north side. A hundred yards farther on, she could see a garland of fire lace the competing parts of the conflagration together to form a fiery gauntlet. On the other side, the mill. She had to get through.

There was no telling where on the other side of the blazing canopy the tunnel of smoke and flame ended. Or if it ended at all. She could dash beneath the flaming overhang, only to run headlong into an impenetrable cul-de-sac of flame.

Suddenly, through a break in the smoke, she saw sets of lights evenly arranged in pairs. Headlights. Of vehicles on the other side. She powered up the windows, leaned on the horn, nailed the gas pedal and shot the Caddy toward the canopy of flame.

It was like plunging into a Hollywood version of hell. Trails of smoke streamed over the windshield and ribbons of gray and black obscured the side windows.

Please don't send me to a place like this when I die, she prayed. *Whenever that is.*

She kept the wheel pointed straight toward where she guessed the middle of the road to be. All around her was impenetrable black, randomly lit by bursts of red and orange. Her only link with the world outside the cab was the blaring of the Caddy's horn. If not for the vibration of the steering wheel in her hands, she could well have been flying hundreds of feet above the earth.

Abruptly the tunnel ended and she exploded into clear night air, swerving to avoid the lead car in a line of vehicles pulled up in the opposite lane. Heads spun like tops as she swept past. She had made it through—barely.

Now to get to the mill. And the house too, she reminded herself. But first the mill. She covered the next quarter mile with the pedal to the floor, then braked and turned sharply off 101 into the drive leading past the house. She sent the Cadillac rocketing down the dirt road leading to the mill and the old car protested, its long wheel base bouncing and lurching and banging off the center strip of the rutted road. She skidded the big car to a stop just inside the front gate of the mill.

The pines at the edge of the yard blocked out a direct view of the fire raging in the forest behind them, but the crowns of the trees were eerily back lit and thick smoke clung to the underbrush at their base. In the silence after the engine switched off, Gillian heard loud cracks and pops from just beyond the shadowed border of stacked logs. It wouldn't be long before the ravenous beast in the forest would be snuffling around her doorstep, its tongues of flame lapping greedily, searching for chinks in the armor, desperate to feed.

Her fingers fumbled with the keys to the office, but finally the door gave way. She snapped on the overhead lights. Lit up the ones around the perimeter of the yard. Shimmied into coveralls. The thick canvas would be some protection from flying cinders. Raking fingers through her hair from front to back, she wiped out the last vestiges of Joyce's labors and tucked the mass of ringlets beneath a plastic hard hat.

Like Don Quixote, she was riding into battle with a mish-mash of weapons, ill-suited to the job ahead. But the foe waiting for her outside in the woods was not imaginary, the figment of a befuddled imagination. It was as real as the love she held for her business, her town, and her life. Her chest swelled. She remembered the mother bear defending her cubs that she'd run across years ago. Now she completely understood the huge animal's instinctive, defensive reaction. This fire was a threat to her own future, Gillian thought, to her progeny, her children. And to her past, she could admit now. She would defend them all with her life. A feeling of peace in the midst of turmoil, of resignation to the dangers of the task ahead, descended upon her.

The thickest gloves she could find in the miscellany behind the counter went on last. She took the steps of the office in one flying leap.

In the scant seconds she'd been inside the office, the predator in the woods had inched noticeably closer, emboldened by the promise of fuel. The underbrush at the edge of the clearing was ablaze now, and tendrils of orange and red were licking the bark of the log stacks bordering the woods. In minutes, the main body of the beast would pounce upon the piles. She had to drag them back and out of its reach. With fifty yards between them and the blaze and everything in between soaked down, there'd be a chance of the fire choking on its own ash before it reached the heart of the mill.

She dashed the length of the yard, headed for the river, hacking on the acrid smoke that assaulted her windpipe. The pump for the water cannons was set on a concrete platform thirty yards back from the high water mark of the Mohasset, with the uptake pipe running deep into the river, close to the pool where Jack had first come upon her. She reached the spot in twenty seconds flat, cracked open the valve in the fuel supply line leading from the fifty-gallon gas tank set on the platform next to the pump, gave the engine full choke, and yanked on the starter rope with both hands.

The engine fluttered, coughed once and settled obstinately into silence. She hauled on the starter rope again.

Nothing.

Pulled again. And again. Still nothing. She smelled raw gas. *Shit.* It was flooded. Back off the choke and the throttle. Pull a half a dozen times on the rope to cycle the engine through some clearing strokes. The snapping and popping of the advancing fire line lent a frenetic urgency to her actions.

Stay calm. It had always started before. Eventually. She eased in a little gas and tugged again.

Nothing. She advanced to quarter choke and hauled pleading on the starter rope. *Start, you lousy piece of sh—*

Vroom!

The engine roared to life, belching black smoke, knocking her backward. She struggled to her feet and cut out the choke. She forced herself to count to ten before engaging the pump drive. The engine roar deepened and slowed as water was drawn up from the Mohasset. The heavy canvas hoses leading from the pump and branching off into the log piles swelled and spurted water at the joints. Seconds later the stacks were buried under a curtain of water shooting from the cannons. Puddles formed on the hard dusty earth.

Thank God. She'd bought some time.

The loader was parked at the rear of the saw shed. She dashed frantically for it and awkwardly hiked herself up into the operator's seat. Her dress was bunched around her waist under the coveralls, so she could barely lift her feet to work the pedals, but there was nothing to be done about that now. Mercifully, the loader fired up on the first try. She gunned the engine and the ancient machine lurched and bumped across the yard toward the log piles.

Turning the last corner of the shed revealed that the fiery creature in the forest had wrapped flaming hands completely around two piles closest to the woods. They were goners, libations to the gods of fire. She would sacrifice them to save everything else.

She jockeyed the loader into a position perpendicular to

the pile nearest the ones ablaze, leaned on the hydraulics and slammed the jaws home underneath the bottommost log. Her plan was neither the safest nor the brightest in the world, and would have earned her a severe reaming out from anyone who knew anything about moving lumber. Especially from her father, who'd earned his cane learning this very lesson the hard way. But desperate times, desperate measures.

The upper jaw of the loader whined, biting into the pile, getting but a meager hold on a few logs. But it wasn't her intention to pluck them cleanly from the stack. Her aim was to unbalance the pile so it would roll down in a semi-controlled avalanche toward the loader. Once the logs were down and lying on flat ground, she could back drag them for thirty or forty yards, creating a firebreak. If it held here, on her side of the yard, the Mohasset would offer protection at the rear and quarter-mile expanses of open fields would act as a buffer on the flanks. Directly in front of her—in the heart of the maze of treacherous piles—was where the battle would be won or lost.

She ground the gears into reverse and gunned the engine. A claw's worth of logs ripped loose from the guts of the pile, and a clumsy chain reaction began as other pieces higher up on the pile tumbled down to fill the gap. With the gas full on, Gillian scooted the machine back and out of the way as ten tons of out-of-control lumber bore down upon it with a vengeance. Logs cascaded, bounced unpredictably, slammed savagely into the forks, skidded up the arms of the loader, threatened to join Gillian in the cab.

But she'd done it. The first pile was down in record time.

The lead log had rolled a good forty feet from where it had initially sat at the top of the stack. Gillian dropped the forks down over it, and a few others behind, and back dragged them another fifty feet for good measure. For the next ten minutes, she cut in and around the downed pile, extracting pieces, dragging some, getting behind others and rolling them along like a line of pencils on the floor in front of a push broom. The loader was a cranky old beast, but a powerful one. With Jack's work on the hydraulics, it was working better than it had in years.

But despite the protective water curtain, heat from the fire in the forest and the inferno in the two outer woodpiles washed over Gillian in waves. She remembered an expression of her father's: *Hotter than the hinges of Hades.* Well, it was that right now, all right. Flaming branches rained down on her from the blazing crowns of the trees closest to her. The roll cage and roof of the loader deflected most of them, but the odor of burned hair and plastic reached her nostrils after one particularly spectacular crash.

Three piles left. The first took ten minutes. That meant thirty minutes for all of them. Judging from the looks of the solid wall of flame extending almost to the very borders of the yard now, that was about twenty minutes more than she had. The time for finesse was over. The battle for the mill would be decided in the next few minutes.

She wheeled in a tight circle and charged the second pile of logs, grabbing twenty-foot lengths of pine trunk by their middles, squeezing them, the powerful jaws of the loader like a terrier grabbing at a rat. Snarling, the machine fought for backward purchase on the muddy ground, its wheels slipping, slipping, finally finding a bite.

Without warning, a chunk of pile unexpectedly ripped free. Mortally wounded, a mass of logs tumbled to fill the gaping void, individual timbers tumbling over each other in their rush to seal the hole. Gillian floored the gas and cut the wheels of the loader sharply to the right to avoid the brunt of the onslaught.

She was almost clear when a falling log ricocheted and jammed itself between the jaws of the loader. A second rolling trunk followed the line of least resistance set by the first, and piled onto the side of the loader. Frantically Gillian spun the wheel side to side, scrambling to find traction on the wet ground. A third trunk, then a fourth, joined the scrum. A rear tire exploded, the loader teetered precariously under the weight of the pile. The roll cage crumpled.

Like a sinking ship sliding under the waves, the front forks of the loader pointed briefly at the sky before the machine disappeared beneath a sea of angry timber.

The speedometer said ninety-five. Jack couldn't remember what he'd done to get Luke's truck up to that speed. It seemed to have a life of its own. He swept around a dump truck towing a bulldozer. Visions of Gillian filled his mind to bursting. Long naked legs, buttocks flexing as she climbed the boulder stairs near the swimming hole. Her sinewy strength fighting him off in the saw shed. Rolling around in the sawdust, with her legs straddling his hips. The feel of her breast against his lips. He realized he would die to save her.

Ahead of him, 101 straightened. A wall of flame suddenly towered before him. Running on instinct and adrenaline, he slammed the gas pedal to the floor. The Bronco broke accelerated past pump and ladder trucks and long lines of firemen toiling to clear underbrush at the sides of the road. Somebody, their face unrecognizable behind a Plexiglas mask—Peter Dunn, maybe—barely had time to raise a warning hand before Jack had streaked past him.

Jack plunged headlong into the inferno. Inside was hell itself. A tunnel of heat and flame and smoke enveloped the Bronco. Visions of a fiery death assailed Jack. He prayed for deliverance if only to be there for Gillian. He shut his eyes, certain he had but moments to live, then realized he wanted to see the end of his days. He opened his eyes to a speedometer that read one hundred and ten and a road cluttered with half a dozen fire vehicles, their yellow flashing strobes adding a macabre touch to the flickering of the flames in the woods at the sides of the road. Out of the corner of his eye Jack caught the word *Bertram* stenciled on the side of a yellow vehicle. The reinforcements Luke had been talking about.

He was on the other side. He had made it through. The road itself looked clear from that point on, too. It seemed that the two advancing armies of firefighters would soon meet in the middle of the conflagration, reopening the road. Just like Peter Dunn had said: The key to beating the blaze.

All this passed through Jack's mind in but nanoseconds, as he let up on the gas and jockeyed Luke's speeding bullet through the throng of trucks and workers. Just like on the Rocky Falls side of the blaze, arms were raised, certainly not to cheer the fool who'd come hurtling out of the brilliant wall of flame—more likely to curse him. Only by the grace of God, and Luke's considerable work on the Bronco's suspension and handling, had he avoided killing someone.

But Gillian's spirit was in the car with him though, urging him on. He was sure of that. As sure as he understood that she was his other half, white to his black. Yes, they could be steel on steel, too, sparking when they clashed. Maybe their union would never be a completely peaceful one, but in strength there was calm. You fought tooth and nail to build something strong, but after you did—and you jumped up and down on it like a fool trying to break it and it actually survived—you never had to worry about it again. Probably a stupid way to think about a relationship, but that's the way he thought of it with him and Gillian.

Suddenly, his longing for her kept him from drawing breath. He was compelled to pry one hand from the wheel and press it to his chest. She was with him. God, he could feel her presence like he'd never felt anything in his life before. Mixed in, though, was a sudden feeling of sadness, of opportunity lost, of something precious slipping away.

Tick, tock.

She was fading away, as if their spiritual connection was losing its power. Gillian had to be in deadly danger.

He let up the gas as her house flashed past on the left. He cursed, braked and banged a hasty U-turn. He took the rutted road so fast that the Bronco only hit the high points. The truck fishtailed into the brightly lit yard and, in a backwash of dust, skidded to a stop next to—the Twins' Caddy?

Chapter 34

He jumped out, his mind furiously working through possibilities, and peeked in the open door of the Caddy, its plush interior lit up by the dome light. He looked around the yard frantically, expecting to see one, if not two, old men working over the flames that looked to have invaded the perimeter of it.

The yard was deserted.

But water cannons were running, their drifting spray casting eerie shadows over the dark piles of lumber. Some of the stacks looked to have been recently and hastily disemboweled.

He had expected to see Gillian at work like a dervish. Doing what, he didn't exactly know. He was prepared to either help her or save her, depending on the situation, but she was . . . nowhere in sight.

Think! The only animate thing in the yard area besides the streams of water from the cannons was an enormous wall of flame that had stalked its way up to the first few woodpiles at the edge of the yard. Another pile had been hastily dragged backward to safety, and water spray was blanketing the rest of the area next to the woods. But aside from the snapping and popping of the blaze, and the steady roar of a gas engine down near the river—the pump, he realized—it was as quiet as death in the yard.

Chilled by the analogy, Jack ran toward the blaze, wildly seeking Gillian. The yard looked like a war zone. The muddy ground around the piles was a myriad of crisscrossing tire tracks, filling now with water from the guns. The freshest set of tracks disappeared beneath a huge pile of logs. He mentally drew a line from the point where they originated to the place they would logically terminate. That brought his gaze to the exact middle of the highest section of the pile. He squinted, his eyes tearing with smoke, and saw a patch of dirty yellow where it definitely did not belong. He splashed closer and carefully ascended the shifting pile.

His hand groped blindly and closed around what felt like a narrow branch. That made no sense. He wiped tears from his stinging eyes. Neither did finding a hydraulic line. A new one. Recently installed. By him. He was looking at the upper jaw of the loader. His mind struggled to put the discovery into context. It succeeded: the big machine was almost completely buried under the mountain of timber he was standing on. Gillian must have been trying to move this pile when . . . Good God in heaven. He couldn't think about it now. The horror would paralyze him.

"Gillian!" he screamed into the tangle of logs at his feet. "Gillian!"

A pinging sound of metal on metal returned to him. He fell onto his stomach and slid his head and shoulders into a gap in the trunks.

"Help! Down here!" A faint cry.

Sweet Jesus, she was alive.

"Gillian, it's me, Jack!"

"No shit? Cripes, what took you so long?"

"Funny!" he screamed into the pile, relief filling his heart. "Are you hurt? Can you move?"

"I'm okay. But I'm stuck inside the frigging roll cage. Hurry up and get me outta here, okay? My ass is sitting in a puddle of gas."

Jack sniffed. There it was. The unmistakable odor of

diesel fuel. He pulled his head out of the hole and looked at the ground around the pile. The surfaces of the puddles were slicked with multicolored hues. He looked toward the forest. Less than fifty yards away, the bright orange beast was greedily licking up what was left of two lumber piles. Gillian's was next on the menu.

"Jack!" His name drifted up from the heart of the pile. "Jack! Get the forklift! Behind the shed. The forklift!"

"Hang on!" he screamed, setting his feet under him.

The voice again. "Jack, wait! The keys. I've got them. . . . Stick your arm down." He shimmied his upper body vertically downward through the gap in the logs where her voice was coming from and extended one arm as far as he could. He felt fingertips, warm to the touch despite the cold water dripping from them. He took a moment to curl his around hers. At the base of one of them he found a hard metal ring. The keys. The hardest thing he'd ever done in his life was to withdraw his arm from the tangle of timber.

"Jack," the voice under the pile said unevenly, "I—love you, you know?"

His throat seized. "Me, too. Back in a sec."

He wormed out of the hole, and picked his way carefully down the pile, hopping from log to log. Some of the trunks, as massive as they were, shifted delicately on balance points under his weight. He lost his footing in the final few feet and landed awkwardly in the mud at the base of the pile. He spit grit from his mouth, rose unsteadily to his feet and slipped and slid his way across the yard to the forklift. It was a newer piece of equipment than the loader, not as powerful likely, but hopefully better behaved. He fired up the engine, then bounced the machine around the shed, aiming for the pile beneath which Gillian was trapped. From the looks of it, he had no more than a few minutes to get her out before . . .

He forced himself to concentrate on the job at hand. He inched the forklift up to the confusion of trunks and studied the pile for a moment. Deciding which log to attack first without burying Gillian further was like playing a giant game of pickup sticks. Which log should he yank out first so the others wouldn't shift?

There was no way he'd be able to just pick up a log with the forklift either, he realized. It was designed to move bundled stock from one flat stable surface to another, not to wrestle ungainly tree trunks in six inches of mud. But it could lift one end of a log and swing it clear. He clumsily raised the forks and slowly inched forward, sliding them gingerly under the log he'd chosen to move first. He fumbled with the unfamiliar lift controls. Finally, he found the secret and the forks obeyed his commands, tilting backward, shaking the trunk down against the body of the lift. *Gotcha.* Now to swing it back and away.

The log resisted, but Jack fed power to the wheels of the forklift and the trunk broke free. Another log rolled down and filled the space left by the first. The ground trembled as the second timber shifted. Jack's heart froze, but he continued backing up. Finally, he extracted enough of the log to maneuver around the other side of it for another attack on the pile.

Three logs were stripped off in the same way. Spaces between the trunks piled on top of the roll cage were beginning to open up. Jack jumped down from the forklift and landed ankle deep in mud, scrambled up the slippery mountain of wood and peered down through the voids. He could see a yellow helmet and a brown jumpsuit. "Almost there!" he yelled.

"I'm not going anywhere, Jack, but make it snappy for Chrissakes! The fumes are killing me down here."

Here he was rescuing her and all she could do was complain about the service. God, he loved her. His plan would work. It had to. Just three or four more logs to go . . .

With a nervous eye on the tendrils of flame advancing toward isolated puddles of gasoline, he returned to the loader and dug into the pile again. Choose, pray, lift, drag, drop, check progress of the fire. Two more times he went through the routine. On the third try, puddles close to the edge of the pile ignited. Like channels to the underworld, they glowed eerily as fuel trapped in the muddy tracks burned off.

Time was running out. Jack gunned the forklift toward the last two logs covering the cage area of the loader. He slipped the forks under the ends of them, and engaged the lift hydraulics. He let the forks drift up, while he jumped from the cab and frantically scaled the mountain of logs. The hydraulics would continue to automatically raise the load until they reached the limit of their lifting capacity. Jack prayed they'd reach that point *after* Gillian was free.

He screamed down to her. "Gillian!"

"What?"

"Get ready to move when I tell you. You've only got one shot at this, so get it right." He didn't want to fill her in on his plan. That would give her an opportunity to contemplate the grisly cost of failure. But part of him was savagely aware that should his idea not work, it would be more merciful for her to die a quick death under a load of falling timber than it would be for her to die a painfully slow one at the hands of the fire.

He watched the final two logs inch up and off the cage of the loader. He could see her face below.

"Who's running the forklift?" she cried.

He screamed at her. "Don't worry about it, damn it! Just get ready. Give me your arms when I say!"

The forklift was quivering under the strain, but still the logs inched higher. Suddenly, Jack heard a bass *whump* and a searing wall of heat washed over him, almost knocking him down. The main body of diesel fuel under the pile had ignited.

"Jack!" Gillian screamed. Another six inches was all they needed. Three inches more now. The tires of the forklift were sinking into the mud almost as fast as it was raising the logs. The final two inches opened with agonizing slowness.

"Now!" he screamed. Gillian thrust her arms up through the narrow space between the roll cage and the raised logs. Jack hauled, his spine cracking and snapping in protest. Gillian popped free. He lost his balance and fell backward down the pile, pulling her with him. The log ends slipped from the forks and their cargo came smashing back down onto the roll cage. Jack heard the heavy steel bars crumple in upon themselves like so many pipe cleaners. He picked himself up out of the mud again and, hoisting Gillian up by the armpits, half-dragged, half-carried her foot by agonizing foot away from the hill of rolling death.

"My legs," she cried, terror in her voice. "I can't move them!"

A mental picture of Charlie leaning heavily upon his cane in Meg's kitchen swam up in Jack's mind, but he brushed it aside. Gillian was alive, that was all that mattered. When they reached firmer ground, he stopped and slung her over his shoulder in a fireman's carry.

Fifty yards from the pile a blast from behind flattened them. Jack twisted as he went down, shielding Gillian from the impact of the fireball that washed over them. Cinders rained down and an orange mushroom cloud lit up the yard as bright as day. The loader had exploded.

Jack came to his senses first.

Flame was all around them. The explosion of the loader had showered the yard with glowing incendiary bombs. He struggled to get his bearings. The office? There. But fire was lapping at the cedar siding. The saw shed? A boiling mass of red and orange was chewing on the end closest to the woods.

An icy shaft of dread pierced him through the heart. Fuel tanks. For the pumps. Others for the loaders. Anytime now they could—he didn't waste time on the possibilities. Had to get Gillian out of there. He shook her. She was a limp moaning log.

The fireball from the blast at the edge of the river lit up the night. Jack shielded his eyes from the intense glare and pulled Gillian tightly to his body. For several seconds the water cannons gallantly spurted their last drops onto the inferno, not yet aware they were mortally wounded. In the eerie silence that followed their final spasm, Jack gathered Gillian into his arms and ran. Like the hounds of hell were upon him, not slowing even when the heated draft of a second explosion threatened to steal his feet from beneath him, he ran. Ran for where he thought the front gate should be, momentarily startled when he glimpsed through the drifting veils of smoke a winged mythological beast with gleaming eyes, hunkered on its haunches, poised as if to spring upon him and Gillian.

The Cadillac. Left idling, with one long, sculpted door hanging open. The headlights glowed like eyes in the smoke. Wonderful: his gal was not only brave, gutsy, and a poor decision maker, she was a thief as well.

Something was seriously loose under the floor of the Caddy, Jack discovered. It banged against the undercarriage as he bounced the huge car along the rutted road leading between the mill and the Wilcox house. *Don't blame me*, he said to The Twins. As if damage to the car or the mill or anything mattered now with Gillian—

A moan came from the back seat. Then a stream of disconnected profanity. Jack breathed an enormous sigh of relief. He skidded the Caddy to a halt in front of the rear porch. Dragged Gillian, cursing and kicking, out of the back seat. Her legs were just fine now. One boot caught him a glancing blow, causing him to speculate where she had ditched her glass slippers.

He sat her down on the back steps, propped up against the newel post. Felt his pockets. Nothing. He needed a phone.

Prayed silently the Wilcoxes wouldn't have a hand-crank version. He yanked open the screen door to the mudroom, remembering just in time its nasty habit of smacking the unwary visitor in the face. As he placed his foot upon the threshold, the earth moved under his feet. Literally.

"What the hell . . . ?" Gillian mumbled, lifting her head to look around her. She saw him standing halfway into her house. "You're not getting my land," she said, pointing at him, wrapping her other arm around the post to steady herself.

"Yes, dear," he said. Her bells were ringing. He hoped they were still all there.

The entire house began to vibrate. He braced himself stiff-armed against the door jamb. To survive an inferno only to be killed by an earthquake. What a crazy town. He peered up the gravel drive in the direction of Route 101. Laughed.

"Go ahead, laugh, smartass. You're not getting it," Gillian said. Then, following his gaze, said, "What the hell . . . ?"

"It's Riley," he said. "Charging, so to speak, to the rescue. He's driving the 'dozer."

"Day late and a dollar short, eh?" Gillian said, rubbing her head.

"A-yup . . . you got that right." He adored her, he realized. Couldn't help it. From the first time he'd laid eyes on her. Crazy town. Crazy woman.

She smiled crookedly up at him then, her eyes and teeth unnaturally white against the sooty blackness of her face. The lights came back on in her eyes.

His heart glowed brighter than the woods.

Chapter 35

"Wake up."

Jack's voice. It seemed she'd only been asleep for moments. She rolled away from it and shoved her head under the pillow. She was never getting out of bed. Ever.

Especially this bed, with its tacky, dated, marvelous, mechanical fingers. Slept like the dead in it last night she did, not that a park bench in the square or the slat seats of the cupola jammed into her barn wouldn't have been as inviting. Anywhere to shut her eyes on the horizontal for a few hours. Or days or weeks. Because what was the point of getting up, after all? There was nowhere to go, nothing to do. The stench of burning diesel fuel and wet, charred wood assaulted her memory. She tugged the quilted comforter completely over herself and curled up in its puffy darkness.

She felt herself being shaken. "Go away."

A hand grabbed her ankle. For a moment she thought she was back in her old dream. Jack Turner dragging her down, down, down. . . . Where was an oilcan when you needed one?

"Get up," Jack said again. "Places to go, things to do."

Sure, straight to hell then rot there. "Jack, everything's gone," she murmured into the blackness of her cocoon. "What's the point?"

It seemed so wonderful just to be alive last night, but daylight ushered in greater expectations. She laughed bitterly. "Yup, Wilbur, or Orville or whoever you are," she said, "I just fished the punch clock out of the rubble pile, so come in like you always do. But careful, it's still hot, yup, yup. Don't burn your fingers on the time card. Oh, and bring a rake and a shovel so we can neaten up a bit."

"What you need is a change of perspective," Jack said. He whipped off the coverlet, leaving her exposed upon the bed. She hugged herself and moaned like a little kid with a stomach virus. Didn't he realize—?

He came around to her side of the bed and waved a ceramic coffee mug with Eagle House imprinted on the side in front of her face. "We're taking a little walk."

She sniffed at the heady aroma, but stuck to her guns. "We saw everything there was to see last night, Jack. There's nothing left." Of the mill anyway. The rest of the town had mercifully escaped. Along with the Vibrobed. She sat up tentatively. Blinked at the strong morning light flooding through the windows of the room. Tried a sip of coffee. Then another. Maybe life still had some possibilities.

She sat herself cross-legged upon the bed. Leaned back against the headboard and curled herself around the coffee cup. Soul-deep sadness muffled her heartbeat, numbed her throat. The phone rang. Jack answered it, then handed it to her.

"Dad, hey." The words fell like lead from her lips. The hand holding her coffee cup trembled. She rested it on her thigh. "Un-huh. Right, Dad. I know. Everything. All gone." Fat tears formed in the corners of her eyes. She blinked. They ran down her cheeks and dotted her T-shirt.

"Right. Right. Maybe we can. Un-huh, okay. . . . Love you too. Bye." She dropped the phone onto the comforter. Watched Jack place it back in its cradle on the bedside table. The mill had always been there for her and her family. For four generations. Her dad. Then her. Scenes of her and Charlie working there together flashed through her mind. She cried, gave in to the great heart-wracking sobs. Jack held her.

"This is so stupid," she said a while later, although she

couldn't have said how much time had passed. "I feel like I've lost a . . . friend."

"In a way you have," Jack said.

"You know the really funny part in all this?" she said, reaching for tissue from the box Jack had placed beside her on the bed.

Jack shook his head.

"My dad didn't seem all that upset by it."

"Really."

"Yeah. He wasn't jumping for joy or anything, but he wasn't exactly down about it either. He gave me the 'everything changes' speech." A giggle bubbled up out of her.

"What?" Jack said.

"I don't think he was calling from Meg's house."

"So, he's not an invalid. I mean, he still drives, gets around—" Jack stopped, his mouth open. "You mean . . . ?"

Gillian laughed at the ceiling, the mirth throwing her head back. "He was 'around' all right," she said. "You know that funny sound your voice gets when you're lying down and talking? Like in bed? There was that *and* another voice in the background."

"Female?"

"*Oh*, yeah . . ." Gillian laughed again. Too much. She wiped new and different tears away with the back of her hand.

"Rachel will know who," Jack said.

She regarded him speculatively. "My, my. You're getting to know the ropes around here. Care to speculate?"

"Yes, but not now. C'mon, get up." He tugged on her hand and brought her to her feet and into his arms. He kissed the crown of her head, then sniffed her hair. "High octane," he said.

"*L'eau du diesel*," Gillian said. "Like it?"

He hugged her tight. "Not anymore. I think my heart will stop now every time I smell it." He shuddered. So close.

"I'll take another shower." She turned to go.

Jack reached for her. "No, I got me a plan. No time to waste." He fished a clean pair of shorts from her overnight bag and handed them to her. "Let's go."

Chapter 36

"Jack, this truly sucks," Gillian said, an hour later. "You are a monster."

Jack swatted her rear end. It was bobbing enticingly at eye level. He'd spent much of the climb up the Haystack Mountain trail replaying the Naked Lady Climbing the Rocks scene that had transpired when he'd jumped into the Mohasset to save her. He wondered who he had really saved with that hair-brained rescue attempt.

"Move," he said. He was tired too, he realized. He'd been up all night working while Gillian snoozed in the velvet embrace of the Vibrobed.

"And what the hell do you think you're going to catch up here?" Gillian asked.

She meant the fly rod case he was carrying slung over his shoulder. That, two water bottles and a couple of Granola bars in his small pack. They were traveling light. "Air trout," he said. "Keep moving."

Just when he thought he was going to have to place an emergency call to the helicopter in Bertram, they broached the crest of Haystack Mountain. It was the highest point for dozens of miles around and it overlooked the whole of Rocky Falls and beyond. From here they had a view of the entire river valley, from where the Mohasset emerged from the trees to the west, to where it disappeared around a shoulder of Mount Resolute to the east. In between, nestled in its protective oxbow, was Rocky Falls.

They stood, hands on hips, breathing heavily from the final two hundred yards of especially steep climb, taking in the scene. Last night, the beast in the woods had hissed and sizzled and snapped in frustrated fury, because in less than four hours it was cornered. Then crews in the woods had worked through the night hosing down hotspots, ruthlessly crushing the vestiges of the thing under their heels, making it well and truly dead for another hundred years. The rain had helped, too. Almost perfect timing. From their vantage point on top of Haystack Mountain, flashes of sun on metal in the dense carpet of forest below told Jack and Gillian that some crews were still at it.

"Unbelievable," Gillian said, assessing the damage, shock and awe parsing her words. The greedy black fingers of the fire had left morning-after smears on the yellow walls of the Eagle House Inn, attesting to the range of its midnight foray. But other than having to touch up some paint, air out the linens and sweep ash from the walkways, Lynette, Arthur, their inn, and the precious Vibrobed had escaped the beast's fiery wrath.

The rest of the town had lucked out, too.

Not so Wilcox Lumber. A blackened skeleton filled with twisted steel marked the foundation of the saw shed. Riley had been working the firebreak just down the road from the mill on Route 101 and had heard the loader explode, they'd found out later. He'd come running only to find most of the mill ablaze. He and Jack had done what they could to save it. When the office caught fire, they abandoned it and went on to protect the saw shed. They cleared a firebreak around it with the dozer, but hungry leaders of flame leaped from the trees around the yard and finally set it completely ablaze.

Gillian and Jack had stood and watched the yard burn

until she could stand it no more. It was the rain that finally turned the tide, sweeping over them in drenching torrents. The steamy smell of a doused fire was never so sweet. Riley went back on station down the road. Jack drove Gillian downtown for a once-over by the emergency medical team set up in the clinic, then ferried her all over Rocky Falls so she could check on people and places and things. At two A.M. Gillian had fallen into an exhausted sleep in Jack's bed at the inn.

Now the bright morning sun reflected off the perpetually wet walls of Coldwater Cliffs across the valley to the north. The sheen was dazzling. Jack and Gillian flopped down onto a knee-high ledge of pink granite and dragged the water bottles out of the pack.

The black scar that had replaced the Wilcox Lumber yard extended into much of the woods around it. The path of destruction followed the south bank of the Mohasset, then clawed its way east. It swerved around the elementary school, tucked safely into its engineered clearing, and swept to the very borders of the downtown.

Her town, Gillian thought, unwrapping a granola bar. The people in it and the only life she'd ever known. The place her life had begun and where she'd most likely end her days. She tore her eyes from the destruction below and looked over at Jack. She watched him watch her town.

"We've got to talk," he said quietly, without looking at her.

"I thought the woman was supposed to say that."

Jack laughed. "I know, huh? The four most dreaded words in the English language."

She took a bite of granola. A circling hawk took up station in the sky above them. She couldn't do this now, she realized. Open negotiations. She was at the end of her rope. Mentally, physically, spiritually.

"Jack, I can't—"

"Ssh," he said. He scooted next to her on the ledge and

put his arm around her. She leaned hesitantly into him. He rested his chin on the crown of her head.

"I know I should think about what to do next," she said, feeling his closeness revive her. "I mean, now that the mill is gone, it's time to make decisions, right. Rebuild on the ashes?" Deep down weariness settled into her. "Or maybe leave town, buy a motor coach and tour the country? Join the circus? Sell encyclopedias door to door? Mary Kay? Fuller Brush? Do they even do that anymore?"

"Will you please shut the hell up?" he said, not unkindly.

He was tired too, she realized. She laughed derisively. "This is all so strange, Jack. And I'm so damn exhausted." She leaned forward and cradled her forehead in both hands.

Jack rubbed her back. Jack wanted her land. One thing felt so good and the other so bad. There was the rub. She snickered. It hurt to laugh.

"What?" he asked.

"Nothing. I kill myself is all."

"What you need is a nice fish dinner."

He was babbling. Again. "Jack, I'm really not in the mood—"

He held up a silencing finger. A Meg shushing finger. He was treating her like a child. Which was remarkably like how she felt right then. She watched him reach behind them and pull the fly rod case onto his lap. He unzipped one end. Out slid a loose roll of papers. Plans. He'd traded in his wallet for a two-suiter.

Her world turned red. "You fucker."

Indignation pushed her to her feet, but exhaustion dragged her back down onto the ledge again. "Get me when I'm down, right? When I'm vulnerable? Pitch me the latest scheme when I'm too damn tired—"

Her voice cracked. *To fight.* It was all too much. The back-rubbing bastard. Had she been wrong? Worse, was she right? Bonded for eternity to this man who wanted to screw her then . . . screw her? Tired, tired, tired. She scrubbed her face. Picked up a twig. Angrily traced some random designs in the thin stony soil between her feet.

He'd been up all night, she remembered. Yes. While she'd been having yet another weird dream. About being chased around the mill yard by The Twins brandishing pitchforks while jets of flame shot from the ground around her feet. She'd felt for Jack in the bed next to her but the space had **been cool and vacant**. A glow of light at the writing desk and a shifting shadow on the floral wallpaper had told her he was there in the room. That had been enough for her. She had gone back to sleep.

He had been working on these plans.

His fucking plans. Rolling endlessly down the line at her like candies on a conveyor belt in a chocolate factory. And she was Lucy, stuffing them here, throwing them there. Now, finally, she was up to her neck in the pile of paper. Jack had saved her from the logs, only to bury her under the endless deluge of his plans.

You can have all of it she wanted to scream at him. All of her land. Or none of it. Whatever left her in peace.

"I don't want any of it," he said.

Had she spoken aloud?

"But *you* might want this." He peeled the top sheet out of the curled sheaf and handed it to her.

Wearily she accepted it. Spread it out on her lap. It featured the front-on renderings of a half-dozen houses. She smoothed the paper. But not cookie cutter. Cute. A Victorian with whoa, actual gingerbread trim. Expensive. A classic Greek revival with its gable end to the street. A colonial. Not really her style but accurately drawn. A couple of cozy bungalows rounded out the collection.

"This is what you want?" she asked. *On my land* lay unspoken.

"No, but you might."

She straightened up. "Jack, look, I give you credit, these are really nice. A lot nicer than I expected. But they're gonna be a bitch to build with all this detail and I don't know who's going to be able to afford them—"

"Almost anyone," he said.

She looked at him. The gas jets were full on. She shook her head dumbly. "I don't . . ."

"Check the scale."

She slid her index finger down to the legend at the bottom of the rendering, into the box that labeled the renderings as Forest Queen Products. *Forest Queen Products?* What the hell was that? She shaded her eyes against the morning sun. Ah, the scale.

One-quarter inch to the—out of habit she filled in *to the foot.* Pretty standard sizing on architectural drawings. But, wait, no. It wasn't that. She squinted. One-quarter inch to the . . . *inch*? These buildings were tiny. Miniature. They were miniatures. A bizarre picture popped into her head of her land bulldozed with each of these tiny houses centered on its own half-acre lot. Step on one and you'd crush it to dust.

"Jack, I'm not . . ." She made a vague gesture with one hand. He once said *he* felt like he'd fallen down the rabbit hole? "These are tiny."

"Correct. Otherwise they would never fit inside this." He handed over another sheet of drawing paper.

A low wood-sided building with a tastefully landscaped parking lot. Behind it a river. To the side, a what? It took her a moment. A waterwheel. Powered no doubt by a sluice-way channeled off of the river. *Forest Queen Products* the sign on the building declared. What could have been a school group was clustered around the wheel. Jack wasn't as good drawing people as he was drawing buildings. The flaw made him somehow more human.

The gears in her head ground painfully but produced nothing. "Help me here, Jack," she said, struggling.

"I've never fallen in love before," he said. "With a place

or a town or a . . . forest queen." His eyes glistened like mica.

She smelled bubble bath. *He tried to save her . . .*

Holy hand grenades.

This—she looked down at the long, low building on the paper—was her what? Castle. Hardly. It was a factory. Jack had drawn a factory that made model homes, heavy emphasis on *model*. Miniature house kits.

A factory. Right on the Mohasset. Right where the mill was until last night. It was the plywood plant all over again. An ecological nightmare waiting to—

"Vegetable dyes," Jack said.

"What?"

"Vegetable dyes on the components. Water treatment built right into the plant. The water it uses is returned to the river in better condition than it started out in. The water wheel helps generate some electricity, too, but mostly it's an attraction."

"For what?" She was dazed. Truly. Like she'd been plunked down in the middle of Kazakhstan or Timbuktu.

"Tourists. School groups. There's a small museum of Maine logging history in the lobby."

Her mind began to wake up. "But it—I mean, the building—must be huge." She looked dubiously at the drawing.

"It is. Most of it's hidden in the landscaping."

"Parking?"

"Also hidden, mostly. I haven't got every detail worked out yet."

Sure. Right. The details, the devil, all that. "Meg will love it," she said.

"Instant field trip."

"Exactly."

"Tax base for the school system, too."

"Again, bingo. Your Meg is going to be superintendent of the whole district someday."

"Don't tell her that. She's hard enough to live with now."

Jack laughed. "Your dad thought this was a pretty good idea, too."

Gillian eyed him suspiciously. "You *were* up all night, weren't you?"

"He was hard to track down, but I finally found him."

"Through Rachel."

"Un-huh. Who also thinks this is a good idea."

"She'd take any kind of job right now. Don't go by her." My, my. Wasn't Jack just the busiest little networker ever? Arranging everything so beautifully while she was unconscious, a prisoner of the Vibrobed. She didn't know whether to be angry or impressed. But maybe, for a change, she could be something else. Her heart gave a little skip. It hadn't skipped in a very long time.

"My dad thought this was okay?" she asked. Amazing. He'd given his life to the mill. Then the greater part of his mobility. It was in his blood. Yet he gave it up. Moved on.

"Remember the 'everything changes' speech you said he hit you with?" Jack asked.

She nodded, recalling.

"It was rehearsed."

"What?" It was an outrage. She tossed her scratching stick aside. It was unthinkable. The two of them up all night scheming how to get her to change her life, her beliefs, the way she had been doing business? Incon*ceiv*able, like the guy in *Princess Bride* always said. An incredible affront. They had complete disregard for her. She looked down at the blackened scar in the forest. It was high handed and arrogant and presumptuous and, and . . . crap.

It was time.

"Do Orville and Wilbur know?" she asked.

"Yup. After you pay for repairs to the Caddy they want an assurance of a dedicated handicapped space out front for the beast. 'Planning for their retirement' they called it. They may never actually retire, you know."

She did. But was a little surprised that *he* did. "And Riley?"

"I told him to hold on ordering a second 'dozer for the planned community job until I talked to you."

"Everybody is pretty much thrilled then, huh?"

"Pretty much."

She sat back down on the ledge. Fished the remains of the granola bar from her pocket. Contemplated it. Picked off a piece of lint. She was suddenly ravenous. She took a ragged bite and broke up the rest of the bar, throwing it into the woods for some equally hungry forest critter. Chewed thoughtfully, looked over the rendering again. Noticed something new.

"What's that?" she asked, pointing at a small octagonal structure behind the plant, adjacent to the river.

"The gazebo," Jack said. "The one from your barn. There's a picnic area there." He circled the tip of an index finger on the rendering.

Gillian felt like a weight had been lifted from her shoulders. "God, I won't have to fix it." She leaned forward, resting her forearms on her knees, hung her head and felt the relaxation spread across the muscles of her back. "You'll get it out of the barn? Transport it? Rehab it?"

Jack nodded.

"I won't have to have a fricking thing to do with it?"

"Yup."

Without straightening up, she stuck out her hand. "Deal."

They shook. He pulled her upright, pulled her tight against him.

"I am so damn tired," she said. She opened her eyes and stared down into the valley.

Her world began somewhere out there in the hazy distance, she thought, looking to the blue rows of mountains filling the horizon in the east, and would undoubtedly end somewhere in the mist clinging to the long ridgeline descending the far side of Mount Katahdin to the west. In between, in the bend in the river below, was the place she lived in. A place that lived in her. And apparently in the man sitting beside her. Of that, she no longer had doubt.

As unlikely as it seemed, this man—a complete stranger to her a few months before and an adversary until just a few weeks ago—was her soul mate. Whatever else lay ahead for them, whatever battles and blowouts were in store, they would ultimately be footnotes to this one simple, uncontestable fact. He had found something new here, something she had always known. He had brought something here that she could never have imagined.

"I've never fallen in love with a handsome stranger before," she said, without taking her eyes from the valley. "Or his factory. I'm all in a whirl."

He chuckled. "Imagine that, the irrepressible Ms. Wilcox, all in a dither." He slid cautiously closer to her on the ledge. Her eyes were sea-green now, with the blue vault of the sky reflected in them. At every moment he learned something new about her, he realized. Some small physical detail was revealed or a hidden corner of her was suddenly illuminated. She was a lifetime of wondering and learning.

"You're quite a vision," he said.

"Aw, shucks." She giggled, blushing. He *did* give good patter. A flutter rose under her ribs then slid lower, warming her insides. They were quiet for a while. A light breeze stirred the pines. The hawk above carved lazy circles across the valley, riding the warm air currents rising up from the cliff faces.

Finally, Jack spoke. "I'm starting to like it down your rabbit hole, Gillian Wilcox," he said. "And tea is becoming my favorite thing to drink."

Her heart sang. She smiled and prayed. *I love you, Jack. Keep going.*

"But I'm—" He bowed his head.

Gillian squeezed him tighter around the waist. He cleared his throat. "But I'm not used to all this . . ." He swept the town with his hand. "You all have each other. In this amazing little corner of the world. I don't know how I could have been so blind to this . . . stuff. My whole life has been a series of acquisitions. Land, people, possessions. *Collect 'em all, trade 'em with your friends*," he mimicked.

She jumped in to protect him from himself. "Jack, it's like I told you at the dance: we all get dealt a hand. I ended up with this one, you got something else. Somewhere along the line you find out you don't like the cards you're holding, you Go Fish." She laughed, amused at herself.

The sound, to Jack, was a silvery lilting thing that echoed among the tall pines.

"We both got a lucky draw here, you know?" she said, thinking. "I mean, look at me. Old maid city, right? Oh yeah, in another forty years I might finally slow down enough for Riley, God bless him, to catch me, but by that time we'd be so old we'd probably just fall down and break something. Too senile to even remember what the big deal was all about."

"But with you," she said, tears stinging the corners of her eyes, "I got a second chance to get things right. Your wheeling and dealing got you here, right? If you weren't such a land shark you never would have swum up this end of the cove, right?"

She scowled at his raised eyebrow.

"Don't be giving me that look, Jack Turner," she said, poking his shoulder. "I'm just saying that everything happens for a reason. I know it's wacky logic, but I've never been happier in my life than I've been—at times—" she laughed, finishing—"in the last few months. All because of you."

Jack pinched the bridge of his nose, then briskly rubbed both cheeks. "As weird as it sounds, I know what you mean. It's crazy and totally unexplainable, but I really do. I've never been happier either—which scares the hell out of me, incidentally—but I feel like I've come home. To you."

He kissed her lightly on the lips. "Is this a dream?"

She brushed a lock of his hair behind his ear. "Not a chance, my dear. You're cursed with me forever." They sat quietly again, their arms around each other. Felt the final pieces slip into place.

An iridescent dragonfly alighted on Gillian's sleeve and assessed her with its multifaceted eyes. A jay screeched in the brush near them. The sun was warm on their faces and bare arms.

Jack said suddenly, "Do you like stories?"

"I . . . um . . . yeah, sure." She wasn't sure she would ever get used to his abrupt changes of direction. He shifted positions and brought his face closer to hers. He lifted a hand thoughtfully and brought a warm, round inflection into his voice. *"Once upon a time, in a little town far from the nattering crowd, there lived a cranky, cranky—"*

Gillian opened her mouth to protest, but Jack hurried on. "Cranky but *beautiful* woodland queen . . ."

Gillian beamed. "Better."

"Anyway, one day, a lonely, bitter—"

"But *handsome*—" she inserted.

"Okay. A lonely, bitter—but *handsome*—stranger came into the queen's magic woods and tried to persuade her subjects to sell him her precious lands. The queen heard of his evil—"

"Misguided—" she amended.

"Right—*misguided*—plan. Anyway, she became so angry one day that she tried to kill him with an oilcan—"

"Jaaack? Stick to the script. No editorializing."

He chuckled. "Right. Anyway, a raging, towering beast tried to eat all her kingdom up one scary night. The brave—but stubborn—queen tried to fight the beast all on her own."

Gillian raised her eyebrows critically, but remained silent.

"The misguided land grabber came to his senses just in time and rescued the beautiful queen. For his reward, she allowed him to live forever in her enchanted land if he'd renounce his former ways." He stopped.

"The end?" she queried.

"Or the beginning. Will the beautiful queen let me live in her land?" He was on one knee now.

"She would be delighted to have you," she said, pushing him back into a sitting position against the trunk of a white spruce that had fought its way through the granite ledge. She leaned over and nibbled gently on his lower lip. He tightened his grasp around her waist, pulling her closer to deepen the kiss.

"I love you, Jack," she murmured against his lips.

"And I love you," Jack said, reaching beneath the back of her shirt, running his hands up her spine. Gillian gently pulled his hands away from her body, held them prisoner within hers. She kissed his throat, trailing a string of kisses down his chest as she slowly undid his shirt.

Button by button, she descended, watching his face change as she went. The gas jets ratcheted up from simmer to high heat to rolling boil. She slowly and carefully removed all his clothes then pulled away and stood tall before him. With the sun full on her, she looked directly into his eyes and removed her own clothing. She stood tall and arched her back, stretching.

Just like that day on the rock ledge above the Mohasset, Jack realized. Except this time, he was not an interloper but an audience. She drew her hands up her stomach and rested them just below her breasts, making him groan again at the vision poised there, a creature composed of equal parts flesh, sky, and woods.

"God, Gillian. Come . . ." he said huskily, beckoning her down to him. The power of coherent speech deserted him.

She smiled, a slow, lazy, slit-eyed cat smile, one that spoke of new beginnings and ancient knowing. "Oh, my dear," she murmured, "that's just what I intend to do."

She straddled him, burying him deep inside her heat and promise.

A second hawk joined the first overhead, and together they wheeled through the bright morning sky, riding the thermals higher and higher. Below them, two human spirits, at long last set free, soared above the bend in the river.